POINT CRIME

For Thomas.

The David Belbin Collection

Avenging Angel • Deadly Inheritance • Final Cut

David Belbin

Three degrees of murder

SCHOLASTIC

Scholastic Children's Books,
Commonwealth House, 1-19 New Oxford Street,
London WC1A 1NU, UK
A division of Scholastic Ltd
London ~ New York ~ Toronto ~ Sydney ~ Auckland

First published in this edition by Scholastic Ltd, 1997

Avenging Angel
First published by Scholastic Ltd, 1994

Deadly Inheritance
First published by Scholastic Ltd, 1996

Final Cut
First published by Scholastic Ltd, 1994

ISBN 0 590 54327 X

Typeset by TW Typesetting, Midsomer Norton, Somerset
Printed by Clays Ltd, St Ives Plc

10 9 8 7 6 5 4 3 2 1

Contents

AVENGING ANGEL

For John Harvey

Summer

Prologue

Angelo Coppola left the paper shop, threw his fluorescent yellow bag around his shoulders, and mounted his bike.

"Hey, Angel!"

Angelo cringed, then nodded at Carol Ward, one of the other paper deliverers. Carol was always teasing him. Angelo hated his Christian name. He'd heard every different nickname that you could possibly make out of it: Angel Features, Angel-face, et cetera, et cetera. Older people were always embarrassing him by commenting that the name fitted his clean-cut looks. He would never forgive his mum and dad for calling him Angelo. Didn't they realize what they were doing?

It would have been much more sensible if they'd called his sister Clare "Angela". Clare, five years older than him, could look angelic on occasion. She was tall, with deep blue eyes and long, flowing black hair. Why did they have to name her after Mum's mother? Oh no: the family name had to go to the boy. Dad claimed it was an Italian family tradition.

Traffic was building up on Alfreton Road. Angelo was late starting his paper round because he'd been round at Paul's, playing Subbuteo. It was halfway through the long summer holiday. He and Paul were playing an entire FA Cup series and this afternoon was the first Quarter Final. The game went into extra time before Angelo's Sheffield United beat Paul's Chelsea, five–four.

Sometimes the road was too busy for Angelo to cross it on a bike. It was quicker to cross at the pedestrian lights instead. Today, however, the two lanes behind Angelo were clear. He cycled over into a third, right-turning lane. On the other side of the road, both lanes of traffic going into town were backed up. He would be able to weave between the cars on to Bobbers Mill Road, where his round began.

The cars behind Angelo on his right began to move, but the two nearest the road entrance stayed put, leaving a gap for the bike to get through. Angelo raised his hand in thanks and cycled through the gap. As he did so, one of the cars sounded its horn. Why?

A woman and child were about to cross the road but, seeing Angelo, stopped. There was a look of fear on the woman's face which Angelo couldn't understand. Then the engine noise was upon him and he realized why they were scared. He looked round quickly. There was a car coming at him, way too fast. The woman and child both screamed.

The car was almost upon him. Angelo could see the panicked face of the driver. He tried to throw himself out of the way, into the row of stationary cars in the other lane. But he didn't have time. For a moment, the whole world went black. When his vision returned, the car had gone. Angelo was on the road, with his bike on top of him, in agonizing pain.

1

Summer had lasted too long. That afternoon, the patrol car's calls had included: a bunch of joyriders who'd managed to boost a Jag; two sets of drunks who refused to leave city pubs; a streaker on Maid Marian Way and a knife fight bang in the middle of Slab Square, the heart of the shopping centre. Still, it was sweltering. As the evening began, more tempers would fray. When it got this hot, violent domestics sky-rocketed and the smallest traffic incident could turn into World War Three. Neil Foster was glad that today's shift was nearly over.

He looked at his watch. Ten to five.

"I could do with a break for something to eat soon," he told Jan, who was driving.

His partner made no comment, but turned left on to the Boulevard, where the home-time traffic was at its peak. They were nearly at the junction with Alfreton Road now: a major bottleneck with a left filter and an illegal right turn. They would be stuck here for up to five minutes. Jan began to drum her fingers on the steering wheel. Then a message from the traffic department came through on the radio.

"RTA Junction of Alfreton Road and Bobbers Mill Road. Possible fatality."

Jan radioed back.

"Unit 63 responding."

She switched on the siren, but there was nowhere for the cars in front to get out of their way. Neil unbuckled his seat belt.

"I'll run over there. It'll be quicker."

Jan nodded. Neil got out of the car and ran towards the scene of the RTA. He would be there in two minutes, provided he could get across the busy four lanes of traffic.

Meanwhile, Jan sat behind the wheel, frustrated. The accident couldn't have happened at a worse place, at a worse time. The cars in front tried to get out of her way, some moving into the centre of the road, some pulling on to the kerb. She edged the Panda forward in the narrow gap that they had created.

Neil would be at the accident by now. She hoped that he would do his job properly. He could be impulsive. Sometimes that was good, like the initiative he'd just shown in running over to the accident. But other times he was careless. He had only been on the job eight months, to her eight years. She was his "mentor" and, since her promotion two months before, his sergeant, too.

She was at the lights now. Cars stopped to let her through. Jan accelerated a hundred metres down the road. The cars on the other side of the road were all stationary, bumper to bumper, except for a small gap where a knot of people stood, gaping at something.

That was where the accident was.

As Jan got out of the car, people moved back off the road. That left Neil Foster and the victim, a boy dressed in T-shirt and jeans, with trainers. Next to him lay a mangled bicycle. The boy looked about thirteen – fourteen at the most. Round his shoulders was a bright yellow newspaper bag with *Evening Post* written across it. Neil was giving him the kiss of life.

Jan turned her attention to the onlookers, who were standing sheepishly by the side of the road.

"Did the car stop?" she asked.

They all began to speak at once. No, the car had not stopped. A hit and run. That was all Jan wanted to know for now. If the car was to be found, it would have to be quickly. Some of the people standing around were already beginning to walk off.

"I don't want anybody to leave!" she shouted at them. "We're going to need you as witnesses. That includes you, sir."

A middle-aged man in a cheap off-the-peg suit stopped by the chip shop, looking guilty.

"Did anybody get a good look at the car?" Jan asked. "I need the colour, the make, the number-plate..."

There was a babble of replies. It was something you learned to do in this job – listen to a dozen people talking at once and pick out the one or two who actually knew what they were talking about. Unfortunately, the best witnesses were probably sat behind the wheels of their cars, at the front of the noisily expanding traffic jam. But Jan didn't have time to go round each one of them.

"It was green..."

"No, yellow..."

"A Ford."

"What kind of Ford?" Jan asked.

"A Sierra..."

"No, an Escort."

It was no good. There wasn't enough consensus among the witnesses for Jan to radio a description to headquarters. In the distance, she heard an ambulance siren. She turned to Neil. He was still leaning over the boy.

"How is he?"

Neil replied breathlessly.

"I think his chest's been crushed. There are head injuries, too."

Jan could see that. There wasn't a lot of blood, but that didn't mean it wasn't bad.

"Can you find any identification?"

Gently, Neil pulled a small pocket book from the boy's trousers. As he handed it to Jan, he spoke again.

"Just before he passed out, he said something."

"What?"

"It sounded like 'blaze'. Any idea what it might mean?"

Jan shook her head. As the ambulance pulled up, Neil began to give the boy the kiss of life again. Jan opened the pocket book. There was a bus pass with a photograph: a grinning, fresh-faced boy with short, blond hair. His name was Angelo Coppola. From his date of birth, it appeared that he had turned fourteen the month before. He lived only a few streets away.

The ambulance men had the boy, Angelo, on a stretcher. Further down the road, Jan could see three more police cars trying to get across two lanes of traffic, and failing.

"You'd better go with him," she said to Neil, "in case he recovers consciousness, can tell you some thing about the accident."

Neil did as she asked. Jan went to the front of the ambulance.

"What are his chances?" she asked the driver, as he got back in his seat.

Without looking at her, the man shook his head. Then he switched on the siren.

Jan sighed as the ambulance sped off. She walked slowly across the part of the road where it had happened, looking for fresh tyre marks. All she could see were endless newspapers strewn across the road, one of them bearing a small patch of blood. For no reason she could put words to, Jan picked this paper up. She put it under her arm and folded it so that the blood didn't show. Then she stepped on to the pavement and joined the waiting witnesses.

Clare Coppola was helping her mother prepare the evening meal. She sliced garlic thinly and tossed it into the pan, watching the heat carefully to ensure that it didn't burn. Mum came in from the garden with some basil leaves from the plant outside. Clare went to work on a red pepper while Mum took the biggest, sharpest knife from the rack and chopped the steak into precise two-centimetre cubes.

Clare checked the cooker clock. Five. She switched on the radio for the news. It was tuned to Radio Trent, the local commercial station, which Mum liked best. Clare preferred the news on Radio Four. It had more depth. But the only time she'd suggested this to Mum, it was as though she'd proposed going to an Anglican church rather than a Catholic one. Mum *liked* all the minor local stories. She found the trite adverts informative. She even seemed to enjoy the endless traffic reports. It drove Clare crazy.

Clare chopped shallots to go with the peppers and opened a can of tomatoes. Mum was a bit behind schedule today, and Clare had offered to help, though she wasn't expected to. Dad would be home from work at six. He liked his dinner by half past – or seven at the very latest. Clare's brother had just got a paper round, so he was no use. Anyway, Clare quite liked cooking. She didn't find it demeaning, as some of her friends claimed to.

Now the announcer was saying: "And word is coming in of major hold-ups on the north side of the city. There's been an accident near the junction of Alfreton Road and Radford Boulevard. Police are still interviewing witnesses, so no traffic is moving at all, causing tailbacks on all northern routes into the city. Police say that it will be some time before traffic starts moving again."

"Your father'll be late," Mum said.

"Less hurry for us," Clare replied.

"You go back to your books. I can finish here."

Clare didn't feel like reading, but there was nothing left for her to do in the kitchen, so she washed her hands and went into the front room. Maybe she would put a record on, drown out the boring radio. Also, Angelo would be back soon. If he got in the front room before she did, he would take over the TV set for his computer games, and she would be driven upstairs until dinner.

Clare wished that the summer vacation was over. There was another month before she could return to Manchester. The other week, she had mentioned the possibility of going back early. After all, her shared flat was available from the middle of September. Dad nearly blew his top. What was wrong with living at home, he wanted to know. Was she getting too high and mighty for her old friends and family? Who did she think had paid her share of the deposit on the flat?

Mum defended Clare. She pointed out that when she was Clare's age, she'd already left home. She'd married Dad, despite her parents' objections that Nick Coppola was a no-good Italian labourer.

However, Mum warned Clare: "There's no more money for you. It's a lot cheaper, living at home." Which was true. Practically all of Clare's friends were stuck with their parents. There were no summer jobs to be had. The grant wasn't even enough to keep you going in term time.

At twenty past five the doorbell rang. Clare went to the door. She assumed that it would be Angelo. He'd have forgotten his key again. Clare wished that she had a part-time job. It would be better than scrounging off her father all the time. And it took seven years to qualify as an architect. She must have been crazy to—

She saw the dark figures on the other side of the glazed glass. It wasn't Angelo.

"Mum!"

Clare opened the door as Mum came through from the kitchen, complaining about the interruption. There were two of them, both in uniform – a man and a woman. The woman looked over Clare's shoulder and spoke directly to Mum. Clare stared at their faces, reading everything into them.

"Mrs Coppola?"

Clare turned to look at Mum, who was nodding, her eyes red with fear.

"May we come in, please?"

Mum kept nodding and Clare stepped aside. She could feel her stomach tightening as the policewoman spoke again.

"I'm afraid we've got some bad news..."

2

Mum was collapsed in Clare's arms, sobbing. Clare kept blinking, unable to react fully, almost numb. The policewoman was saying:

"We'll drive you to the hospital. What about Angelo's father? Does he live with you?"

"He'll be on his way home," Clare told her. "But with the traffic—"

"I can wait here for him," the policeman offered.

The policewoman was helping Mum to stand up. Clare thought about Dad, coming home to find a stranger with tragic news.

"Dad's a builder," she said, as though this was important. "He's got a mobile phone. I think it's best that I ring him, tell him to go straight to the hospital."

"Yes," said the policewoman. "I think that's a good idea. Will you be…?"

Clare nodded. The policewoman gently guided Mum away. Clare went to the phone in the kitchen. The stew was starting to burn. She turned it down, then thought again, and turned it off. She dialled Dad's carphone number automatically, without thinking how she was going to put the news. What difference would well-chosen words make? The effect would be the same.

The phone rang three times before Dad answered.

"Yes, hello?"

"Dad, it's Clare."

"Clare? What is it?"

"It's Angelo, Dad. He's had an accident."

There was a pause. Clare knew that she couldn't tell Dad everything the policewoman had said. He would be too upset to drive to the hospital.

"How bad?" Dad asked.

"It's serious, Dad. A car knocked him off his bike. We won't know how bad it is until we get to the hospital. He's at the Queen's. The police are going to take Mum and me. Can you meet us there?"

Dad's voice became gruff, the way it always did when he was covering up emotion.

"Yes, yes. Where's Maria? Can I talk to her?"

"I don't think Mum's up to talking, Dad."

The policewoman had come back into the kitchen.

"I think we need to go, Dad."

"I'll be as quick as I can. The traffic's hell tonight, though."

"I know. Drive safely. I'll see you there. I love you, Dad."

"I love you, too."

Clare put the phone down. Her body was shaking. Tears streamed down her face. The policewoman put an arm around her.

"Come on, love. Let's take you to your brother."

"They're still operating," the nurse told Neil Foster, "but there's really no chance of him recovering consciousness. You might as well leave."

Neil got up as though to go. He'd been waiting around in case Angelo Coppola was able to give a description of the car that hit him. Still, he was reluctant to go. He had held the boy in his arms, had spoken to him before he passed out. He ought to talk to the family before he went home.

They arrived two minutes later – mother and daughter, arms around each other. The mother was small, fortyish, with short brown hair. The daughter was much taller. She had long, thick black hair and was stunningly attractive, even though she'd been crying. The two women began to ask the doctor a lot of questions, which she avoided answering. To Neil's surprise, neither of them sounded Italian.

"This is Police Constable Foster. He was the first to reach Angelo. He gave him resuscitation, which may have been what kept him alive."

"Thank you," the mother said. "Thank you for helping our son."

Neil wanted to say "it was nothing", but didn't, because he knew that it *was* nothing and he didn't know if they knew that yet.

"What happened?" the girl asked. "No one seems terribly sure."

"A hit and run," Neil said. "A car cutting across the main road didn't see your brother in time. That's what it looks like, anyway."

"Was he in a lot of pain?" the girl asked.

"I don't think so. He was still conscious when I got to him. He said something to me. I don't know what it meant."

"What did he say?"

"Just one word: 'blaze'."

He looked at the girl. Her face was blank.

"Does that mean anything to you?"

The girl shook her head.

"The make of the car that hit him, maybe?"

"That occurred to me. We'll check it out."

They were interrupted by the arrival of a large, dark-haired man in a sweat-soaked, open-necked shirt. He spoke with a slight Italian accent.

"Maria, Clare. How is he?"

"They won't let us see him until they've finished operating, Nick," Maria said. "They say it's very bad – his head and his chest."

Nick Coppola hung his head.

"*Dio*."

Neil shuffled uncomfortably as the three of them hugged. It was time for him to go. Nick Coppola broke away from the two women and spoke to Neil.

"You'll find him, won't you? You'll find the *stronzo* who did this to my son?"

"We'll do our best, sir."

A middle-aged man in a white coat was walking down the corridor. Neil recognized the surgeon who had been operating on Angelo Coppola. It was over already. Neil had hoped not to be here when this happened.

"I'm very sorry," the surgeon was saying to the Coppolas. "We did all that we could do, but his injuries were too severe. We lost him five minutes ago."

The father broke down first, then the daughter. The mother remained calm.

"Can we see him?" she asked. "Can you take us to my son?"

"Yes, of course."

The surgeon led them down the corridor.

Neil phoned Jan at the station. He told her what had happened.

"Any leads?" he asked, when he'd finished.

"Not enough to go on. The only thing the witnesses agree about is that it's a light-coloured car of 'normal' shape – not a hatchback, in other words. We're still interviewing people. Hopefully, something will come up. Why don't you get a meal before you come in? You deserve a break."

"Thanks, Jan, but I'm not hungry right now."

Neil stepped outside into the sweltering evening, thinking about the dead boy. He remembered his promise to the Coppolas. It was true. The police would do the best they could. But he knew from his training – if they hadn't got the car within an hour of the incident, the chances of catching the driver were poor.

Neil told the taxi-driver where he was going.

"Might take a while," the cabbie told him. "Traffic's murder tonight."

"You're right," said Neil. "It is."

3

"It's like I told you yesterday…"

"It's too hot to concentrate in here. Can't you turn that fan on?"

"I'm sorry, sir, it's broken."

Several witnesses were being interviewed for a second time. They weren't happy about it. The Traffic Superintendent had been informed of Angelo's death and he had put Inspector Thompson in charge of the investigation. It was Thompson who had insisted on the re-interviews. Jan and Neil were still on the case, but their opinion didn't seem to count for much.

"What about the boy's last word, sir, 'blaze'? Shouldn't we be checking that out?"

Thompson, a career policeman with a greying moustache and a growing bald patch, gave Neil a supercilious look.

"You asked the family and it meant nothing to them, right?"

"That's right," Neil replied. "But I thought that it might be the model of the car that hit him, or even a design on the side of it. You know the way that some people—"

Thompson interrupted him.

"Think about it, lad. You're about to be run over by a big car, speeding straight at you. What do you do?"

Neil didn't reply. The Inspector carried on, his voice dripping with sarcasm.

"You don't drop your bike and run to try to somehow get out of its way. No, you stay there in the middle of the road and see if you can recognize the model of the car about to hit you. Smart move, eh? Mind you, if Coppola was in such an observant frame of mind, you'd think he'd have memorized the number-plates too, wouldn't you?"

Neil swallowed and tried again.

"Surely it's possible that he recognized the car in some way and was trying to tell me about it."

Thompson shrugged his broad shoulders.

"Possible, yes. Likely, no. We'll get to it when we have time, Foster. Now, do you think that you could interview Mrs Ohagi again?"

Neil went back to the interview room. Mrs Ohagi was a Nigerian woman who had been coming out of the chip shop on the corner of the road where Angelo Coppola was knocked down. The officer who first interviewed her had described her as a "very clear" witness.

"I've no idea of the make," she told Neil, "but the car was green, I'm sure about that."

"What shade of green?"

"Quite light. A sort of lime green, I think."

Neil made a note. This was an advance on the previous day.

"New? Old?"

She shook her head.

"Not old and rusty, but I'm not sure how new … you see, I was looking more at the boy. He was right in the middle of the road. There was no way that he could get out of the way in time. I think I screamed."

"Any idea what speed the car was doing?"

"I don't know. Forty? Fifty? It would have to have been pretty fast, wouldn't it?"

Neil nodded, though this wasn't strictly true. Ninety per cent of people hit by a car doing forty miles an hour died.

"What about the driver? Did you see who was behind the wheel?"

"Only a glimpse."

Again, she hadn't said this yesterday. Or, if she had, the interviewing officer hadn't written it down.

"What can you tell me about the driver?"

"Not much."

"A man or a woman?"

"A woman, I think."

"Black or white?"

"White."

"Age?"

"No idea."

"What was she wearing?"

Mrs Ohagi paused.

"I'm not sure. No, wait. I think she might have had something on her head. Something bright. A headband, perhaps."

Neil let the silence linger, the way he'd been taught to, in case Mrs Ohagi's subconscious came up with another gem. Finally, he asked:

"Anything else?"

"Sorry, no. Even what I've just told you is very hazy. It was such a shock."

"And you say this woman was alone in the car?"

"Yes. I'm sure about that."

Neil offered her his hand.

"Thank you. Thanks for coming in. You've been a great help."

Jan was in a small terraced house on Hazelwood Road, five minutes' walk from the place where Angelo Coppola had been fatally injured. She was interviewing one of the two people who'd been crossing the road at the same time as Angelo Coppola. Tracey Lord was a thin girl, barely out of her teens. She sat on the sofa, chewing gum, while her three-year-old daughter Jade played on the floor.

"Just take me through it again slowly, Tracey."

Tracey sighed. "I don't see the point. I'm not going to remember anything else. I keep telling you. I was just bothered about getting Jade out of that maniac's way!"

"You'd already started to cross the road?"

"I was on the road, yeah. The lad who was killed, he came across on his bike – cocky as anything, they are, those kids on bikes – he came right through the cars on Alfreton Road. Well, I wasn't going to get out of his way, but then I saw the car behind him. You know, if he'd heard it, he might have got out of the way, mightn't he? But it's really noisy along there, with all that traffic..."

Jan let Tracey go on in the way she wanted. Let a witness tell it her way, and it was possible that she'd come up with something she didn't know she remembered.

"Did you get a good look at the car?" Jan prompted.

"It just came from nowhere, dead fast, straight at us, you know, like a bullet, dead fast."

"Straight at *you*?"

Tracey nodded.

"I was sure it was going to hit me and Jade, yeah. But then it sort of swerved and went into the boy instead."

"You were still on the road? You didn't have time to get back on to the pavement?"

"Jade and me just stood still, on the edge of the road … he came this close."

She held out her arms to indicate a distance of less than a metre. The thin material of her cheap cotton blouse flapped around her shoulders. Jan wished that she was wearing lighter clothing. It was so hot that she found it hard to concentrate. Her head felt like mashed potatoes. It would be easy to miss something. She consulted her notes.

"He … you said 'he' just now."

"Yeah."

"Only, yesterday you said that you didn't see who was in the car at all, couldn't even remember what colour the car was."

Tracey stared into space. Jan couldn't tell if she was concentrating or her mind was as blank as she looked. Finally, she answered.

"Got to be a man, hasn't it? When did you ever hear of a woman driving like that?"

The road looked the same as ever. Traffic flowed smoothly. There was no sign of what had happened to Angelo there. Why should there be? It was important, Clare had decided, to come here quickly, to cross the road, to go to the shops, not to build up some kind of taboo about the place where her brother was knocked down.

Anyway, she couldn't stand it at home any longer. All day there had been calls of condolence. It was good to know that so many people cared. It kept Mum and Dad occupied, too. But it was driving Clare round the twist. She didn't want to hear one more person tell them how pointless Angelo's death was, how tragic. She wanted to be able to do something about it.

Clare had spent the morning fielding phone calls. Close friends were put through to Mum or Dad, if they could come to the phone. Business colleagues and more casual acquaintances, Clare spoke to herself.

Hardest to deal with were the calls from Italy. Clare's Italian was rusty, but Mum or Dad couldn't always come straight to the phone.

Dad had phoned her uncle that morning. He'd agreed to tell the relatives in Napoli. Just before Clare left the house, her grandmother rang, immediately bursting into floods of tears.

Since the *Evening Post* came out there had been more calls. Clare told Mum and Dad she was going to buy a copy, see what it said. Now, as she walked into the shop, a silence descended. Mr Malik came out from behind the counter.

"We are so, so sorry. If there is anything we can do, anything..."

Clare nodded blankly.

"He was a good boy, Angelo, the best. He had so much life to live."

Clare picked up a paper off the counter. Mrs Malik came out from the back of the shop. Clare reached into the pocket of her jeans and realized that she didn't have her purse with her. Before she could explain this, Mrs Malik shook her head.

"Take it, please. Do you need anything else?"

Clare shook her head. Mrs Malik took Clare's arm and squeezed it.

"We feel so bad about what happened. If we hadn't taken Angelo on..."

"You mustn't even *think* that sort of thing," Clare said. "Only one person is to blame for what happened – whoever was behind the wheel of that car."

"I'm sure they'll find him," said Mr Malik.

"They'd better," Clare told him, clenching her fist beneath the newspaper. "They'd better."

Anger made her feel stronger. Instead of walking back to the house, she walked down the road a little, to Churchfield Lane. This was where the car which ran over Angelo had come from. It was a rat run. By cutting across Alfreton Road to Bobbers Mill Road you could get to Hyson Green without meeting any traffic hold-ups. A lot of drivers did it, though, and, sometimes, like now, there was a queue of cars waiting to drive across the busy main road.

There was a patch of land at the end of Churchfield Lane, the one which gave the road its name. Clare sat there sometimes, in the shade of St Peter's Church, and sketched. Sometimes she drew the trees around her, sometimes the buildings. Other times she would draw cityscapes. Over the years, she had a record, not just of her improved drawing skills, but also of how the city had changed.

When Clare first visited the churchyard, there had been a giant Players Cigarette factory behind her. Now it was a retail park. All that remained of the old factory was its clock, set on a plinth in the corner. Clare sat down on a bench and looked at the paper for the first time. Angelo's death did not appear on the front page. She had to scan page three twice before she found the story, just beneath the fold of the broadsheet.

"HIT AND RUN" DRIVER SOUGHT

Police are appealing for the driver of the car which killed Angelo Coppola, 14, yesterday to come forward. Paperboy Angelo died from massive head and chest injuries within an hour of being knocked from his bike.

"We will find whoever is responsible for this death," said Inspector Brian Thompson, who is in charge of the investigation, "and it will be easier for them if they give themselves up now, rather than making us spend numerous police hours on the investigation."

Angelo was run over at the junction of Alfreton Road and Bobbers Mill Road, at ten to five yesterday afternoon. The incident caused grid-lock conditions on the north side of the city, delaying many drivers for over an hour.

Inspector Thompson thanked motorists for their patience and co-operation. "We would appreciate it if any witnesses whom we have not interviewed would contact the Radford Road Police Station," he said. Angelo is survived by his parents, Nicholas and Mary, and his older sister, Clare.

It annoyed Clare that the paper had printed her parents' names that way – no one ever called Dad anything but Nick, and his full name was Niccolo, not Nicholas. Mum's parents were the only ones who still called her Mary – to everyone else she was Maria, the name which Dad gave her when they first started courting.

Clare got up and left the churchyard, thinking about Angelo. She and her brother weren't that close. There was five years between them. Clare had been an "accident", forcing her parents to marry before they were ready. Angelo was a planned baby, born shortly after Mum and Dad moved to the house where they still lived. Clare loved her brother, but she envied him, too. He always seemed to have so much more freedom than her.

Clare had expected that she and Angelo would become closer as they got older. The age difference would stop mattering so much. Now that would never happen. She'd been so happy when he was born, so keen that the new baby would be a boy.

Now she would never be able to give him the benefit of her experience in passing exams, never give him advice about his first girlfriend, never swap notes about how each of them *really* felt about different members of the family. He wouldn't be there at her graduation ceremony or her marriage. He would never be an uncle to her children.

Clare knew that she ought to be sad, but instead she was angry. She was so preoccupied with her anger that she started to cross the quiet road without looking. A horn sounded. She turned round to see a fast-moving Ford Escort coming out of nowhere.

As Clare stepped back on to the pavement, two teenage heads poked out of the back window and jeered at her: the usual insulting, sexist obscenities. She gave them the finger. It was the wrong thing to do. You didn't provoke louts. But she was mad. She didn't care.

The car squealed to a halt and did a "U" turn in the middle of the road. A yellow Escort. Clare stood her ground. She made herself memorize the first part of the licence plate number, Y642... The car hurtled towards her. What could these lads do? she thought. Beat her up in broad daylight? Hardly. There were people up and down the street.

The Escort sounded its horn. There were four boys in it, two in the front and two in the back. All but the driver leant out, shouting at her again. She couldn't make out all the words, but their intention was clear enough. She stepped back as the car came crashing towards her, mounting the pavement, making her throw herself out of its path.

The next thing Clare knew she was on the ground. Her shoulder ached where she had flung herself against someone's garden wall. The Escort was beside her, both its left-side doors open. They were going to come for her. They were going to get her ... she tried to get up, and failed. She didn't care if there were four of them. She was going to fight.

But they didn't get out of the car. Instead, they leant forward and spat at her.

"Next time," said the one in the front passenger seat, "we'll run you over, or worse. That was just a warning..."

He finished the sentence with a torrent of obscenities. Then, still sounding its horn, the car drove off, leaving Clare stranded on the pavement. Ignored by passers-by, she forced herself up, using the garden wall as a support.

4

Slowly, painfully, Clare walked home. She felt dirty, defiled. She wouldn't tell Mum and Dad what had happened. Not on a day like today. But she had to tell someone. Suppose – just suppose – those four had had something to do with what happened to Angelo?

Clare threw the paper on the table and went upstairs for a shower. Undressing, she found a bright red bruise on her shoulder where she'd hit the wall. Hot water soothed the ache but not the anger. She tried to remember the faces of the boys in the car. Not one of them looked old enough to drive. Downstairs, the doorbell rang.

Mum came upstairs as Clare left the bathroom.

"Are you all right, Clare? You shot up those stairs like an alley cat when you came in."

"I'm OK, Mum."

"There's a policeman downstairs – the one who was at the hospital. He wants to ask us some questions."

Clare remembered the policeman from the hospital – a lanky, nervous youth.

"I'll be as quick as I can," she told her mum.

"And another thing..." Mum hesitated. "You're going to think this sounds silly..."

"What?"

"You know how old-fashioned some of the family are. It would be best if you wore black."

"I've been wearing black jeans."

"Not jeans – a dress."

Clare couldn't believe this. Exasperated, she replied: "Mum, the only black dress I've got is the short cocktail one. I can't wear that."

"No," Mum said, patiently, "the long one. That's still in your wardrobe."

"I haven't worn that since I was fifteen!"

"You're exaggerating. Put it on – for your father – please."

Clare gave in.

"If you insist."

Mum was right. The satin dress was still there, at the back of the wardrobe, with the rest of the clothes that she hadn't taken to university. Reluctantly, Clare put it on. Then she sat in front of the mirror and brushed her hair.

Four years ago, when she and Mum bought this dress, black was the height of fashion. Then, the dress seemed daringly low cut. Now it looked modest, if a little tight. Clare had put on weight around the shoulders and thighs. She wished she'd inherited her mum's small build rather than her dad's big bones. Then she felt angry at herself. She shouldn't be thinking about her weight on a day like today. Clare went downstairs to meet the policeman.

She could hear Dad's voice booming before she got inside the room.

"Angelo … enemies? That's ridiculous! He was only fourteen years old."

"It's just a routine question, Mr Coppola. We have to explore every—"

"Here's Clare," Nick Coppola announced. "Tell Constable Foster, Clare. Angelo had no enemies."

The constable was sinking into one of the huge old armchairs. He looked at Clare nervously, apologetically. His shirt, Clare noticed, wasn't tucked properly into his trousers.

"None that I know of," Clare said slowly. "But I've been away at university for a year."

"Do you know who his friends at school were?" the constable asked.

Clare shook her head.

"We did go to the same secondary school: Greencoat. But Angelo started the term after I left to go to Sixth Form College."

"Did he ever talk to you about things he was interested in?"

"The usual stuff – football, computer games, videos…"

She hesitated and the constable made another suggestion.

"Did he talk about cars, for instance?"

"He was more interested in cycling," Dad interrupted. "He'd passed his cycling proficiency test, did I tell you that? Not that it helped him yesterday."

"Cars?" Clare returned to the subject. "How do you mean?"

Constable Foster shuffled in his armchair.

"A lot of boys round here get involved in taking without the owner's consent – that is, someone breaks into a car and then they take turns at driving it. It's what the media call 'joyriding'. Did Angelo ever mention anything like that?"

"That's ridiculous!" Dad said, angrily. "Angelo was a good boy. Never in any trouble."

Mum hushed him this time. Clare shrugged.

"He never mentioned anything like that," she said. "But then, even if he knew anything about it, I can't see him discussing it at home, can you?"

There were a few more general questions about school and Angelo's friends, then the interview was over. Clare insisted on showing the policeman out.

"Look," she said, "Constable…"

"Please, call me Neil," the tall youth said, awkwardly.

"Neil. Something happened to me an hour ago. There were these boys, in a yellow car, driving really fast on Churchfield Lane…"

Quickly, she told him the story. Neil Foster made some notes.

"Do you want to press charges against these lads?"

"No, no," Clare insisted. "And I don't want to worry my parents with it. But I thought they might be some of those joyriders you were talking about. They could have been the ones that ran over Angelo."

Neil nodded slowly.

"I'll look into it – see if what you've given me matches a stolen car – though they'll probably have dumped it by now. I might need you to drop into the station later to look at some photographs."

"OK," Clare said. "Anything you want."

Neil opened the door. He held out his hand. Clare shook it.

"Thanks for your help," he said. "I know what a hard time this must be for you."

"What were you talking to the policeman about for so long in the hallway?" Dad wanted to know.

"Not much," Clare replied. "He was just being sympathetic."

Dad frowned. Luckily, the phone rang, so Clare went to answer it before Dad could question her further. It was her Great-Uncle Angelo, calling from Bedford. Clare brought Dad to the phone.

"No need to tell me why the young policeman was chatting to you," Mum said, when they were alone in the front room.

"How do you mean?" Clare asked, thinking she'd been overheard.

"I saw the way he was looking at you."

"Oh, Mum, don't be disgusting."

"There's nothing disgusting about being admired. But maybe you were right – that dress is a mistake. We'd better get you something else."

"Nothing," Neil Foster was saying to Jan Hunt in the incident room later that afternoon. "Just an ordinary lad who happened to be half Italian, who happened to be in a hit and run. What did you get?"

"Not a lot. Every time we get a witness who seems definite about something we get another who contradicts them."

Neil looked at the board. There had been fourteen witness interviews. A chart showed how they matched up.

Colour of car: green 3, yellow 4, red 1, "light" 2, "metallic" 2, don't know 2.
Number of occupants: one 6, two 2, more than two 2, "didn't see" 4.
Type of car: estate 2, large 5, hatchback 1, Volvo 1, Ford Escort 2, "foreign" 3.
Sex of driver: male 5, female 2, "didn't see" 7.
Description of driver: white 6, black 1, middle aged 2, young 2, wearing bright headband 2, underage 1.

"All we can say," Neil summed up, "is that it was probably a single white male driving a light-coloured car of average size or above. We don't even know for sure whether the car turned right from Alfreton Road, or cut across four lanes of traffic from Churchfield Lane. The witness reports are conflicting on that, too."

He drew the sketch which the Reporting Officer was obliged to fill in.

Inspector Thompson looked at the board and the sketch. Then he asked Neil about his interview with the Coppolas. Neil told him what he'd told Jan.

"That's the lot?"

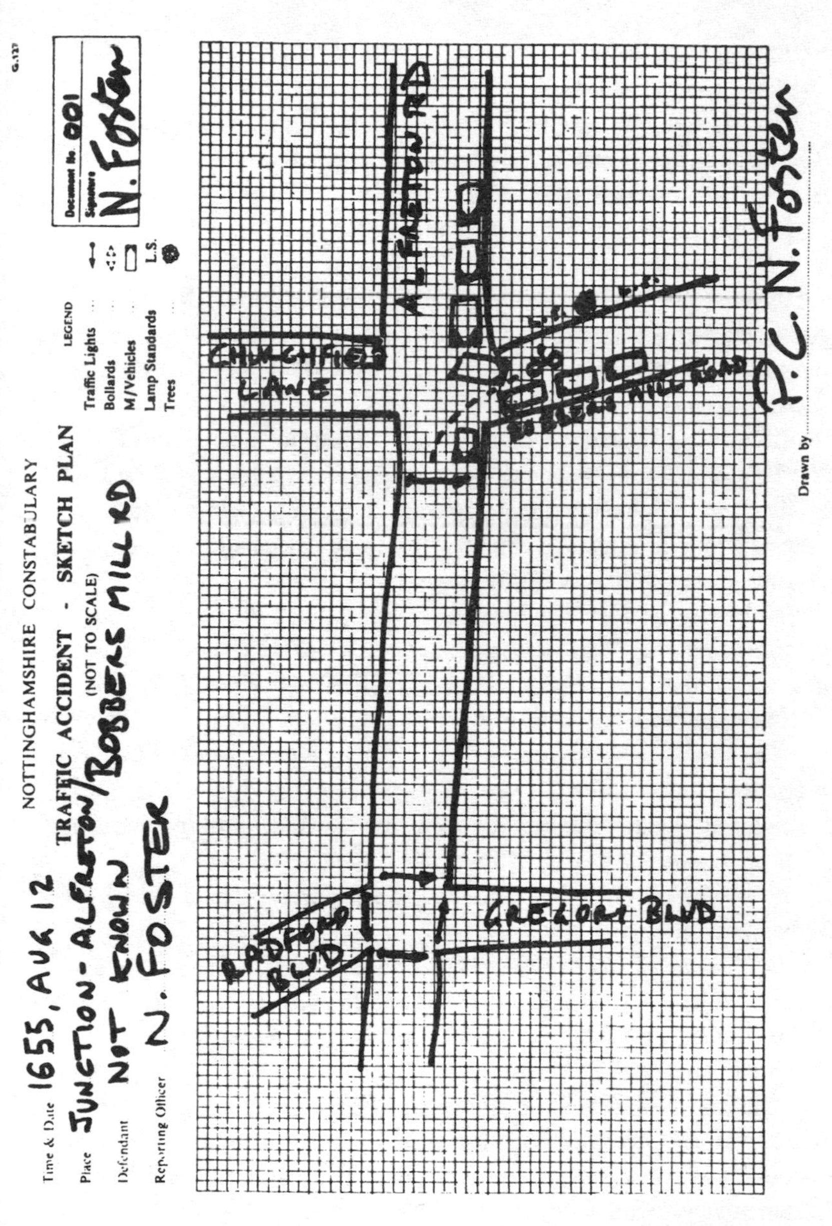
G.127

NOTTINGHAMSHIRE CONSTABULARY

TRAFFIC ACCIDENT - SKETCH PLAN

(NOT TO SCALE)

Time & Date 1655, AUG 12

Place JUNCTION-ALFRETON/BOBBERS MILL RD

Defendant NOT KNOWN

Reporting Officer N. FOSTER

LEGEND

Traffic Lights

Bollards

M/Vehicles

Lamp Standards L.S.

Trees

Document No. 001

Signature N. Foster

ALFRETON RD

CHURCHFIELD LANE

BOBBERS MILL ROAD

GREGORY BLVD

RADFORD BLVD

Drawn by P.C. N. Foster

"There was one other thing, sir. Probably not relevant."

"Yes?"

"The daughter, Clare – she's nineteen, a university student. It seems she had a run-in with some joyriders this afternoon. Tried to knock her over."

Thompson frowned.

"Did they say anything to her?"

"No. It sounded like some of the usual lads messing about, sir. Trying to give a pretty girl a scare. But she thought it possible that there was some connection with her brother's death."

Thompson didn't look impressed.

"Do you agree with her?"

"Not really," Neil had to admit. "Joyriders usually work in packs, and most of the witnesses agree that there was only one person in the car. Though I see from the chart that one witness did say the driver was underage."

"What do you want to do about it?" Thompson asked.

"I thought I might check the cars that were stolen this afternoon – I've got a good description and a partial plate from Clare Coppola. Then, if it turns out that the car was nicked, bring the girl in and get her to look at some mugshots."

Jan began to moan.

"Oh, come on, Neil. Joyriders are ten a penny. Even if you get a conviction they only end up with a slap on the wrist."

She turned to Thompson.

"This is a manslaughter enquiry, sir. There are lots of better ways of getting results."

Neil felt like kicking her. Thompson frowned, thinking about it.

"You say they threatened the girl?"

"She says they tried to run her over. Hard to tell how serious they were."

"Well, none of our other lines of enquiry seem to be getting anywhere. I'll let you spend tomorrow on it. Oh, and ... Sergeant Hunt?"

Jan looked up.

"Sir?"

"You may be right about this being a manslaughter investigation, but we haven't yet ruled out the possibility of murder. Two of the witnesses say that the car seemed to be driving at the Coppola boy."

Jan gave him a disbelieving look.

"You don't—"

"There's an old Italian custom that you might have heard of: the vendetta. Yesterday, the boy; today, the girl. Keep it in mind, eh?"

He walked off, leaving Jan fuming.

"'*There's an old Italian custom you might have heard of.*' He talks like he's in a spaghetti western. You don't really buy any of that do you, Neil?"

Neil shook his head.

"Lots of easier ways to kill someone."

"So why do you want to follow this thing up with the girl?"

Neil shrugged.

"She told me about it. I said I'd check it out."

Jan gave him a sly smile.

"Good looking, is she?"

Neil tried to sound casual. He hoped his face hadn't gone red.

"Gorgeous. Like Sophia Loren must have looked when she was a teenager. But that's got nothing to do with it."

Jan gave him a sceptical look.

"If you say so. But bear this in mind. We've only got two, three days at the most before this investigation gets put on a back burner. You've just committed your morning to chasing up joyriders and you're doing overtime at the inquest for most of the afternoon. So that's a wasted day in prospect. G'night."

Neil waited until she'd gone, then picked up the phone. The information he wanted took less than five minutes to get hold of.

"The car you describe was taken from the car park of a leisure centre in West Bridgford at around two this afternoon. It hasn't been recovered yet. Do you have anything for us?"

"It was seen in Radford about an hour later," Neil replied. "I have a witness. There might be a connection with a case I'm working on. All right with you if I interview her and get back to you?"

"Might as well leave it until the morning," Neil was told. "Car should have been found by then. Ninety-nine out of a hundred are."

Neil arranged to get photos of frequent young offenders to show Clare Coppola the next day. They made depressing reading. Some of these lads had been caught ten times before they were old enough to get a provisional licence.

You got kids of fifteen who claimed to be "addicted" to driving, the same way some kids were hooked on slot machines. It was rubbish as far as Neil was concerned: these kids had dull, drab lives and all they were "addicted" to was anything that gave them a cheap thrill. You could feel sorry for them – until it was your car they took, or your brother they ran over.

He could call in on Clare Coppola on the way home, give her the news that she'd got it right about the joyriders, arrange for her to come in the next morning. Or he could talk to her on the phone. But he would like to see her again.

That stuff he'd said to Jan about Sophia Loren wasn't quite true. Clare's nose was slightly too big and her cleavage was more modest than the film star's. But there was something arresting, almost aristocratic about Clare. She had deep blue eyes with a sad, faraway look in them which wasn't just to do with her brother's death. Since the interview that afternoon, Neil had found it hard to keep her out of his mind.

He checked his watch. Going on for ten. On the late side. Tomorrow he moved from a late to an early shift, with only eight hours' sleeping time in between. He'd better go home. It would be wrong, too, to intrude on the Coppola grief for the second time in a day. A phone call would have to do. He looked up her number in the book.

"Hello?"

The voice was slightly breathy, somewhat formal. She sounded like she'd been answering the phone all day.

"Clare, this is Neil Foster at Radford Road Police Station."

"Oh, yes. Can I help you?"

"You were right about that car this afternoon. It had just been stolen."

"Really?"

She sounded excited for a moment, then her voice calmed down.

"Do you think there's any connection with—"

Neil tried to sound mature, responsible.

"I don't know. It's possible. I've been given the go-ahead to spend tomorrow morning having a look at it. Do you think you could come into the station and have a look at some photographs for me?"

"Sure." She hesitated, then added, "It'll give me an excuse to get out of the house. What time do you want me?"

"Is ten OK?"

"Ten. I'll see you then. 'Bye."

She hung up. Neil put down the phone with a big smile. As he got into his car to go home, he had to remind himself that this was an investigation into a death. Clare Coppola wouldn't be thinking about romance at all. Neither should he.

5

It was awkward, explaining to Mum and Dad why Neil Foster wanted to see her.

"He has some photographs he wants me to look at."

"Doesn't he want us to see them, too?"

"You wouldn't recognize them – kids Angelo might have known at school."

"But you weren't at school at the same time as Angelo."

"I know – it's probably a waste of time."

Clare walked to the police station. Normally, she would have used her bicycle, but times weren't normal. Should she have told Mum and Dad the truth about the joyriders? Sometimes it seemed she spent half her time avoiding telling her parents what she was really doing. Dad could blow his top at the slightest provocation. Mum would try to calm him down, but Dad always held sway.

Clare kept quiet about her boyfriends at home. Once she'd dated a boy who was Italian–English, like herself, and made the mistake of telling Dad. He tried to insist on a chaperone. Mum put a stop to that. She pointed out that Dad had married a Nottingham girl and his daughter was a Nottingham girl, too. Dad backed down. Clare learned that it was safest not to mention the boys she was seeing.

University was the other big conflict. Dad wanted her to have a *liceo classico* – a classical education, preferably studying Latin or Greek. But they didn't teach those subjects at Greencoat. Architecture was the nearest discipline to her parents' ideals that Clare could find. Even then, Dad warned Clare that it would be years and years before she earned real money, and he was aware from his position as a builder that the country was full of unemployed architects. But he was proud of Clare because she was getting the education he'd missed. Also, in a way, she was following the family tradition. Dad used to joke that he and Angelo would build the houses Clare designed.

It was another baking hot day. By the time Clare arrived at the Radford Road Police Station, sweat was trickling down the back of her grey cotton dress. She had the matching jacket draped over her shoulder for wearing later. However, it looked like she would have to change again before going to the inquest that afternoon. All this heat used up clothes.

She had to wait only a few seconds for Neil Foster. He appeared from a side door, in his shirt sleeves.

"I appreciate your coming in at a time like this. It won't take long."

He offered her coffee or a soft drink. Clare accepted lemonade. She looked around. The police station had been built only a few years ago. It didn't have the shabby look that Clare associated with such buildings. The anonymous, small rooms reminded her more of a portakabin. She'd worked in one during a placement for the architects on one of Dad's construction jobs last summer.

Neil set out the photographs.

"Take your time," he told her. "Look for as long as you want."

The pile was huge.

"It's hard to believe there are so many criminals under the age of seventeen," Clare said.

"These are just the ones associated with taking without consent," Neil told her. "Actually, the majority of petty crime in this country is committed by kids of fifteen or under. Makes you think, doesn't it?"

In the black-and-white photographs in front of Clare, everybody *looked* like a criminal. It occurred to her that if there was a photograph of Angelo here, he would look like a criminal, too. It was the guilty, suspicious way they looked at the camera. The pictured boys knew that they were being entered into a gallery of the damned.

"I only saw one of them clearly," she told Neil. "I half saw another one. It's difficult."

"Take your time."

It was tempting to pick out faces which loosely resembled those of the boys she'd seen. However, Clare was aware of the responsibility involved. Anyone she pointed out would be picked up and interviewed about his whereabouts on the previous afternoon. She had to get it right.

The other strange thing was that, now and then, she recognized someone she vaguely knew. There was a skinhead boy who lived down the street from her, and another with red hair looked like a kid at her old school. How many cars had they stolen? Every so often, she commented on one of the faces in front of her, but only to emphasize that it wasn't quite right.

"His face was a little longer than that. The hair and the eyes are right, but the jaw is wrong."

"It's no use," she said, when she'd gone through all the photographs for a second time. "They're not here. Or, if they are, I don't recognize them."

"Don't worry," said Neil. "I'd like to you try something else."

He left the room. When he returned, he was wheeling in a trolley, on which was a video recorder and a TV set.

"Some of these people don't appear on photographs," he explained. "They're too recent or they haven't been convicted yet."

The videos were taken in the entrances of police stations throughout the city, as suspects were brought in past the security camera behind the front desk.

"It runs all the time," Neil told her. "You'd be surprised how many incidents there are in the waiting areas. It's worth its weight in gold."

The quality of the pictures wasn't very good and the editing was crude. A date appeared at the bottom of the screen, beginning with January the first and slowly moving forward, day by day. As soon as a suspect had been in front of the camera long enough to be identified, the image cut to the next one.

The people in the video pictures were sadder than the ones in the photographs. You saw their whole bodies – slumped, defeated, most of them. Others tried to look jaunty, like rock musicians affecting rebellion. Many had a dazed look in their eyes which Clare assumed meant that they were on drugs.

"Just tell me if you want me to rewind any of them," Neil said.

Clare shook her head. The tapes went on and on – a badly lit video with no soundtrack, nothing to hold your interest. Some of these people are probably innocent, she told herself. But none of them *looked* innocent. Innocence didn't belong here.

"I've seen so many faces," she told Neil, "I'm not sure that even if I saw him now I'd recognize him – you know what I mean? I might end up identifying one of the people from the photographs you showed me earlier."

"We can stop if you want," Neil told her. "Take a break."

Clare looked at her watch.

"I've got to be at the inquest this afternoon. I need to go home and change."

"You look fine as you are."

Clare gave him half a smile. The fan had kept the room cool, it was true. She no longer felt dishevelled.

"I could give you a lift to the inquest."

Clare thought. If Neil drove her there, she wouldn't get sweaty again, walking home.

"OK," she said. "Can I ring my mum before we continue?"

The tapes ran for another half an hour. Slowly, the date at the bottom of the screen edged into July, then August.

"Nearly over," said Neil, unnecessarily. "We should have time for a spot of lunch before we go to see the coroner."

Mention of lunch made Clare's stomach rumble. She hadn't eaten breakfast. No one at home had. They acted as though it was impolite to eat in the face of death.

Her mind was wandering. Clare was convinced now that the boys she had seen would not appear, that she was wasting her time. Her thoughts were moving forward to the inquest and after, to the relatives who would be arriving from Italy for the funeral. When her assailant appeared, she almost missed it.

"Wind that one back, would you?" she said to Neil.

He did it without comment. On the screen a wiry, angry-looking boy walked into a police station, this station, with his head held high.

"That's him!" Clare announced. "The driver."

"You're sure?"

"I'm positive."

Neil freeze-framed the boy's image, then checked the date at the bottom of the picture.

"I just have to make a phone call," he explained. "Watch the rest of the video while I'm gone. You might see the others."

The other boys weren't there. Neil returned to the room five minutes later.

"I've got his name," he told Clare. "We'll pick him up later. You may have to ID him at an identification parade to establish that it was definitely him yesterday."

"It's not yesterday I'm bothered about," Clare told Neil, "it's the day before. When you interview him, you will find out what he was doing when Angelo was killed?"

"Of course." Neil smiled and opened the door. "Now, shall we get some lunch?"

Where did you take a girl like Clare Coppola? They had only half an hour, so Neil settled on the Playhouse Bar, a short walk from the coroner's offices on East Circus Street. Clare drank orange juice and wolfed down her cheese cob in seconds, so he bought her another.

While Clare ate, Neil tried to think of things to say to her. He'd never been much good at small talk. He found it hard to get beyond the football scores and station gossip. When in doubt, the other blokes at Ryton training college used to say, ask them about themselves, show them that you're really interested in *them*.

"Clare's not an Italian name, is it?"

Clare swallowed the last morsel of bread and wiped her lips before replying.

"Not a very common one. But my mum's English, as you must have noticed."

She said this in a slightly teasing way, as though he was being a bit thick.

"But your brother was called Angelo..."

Clare nodded her head slowly.

"It's an old family name. My Uncle – Great-Uncle, really – Angelo gave Dad his start in the building trade over here. Mum and Dad had an agreement – Mum got to choose the name if I was a girl, Dad did if I was a boy. If the agreement had been the other way round I suppose my name would have been Angela."

She looked a little uncomfortable, discussing her dead brother. Neil quickly began asking her about university. It turned out that Clare was studying architecture, so he got her talking about buildings she liked. He acted interested, but inside he was depressed. It was obvious that Clare Coppola was out of his league. He guessed that she had a boyfriend, too, back in Manchester. But he couldn't work out how to get that information out of her.

"We'd better get going," Clare said, finally. "The inquest's in ten minutes."

Technically, Neil was off duty at two, so he could claim some overtime for his court appearance, which was good news. The couple walked to the coroner's together. Once they got inside the building, Clare put on the grey linen jacket which matched her dress. Then she brushed her black hair back over her shoulders. This more formal look seemed to age her by about five years. Neil followed her into the court at a distance. For the first time, he remembered that he had to give evidence himself, and became nervous.

When he was called, it was less stressful than other court appearances he'd made. Then, he'd always been for the prosecution. Here, no one was trying to catch him out. The only pressure on him was performing in front of Clare. He tried to avoid looking at her, as she sat between her mother and father on the front row. Behind them were several other family members and a couple of journalists.

"I held him in my arms," Neil said quietly. "He was conscious at that point. He said one word to me – 'blaze'."

"You're quite sure that was the word he used?" the coroner asked.

"Positive. It was very clear. Then he passed out."

"And what happened after that?"

"I attempted mouth-to-mouth resuscitation several times, until the ambulance came."

"And he was alive at that point?"

"He was breathing spasmodically, yes."

"But he did not regain consciousness?"

"No."

The coroner congratulated Neil on his evidence and on his exemplary conduct. Then came the medical evidence. The surgeon explained that the immediate cause of death was the chest injuries.

"But he also sustained severe injuries to the head which made his recovery extremely unlikely."

The pathologist expanded on this.

"I found brain damage of such an extent that Angelo would never have recovered full consciousness. He was almost certainly brain dead before he reached the hospital."

She was asked about the speed of the car which had hit him.

"His injuries were consistent with being hit by a motor vehicle travelling at between forty-five and fifty miles per hour."

The traffic accident investigation officer confirmed the pathologist's estimate of the car's speed. Photographs of the scene were shown. It all went very quickly.

The coroner recorded a verdict of death by misadventure and it was all over. The whole process had taken less than twenty minutes. Maria Coppola thanked Neil again on their way out. Clare didn't talk to Neil. She was busy calming down her father.

"It wasn't 'death by misadventure'," Nick Coppola was saying to a TV camera. "It was murder. And someone has to pay!"

6

"His name's Mark Crowston," Neil told Clare on the phone. "No criminal record, but his name's come up twice in connection with TWOC offences."

"*Twock?*"

"Taking without the owner's consent. Seems that Crowston's a dab hand at boosting cars."

"Should you be telling me this?" Clare asked. "I thought you said that there might be an identity parade."

"There's no point, I'm afraid," Neil said. "He admits having an altercation with you. He denies trying to run into you – naturally – and he has three witnesses who were in the car with him. They'll swear that you made abusive gestures and used foul language for no reason at all. He's lying, of course, but there are four of them against one of you."

"But the car was stolen. Surely—"

On the other end of the phone, Neil's voice became even more apologetic.

"We can't prove that, I'm afraid. Crowston claims that he was driving his brother-in-law's car, which is a similar make and colour. We've found the stolen car whose plates you gave us. But it had been burnt out on the Bestwood Estate. The fire removed the prints. Your evidence isn't enough to tie Crowston to it."

Clare was getting exasperated.

"But what about Tuesday? Couldn't that have been one of them?"

"I'm afraid Crowston has an impeccable alibi," Neil told her. "He and two of the other lads in the car were in court, charged with two TWOC offences from back in the spring. They got off. That was why they were out joyriding yesterday. They were celebrating."

"What about the fourth one?"

"He couldn't have done it either, I'm afraid."

"Why?"

"He's broken his right arm."

Clare wanted to scream.

"We'll get them in the end," Neil told her. "Crowston's already been arrested again for another offence. That was why he was on the video you saw."

Neil was trying to make his voice soothing, to calm her down. Clare hated it when people treated her that way. As far as she was concerned, the conversation was over. Neil Foster, however, kept talking.

"How are you keeping?" he asked.

"I'm OK. I'll be glad when the funeral's over."

"That's not till Monday, is it?"

"That's right."

"I was thinking..."

"Yes?"

Neil's voice stumbled over the words.

"I've got the weekend off. I thought you might want to do something to take your mind off things – go to the pictures or something like that."

Clare waited for him to finish, but Neil clearly thought he had made himself clear.

"You mean, with you?" Clare prompted.

He laughed nervously.

"Yes. Sorry. Didn't I say that?"

Clare took a deep breath. She was used to dealing with boys asking her out, but not in circumstances like this.

"It's very nice of you, Neil. But I've got loads of relatives arriving this weekend and I'm expected to be here. You know how it is."

"Sure. Another time, maybe."

"Maybe, yes. Thanks for asking. 'Bye."

She put the phone down before he could say anything else. It was supposed to be flattering when someone asked you out, but Clare usually found it embarrassing. She had been thinking of Neil as a police officer, not a potential boyfriend. Men should be able to tell if you liked them, then they wouldn't risk the humiliation of being turned down. But most of the men she met seemed to know less about women than they did about modern architecture. Which was nothing at all.

"Neil, I don't want to be funny, but..."

"What?"

"I couldn't help overhearing your conversation with the Coppola girl."

Neil blushed. He thought Jan was going to tease him about asking her out. She wasn't.

"What about it?"

"You were giving her information which wasn't necessary – the guy's name for a start, not to mention his alibi. You're only meant to tell her what's pertinent to her involvement in the investigation."

"Oh, come on, Sarge. What possible harm—"

Neil called Jan "Sarge" only when he was annoyed with her.

"I'm just warning you, that's all. Suppose some of her friends were to find out where Crowston lives, harass him..."

Neil laughed.

"You're almost as bad as the Inspector, with all that 'vendetta' nonsense."

"And you're as bad as all the rest, giving the girl special treatment because you fancy her!"

Neil came over and put his hand on Jan's shoulder. Jan hated it when coppers behaved in that patronizing way, particularly when they were younger than her.

"You're over-reacting," Neil said. "He was in court. It's a matter of public record."

"All right," said Jan, shaking off his hand. "So now you can give me some help. I persuaded the boss to let me check out that car model angle, the one you were so keen on, but I can't work out how to access it on the computer. Give me a hand, would you?"

Neil grinned.

"Not entirely computer literate, are we?"

Jan gritted her teeth.

"I know how to use the system, but not for this. And your training is a lot more recent than mine. The programs change constantly, don't they?"

Neil nodded.

"Yeah, well I've had a load of 'hands-on' experience, it's true..."

Jan flinched. She'd had enough weak sexist jokes to last her a lifetime. She knew all the put-down replies, but was getting tired of using them.

"I know the only thing you've had your hands on, my lad."

Water off a duck's back. Neil didn't even bother replying. He was busy playing with the keyboard. Two minutes later, he pressed the button marked "print" and paper began to spew out of the bubble jet. Smart alec!

"I can't access the cars with 'blaze' in the model name," he told Jan. "The computer doesn't allow that. So I'm getting a printout of all the different types of cars and model names, going back ten years. We can go through them manually."

He meant by looking at them.

"How long will that take?"

"Not long."

The printout was on its third sheet. Jan looked at it. The list was only halfway through the Alfa Romeos. She handed it to Neil.

"Not long, huh?"

He frowned, then gave her another of his silly grins.

"Good thing you've got me here to help you."

Clare's grandmother arrived on Saturday afternoon, along with two of her uncles and her Aunt Rafaella. Clare hadn't seen any of the Italian side of the family since she last visited their village, two years before. She accompanied Dad as he drove down to meet them. They didn't talk much on the way, but spent the entire journey listening to classical music on Radio Three, each engrossed in their own thoughts.

The reunion at the airport was sombre. Only Uncle Roberto spoke to her in English.

"You look wonderful, Clare."

She was wearing the new black dress Mum had bought her in Jessops, after the inquest. Roberto went on.

"Like your Aunt Rafaella did when she was your age – a real beauty."

Clare let the rest of the conversation wash over her. Her Italian wasn't too strong, but she caught the general drift, which was the same as everybody had been saying for the last five days – it was a tragedy, a terrible waste, and something dreadful should be done to the villain responsible.

Once they got home, the atmosphere was claustrophobic. The house was too full. Her uncles shared Angelo's bedroom and Grandma had the spare. Rafaella shared with Clare. On Sunday morning, it was impossible to get into the bathroom before church. When they got back, Uncle Angelo and three more Coppolas had arrived. Since only Roberto spoke much English, most of the conversation was in Italian. Clare joined her mum in the kitchen. Maria was upset.

"You know, when I was pregnant with Angelo, before Nick started the business, he had a chance of a job back home in the village. He tried to persuade me to go back with him. We'd have less money, he said, but we'd be happier. The village was a good place to bring children up. And I … and I…"

She was on the verge of tears. Clare held her hand.

"I said no. I don't remember what reasons I gave Nick. He didn't press me. Both of my parents were still alive then. It was the end of the seventies and unemployment was just starting to get high. We could see that things were going to get worse, but I thought Italy wouldn't be any better. I hardly spoke the language and your dad's family frightened me a little. They were all older than me. They didn't really approve of Nick marrying an English girl. Yet now…"

Tears were streaming down Mum's face, but she didn't dry them.

"Now they've all come over to grieve for Angelo. And they're all warm, loving people who've borrowed money to get the air fare and I think – if I'd gone over there, this wouldn't have happened. Angelo would be alive, with all his relatives around him. We'd be happy. Instead…"

She broke down. Clare hugged her.

"You can't change the past, Mum. No one can say what would have happened if we'd lived in Italy. I'm not sure if I'd have been as happy as I have been, but that isn't the point. What's done is done. Please stop crying."

Mum shook her head as her tears soaked into Clare's dress.

"No. I need to cry. It helps."

Clare was crying, too. She was dimly aware of people looking into the kitchen, then moving quickly away, allowing them to grieve with dignity. After another minute, Mum broke away from Clare.

"Thank you," she said. "I needed to do that."

She washed her face in the sink. Clare wiped her own eyes.

"Will you be all right now?" she asked.

Mum nodded.

"I'd better go and talk to your aunt and uncles. What are you going to do?"

"I really need to get out of the house for a while," Clare told her. "There's some kind of festival on at the Forest, with music and stuff. I think I might walk over there and have a look."

"Go on," Mum said. "Get going. There's only your dad'll notice. I'll square it with him."

Clare changed into jeans and a light T-shirt. It was a great relief to get out of the house and its stifling atmosphere. She walked over to the Forest recreation ground. The Rock and Reggae Festival was held there, on the large grassy area where Nottingham Forest, the football team, used to play. It was a free festival. Every year the Council threatened to close it down because of noise, or damage or drugs or something. Yet, somehow, it always survived.

The afternoon was at its hottest, and there was a pleasant lethargy about the festival. Children played on the grass. Many of them had had their faces painted at one of the stalls. Exotically dressed people were picnicking on the grass, enjoying the rough and ready music.

Two hundred metres away, on Sherwood Rise, was the Italian Community Centre. It might as well be on another planet. Here, unkempt crusties played thrash metal on the main stage. The latest rave sounds came from one of the marquees. There were a few police around, in their shirt sleeves, maintaining a low profile. It was a relaxing place to be.

However, after an hour, Clare had looked at enough stalls selling trinkets and tapes and the music bored her. She wasn't ready to go home, so she decided to walk up the hill to the tree-lined slopes of the upper part of the Forest.

A road ran across the middle, separating one half from the other. Beyond it, on the left, was an old graveyard, long full up. Clare walked there sometimes, on her own. In the middle was a vast hollow where the city's paupers used to be buried. It would be cool there. Clare decided that she needed to walk around for a while, to spend some time thinking about Angelo.

The entrance was on the main road. Clare left the festival, passed the all-weather soccer pitch and joined the slip road that led on to the Mansfield Road. Cars were coming down the slip road and parking in order to visit the festival, although they weren't supposed to stop there. Clare hardly paid any attention to them. She didn't look back, even when one of them slowed to a crawl behind her.

The front of the car nudged Clare's left buttock and she spun around.

"What do you think you're playing at?" she yelled.

The car stopped and the driver got out. It was the youth she'd identified two days before: Mark Crowston.

"You and I need to have a talk," he said.

Clare stood her ground.

"We've got nothing to talk about," she told the ugly youth.

His hair was cut shorter than it had been on the video. He wore a torn T-shirt. His three side-kicks were in the car, leering at her through the windows.

"She looks a bit tasty today," one of them called. "Why don't we take her for a ride?"

Clare flinched.

"Leave me alone," she said loudly. "I don't want anything to do with you."

She turned on her heel, intending to walk off. Crowston grabbed her shoulder. The other youths got out of the car, blocking her path.

"You went to see the police about us, didn't you?" Crowston sneered. "That wasn't a very nice thing to do, was it?"

Clare was silent. Crowston continued.

"A little bird told me that your brother got run over. What a shame."

Anger replaced fear. Clare was livid. She slapped Crowston hard on the face.

"You—"

Stung by the pain, Crowston let go of her for a moment. Clare seized her chance. She ran between Crowston's henchmen, up the hill.

Immediately, she knew she'd made a mistake. She should have headed downwards, towards the safety of the festival crowd. The hill was steep and the joyriders were taller than her, would run faster. Already she could hear them getting nearer and nearer. She had only one advantage over them. She knew her way around the graveyard and they probably didn't. But first she had to get in there.

Clare charged into the cemetery and took the path that ran diagonally across the centre, through the gravestones. The yobs were advancing on her. She had to put them off. Gasping for breath, she ducked between a white, crumbling sepulchre and a grassy, unmarked mound. The four youths ran past her.

On her left was the path which led down to the paupers' graves. She might be able to hide there, but if these boys found her, she'd be trapped. She decided to double back on herself and get out of the cemetery. She joined the path and began to run. A high wall hid her from watching eyes, then dipped again. Suddenly, she could see two of them. And they could see her.

"There she is!"

They were on the same path, running straight towards her. Clare made for the path she'd just run down. But there, at the other end of it, were the other two. She froze, not knowing what to do. The only way she could go now was down into the huge hollow where the paupers were buried. But if she ran down there, she would be trapped. There was only one thing for it. She would have to try to scale the wall to her right, then jump over the other side.

Quickly, Clare jumped on to the sandstone wall, at a point where it was only a little taller than she was. She was wearing trainers, and managed to get some purchase with her feet. She looked over the edge of the wall, knowing that the drop on the other side was going to be bigger than the one she'd just climbed. It was at least five metres. She could easily break something. But she had to try. Behind her, she heard Crowston's voice.

"We'll have her now!"

Clare tried to swing her body over the wall, but it was no good. A rough hand grabbed her foot.

"Gotcha!"

The sandstone crumbled away at her feet and she fell to the stone floor, knocking her ankle.

"No!" she screamed.

She heard a loud, piercing whistle coming from behind her. Crowston yelled, "You asked for this!"

Clare looked up to see a large boot heading directly for her face.

7

In the end Jan brought the work home with her. Kevin hated it when she did that. He said her weekends off were for them. He would never let Jan pull overtime when Forest were playing at home, even though sometimes they could do with the money. Especially, as it turned out, now.

The printout was a hundred and two pages long. Jan was on page ninety-two. In ten minutes, she would have found out if a car with the model name "Blaze" had been sold new in Great Britain during the last ten years.

"Jan!"

Kevin had come in from his game of badminton. He walked into the living-room, leant over her armchair, and kissed her on the neck. His hair was still wet from the shower and it dripped on to her, refreshingly cool.

"You're not still doing that? You were at it when I went out."

"I know, but Mum rang up."

Kevin's eyes widened.

"Did you tell her?"

Jan's eyes met his. Let him work it out.

"You didn't tell her?"

Jan nodded.

"Wait another week. Until I'm sure."

"Whatever you say," Kevin told her. "As long as you haven't changed your mind."

Jan smiled.

"I haven't changed my mind." Kevin grinned. "Are you ready for the monthly ritual?"

"I told you – ten minutes."

"Leave that until tomorrow, when you're being paid to work on it."

"I'll be ready by the time you've got changed and dried your hair."

Kevin kissed her again and left the room.

The "monthly ritual" was the visit to Jan's in-laws for Sunday dinner. They were nice people, but they were boring. And they couldn't understand why their successful doctor son had married, of all things, a policewoman.

Jan's eyes moved down the page at double speed. Once, she'd planned to make Inspector by the time she was thirty-five. It would never happen now. She moved on to the next page. Astonishing, the number of cars that Volvo made. None of them with a model name of "Blaze". The next page. More Volvos. It was going to be a Sunday roast, of course. Who wanted to eat a roast dinner when the weather was as hot as this? All Jan fancied was a salad, maybe a little shellfish. Was she allowed to eat shellfish any more? She didn't know. Another page. Another.

There was actually a car called a Yakimoto. She'd heard of Yamaha, Honda and, of course, Toyota. But Yakimoto? She'd never seen one of them. Mind you, there were only three models: the compact, Stella, which had an 1100 cc engine, the standard 1300 model, Lone Star, which sounded like it ought to be American. Then there was the souped-up 1.6 GTI version, which she had to turn the page to get the model name for: Blaze.

She read it again to make sure that she wasn't hallucinating, that it didn't read "Black" or "Blazer" or "Daze". No – there it was, at the top of the page. Jan gave a whoop.

"Got it!"

"That's good. Can we go now?"

Kevin had come back into the room wearing his plaid cotton button-down shirt. He always wore his best clothes to go to his mother's.

"In a minute," Jan said, with a smile.

"But you said you'd got it."

"I need to make sure."

There was a possibility – remote, but nevertheless a possibility – that there was another car with the model name Blaze. The secret of good police work was thoroughness. Jan was always thorough. Before carrying on, though, she read the model details again – the

Yakimoto was a hatchback, which didn't tie with most of the witnesses' statements, but it came in three colours: yellow, dark green and, lastly, lime green, which did. And the speed made sense, too. It was the sort of car that people who drove fast used.

Best of all, only a tiny number of Yakimoto 1.6s had been imported to Britain, according to this report – a little over a hundred. If the car which knocked over Angelo Coppola, causing his death, was a Yakimoto Blaze, then the police had an excellent chance of catching the driver.

But just to be sure, Jan went back to the last five pages of the printout.

Clare covered her face with her arms, but the blow didn't come. Instead, she heard the loud whistle again, nearer this time. She looked up and the youths were running away.

"Next time!" Crowston yelled, as he vanished into the endless tombs.

Neil Foster, in his short-sleeved light blue shirt, came running around the corner. Clare had never been gladder to see anyone in her life.

"Are you all right?"

She tried to stand up, but stumbled. Neil caught her and held her close. Clare realized that she was shaking.

"I was so scared," she told him.

"You're all right now."

They sat down on a grassy knoll, next to what looked like a crypt.

"Was it Crowston?" Neil asked.

Clare nodded.

"They ran into me – literally – as I was leaving the festival."

"I know," Neil said. "I saw. I didn't notice you until you were leaving. Then, when I saw the lads getting out of the car, I came as quickly as I could."

"I'm glad you did."

Neil smiled. He squeezed her arm, gently.

"I'll go and see Crowston tomorrow, drag him into the station for a caution, tell him what'll happen if he comes near you again."

Clare was beginning to feel calmer. Her shoulder and her ankle ached from the fall.

"Won't it be like before?" she asked. "My word against him and his mates?"

Neil shook his head.

"I'll tell him I saw him, too."

"But you had to ask me whether it was him."

"Only you and I know that."

"Wouldn't stand up in court," Clare said.

"It doesn't have to," Neil assured her. "I just need to keep him away from you. But you'll still need to watch out. Crowston hangs around with some violent people. Have you told your family about him?"

Clare didn't answer.

"You haven't, have you?"

"No. They've got enough on their plate."

She remembered something.

"He knows about Angelo," Clare told Neil. "He made a joke about it."

"I think you ought to tell your parents," Neil said.

Clare didn't answer this.

"Would you like me to get you a car to take you home?" Neil asked.

"No, I'll be all right, really," Clare said. Then she added, more warmly, "Is that offer of a film still open?"

Neil's eyes brightened up.

"Of course."

"Everyone should be gone by Tuesday afternoon," Clare told him. "I'll need to get out of the house by the evening."

"What would you like to watch?"

"I don't know. Why don't we go down to the Showcase, see what's on?"

"Fine."

They exchanged awkward goodbyes. Clare walked home slowly, trying to ignore the pain in her leg where she'd fallen on it. She wasn't sure why she'd given Neil a date. Partly it was gratitude. He had saved her from a beating. Partly it was because he looked so eager. She knew that look. Neil was smitten with her and Clare felt bad about disappointing him. Yet also, she had to admit to herself, she was going out with Neil because she wanted to get close to the investigation into her brother's death. But there was nothing wrong with that. Was there?

* * *

"What do you want to see Crowston for?" Jan asked Neil. "I thought you'd eliminated him and his cronies."

"They had a go at Clare Coppola on Sunday afternoon."

"How do you mean, 'had a go'?"

"Chased her up the Mansfield Road to the old cemetery. I think they were going to beat her up before I got there."

"So you played the knight in shining armour, did you?"

Neil gave her a sly grin, which was rather unlike him.

"Something like that, as it turned out."

"But no offence was committed?"

"Not as such. No."

They parked the car halfway up a side road on the Whitemoor Estate. Jan knocked on the door of a dowdy semi-detached house with crumbling brickwork. It was answered by a woman of indeterminate age.

"Mrs Crowston?"

"What do you want?"

"Is Mark in?"

She gave them both hostile looks.

"What's it about?"

"We want to speak to him. Is he in, Mrs Crowston?"

"He's in bed."

"Would you get him up, please?"

It was eleven in the morning. Jan and Neil waited in the dingy, fusty-smelling front room of the house, trying not to look at the peeling wallpaper, the carpet covered in cigarette burns. They'd both spent time in much less pleasant places. Jan had been brought up in a series of them: run-down, squalid flats which her single-parent mother was always having to leave because she was behind with the rent. According to the sociologists, a background like that should make you become a criminal, not a copper. Jan didn't have a lot of time for sociologists.

Mark Crowston took five minutes to emerge from his bedroom. When he did, he was wearing ripped jeans and had a bare torso, exposing two tattoos: one was of a coiled snake; the other, almost touchingly, read "Mum". He lit a cigarette and sat down in a decrepit corduroy-backed armchair. He spoke before they did.

"I told you on Friday I had nothing to do with the Coppola kid."

"How come you know the name?" Neil asked.

Crowston sneered.

"Read the papers, don't I?"

"But that's not what we're here about," Jan told him.

Crowston squinted at them. Probably needs glasses, Jan thought. Too vain to wear them.

"Well?" Crowston asked.

He was looking at Jan. She should be dealing with this, not Neil. She was more experienced. But for Neil it was personal. So she let him get on with it.

"I saw you yesterday," Neil told Crowston.

"Oh, yeah? In the White Lion, were you?"

"No. I was patrolling the Rock and Reggae Festival, on the Forest."

Crowston laughed.

"You wouldn't see me near there – load of hippies, crusties, lousy music … you're kidding, right?"

Slowly, Neil shook his head.

"You didn't go into the festival itself."

"I didn't go near the festival. I told you, I was in the pub when—"

Neil leant forward.

"When *what*? I didn't tell you a time, or what happened."

Calm down, Jan wanted to tell Neil. Let him find enough rope to hang himself with.

"I was in the pub," Crowston repeated.

And Neil blew his cool.

"You were harassing a girl called Clare Coppola, whose brother died last week, and who you tried to run over the following day. There's no point in denying it, because I was there!"

Crowston shrugged.

"If you say so. What's the problem? Harassment? Big deal!"

"You also assaulted her…"

That wasn't what Neil had told Jan earlier. The young policeman went on.

"If I hadn't arrived, you'd have beaten her up!"

Crowston stood up.

"Says who? You reckon you saw me – there are a hundred blokes who look like me. How close were you?"

Neil didn't reply.

"You say this Coppola girl *nearly* got beaten up. So where's the crime? All I know is this girl's got a grudge against me because I drive a car the same colour as the one that killed her brother..."

Neil stood too, now, looking triumphant.

"How do you know what colour the car was?"

Crowston stubbed his cigarette out in the fireplace.

"Don't make me laugh."

Jan put a gentle arm on Neil's shoulder. Then she spoke to Mark Crowston, very softly, but very firmly.

"Mark Crowston, I am cautioning you for threatening behaviour towards Clare Coppola yesterday afternoon. No charges are being brought at this stage, but if there is any repetition – indeed, if you ever go near Clare Coppola again – you will be in deep trouble. Do you understand me?"

"I understand that you've got nothing on me."

"Well, then," Jan said, at the edge of her patience, "you'd better make sure that you don't give us any reason to arrest you. Because if you do, we'll throw the book at you! Got that?"

Crowston turned his back on them. Jan grabbed Neil and got him out of the house before he made more of a mess of things. Once they were in the car, she blew her top at him.

"Crowston's been avoiding the law since he was ten years old! He knows the rules better than we do. You've got to be more subtle, Neil – draw him out a bit at a time. All you did was raise his hostility – he hardly took in the warning we were there to give him."

Neil was indignant.

"What about the things he said about the colour of the car? Maybe he was out of court by the time the accident took place. Maybe he was driving that car."

Jan shook her head.

"He was winding us up. He doesn't know the colour of the car that killed Angelo Coppola any more than we do. By the way, was he right? Were you too far away from the incident yesterday to identify him properly?"

Neil was silent for a moment.

"It looked like him," he mumbled eventually. "Clare said it was him."

"You're impossible," Jan told him. "Let's just hope it's the last time we see that excuse for a human being."

She turned the car out of the estate, heading right, away from the station.

"Where are we going?" Neil asked.

Jan didn't reply for a while. Neil asked again. This time, she replied.

"We're going to see one of the two people in the city who own a Yakimoto 1.6," she told him.

"A what?"

"A car with the model name, 'Blaze'."

8

Brian Boland's Yakimoto Blaze was parked outside his insurance office. It was yellow. There was nothing special about the car. You'd have been hard pushed to say what separated it from at least a dozen other cars on the market.

Before going in, Neil and Jan examined the front of the car very carefully. No dents, no suspicious scratches or cracks on the bumper. Nothing which could be the consequence of a head-on collision with a cyclist. Nor were there any signs of recent bodywork which might have been done to cover up such a collision. Appearances could be deceptive, though – new work could be made to look old and some car deaths left no traces of the incident on the car itself. Not even blood.

And there was one thing: on the front left-hand wing, written in bright red letters, was what must have been the last word that Angelo Coppola ever read: *Blaze*.

Boland was in his forties and overweight. His nose had exposed veins and the mottled look which indicates a heavy drinker. He was an insurance broker.

"I often find," he told Jan and Neil, "that police officers, as a breed, are under-insured. They tend to think that it'll never happen to them, because of their jobs. Whereas you'd think, with their jobs, that they'd know the risks and take action to avoid them. Am I right or am I right?"

Neil didn't answer. He didn't have any insurance, other than for his car. Who needed it, when you lived at home with your parents?

"Take life insurance, for example. Do either of you have life insurance?"

Before Neil could answer, Jan made her point.

"We're here to talk to you about your whereabouts last week, Mr Boland."

Boland sighed. He got a packet of mints out of his pocket and offered them to each of the officers, both of whom refused. Then he popped one into his mouth. Probably used them to mask the smell of alcohol, Neil decided.

"Am I in some kind of trouble?" Boland asked, politely.

"Not at all," said Neil. "We just need to eliminate you from our enquiries."

"What enquiries?"

The phone rang. Boland reached over to pick it up, looked at Jan and Neil, then changed his mind. Instead, he pressed the button which activated the answering machine.

They heard his voice saying:

"This is Brian Boland Insurance Associates. I'm afraid that we can't take your call right now, but if you..."

The voice cut off as the caller hung up. Boland shook his head ruefully.

"Up to fifty per cent do that, you know. Can't stand talking into a machine. If I had the—"

"Mr Boland," Neil interrupted, "can you tell us where you were on the afternoon of Tuesday last?"

"Certainly."

Boland opened a desk drawer and pulled out a filofax. He flicked to the right page and pushed it across the desk to Jan and Neil. Too casual, Neil thought. He behaved like he was used to being questioned by the police.

The diary read like this:

10.00 Drexel Ltd
11.30 Simon Harrison
12.00 Karen Black
02.00 Market

"'Market'?" Jan asked.

"The Market Club. It's just off—"

"I know where it is," Jan said.

The Market Club was an all-day drinking bar, and had been since before all-day licensing was introduced. Its clientele were mainly market traders, but also included fringe elements of the criminal fraternity. It wasn't the sort of place you'd expect to find a businessman like Boland.

"Kind of a short working day, isn't it?" Neil asked.

"I do a lot of business in the Market Club," Boland replied. "You'd be surprised."

"Life insurance?" Jan suggested.

"Yes. And other things."

"What time did you leave?" Neil said, almost casually.

"Now there's a question."

"Try to answer it, please," Jan said, without a trace of impatience.

Boland appeared to be thinking about it.

"Could have been three. Could have been four."

That was too early.

"Which?" Neil asked.

"I guess that it would be the later time," Boland said. "But I'm not sure."

"Can you give us the names of anybody there who'd remember?" Jan asked.

Boland looked shifty for a moment. He's been lying, Neil thought. We're going to get him.

"There's the barman, Dave," he said slowly.

"We'll need more than that," Jan told him, firmly. "The names of everyone you met there."

"I'm not sure I'll be able to remember," Boland said slowly. "You see, I had a few."

"Please try."

He gave them some names and Jan wrote them down. Finally, she asked, "And you're sure you don't remember what time you drove home?"

Boland frowned.

"It may have been a bit later than four," he said. "I seem to remember that the traffic was bad."

Neil felt like cheering. Wait till he told Clare Coppola about this.

"Oh, but I didn't drive," Boland added, almost as an afterthought. "Not after drinking, obviously. I caught a bus."

* * *

Ten minutes later Jan and Neil drove back to the station. According to Boland, after failing to sell some life insurance to Karen Black, he had driven to his home, where he had deposited the car, then caught the bus into town, walking from Slab Square to the Market Club.

"I suppose it saved on the parking fees," Jan said.

"You believe him?" Neil asked, incredulously.

"No," said Jan. "I don't believe him. But if you were being interviewed by the police you wouldn't admit to drunken driving, would you? Doesn't mean he's guilty of killing Angelo Coppola."

"Makes it a darn sight more likely, though," Neil said.

"Agreed."

Neil checked the time. Twelve-thirty. Elsewhere, he knew, just a few kilometres away, Angelo Coppola was being buried.

"So who's got the other car?"

Jan checked her notes.

"A woman called Dawn Miller. We can't see her until this evening."

"This evening?" Neil groaned. "Why not?"

"Because she's in court this afternoon."

"Another one in court – what's she done?"

"Nothing, as far as I know. She's a probation officer."

Clare had been to funerals before, but never one where someone had died young. There was so much grief, and no one trying to hide it. Clare found it impossible to hold back her tears.

"It's right to cry," Aunt Rafaella said, her own eyes moist. "You cry as much as you want."

Somehow, Mum and Dad stayed in control, even when the priest delivered a eulogy to Angelo which made him sound like a saint. Perhaps he went too far. To Clare, her brother had been a normal, naughty boy, always getting in her way. Now he would never be anything else to her.

The chapel was full, not just with family. Many of Angelo's schoolfriends were there. Some of Clare's came, too: Denise, Sarah, Helen. Denise had been her best friend before she went to university. Now she was a secretary. Inevitably, they had drifted apart. Sarah and Helen both went to different universities, doing different courses. They saw each other much less than before, too.

With them, though, it didn't matter so much, because they were having similar experiences.

This afternoon the four girls were as close as ever. Each of them hugged Clare in turn. It had never felt more important to have friends.

"You must come out soon," Denise said. "Take your mind off things."

The four of them arranged to go out on Wednesday. Then Clare went home to a house full of grieving relatives.

Soon everyone was eating. A feast of food was laid out – much of it more suitable, Clare thought, for a wedding than a funeral: fancy breads, pickles, salami, hams, gherkins, huge, ripe tomatoes, endless different cheeses and, on another table, an array of cakes which Clare would have found mouthwatering any other day. Today, the sight of people tucking in made her feel sick. She retreated to her usual hiding place, the kitchen, expecting to find her mum there.

Instead she found Dad, with Uncle Roberto. They were talking in Italian, but Clare could work out what was being said. Roberto was saying, "And if you find him, you know what you must do. It's a matter of honour."

"Roberto, Roberto..." Dad shook his head. "We're not in Italy..."

Then he noticed Clare, and quickly changed the subject.

Dawn Miller had told Jan that she would be home by a quarter to six, so she and Neil arrived at ten to. The door was answered immediately. Dawn was a handsome Afro-Caribbean woman about the same age as Jan. She wore a white linen suit and a plain but expensive red silk blouse.

"How come you people are only ever early when it's inconvenient?" she asked. "I haven't had time to get changed yet."

Jan apologized.

"This'll only take a few minutes," she said. "We're anxious to get home ourselves."

"Tell me about it."

Jan went through what she wanted to know. Dawn consulted her diary.

"I was in court between three and four," she told them. "Then I went back to the office. I guess that I would have come home about five – that's the normal time."

"Do you remember the journey home?" Neil asked.

"Any reason why I should?"

This interview was totally unlike the one with Boland. Dawn Miller had nothing to hide. They were three professionals, going about their business. Nevertheless, Jan played it by the book.

"You were travelling by car?"

"That's right. Oh, hang on, that was the grid-lock day, wasn't it?"

Jan nodded.

"Yes, I remember now. I just missed it. I was listening to the reports on the radio, counting my blessings."

"How come?" Neil asked. "I mean, if you left work at five ... the whole city was snarled up."

"But I didn't leave at five," Dawn told them. "I left just after four to visit a client, in Radford, on my way home. I left him just before five."

Jan smiled at her.

"Could you tell me the client's name?"

"Nick Shears. Male. Thirty-nine. On parole after being released halfway through a three-year sentence for drug dealing."

"And you were visiting this guy on your own?" Neil asked. "Is that usual for a female probation officer?"

"Not usual, no. But, to be honest, I wasn't expecting him to be home. He hadn't turned up for his last two visits to the office. I wanted to check that he was still at the same address."

"And he was?"

"Yes. He said he'd been ill, apologized."

"And was that all right?" Jan asked.

Dawn shrugged. Sometimes, Jan couldn't believe how soft the system was. The way she saw it, parole shouldn't exist. Someone got three years, they should serve three years. But the prisons were overcrowded, so if you kept your nose clean, you might get out after one. In theory, you would be sent straight back if you committed another crime. In theory. But Jan kept her views to herself.

"How long had he been a client?" Neil asked.

"Nearly four months. He'd served eighteen months, which meant he had to do six months on parole. He was still on weekly visits. We would have relaxed that, but then he went AWOL."

"You'd better give us his address," Jan said. "Just a formality, you understand, but we have to make sure."

Dawn shrugged, then dictated it to Jan, from memory. Jan's ears pricked up. The address was a road off Churchfield Lane, which was the road they thought the hit-and-run driver had come from.

"Which way did you drive home?" Jan asked.

Dawn thought for a moment.

"I went along Churchfield Lane, turned right on to Alfreton Road, then left along the boulevards until I got to Mansfield Road. Why? What's all this about?"

"Just routine," Neil said. "Before we go, do you mind if we take a look at your car?"

"Of course not," Dawn Miller told them. "It's in the garage."

She offered them the keys, then paused.

"You don't think I knocked over that boy, do you? Good God!"

"Just routine," Jan repeated. "Nothing at all for you to worry about."

They went out to the garage. Neil opened it. Inside was Dawn Miller's lime green Yakimoto Blaze.

"Look at that," Neil said.

Beneath the headlight was a long angular scratch, nearly two centimetres wide.

"It looks as though she bumped into some thing," Jan said, thoughtfully.

Neil's voice was more angry.

"It looks like she ran into the handlebars of a bike."

9

The film they chose in the end was a light comedy. Clare didn't laugh much, but it took her mind off her troubles. Afterwards, they went for a drink in the Boat Inn. Neil off-duty, in jeans and a rugby shirt, was a different, more relaxed person. Clare was surprised to realize that she quite fancied him.

"What were you doing at the Rock and Reggae Festival?" he asked. "I wouldn't have thought it was your sort of scene."

"I just needed to get out of the house," Clare told him, wondering what he thought her "scene" was. "What were you doing there, anyway? You told me you had the weekend off."

Neil shrugged.

"I did, but I had nothing special to do, so I decided to earn some overtime. I'm saving up for a house."

"Where do you live now?"

"With my mum and my younger sister, in Wollaton."

"Mmmm, Wollaton," Clare teased him. "That's quite posh."

"On the council estate behind the park."

Embarrassed, Clare quickly moved the conversation on.

"How long have you been in the police?"

"Eight months. I've just finished my foundation period."

"Tell me about the training."

Neil gave her a look, as if to see that she was really interested, not just making up for her gaffe about Wollaton. Then he told her.

"It takes two years. The first 31 weeks is the foundation period. You do ten weeks at the Regional Training school at Ryton."

"What do they teach you?"

"All sorts. Experiential learning, they call it. You do lots of role-play. How to deal with the public. How to manage stress. The law, of course, and all the different police procedures."

"Your course sounds a lot more interesting than mine. What happens next?"

"Then you do five weeks with your tutor constable, working the area where you're going to work eventually. Then a week off, then another five weeks with your tutor and, finally, a week at Epperstone training school for what they call 'smoothing over' and final assessment."

"Which you passed?"

"Yes."

"So what happens now?"

"For the rest of the two years, I'm on my probationary period, monitored by my sergeant. I'm driving with her at the moment. Jan Hunt."

"What's she like?"

Neil smiled hesitantly.

"Jan's a good officer – very efficient. She gets a bit uptight sometimes, but nobody's perfect."

"What made you become a policeman?" Clare wanted to know.

Neil looked bashful.

"The usual reasons."

"Don't tell me – you like wearing a uniform and your favourite TV programme is *The Bill*."

Neil shook his head.

"I wanted a steady job with good money. My dad got made redundant when he was forty-five. He was on the dole for ten years before he died."

Clare was ashamed of being flippant. Other people had their troubles, too.

"I'm sorry," she said. "How long ago was that?"

"Last year," Neil told her. "Heart attack."

"Let's talk about something more cheerful."

They struck up a conversation about films and football teams. It was a bit strained. If Clare had come across Neil at university, where most of her friends were arty types, they would never have hit it off. But this was Nottingham. Here, she needed him. She didn't ask too many questions about his work. She didn't want him thinking that she was only going out with him because of her brother, even if it turned out to be true. So far, all he had told her was that Crowston had been cautioned for chasing her two days before. He wasn't allowed to discuss the ongoing investigation, he said. It was against the rules.

By their second drink, the conversation had moved on to Clare's family.

"My Uncle Angelo came over in the fifties," Clare explained. "The London Brick Company brought over whole villages from Southern Italy in those days, settled them in Bedford. In the sixties, Angelo set up his own building firm. My dad came over to work for him in the seventies. He did some jobs for people in Nottingham, met my mum, married her, and Angelo helped him to set up his own firm here."

"And your father named his firstborn son after his benefactor."

"Yes."

"Yours is small for an Italian family."

"I think Dad would have liked a huge family, like the one he comes from. But two of us was quite enough for Mum."

But now she's got none at home, Clare thought. And Dad still works all hours. How's she going to cope with all that time alone?

"Will you find him?" she asked suddenly, in a desperate voice. "Will you catch the person who killed Angelo?"

"I hope so," Neil said. "We've got a couple of good leads, which we're checking out. It should only be a matter of time."

"What kind of leads?" Clare asked.

Neil looked uncomfortable.

"I really shouldn't tell you. It's against—"

"I only meant *generally*," Clare insisted. "Just give me an idea."

Neil sipped his pint.

"Actually," he said, "you suggested it to me yourself, last week, at the hospital. You remember I asked you what the word 'blaze' might mean to Angelo?"

"I remember. I said it might be the model of the car that hit him."

"Right. Well, it turns out that there is a car with the model name of 'Blaze' – just one. And luckily, it's quite an obscure car company."

"Would I have heard of it?" Clare asked.

"I doubt it – the car's a Japanese import. Yakimoto, they're called. Anyway, there are only two of these cars that we know about in the Nottingham area. So we're checking out their owners."

Before Clare could ask anything else, Neil added, "And that's all I can tell you."

"But it looks promising?" Clare pressed him.

"Please," Neil said. "Let's change the subject."

They talked about their old schools and holidays they'd been on – standard first-date stuff. At ten past eleven, Neil drove her home.

"Thank you," she said to him. "I enjoyed myself."

"Can we do it again?" Neil asked, a little nervously.

"Yes. I'd like that."

He leant forward. She thought he was going to give her a peck on the cheek, but then he chickened out. She offered him her hand.

"Good luck with the investigation," she said. "You will let us know if..."

"We'll let you know," he said.

All the house lights were still on. Clare went inside to face the usual inquisition. But tonight, it didn't come. Her parents sat alone in front of the TV set, watching the closing credits of *Newsnight* in silence. Dad turned off the set before *The Late Show* began.

"Have they found out anything?" he asked, when Mum had gone upstairs.

Clare shook her head.

"He says they have some promising leads. They're doing their best."

Dad nodded grimly. He kissed Clare on the forehead, then went to bed, walking out of the room slowly, fists clenched inside the pockets of his trousers. Clare put the television back on with the sound low. She watched it until half past one, when her head became bleary and she knew that, finally, she would be able to sleep.

The other workers in Dawn Miller's office confirmed her story. Someone had blocked her in at the car park, and in the process of getting out, she'd scratched her car on a wall.

"She took it very well," the Senior Probation Officer said. "Put a note on the other car's windscreen – 'next time you park behind me, leave a tin-opener so that I can get out'."

This had happened on Wednesday, the day after Angelo's death.

"Didn't look like a wall to me," Neil told Jan. "Maybe she made a song and dance out of it in order to cover herself. Maybe it happened the day before."

"Don't be so cynical," Jan told him. "We'll see this Nick Shears bloke. If he backs up her timings, she's off the hook."

But Nick Shears wasn't home. According to Dawn, he was unemployed.

"Probably working a fiddle somewhere," Jan said.

"Don't be daft," Neil told her. "Just because you're on the dole doesn't mean you've got to stay home all day."

They drove to Sneinton Market, where they were forced to park on a single yellow line outside the Victoria Leisure Centre. Sneinton Market was in full flow. It was only eleven, but some of the punters in the Market Club were already well oiled.

"Brian Boland?" Dave the barman said. "Course I know him. A regular."

"Was he in last Tuesday afternoon?" Neil asked. "I believe you were on."

"He's in every Tuesday afternoon. Does a fair bit of business here then. People know, if they want to find Brian, he'll be around."

"Do you remember what time he left?"

"There you've got me. Sometimes stays till four, five … I've known him stay till six."

They talked to three other people who remembered seeing Boland the previous Tuesday. None was certain when he'd left. As the two officers walked out of the club, Jan turned round.

"Oh, by the way," she said to the barman, "where does Brian Boland usually park his car?"

"The car park opposite," Dave told them, in a tone which suggested that the answer was obvious. "That's the reason he comes on Tuesday afternoons. The market closes early and you can get a parking place."

"So he was lying about the car," Neil said, as they drove back towards Churchfield Lane to see if Nick Shears had returned. "I wonder what else he was lying about?"

"I think," said Jan, "it's time we ran a computer check on Mr Boland."

This time, the door was answered. Nick Shears turned out to be a small, wiry, good-looking guy, with long, curly hair. He didn't look like most drug-dealers Neil dealt with, more like a mechanic, or a plumber.

"Yeah, she came round about ten past four," he told the officers. "Left about three-quarters of an hour later."

"Long visit," Neil said.

"Yeah, well ... I'd missed a couple. You know how it is."

"Working?" Jan suggested.

Shears laughed.

"Have you tried getting a job round here – with or without a criminal record? There are over four million out of work in this country, if you count all the people the government leave off the books. Did you know that?"

"Yes," said Neil. "I did."

"Thanks for your help," Jan told Shears. "We'll see ourselves out."

"Believe that?" Neil asked as they drove back to the station.

"Why not?" Jan told him. "I can't see many ex-cons wanting to give their probation officer an alibi, unless it were true. Can you?"

Neil shook his head.

"So where does that leave us?"

Jan didn't answer his question. A message was coming through on the radio.

"The suspect you enquired about, Brian Boland, was convicted of driving under the influence of alcohol in May this year. He was fined five hundred pounds and banned from driving for twelve months."

Neil and Jan looked at each other.

"I think we'd better go and see Mr Boland again."

They got to Boland in his office, just as his wife arrived to take him home. Jan confronted him with what they'd found in the National Computer records.

"What you didn't tell us when we spoke last, Mr Boland, was that you'd been banned from driving for twelve months."

"You didn't ask." Boland looked irritatingly smug.

"But your car was outside your office when we interviewed you, Mr Boland," Neil said. "How do you explain that?"

"My wife drove me to work, then caught the bus herself," Boland replied. "She often does that when the traffic's heavy. You're not very keen on driving, are you, Marjorie?"

"That's right," said Mrs Boland. "I'm not."

Mrs Boland, a primary school teacher, was a hard-faced woman with a matronly figure. Jan could see that they wouldn't get much change from her. But she had to try.

"You have your own car as well, Mrs Boland. Why is that? Why do you keep two cars on?"

"A year's ban doesn't last for ever, Sergeant. Brian's fond of that car. There's not many like it."

"That's true," said Neil, "and that's why, Mr Boland, I'd like to put it to you that, on Tuesday last, your car was involved in a collision at about ten to five in the afternoon, while you were driving, illegally, back from the Market Club."

That was Neil, going in feet first. Jan sighed. She knew what was coming.

"That's impossible," Mrs Boland said before her husband could reply. "Last Tuesday Brian came home on the bus, like he always does from the Market. He'd had a few and went straight to bed to sleep it off. He got home just after I did – half past four."

"Why did you have to mention the time?" Jan asked Neil on their way out. "Now he's got an alibi instead of a faulty memory."

"Oh come on," said Neil. "It's obvious she'll say anything to protect him. You don't really believe he's not driving that car around, do you?"

"Of course not," Jan replied, irritated. "But believing and proving are two different things."

"So where does that leave us?" Neil asked.

"Dawn Miller's in the clear. Boland's our best suspect. We'll give his details to all the foot and car patrols. If anyone sees him driving, he's had it. But as far as the Angelo Coppola case is concerned, we're on shaky ground. He could have done it, but all the evidence is circumstantial and there's the wife's alibi. Also, Boland had no reason to turn on to Bobbers Mill Road."

"A short cut home?"

"For Dawn Miller, yes. But not for Brian Boland. No, I'm afraid that unless something turns up, we've had it."

"Back to square one," Neil suggested.

"Worse than that," Jan told him. "A dead end."

Autumn

10

The heat wave broke abruptly, in the second week of September. The children had gone back to school and the streets were suddenly empty. Cold sheets of rain blew across the city. Clare felt trapped inside the house. Dad complained that it was impossible to get work done. Mum sat around, staring into space.

Before long, Clare would be back at university. Yet that life seemed a world away. So much had happened since June. If Angelo were alive, he would be taking his GCSEs this year.

If.

The investigation into Angelo's death was winding down. The "promising leads" which Neil had mentioned seemed to have turned into dust. His sergeant was still responsible for the case – officially – but she had it on a back burner. Clare's patience was wearing thin.

She had been out with Neil twice since their first date. They had some laughs together. Under other circumstances, they might have something more going on than warm conversation and goodnight kisses. But Clare knew it wouldn't last after she went back to university. Neil was keener than she was. Clare meant to let him down gently before time and distance did the job for her. Meanwhile, the house felt like a tomb. The family didn't talk much. The visits of condolence tailed off, and they watched a lot of television. Every time there was any kind of a car chase on the screen, Mum would change the channel.

Clare's going out with Neil made things worse. After each date, when Dad got Clare alone, he would ask her, "Have they got anything? Are they any nearer?"

"No, Dad," she would tell him. "And Neil wouldn't tell me if they were near – not until charges were brought. We have to be patient."

Clare doubted that she was convincing her father of the need to be patient. She certainly wasn't convinced herself. Clare needed to do something, *anything.*

"It's hard to be patient, *tesore.* Not when a hundred things every day remind me of Angelo, and why he isn't here. How can I sleep at night, knowing that my only son is dead and his killer is free? Tell me that."

Clare squeezed his hand.

"But Dad, even if we did find out who did it, we have to leave it to the law. Trying to take our own revenge would only make things worse."

"I'm not talking about revenge," Dad told her. "Revenge is bitter. But I am talking about vengeance, about just retribution. When your Uncle Roberto talked about avenging Angelo's death, I said no – we must leave it to the law. But if the police don't find out who did it..."

He put his head into his hands.

"Then what?" Clare asked, softly.

"I don't know," Dad replied.

Clare looked lovelier every time Neil saw her. Tonight, in Browne's wine bar, she wore a black lambswool top with a simple, silver necklace. Neil was sure that every other man in the place envied him.

"A fortnight ago," Clare said to Neil, "you told me you had two promising leads. What happened to them?"

"Their stories checked out," Neil told her. "That's all."

"But you seemed so sure."

Neil grimaced. He had been trying to avoid this conversation. Jan had warned him – going out with someone who was involved in one of your cases was asking for trouble. But he couldn't help himself.

"Look," he told her. "It's true. There was one person who looked like a very likely candidate, and we're still investigating that person. But, so far, we don't even have circumstantial evidence. No damage to the car, no identification by witnesses, nothing. I don't want to build your hopes up."

"So it's possible," Clare said to him, "that you know who killed my brother, but you can't prove it?"

"No," said Neil. "We can't *know* who killed Angelo without evidence. It's possible that we've *found* your brother's killer, but we have no proof. And without proof, in the eyes of the law, that person is innocent.

"Look," he went on. "I'm afraid that police work is littered with cases where we've got a fairly good idea of who committed a crime, but we can't pin it on them. Now, can we change the subject, please?"

Clare listened while Neil told her a long story about a credit card thief they'd caught in the city. But he could see that her mind was elsewhere. The angry look on her face told him what she was thinking. Telling Clare that they might have already found Angelo's killer, but couldn't prove it, only made things worse.

However, she'd have been angrier still if he'd told her the full story: that Brian Boland was serving a year's suspension of his driving licence for drunken driving. If Boland was the one who knocked over Angelo Coppola, he had probably been over the limit, and driving illegally. In Neil's book, that was cold-blooded murder.

Every traffic cop in Nottingham had been alerted to look out for Boland driving, but, so far, he hadn't been behind a wheel. His wife drove him to work in the morning, in her car, then went on to the school where she worked. Boland's Yakimoto Blaze stayed resolutely parked outside his house.

It was no good knowing that Boland had driven illegally in the past – they had to catch him doing it now. Just a matter of patience, Jan told Neil, but Neil didn't agree. Boland might be an alcoholic, but he wasn't a fool. He would obey the letter of the law until his ban ran out.

It was frustrating, not being able to share all this with Clare. Now, as he asked when he could see her again, Neil sensed hesitancy in Clare's reply.

"Leave it a few days," Clare said. "My friends are feeling neglected. There's only a couple of weeks before we all go back to uni."

"That's what I'm worried about," Neil said, trying not to sound wimpish.

"Don't get too serious," Clare whispered, and kissed him on the cheek.

It was all very well for her to say that, Neil thought, as he watched Clare walk out of the room. If he could hold back his feelings for Clare until he was sure of hers for him, he would. Jan Hunt was always after Neil to think before he acted, and he was getting better, more methodical, in his police work. But falling in love was another matter, out of his control. There was a song he half remembered. How did it go? Something like: *mere reason alone can never explain how the heart behaves.* It was true. He could see that Clare was going to hurt him, but nothing he could do would stop it happening. He was too far gone.

Clare looked through the Yellow Pages section on car dealers. There were thirteen pages, full of ads. Nothing under Yakimoto. This was hardly surprising, she thought. If a dealer had sold only two cars in the last ten years, they'd long since have gone bust. But some dealers handled a variety of different makes. She went through the whole section again, this time with a fine-toothed comb. She found two possible contenders: Glaxon Cars in Arnold, specialists in exclusive imported models; and "Big In Japan", the Japanese car specialists, over in Ilkeston.

Clare took a deep breath, then dialled the first number and asked to speak to the manager.

"Who's calling, please?"

"Clare Coppola. I'm doing a story for BBC Radio news."

At university, Clare did a bit of work for the student radio station.

"How can I help you?" a young, over-confident voice asked.

"Hi. I'm doing a story about what makes people buy obscure cars."

"Then you've come to the right place."

Clare tried to project bubbly enthusiasm.

"Great. I wonder, do you stock a car called the Yakimoto?"

The manager ummed and aahed.

"I'm sure we have done, in the past. Never a big seller. Nothing particularly distinctive about them, you see."

"Would you have a record of the ones you've sold?"

"Our service department would, yes. Why are you interested in that particular make?"

"Er ... we want to feature cars that nobody's heard of."

The manager started to bore her with details of cars so obscure that she was bound to love them.

"Eastern European cars – they're the coming thing. Not very fast, not very sturdy, but *extremely* environmentally friendly. Now, everyone's heard of the Trabant, but have you heard of—"

"Perhaps it would be a good idea if I came in to see you," Clare said. "Would this afternoon be all right?"

"Certainly, certainly. Any publicity for our new registration models would be much appreciated."

"And if you could look up the details of the Yakimotos you've sold … You see, there's this angle there that I'd like to pursue."

"No problem."

Clare made an appointment, then rang up "Big In Japan". The manager there seemed quite knowledgeable about Yakimotos.

"Nah, don't stock 'em. Thing is, we've only been open three years, and Yakimoto merged with one of the big boys just before then – Toyota, Honda … can't remember which. Anyway, they stopped making cars under their own name. No great loss. There was nothing original about their designs. They were a bit cheaper than some of the equivalent models, that's all."

Clare thanked him and hung up. Then she got her bicycle out of the shed in the garden, pumped up the tyres, and put on her cycle clips. As she was wheeling the bike out by the path at the side of the house, Mum called to her: "If you're going out on that, you'd better wear this."

"This" was the cycle helmet that Angelo had been given for his fourteenth birthday. He had worn it for a while, but then complained that he found it too hot during the heat wave. Clare took the helmet, and adjusted the strap so that it fitted her head snugly. At least it'll keep the rain off, she thought.

Cycling to Arnold took her twenty-five minutes. The garage was easy to find. The manager was in his early twenties, with short, straight hair and a baggy designer suit. His tie was almost as loud as his voice.

"BBC not pay well?" the manager asked. "Can't even stand you a taxi?"

"I'm freelance," Clare explained. "I don't get expenses. Anyway, I like cycling."

"To each their own."

Clare had to listen to an endless spiel about the glories of Glaxon

Cars and the different makes they serviced and supplied. Dutifully, she took notes in what looked like shorthand, until you tried to read it back. Finally, she asked, "Did you manage to find out about those Yakimotos I mentioned?"

"Sure did, though I don't know why you're so interested. The last one we sold was before my time, just over three years ago. In fact, we've got one in today, having its first MOT. Want a look?"

Clare nodded. What she saw was a small, compact car with bright red metallic paint. She looked all over it for the word "Blaze". It wasn't there.

"Actually, I was particularly interested in another model. The one called Blaze."

"Never heard of it."

Grudgingly, the manager flicked through his card index.

"No, you're right. 'Blaze' is the GTI model – very obscure. We did sell one once. No, I tell a lie. Two."

"Who did you sell them to?"

The manager gave her a funny look.

"Who did you say you were working for again?"

"The BBC. Look, I'll make sure you get some good publicity out of it."

Grudgingly, the manager pulled out the card.

"We'd better. Here they are: the first one brings hers back for regular services. The second one's a cheapskate – never been back since his parts guarantee ran out."

"Thanks," said Clare, hoping that he wouldn't notice how her notes had suddenly become legible. "I appreciate this a lot."

She put her bike helmet back on. The manager handed her his card.

"Aren't you going to give me yours?"

"Haven't got any at the moment. I'm having some more printed up."

He gave Clare a look which said that he wouldn't believe her in a million years.

"How about your phone number, then?"

"Sorry," she told him as she unlocked her bike. "I've got a boyfriend."

Before he could come back on that, she cycled off. She had the information she needed. She was ready to begin.

11

Brian Boland's address turned out to be a smart semi in one of the city's hinterland estates. Parked outside the house was a yellow car. As Clare cycled up to it she saw the lettering, clear as anything, on the wing near the front: Blaze. It really existed. She hadn't expected the car to be there, nor for anyone to be in. She'd only cycled here because it was more or less on her way home.

What to do now? The house looked empty, but she could ring the doorbell, find out. Clare assumed that a man living in a house like this must have a job. But, if so, why had he left his car at home?

She decided to inspect the Yakimoto more closely. There was no sign that it had been in an accident of any kind. She looked inside. Expensive radio-cassette. Leather upholstered seats. Fitted rear seat belts. Nothing out of the ordinary.

Then Clare noticed something, something so obvious that she felt foolish for not spotting it at once. There was some gilt lettering etched on to the rear windscreen, beneath the rear window heater. Clare walked behind the car, trying to look casual, and read what it said: "Boland Associates. Best cover, best prices for all your insurance needs. Call us now on..." There was a phone number and an address, on a main road not far from where she was now.

Was Boland the one the police suspected? Clare considered this as she cycled through the spitting rain to Boland's office. The other Yakimoto owner was a woman who lived in Mapperley. Maybe it was her. Clare had expected the driver to be a man, but that was just casual sexism on her part. After all, Boland didn't need to drive down the Alfreton Road to get back from work. Maybe Dawn Miller did.

The office of Boland Associates was above a shop on the Nuthall

Road. A metal staircase led up to it. There was a light on inside. All Clare had to do was walk in. But what should she say? If she pretended to be buying insurance, she had no excuse for asking where Boland and his car were one afternoon in August. She would have to make it up as she went along.

Through the office window Clare saw a large man, presumably Boland. He was sitting in a leather-backed swivel chair, talking on the telephone. He waved Clare in.

"Only be a minute," he told her, covering the mouthpiece.

As he talked, Clare was able to get her bearings. It was an ugly, square office which contained little more than three chairs, Boland's desk and a filing cabinet, with a plant pot on top of it. There was a small sink, above which was a calendar showing a semi-clad girl photographed in an exotic location. An electric kettle stood on the drainer, and to the left of that was a small cabinet, presumably containing drink.

"Coffee?" Boland offered, extending his hand once he'd put down the phone. "I saw you looking longingly at the kettle. Horrible weather out there."

"Thanks," Clare said. "I'd appreciate that."

She looked at Boland from behind as he put the kettle on. He was a large, overweight man who slouched. His grey suit was slightly too big for him, and crumpled. He had a bald patch which he'd attempted to comb his brown, greasy hair over.

"Like a drop of something stronger in it to keep out the cold?"

"No, thank you."

"Don't mind if I do?"

Boland opened the drinks cabinet and added half an inch of whisky to his coffee. He gave Clare hers.

"Now, young lady, what can I do for you? No, don't tell me – bicycle insurance?"

Clare smiled graciously and put her cycle helmet on the floor.

"I think it's covered under our household policy, thank you."

Boland nodded.

"Cheapest way. What then?"

Clare put on her most ingratiating voice.

"Actually, I may have taken your coffee under false pretences. I don't want to buy insurance. I'm a freelance reporter, researching a series for the *Evening Post*."

Boland raised both eyebrows. There was something distinctly slimy about him, Clare thought.

"About insurance?"

"No," Clare told him. "About traffic accidents."

Boland drank half of his coffee down in one gulp.

"I'm not the man you need to see," he told her. "The big boys in town have all the actuarial tables..."

"I'm not after statistics," Clare told him. "I'm writing about a specific case – the police gave me your name."

"The police?" Boland looked disturbed.

"Yes. I'm writing about unsolved hit-and-run accidents. I gather that you were one of the people questioned and cleared of involvement in a recent accident of that kind – the Angelo Coppola case."

Boland blinked and nodded.

"Well, it's nice to know that I've been cleared of suspicion," he said. "Nice of the police to tell you that without telling me first. But I'm not sure how I fit into your article, Miss ... what did you say your name was?"

"Clare," Clare told him. "Clare ... Foster. The thing is, I'm writing a history of the investigation. Obviously, we hope that it'll jog people's memories and may help the police find the killer ... that is, driver. But we wouldn't want you to be embarrassed by the publicity. That's why I'm here to get your co-operation."

"I see," said Boland. "OK, then. What do you want to know?"

"Just what you told the police."

Boland lit a cigarette.

"So you haven't seen my statement?"

"Oh no, of course not."

Boland nodded slowly.

"There's not much to tell, really. I was at home when it happened, with my wife. I'd been in the Market Club that afternoon and caught the bus home. End of story."

"Why weren't you in your car?"

"My car?"

"Yes. I believe that the make of your car was what connected you to the investigation."

"Was it now?" Boland seemed disturbed for a moment. "That's interesting. But I don't drive for the time being."

"Why not?"

Boland drained his coffee.

"Too fond of this stuff," he said, pointing at the dregs in his mug. "Got a one-year ban for being over the limit."

Clare tried to conceal her reaction.

"But," Boland added, poking a finger at Clare, "your paper'd better not print that. A driving ban's bad publicity for someone in my trade. People tend to think bad luck's infectious."

"I promise to be discreet," Clare told him, finishing her coffee. "And I won't use up any more of your time. Do I take it that you have no complaints about the way the police handled your involvement in the case?"

"None up till now," Boland said, ambiguously, as he showed her out.

"Thanks for your time," Clare told him.

"You're welcome, Miss Coppola."

Only as Clare was cycling back home did she realize what he'd just called her.

Neil finished the report and Jan checked it through for him. She corrected a couple of spelling mistakes, but otherwise it was OK.

"So what do I do now?" Neil asked her.

"File it," Jan said. "If anything else comes up, we reopen the case. Otherwise, it stays in the filing cabinet, unsolved."

"What about CID?" Neil asked. "Do we know if they found anything when they were going round the garages?"

"If they'd found anything, they'd have told us," Jan said. "But, just to make sure ... excuse me, sir."

Neil looked round. Inspector Thompson had come into the room.

"We're just doing the paperwork on the Coppola case, sir. Did CID circulate all the local garages as we requested?"

"Of course they did," the Inspector said, grumpily. "Nothing. Zilch."

"Thank you, sir. Did you want anything?"

"Yes," said Thompson. "I want you in my office, *now!*"

Jan's face paled. She followed the Inspector out. Thompson had a mean temper when you were in the wrong. Neil felt very glad that he wasn't in Jan's shoes.

He filled in form G.126A on the circumstances of the accident.

Or, to be more accurate, he filled in those sections he could fill in. A lot of the paperwork assumed that you knew who the driver was. He wrote "0", which meant "not applicable" by the breath test section, then wondered what to do with the next bit, about what kind of driving licence the driver had. He left that section, and the next one, which was headed "Towing and Articulation", and went on to the next bit, which was the shortest. It was headed "Hit and Run".

There were three choices: "0" meant "Not Hit and Run", "1" meant "Driver Aware" and "2" meant "Driver Unaware". Neil wrote a "1" and went on to the next section, "Manoeuvres", where he filled in a "9" for "Turning right". But they didn't know that for sure, so he ticked 18, "Going ahead other", as well. The next few categories were even more difficult. Neil began to chew his pencil, but was interrupted by an angry shout.

"What on earth have you been up to?"

Jan had stormed back into the room, eyes blazing.

"Pardon?" Neil said.

"Tell me something. Have you been talking to a reporter about this case, giving her details about the investigation?"

"No. Of course not."

According to Neil's training, you were allowed to give confidential details of an investigation to the press, as long as they treated it as background, and didn't use it in their story. However, you were advised to avoid doing this, as some reporters couldn't be trusted not to use the information.

"What's happened?" he asked Jan.

"The Inspector's just been taking a complaint from Brian Boland, about his personal life being delved into, all because we gave his name to someone claiming to be an *Evening Post* reporter."

"I haven't..."

"Only Boland didn't think she was an *Evening Post* reporter, because he thought he'd seen her on the telly, coming out of the Angelo Coppola inquest."

"Oh no," said Neil. "I swear I didn't—"

"Don't get yourself in any deeper before you hear what she called herself," Jan told him, with a trace of humour in her voice. "The woman claiming to be a reporter said her name was Clare *Foster*."

Neil sat down and groaned. Part of him felt proud, in an obscure kind of way. The other part felt like he'd just been punched in the stomach.

The car arrived at twenty to six. The house had a garage, but the rain had stopped, and Dawn Miller left the car outside. Perhaps she was planning to go out later. Clare gave the woman two minutes to get inside, then went and looked at the Yakimoto Blaze. There was a blue, circular parking pass on the front, with "Probation Service" written on it. On the front right-hand wing, just in front of the "Blaze" logo, was a scratch, two centimetres thick, twenty centimetres long, slightly crooked. It could have been caused by a collision with a bike.

That was all Clare needed to know for now. She knew what Dawn Miller looked like, and she had seen her car. Presumably Miller was a probation officer, which meant that she knew the law, and would be even less impressed by Clare's claims to be a reporter than Boland was. She had to try a different tack.

When Clare got in, Dad still wasn't home. Mum was in the kitchen. Clare put her bike away then used the phone in the hall. Dawn Miller's number was in the directory. She answered on the second ring.

"Hello?"

"Dawn, this is Sergeant Hunt from the Nottinghamshire Constabulary. We spoke a few days ago."

"Oh, right. Have you had any luck finding your driver yet?"

"I'm afraid not."

"What can I do for you?"

Clare made her voice a bit quavery. Jan Hunt had a quiet, undistinctive voice, with a bit of a Nottingham accent, much like Clare's own.

"This is a bit embarrassing, Dawn, but we're writing up our report and my colleague has mislaid some of the notes from our interview with you. Is it OK if I go over some of the facts with you again?"

"Of course."

"Your movements on the afternoon of the accident."

"I visited a client, Nick Shears, just after four, and left his house just after five, getting home by half past."

"And the address of Nick Shears?"

Dawn told her the address, which was off Churchfield Lane, close to where Angelo had been knocked over. Then she added.

"But you should have it, surely? He told me that you'd interviewed him already."

"Yes, you're right," Clare said. "We do have it somewhere. Have you remembered anything else that might help us with our enquiry?"

"How could I remember anything?" Dawn said. "I didn't see the accident."

"Of course. Well, thanks again for your help."

"No problem."

Dawn Miller hung up. She sounded just a bit defensive, Clare thought. And she was in the vicinity of the accident, at the right time. She must be the one, Clare decided – the one the police thought had done it. All they lacked was the evidence to back up their suspicions. Clare intended to find it. The police might not have any more time to devote to finding her brother's killer, but she did. She wouldn't rest until she'd worked it out.

12

At last Nick Shears came out of his house. It was gone eight and the light was fading, which suited Clare. She followed him at a distance, trying to look as though she knew where she was going. Shears didn't look back. He turned off Churchfield Lane, up Prospect Street. Clare turned the same corner twenty seconds later. Shears was nowhere to be seen. Clare stopped outside the doors of the Pheasant. If Shears hadn't gone into this pub, she'd lost him.

He was there, drinking quietly on his own in a side bar. Nick Shears didn't look like a criminal. He looked more like an actor. He was smaller than average and his brown hair was a little too long for Clare's taste. He had deep, memorable eyes, and a slight, puckered chin. She would guess his age to be about thirty-five.

Clare bought herself a tomato juice and sat near the bar. It would be best if Shears tried to chat her up, rather than the other way round – more natural. She glanced at him, wondering how a girl who wanted to be chatted up in a pub behaved.

She also wondered what crime Nick had committed. Clare was a little hazy about how the probation service worked. As far as she knew, people got put on probation because their crime wasn't serious enough to land them in prison. Maybe Shears was into cheque book fraud, or a similar minor con.

"On the bloody Marys are we, darlin'?"

A burly bloke with a beer gut was grinning at her.

"Want another?"

"No, thank you. I'm waiting for someone."

"Aren't we all?"

The man took the bar stool next to hers. He wasn't going to go away, so Clare stood up and walked across the room.

"Mind if I sit here?"

"Be my guest."

Clare sat down with her back to the bar. She gave Shears her best smile and hoped he would start talking. But he just sat there, staring into his pint.

"Didn't that used to be Players Cigarette factory next to here?" Clare said, finally, looking around in desperation.

"S'right," Shears told her. "This place used to be a lot busier then."

"I'll bet," Clare said.

"I had my first job there," Shears said. "Cutting Gold Leaf. You wouldn't remember those."

Clare shook her head.

"Class cigarette," Shears told her. "They don't make them any more. Came in a bright red packet with a gold trim and a tiny picture of a sailor."

"Is that right?" Clare asked, wondering how long she could affect an interest in obsolete cigarette packets. "And where do you work now?"

"I don't."

"Oh. Sorry."

Shears shrugged.

"Nothing to be sorry about. I get by."

He asked Clare what she did and Clare gave him a spiel about her architecture course, trying all the while to work out how to get the conversation round to the alibi he'd given for Dawn Miller.

"You know," she said, "I've been trying to work out where I've seen you before. At first I thought I'd seen you on TV or something."

"You're kidding."

Clare smiled.

"No, but I think I remember now. I saw you somewhere with this really good-looking black woman, bit taller than you."

As Clare spoke, she hoped that Shears *had* seen Dawn Miller in public at some time, otherwise this approach was doomed.

"Where would that be?" Shears asked.

He sounded a bit touchy, but then Clare had just brought up the subject of his probation officer.

"Oh, somewhere round here," Clare said. "I live just over the other side of Alfreton Road."

"And why would you remember me and her?"

"Dunno," Clare said. "It just came to me. I guess you must be a memorable couple. She your girlfriend?"

Shears mumbled his eventual reply.

"Not exactly," he said.

"What's her name?" Clare asked, still trying to sound chatty.

"None of your business."

Shears' face turned dark.

"Where are you really from? All that stuff about 'architecture' – don't make me laugh! The DHSS, is it? Or are you a snooper from the probation?"

"No, no. Nothing like..."

Clare realized she'd made a mess of it. There was no way now that she'd get him talking about Dawn, or find out what he had told the police.

"I didn't mean to offend you," Clare said, gently. "I'm sorry if..."

Shears glared at her. Clare looked at her watch.

"Looks like I've been stood up," she said. "Time for me to go."

Shears said nothing as Clare left. There was something funny going on, she decided. Otherwise, why would he be so touchy about Dawn Miller? He had to be protecting her in some way.

But how? Maybe Dawn Miller had threatened to have Shears sent to prison if he didn't back up her story. One thing she was sure about: she didn't trust Nick Shears. And if she didn't trust him, that meant she didn't trust Dawn Miller's alibi, either.

"Neil called," Mum told Clare when she got in. "He wants to see you."

"He'll have to wait," Clare said. "I told him that I couldn't see him for a few days, that I wanted to spend time with friends."

"And is that where you've just been, seeing friends?"

Clare didn't answer. She didn't want Mum to know about her abortive attempts at an investigation. Mum looked pale and worn these days.

"Listen, Clare," Mum went on. "Neil sounded angry. And I'm concerned about you and him."

"How do you mean?"

Mum folded her arms, the way she did when she was laying down the law.

"This isn't a time for you to be getting serious with a boy in Nottingham – not with what's just happened. Anyway, you're going back to Manchester soon."

"Who said I was getting serious?"

Mum wouldn't let Clare interrupt.

"But I don't know if Neil knows that. And I don't know if you're only going out with him because you want to find out about the police enquiry into the accident."

Clare acted affronted.

"Where did you get that idea?"

"Something Neil said earlier. I won't let you do it, Clare. Your brother's dead. His death was an accident. Even if they find who caused it, that won't bring Angelo back. We need to get on with our lives."

"But how can we," Clare pleaded, "when whoever knocked Angelo over is still driving around out there? It drives me crazy. It's like I'm obsessed with it. Whatever I'm doing, whatever I'm thinking about, all the time, it just keeps coming at me – someone killed my brother. I can't rest until we find out who it is."

"Don't you understand?" Mum was raising her voice too, now. "I feel the same way. So does your father. But it isn't helping us. All we're doing is building up all this ... all this impotent rage."

Mum put on her more reasonable voice.

"I know the way some of the family were going on after the funeral – all that Italian machismo talk about vengeance – but it's just talk, Clare. So, if you're going out with Neil to get closer to the case, I want you to stop. He's a nice boy. He doesn't deserve to be hurt."

"Yes," Clare said. "He is nice."

The truth was that she had become fonder of him than she ever expected to. She went on, "But I'm not in love with him, if that's what you're really asking me."

"Then perhaps it's time you stopped letting him get in any deeper."

"Yes," Clare said. "I mean to. I will."

"When?"

"When I see him. But not tonight. I've got things to think about first."

Before Mum could go on at her again, Clare stomped upstairs to her room. She would stop using Neil to find out about the case, but she wasn't going to forget about finding Angelo's killer. She had to go on. If the police couldn't find the person responsible, she would.

13

Heavy traffic piled along the Nuthall Road as Clare cycled back to Brian Boland's house. She passed the office where he worked and checked to make sure that he was inside. He was.

Two potential hit-and-run drivers: Brian Boland and Dawn Miller. One of them was lying. But which? Clare cycled on to Boland's road. There were no lights on in his house, though it was a gloomy day, so Boland's wife must be at work, wherever that was. Clare could get on with what she had to do.

If someone had told Clare, three weeks ago, that she would be knocking on the doors of total strangers and telling outrageous lies, she would have laughed in their face. But here she was, doing just that. She chose a house further along the road. An old woman opened the door.

"Hello. I'm sorry to bother you."

"What is it?"

The woman held the door open on a chain.

"It's OK. I'm not selling anything. I'm making some enquiries for an insurance company. I only need a minute or two of your time."

The suspicious look didn't fade.

"It's about the man next door but one – a big man, drives a newish yellow car. Do you know him?"

"Only to look at."

This was a relief. Clare had avoided the houses on either side of Boland's in case he was friendly with his neighbours.

"Have you seen him driving his car recently?"

"What do you mean – 'recently'?"

"In the last two or three weeks."

"You say it's about insurance?"

Clare nodded. She hoped that she wouldn't have to explain, because she couldn't.

The old woman smiled.

"I don't like him," she said. "This is a quiet road. He drives up it like he's at a Grand Prix, at all hours. Not this week, though. His wife's been driving him. I've seen her. What is it – he's pretending to be injured or something?"

"I'm not really allowed to explain—"

"He beats her up, you know. I've seen her with a black eye. And she teaches little kiddies—"

"Tell me," Clare interrupted. "When did you last see him driving?"

"It'd be early last week, maybe the weekend."

"And before that, you say he drove all the time?"

"Oh yes, you couldn't miss him."

"Thanks," said Clare. "You've been very helpful, Mrs—"

"Johnson. Are they with you?"

Clare looked round. There, much to her distress, was a police car. Neil Foster was getting out of it.

Clare mumbled something and fled down the path. If she could just slink off, cycle away ... but Neil had seen her. She had a horrible feeling that he'd come looking for her.

"*Get in the car.*"

"I don't see why—"

"Get in the car!"

Clare did as she was told.

"My bike..."

"We'll bring you back for it," the woman behind the wheel said. She must be Jan Hunt, Clare realized, Neil's sergeant.

"What do you think you've been playing at?" Neil asked, bitterly.

"I've been finding some things out," Clare said, angrily. "Did you know that, until last week, Brian Boland has been driving his car around quite merrily, despite being banned for drink-driving?"

Jan Hunt stopped the car in front of some garages and turned round to face Clare.

"Yes," she said. "We were aware of that. And we will be dealing with Boland when our investigation into your brother's death is over."

The sergeant put on her official voice.

"You've been obstructing the police in the course of their duties by interfering in this investigation," she told Clare. "Which is an offence. Not only that, but this morning I had a call from a probation officer, wanting to know why one of her clients had been questioned by someone in a pub last night. Mean anything to you?"

Clare was silent. She looked at Neil. He was staring ahead, anger burning in his eyes.

"But that wasn't all Dawn Miller told me," Jan went on.

Clare hung her head.

"She wanted to know if I'd rung her the other evening, because I'd 'lost my notes' about her involvement in the case. How stupid are you, Clare? Presumably you know that it's illegal to impersonate a police officer?"

"It was only a phone call," Clare muttered.

"That makes no difference," Jan said. "Neil, tell her."

Neil turned round, his face red with embarrassment.

"You told Boland that the police had given you details about him. Did I?"

Clare shook her head.

"How did you get them, then?" Jan asked.

"From the garage that sold the car."

"You got me into trouble," Neil said. "I shouldn't have told you anything about the case. People are bound to believe that I told you a lot more than I did."

He raised his voice.

"We're not in some children's TV show, where you can play private detective whenever you fancy it. This is real. What you did might have jeopardized the investigation, as well as mucking up my career."

"I'm sorry," Clare said.

"Sorry isn't enough," Jan told her. "We're going to have to take you to the station so that you can make a statement."

"Whatever you say."

"And after that," Neil told her, "I don't want to see you again. Don't go near Brian Boland, or Dawn Miller, and especially not Nick Shears. Or me, for that matter. Have you got that? We're through."

14

There was a week to go before Clare returned to university. She was looking forward to going back, but felt guilty about feeling that way. Although they didn't talk about it much, it was obvious that Mum and Dad needed her at home. Angelo's death had changed everything.

Dad's work was going through one of its periodic slumps. Normally, things got bad in the winter, but this was September and the only jobs coming in were small ones. Dad was having to lay people off, which he hated to do. Worse, he began to talk about bankruptcy in a fatalistic way Clare hadn't seen before. It was as if Angelo's death had knocked the fight out of him.

Clare was surprised by how much she missed Neil. It seemed like her relationship with him was the one good thing to have come out of the summer. But he hadn't called her, and she was far too proud to call him. She had kept her promise not to go near Brian Boland or Dawn Miller. There wasn't much choice, since Neil's sergeant had threatened to give her a formal caution for impersonating a police officer if she interfered in the case again. But she hadn't given up.

She went to the newsagent's which Angelo used to deliver for. The shop was empty of customers.

"Is there any news?" Mrs Malik asked her. "Have they found anything?"

Clare shook her head.

"It doesn't look like they're going to."

Mrs Malik was sympathetic.

"That's hard on you."

Clare agreed.

"It's hard enough accepting that Angelo's dead. But knowing that the person who did it is just walking round, without being punished at all – it makes me mad. It makes me think that there's no justice. I keep thinking about revenge."

Mrs Malik shook her head.

"My religion teaches me that revenge is bad for the soul. We believe in forgiveness, instead. I know it's hard to do, but—"

Clare couldn't take this.

"What about punishment?"

"Through the courts, yes. But the real punishment is what comes in the next life."

"I'm sorry," Clare told her. "I can't wait that long."

A customer came in.

"Are my photographs ready?" Clare asked.

"Here."

Clare paid for the photographs and put them in her pocket. She chatted with Mrs Malik for a few more minutes about her university course. The Maliks had a daughter a year older than Clare who was studying to be a dentist.

"It's a long time," Mrs Malik said. "But it's worth it in the end, yes?"

"I don't know," Clare said. "I really don't know if anything's worth it any more."

She left the shop and walked down towards Churchfield Lane. She would sit in the churchyard, she thought, look at her photographs and decide on her plan of action.

The road was quiet. Over a month had gone by since the joyriders had accosted her here. Clare guessed that they were back at school now, if they still went. Lost in thought, she crossed the road towards the churchyard.

"Gotcha!"

A rough hand seized Clare's arm and twisted it behind her back.

"Following me again, were you?"

"Stop. You're hurting me."

Nick Shears snarled into her ear.

"I ought to kill you."

"Why?" Clare said, trying to turn and face him. "What have I done?"

"You know full well what you've done, you interfering little—"

He didn't finish, as Clare lifted her knee and managed to catch him in the groin. Shears doubled up in pain and Clare was able to break away from him. She ran as hard as she could.

Back home in her room, after getting her breath back, Clare got out the photographs and looked through them. The camera they'd been taken on was Angelo's. The first pictures she looked at were his. Several were from the day of his fourteeth birthday. Others were shot down at the youth club near his school. Clare recognized a lot of the faces.

Then there were pictures that he'd taken of her, the week she'd come back from university. Angelo kept teasing her about how scruffy she'd become, in her casual student clothes. Clare was struck by how happy she looked in these photos: her on her own, her with Mum, her with Dad, her with Mum and Dad. Then one of Clare standing between Angelo and her father, all of them grinning. It was the last photograph of her brother alive.

Clare put these photographs aside and looked at the ones she had surreptitiously shot the day before. They were all of a lime green car, and had been taken in the probation office car park. The scratch on the front of the wing had been painted over, but the car was still recognizably Dawn Miller's. Clare stuffed the snaps into her pocket, then took Angelo's photos downstairs to show to her mother.

The way Clare saw it, the police had plenty on Boland. If they could prove that he'd done it, they would. Dawn Miller was another story. As a probation officer, she was practically one of them. Therefore, they wouldn't investigate her seriously. But Clare meant to.

From now on, she was going everywhere on her bicycle. If she came across Nick Shears, she wanted to see him first. Clare had considered telling the police about his threatening behaviour this morning, but couldn't see the point. After all, she had hurt him more than he had hurt her.

Dawn Miller worked the west side of the city. Her clients were in Radford, Basford, Forest Fields and Hyson Green, all areas which were riddled with back-street garages. From what Neil had told Clare at the beginning of the enquiry, the police would have done a routine check on the main garages in the city. But it was unlikely that they'd gone round all the back-street garages, which came and went so quickly.

Back-street garages were the sort of places that would employ people on probation, no questions asked. So Dawn would get to know about them. She'd certainly know enough not to take her damaged car to Glaxon, where she had it serviced. Then, finally, the probation officer could have deliberately scratched her car after having it fixed, because anyone looking at the car would notice the scratch, not the recently repaired bodywork.

"Not been near us," the man at the body shop on Birkin Avenue said. "I'd remember a make like that."

"What did you say was wrong with it? A dented body?" another asked. "Did it want knocking out or a new wing?"

Clare said she didn't know.

"Thing is, a new wing would have to be ordered from Japan."

That would take too long, and it would be on record.

"No," Clare said. "She'd have wanted the bumps knocked out, but so that you couldn't see it had ever been in an accident."

"In that case," the owner told Clare, "you'd want a place that does restoration work, not just resprays and insurance jobs."

He gave her a couple more to try.

By evening, Clare had visited a dozen garages, and was exhausted. Her legs wouldn't carry her any further. Her bottom was so sore that she could barely sit down. Tomorrow she would have to go farther afield, but right now she needed a bath.

"Hey, look who it is!"

Clare groaned. She was two minutes from home. A white GTI accelerated past her, then screeched to a halt further down the road, spinning round with its front wheels off the ground, doing a "wheely", a hair-raising turn using the handbrake. Now it was driving towards her. There was nowhere for Clare to run. She was as vulnerable as Angelo had been a month ago. Only these boys weren't trying to kill her. More likely, they just wanted to impress her. They were pathetic, Clare thought, trying to blank out her fear. When would they learn?

The car came to a halt centimetres from her front wheel. There were four boys in it. Three of them were Mark Crowston's young cronies. Then there was a fourth, younger one, who she didn't recognize.

"Pity Mark's not here," the driver shouted to Clare. "He was looking forward to seeing you again."

"Leave me alone," Clare told them.

She considered riding on the pavement, but they might still try to get in her way. After all, they weren't bothered about whether they damaged their car.

"Did you find who knocked over your brother yet?" one called out.

Clare didn't reply.

"Dangerous things, bicycles, you know. I'd have thought you'd have learnt that by now."

"Just leave me alone," Clare repeated.

Behind the car, a large van was coming. It hooted for the lads to get out of the way.

"I hope you've taken your cycling proficiency test," another of the boys called out. "Mind you, it didn't help your brother, did it?"

"Why don't you go to hell?" Clare shouted at them, not caring how they responded.

All four boys laughed. Behind them, the van driver put her hand down on the horn. The white car accelerated off. The boys had got the rise they wanted out of Clare. She felt sick. Slowly, she cycled home.

The next day was the first of October, a Friday. Clare could be moving into her flat today if she wanted. Instead, she was cycling around increasingly obscure back streets, visiting increasingly dodgy garages. The people she met were less and less forthcoming. Clare was sure that half of them were involved in breaking up stolen cars for their parts, or respraying them and changing the number-plates. The funny thing was, she found her search fascinating. If her cause hadn't been so desperate, she would almost say that she was enjoying herself.

Dad came home for lunch.

"When do you want me to drive you to Manchester?" he asked Clare.

"I'll catch the train on Monday," Clare told him. "There's no need for you to waste your day off."

"Nonsense," Dad told her. "You'll need to take lots of things for your new flat. Anyway, I want to see it."

What he meant was he wanted to make sure that the people she was living with were all girls, like she'd said. Which he wouldn't, because they weren't.

"Really, Dad, I don't have that much stuff. I'd prefer to go on Monday."

"You must be sick of this place by now," Mum said.

"There's something I have to do."

"And what's that?" Mum asked.

Clare didn't answer.

"Haven't you got into enough trouble with the police already?" Mum asked. "You shouldn't be trying to do their job, Clare. You're only hurting yourself, and hurting us, too."

"Maria's right," Clare's father said. "It's time to put it all behind us. Leave it, Clare. Go back to Manchester."

"There's one thing I need to finish," Clare said. "When it's done, I'll feel like I've done everything I could to find … to find…"

Dad gripped her hand.

"If that's how you feel, do whatever you have to do. But let me drive you to Manchester on Sunday. All right?"

"All right."

There was no point in arguing. Garages wouldn't work on Sunday, anyway. Clare had a day and a half to find the place which had fixed Dawn Miller's car, if it existed.

Neil called round on Saturday morning just as Clare was getting ready to go out. Mum let him in, despite Clare's complaints.

"I look a mess!"

She was wearing the dirty jeans she cycled in and a sweatshirt which was too tight. She was glad to see him, but tried not to show it.

"You look great," Neil told her. He was in uniform.

"More overtime?"

"No. It's my weekend on. I'm driving on my own now."

"Congratulations. Did you come round to tell me that or to remind me that you're still mad at me?"

Neil smiled.

"I've got over being mad at you. I came to say goodbye before you go back to university."

"Goodbye," Clare said.

"Don't be like that. There's something else, too." He looked over at Clare's mum.

"You'd like some coffee, Neil?" Mum asked, tactfully.

"Please."

When she'd gone, Neil leant forward and lowered his voice.

"I thought you'd like to know, Mark Crowston's been sent down. He got a year for the two taking without consent charges we had him on last month, so he'll serve at least six months."

"Good," Clare said, "but that still leaves all the other kids he's taught to steal cars. I saw three of his pals the other day, flashing about in a stolen GTI, trying to give me a scare. How come they got off?"

"They're all younger than him," Neil explained. "And he was the ringleader."

"Well, they've already got a new recruit to replace him," Clare announced, bitterly. "You may have cut off the head but that still leaves a live worm."

"Sometimes," Neil told her, "that's the best you can hope to do. At least we got Crowston."

"But you didn't find out who got my brother."

"No," Neil admitted. "We didn't."

He went on, more tenderly.

"Look, I'm sorry I lost my temper with you last week."

"You had a right to..."

Neil acknowledged this with a nervous nod of the head.

"I wondered if I could take you out tonight – finish on a better note."

"I don't think so," Clare said.

"I'd like us to be friends," Neil told her. "I'll be home by half four, if you change your mind."

"I won't."

Neil left just as Mum was bringing in his coffee.

Clare cycled off a few minutes later. This morning, she'd been missing Neil. But now she was annoyed with him. How could he think he could walk back into her life so casually? She would like very much to prove him wrong, to finish the investigation that he'd given up on. But it was no good. She had to admit it to herself – she was on a wild goose chase.

Clare's searches had taken her right to the edge of the city, almost to the Cinderhill roundabout, near to the office where Brian Boland worked. But Boland wouldn't be working on a Saturday. She was unlikely to bump into him. She checked her *A to Z* and wove in and out of back streets. She didn't find any garages. Anyway, even if she did, how would Dawn Miller have known about them? It was time to give up.

Clare checked her map again. She was on one of the countless small private estates that had sprung up all over the city, wherever there was some space. This one wasn't marked on the map. She would have to get out of it by guesswork. She took one street, then another. From the heavy traffic noises, she could guess that she was almost parallel with the Nuthall Road. The next corner would take her to it.

But the next turning was a dead end. Clare was about to turn back when she realized what was in front of her: a block of four workshops, smart ones, with roll-down steel doors, not like the tacky cowboy outfits she'd been visiting for the last few days. Three of them were shut. The fourth was on the verge of closing, as a man in overalls was pulling down the door. Inside the workshop, Clare could see familiar machinery. Above the door, a sign read: *P. Mulhaire, Expert Body Repairs, Classic Models Restored.*

"Excuse me."

The man, in his twenties, stopped closing the door and looked Clare up and down.

"I don't fix bikes," he said.

"It's not about my bike. Are you Mr Mulhaire?"

"That's right. Paul."

"This won't take a minute. I'm trying to trace whoever repaired a car..." Clare gave him the vague story she'd invented, claiming that it was a matter of life or death for her brother, who'd been in a collision with the car. She showed him the photographs.

"It's an obscure model," she said. "Would you remember if—"

"Oh, I recognize this one all right," Paul Mulhaire said. "It's a Yakimoto GTI. I did some work on one once, yes. Might have been this one."

"What kind of work?" Clare asked.

Mulhaire shrugged.

"Nothing major. A few dents in the wing, that kind of thing."

"And would you happen to remember who you did it for?"

"I'd have a record, but it's alphabetical – take me a fair while to go through all the names."

"I've got a name you could try," Clare suggested. "Dawn Miller. She's a tall, attractive black woman. Does that ring a bell?"

Mulhaire gave her a grin.

"No. I'd remember her."

Clare was disappointed. But then she thought to ask something else.

"How about Boland, Brian Boland?"

Mulhaire smiled.

"Of course, it's Brian's car. You're right."

"You know him?"

"He puts some insurance work my way. This isn't any kind of trouble for him, is it?"

Clare didn't answer.

"How long ago did you do this work?"

"A month, two months – I'm not sure. During the summer."

"Could you look it up?"

"Can't, I'm afraid. You see, I did it as a favour. I think Brian had had one too many – drove into the back of something when he should have been reversing. Know what I mean?"

Clare was quiet. If she spoke, she would give away her emotions. Mulhaire carried on, chatting like the information he was giving her had no real importance.

"He promised he'd make it up to me by recommending his clients use me… Hey, it wasn't you he ran into, was it?"

"No," Clare told him, as the anger welled up inside her. "It was my brother."

15

Neil was taking his uniform off when the phone rang.
"For you!" his mother called. "A girl."
He hurried to the phone.
"Hello?"
"It's me."
Neil's heart lifted.
"I thought you said there was no way you'd be calling me?"
Clare's voice was sombre.
"Something's happened. I've found the proof you need to convict Brian Boland."
Neil groaned.
"I'm not on duty."
"Can't you come round anyway? I'd really rather speak to you. Please."
Exasperated, Neil gave in.
"I'll come. But I hope you aren't clutching at straws, Clare."
"I'm not. Believe me."
Neil hung up, then put his uniform back on, still irritated. Clare was hardly likely to have succeeded where the police force had failed. All the same, he and Jan were sure that Brian Boland was the one who ran over Clare's brother. He would dearly love to be able to prove it.

Clare told her mother the whole story.
"So you think they'll be able to arrest Boland?"
"I don't know," Clare said. "I hope so."
"I'm going to ring Nick," Mum said. "He'll want to be home for this."

Clare went into the front room to wait for Neil. She felt exhilarated. The look of satisfaction on Mum's face when she told her about Boland left Clare feeling – what was the word? – vindicated. People kept saying that the family had to put Angelo's death behind them. Once Boland was behind bars, they could begin to.

The doorbell rang. Clare got up to let Neil in.

The man who barged through the door was not Neil. He was large and ugly and he smelt of whisky. It was Brian Boland.

"I want to talk to you!"

Clare didn't know what to say. Mum came through from the kitchen.

"Who is this?"

Boland's face was red. He began to shout.

"Your daughter's been interfering in my life – lying, pretending to be a reporter, going round my neighbours asking questions about me, then going to my friends, making up stories about me running over her brother."

"They're not made up," Clare snapped.

Boland exploded.

"That's *slander*! I'll have you in court for it!"

"You'll be the first one to appear in court," Clare said quietly.

Boland grabbed Clare's shoulders and began to shake her.

"I want you to leave my life alone, do you hear me!"

"Let go of her!" Mum shouted.

The door opened. Dad stood in the doorway. There was a fierce look on his face which Clare had never seen before.

"Leave my daughter alone," he said.

Boland took a step back.

"Then tell her to leave me alone."

The two men faced up to each other. Boland was a big man, but Dad was bigger.

"Did you kill my son?" Dad asked.

Behind Dad, in the street outside, Clare saw Neil getting out of his car. Boland began to bluster.

"From what the police told me, no one 'killed' your son. He died in an accident, didn't he? Perhaps he'd still be alive if he'd been wearing one of those." Boland was pointing to the cycle helmet which Clare had left on the stairs. Dad's fist was already clenched. Slowly, he raised his arm.

"You … you ran him over."

"No."

Before Dad could hit Boland, Neil charged through the open door, between them.

"Stop! What's going on here?"

There were five people crammed into the small hallway now. Clare spoke.

"I found the garage which repaired Brian Boland's car after he ran into Angelo."

"Rubbish," Boland sneered. "That happened weeks before your brother died. I was nowhere near—"

"In that case," Clare interrupted, in a quiet, assured voice, "how come you knew that Angelo wasn't wearing a cycle helmet?"

"I, I must have…" Boland ran out of words.

Neil was removing the handcuffs from his pocket.

"Brian Boland," he said, "I'm arresting you for driving a motor vehicle while banned. I will be requiring you to take a breathalyser test, as I suspect you of driving under the influence of alcohol. I am also arresting you for unlawfully causing the death of Angelo Coppola. I must caution you that you do not have to say anything unless you wish to do so, but anything you do say will be taken down and may be given in evidence against you. Do you understand this?"

Boland began to shout obscenities. Neil snapped the handcuffs on.

16

"The papers have to go to the DPP," Neil explained to Clare in the pub that night, "but I'm pretty sure that they'll proceed against Boland. There has to be a better than fifty per cent chance, and a lot of the evidence is circumstantial. Even so..."

"How long will he get?"

Neil shrugged.

"If he's found guilty ... I'm not an expert, but for causing death by reckless driving while banned, even if we can't prove that Boland was over the limit – at least three years. Maybe as many as five."

"It's not a lot for a life, is it?" Clare said.

"It's a lot more than what he would have got if you hadn't traced that garage. You did brilliantly."

Clare tried to be modest about it.

"I didn't think it was Boland, you know. I thought he was too obvious, that if he'd done it, you'd have been bound to catch him. I thought Dawn Miller was the driver, especially after what happened with Nick Shears..."

She told Neil about Shears attacking her.

"I couldn't understand why he was so upset," she finished.

Neil smiled.

"I can. Nick Shears and Dawn Miller were having an affair. That's why he was so touchy about the alibi. Dawn hadn't told anyone at the office about her relationship with him. If she had, they wouldn't have let her carry on being his probation officer. Anyway, last week she rang up Jan to tell her. Said she was embarrassed at the time, but now she'd got taken off his case and terminated her relationship with Shears, so she wanted to clear the air. I shouldn't be telling you this, really."

Clare sighed.

"I'm glad you did. No wonder Shears was angry at me. He had every right to be."

"Maybe," Neil said. "But I don't think violence is ever justified, do you?"

"I guess not," Clare said. "Though today, I thought my dad was going to murder Brian Boland. I wouldn't have been upset if he had."

"You would have been when your dad ended up in prison for years and years."

"I guess."

"What now?" Neil asked. "Are you ready to get back to your real life, in Manchester?"

Clare stared out of the window without answering. She made Neil mad sometimes, the way she seemed to be there, but not there. Even on the few occasions that they had kissed, it sometimes felt like she was merely going through the motions. Why did he put up with it? He had humiliated himself, asking her out again only a week after chucking her. His mates said he was behaving like a fool.

But Neil only had to look at Clare to know that she was worth it. Her brother had died, too. That excused a lot. He wouldn't have put up with any other girl treating him in the offhand way she did. But Clare wasn't any other girl. While he had the chance of someone like her, he had to go for it, or he might regret it all his life. Neil decided that he had to ask her now, even though he was sure he already knew the answer.

"What about us?" Neil said, tentatively. "Have we got a future?"

Clare hesitated.

"I don't know," she told him softly.

She gave him an affectionate look. She had treated him more fondly tonight than at any other time in their relationship, but instead of kissing him, she started making speeches.

"Maybe it's best to say that we finish for good. You're all bound up in my mind with what happened to Angelo and I want to put all that behind me. But I really care for you. I want to stay friends, to see you … is that an awful thing to ask?"

Neil gave her a rueful smile.

"Not awful," he said. "But difficult."

He leant forward as she leant towards him. Then, gently, they kissed for what he knew would be the last time.

Winter

17

"Did you need to bring quite so much stuff with you?" Dad asked, as the car handled heavily on the M1. "You're home for less than a month."

Clare didn't answer. She'd wanted to save her announcement until they got home.

"Cat got your tongue?"

"I'm not going back," she said, in a voice so low it was barely audible.

"Pardon?"

"I said *I'm not going back*."

That shocked Dad into silence. Quietly, carefully, Clare explained that she'd never really wanted to be an architect, that she'd done it to please him.

"I couldn't keep it up, Dad. Not for all those years. I'm all grown up now. I have to live for myself."

Dad seemed to be holding back the tears.

"But *tesore*, you can't throw away a *liceo classico*. You could change to another course, one that you'd enjoy more."

"Not this late."

"We'll find the money. Nothing's too good for—"

Clare stopped him.

"Dad, I don't want to be a student. Not that kind, anyway…"

"But what are you going to do?" Dad pleaded. "There are millions and millions of people unemployed."

It was too early to tell him. Mum needed to be there, too.

"Then I'll be one of them for a while, Dad. There's no shame in that."

"I won't allow it. I'll find you a job with the family. Angelo's always needing a secretary in Bedford. We'll find—"

"I didn't get all those A-levels just to be a secretary, Dad."

"Then what?"

"Watch the road, Dad. It's busy."

It was a cold December day. Every so often fog descended, but the cars around Dad's estate hardly slowed down. Even fewer put their fog lights on. It was scary. Clare tuned the radio to a local station for the traffic reports. They drove the rest of the journey in silence.

Mum hugged Clare when she got out of the car. Nevertheless, she seemed gloomy.

"What is it, Mum?"

Mum took a brown envelope from the hall table.

"This came by the second post."

The letter informed the Coppolas that Brian Boland would be tried at the end of February.

"How can it take so long?" Dad asked. "Every time people talk to me, especially the family, they ask 'has it come to trial yet? How long did he get?' And I can't answer. I want it behind us."

"We all do," Clare said. "But Boland's in gaol. There's always a backlog of cases. At least now we know when the trial is."

"Clare's right," Mum said. "Only two more months."

They sat down and drank coffee.

"Clare's got something to tell you," Dad announced.

Mum gave Clare a searching look.

"What is it?"

"I'm not going back to university."

"Over my dead body you're not," Mum snapped back.

"It's too late, Mum," Clare insisted. "I've already packed it in."

Mum looked even angrier.

"Why?"

"I couldn't get involved in the course. I realized that I didn't want to be an architect. I want to do something more useful with my life."

Mum put her hands on Clare's shoulders.

"I knew something was up from the way you clammed up whenever I asked you about your studies on the phone. But don't throw it all away, Clare. Do you know what I'd have given to have the chances that you've got?"

"I know."

Mum began to speak more urgently.

"Has it occurred to you that the way you're feeling at university might be bound up with Angelo's death? They call it delayed shock. It's a common thing, a kind of depression. But you'll come out of it, Clare. Don't make a hasty decision that could ruin your life. There are other courses. Take a year off. Think about it. Nick?"

Dad nodded.

"Your mother's right, Clare. It's a lot to give up. Have you even thought about what you're going to do instead?"

"I have," Clare said. "I've already applied and had an interview. I'm waiting for the results of the exam."

"What exam?"

"They tried to persuade me to finish my degree first, said it would stand me in good stead. But I told them I'd had enough of academia."

Both Mum and Dad looked bemused.

"What are you going on about?" Mum asked.

Clare smiled.

"I'll be staying in the county," she told them, proudly. "I'm going to be a policewoman."

18

The court house was a recent building on the edge of the city centre, between the bus and train stations. You had to cross a five-lane road to get to it. From outside the place looked like a small office block, but inside it was airy and spacious. A guard searched Clare's bag, then ran a metal detector up and down her body – as though, she thought, she were likely to bring in a gun and shoot Boland if the verdict went the wrong way.

In films, court houses were always hectic, crowded places, but this one was incredibly quiet. The decor was calming – all polished wood surrounded by cream and grey, with muted blue carpets. Six out of the nine crown courts were not in use. Clare joined her mum and dad outside Court Six. Around a corner, she could see Neil, awkwardly waiting to begin his evidence.

It was five past two. People began to go in for the afternoon session. It was the third day of the trial. Apart from the Coppolas and a solitary reporter, there were no regular onlookers. Today, however, there was a teacher with five school kids. The usher checked that none of the visitors were witnesses, then made sure that the kids were all over fourteen.

The school party sat by the door, facing the far wall and the judge's red chair. Clare and her parents were directed to a long row, behind the press seats, facing the barristers and solicitors in the middle of the small, square courtroom. Beyond the lawyers were the twelve seats reserved for the jury.

Everyone rose as the judge came in for the afternoon session. Then the jury took their places. Clare couldn't help but keep looking at them as the trial went on. Seven men, five women. Half of them looked like they were concentrating on every point. Clare wasn't so sure about the rest.

The atmosphere in the court was unreal to Clare, like watching a play on television. She couldn't tell how the trial was going. Earlier, a doctor had given evidence. So had Jan Hunt, Boland's wife, and several witnesses to the accident. Still to come were Neil, the mechanic, and (presuming that he took the stand) Boland himself.

It still made Neil nervous when he had to give evidence. He'd be glad when it was all over, especially with Clare watching him, only a few metres away. Boland had hired a good brief. After lunch, in the conference room outside, the Counsel for the Prosecution had warned Neil that they would try to take him apart.

"Just stick to the facts, officer, and you won't go wrong."

But now Neil was in the witness box, under cross-examination, and the facts seemed slippery, two-faced things.

"You did not see my client's car, did you, Constable, on the afternoon of the accident?"

"I couldn't have seen the car because—"

"A simple 'yes' or 'no' will suffice, thank you, Constable."

"No."

"And none of the witnesses identified either my client or his car, is that correct?"

"Yes."

"Indeed, you have been unable to establish any reason why Brian Boland should have driven on Bobbers Mill Road on the day in question?"

"That's true, but—"

"So your only way of connecting my client to this unfortunate accident was an ambiguous bit of hearsay from the deceased?"

"I wouldn't say it was ambiguous."

"No?" The barrister's tone was withering. "You knew this young man well, did you? Well enough to be sure exactly what he meant to say when he was injured, indeed fatally brain damaged and on the verge of losing consciousness for the last time?"

Neil didn't reply.

"In fact, you'd never seen him before, had you?"

"No."

"The word that you say he used – 'blaze' – did you check whether it might have any connotations other than as the name of a model of car?"

"Pardon?"

Neil wasn't sure what the word "connotation" meant.

"You assumed that 'blaze' referred to the car."

"It seemed a reasonable assumption, yes."

"It didn't occur to you, Constable, that, Angelo Coppola being of Italian descent, the word might have, unbeknownst to you, a separate meaning in Italian?"

Neil didn't answer. He hated the way the barrister kept stressing his rank, as though to show how junior the prosecution's chief witness was.

"Very well. Let us move on to some of your other dubious conjectures."

As the barrister leafed through his papers, Neil remembered that he *had* questioned the Coppolas about whether the word "blaze" had any special meaning to them, as soon as they'd arrived in the hospital. But it was too late to bring it up now.

"You say that my client observed that Angelo Coppola might not have died had he been wearing a bicycle helmet?"

"Yes."

"And this was one of your principal reasons for arresting him?"

"Along with the evidence about the repairs done to his car, yes."

"I see. You told Mr Boland that the information about the helmet had not been reported?"

"Yes."

"Then perhaps, Constable, you'd like to explain this video, which, with the court's permission, we will call exhibit three."

A large-screen TV and video was wheeled in. Neil had no idea what the video would be.

Central News flashed on to the screen. It was a report on the Angelo Coppola inquest. A reporter was speaking to camera.

"It emerged during the inquest that Angelo Coppola was not wearing a cycle helmet, which might have saved his life – a clear message there for all paper-boys and girls in the country."

The picture cut to where Nick Coppola condemned the coroner's verdict and pleaded for information that would lead to the arrest of his son's killer. Clare was standing in the background. In a box at the back of the court, Boland smiled. The tape was switched off.

"Well, Constable…?"

Neil became angry.

"I haven't seen that report before," he snapped. Then he added, brusquely, "The reporter was wrong, anyway. Helmets only protect against cuts and fractures – they're no protection against the severe shaking up the brain gets in a high-speed impact like the one that killed Angelo Coppola."

The barrister smiled.

"Thank you for that expert testimony, Constable. However, you must accept that my client, who watched this broadcast along with several hundred thousand other viewers, demonstrated no special knowledge of the case."

Neil was silent. The barrister smiled smugly.

"I'll take that for a 'yes'. One last point, Constable Foster. Although you had no knowledge of the Coppolas before the accident, is it not true that shortly afterwards Clare Coppola – the deceased's sister – became your girlfriend?"

Neil felt himself blushing, but there was nothing he could do to stop himself.

"For a while, yes."

"So you had a particular incentive to find the driver of the car, did you not?"

"It made no difference to—"

"In fact, it was Clare Coppola who found the so-called evidence about the repairs to my client's car. Is that correct?"

"Yes."

"Would you say that your judgement when it comes to matters pertaining to Clare Coppola was entirely, er ... disinterested?"

"I would say that I acted within the guidelines at all times."

Again, that horrible smug smile.

"Oh come, come, Constable. You've just admitted that one of your main reasons for arresting my client was bogus. Is it not also the case that, during the case, you were given a verbal warning for revealing confidential information about the investigation to the victim's sister – your girlfriend?"

"Well, er..."

"And that Clare Coppola, your then girlfriend, impersonated a reporter in order to get Mr Boland to reveal information about the case?"

Before Neil could reply, the prosecution counsel at last stood up.

"I object. I don't see what relevance such tittle-tattle has."

Before the judge could rule, the defence barrister gave a majestic shrug.

"I withdraw the question. I have no further questions for this witness."

"You may step down," Neil was told.

Neil walked out of the court, avoiding Clare's gaze. He didn't need her to tell him that he'd made a pig's ear of the whole thing.

They didn't talk about the court case much on the way home. However, in the evening, Dad began to talk about a story he'd heard on the radio. A lorry driver ran over a twelve-year-old boy on his bicycle. He'd actually seen what he was doing and, rather than stop in time, risking capture, he drove on, crushing the boy to death. At the trial it emerged that the man had never even held a driving licence. He only got eighteen months. To make matters worse, when the driver got out, he went on driving a lorry, illegally, and gave a V-sign whenever he saw his victim's father.

"Anyway," Dad said, "one morning the father wakes up to find that someone's left a loaded shotgun on his doorstep. He knows what it's about. Someone with a grudge against the lorry driver left it there. But something snaps inside the father. He picks up the shotgun, gets in his car, and goes to where the driver lives. He waits in his car till he sees him."

"And what happened then?" Clare asked. "Did he kill him?"

Dad shook his head.

"Finally the father sees the driver walking down the street with his girlfriend. He gets out of the car with the gun. But the driver sees him. He grabs his girlfriend and covers himself with her. Can you imagine a more cowardly act? In Italy, any man who could do a thing like that ... there isn't a word low enough. Eventually, the man lets his girlfriend go, and makes a run for it. The father shoots."

"Did he die?" Clare asked.

Dad shook his head.

"He was badly hurt, but he lived."

"And what about the father?" Mum asked, in a bitter voice. "What happened to him?"

"He was tried for attempted murder," Dad told her, "and grievous bodily harm. He pleaded innocent to both charges."

"But how could he do that?" Clare asked. "After all, he did it."

Dad shook his head slowly.

"I don't know. Maybe he claimed that the balance of his mind was momentarily disturbed, although – obviously – he had planned the shooting, waited in the car, and so on."

"What sentence did he get?" Mum asked.

"No sentence," Dad replied with a smile. "The jury found him 'not guilty' on both counts."

Mum nodded.

"I remember the case now," she said. "It's odd how things don't sink in at the time, but later they come to mean so much more to you."

Clare agreed.

"But Boland won't get off with eighteen months, will he? I mean..."

Dad shrugged again.

"They've got the breathalyser results from when he came round to our house, as well as all the witnesses to his driving while banned. That has to be worth a prison sentence. But when it comes to running over Angelo..."

"He did it," Mum said, firmly.

"I know he did it," Dad said. "And so does anybody who's been following the case. But they have to prove it, beyond a reasonable doubt, and after..."

He didn't say "after Neil's evidence today". He didn't need to, Clare thought. But the trial wasn't over yet.

"Your full name, please."

"Paul Mulhaire."

"And your occupation."

"Mechanic."

"This summer you repaired a car for someone in this courtroom. Can you point that person out?"

Mulhaire pointed to Brian Boland.

"Could you tell us the nature of the repairs, please, Mr Mulhaire?"

"Ah, it was just knocking out a few dents on one of the wings."

"Which wing?"

"I don't rightly remember."

Clare noted the way that Mulhaire was exaggerating his Irish accent. This wasn't the way he'd spoken to her at the garage. He was trying to make himself sound stupid. And he'd been certain about which wing it was when he'd spoken to her.

"And these repairs, were they to the front of the wing?"

"Ah, no. I'd say they were more to the side."

"What kind of dents were they?"

Mulhaire scratched his chin.

"I'd say they were more like scratches – like he'd scraped a wall, something like that."

The prosecution counsel was frowning now. Clearly, he was thinking the same thing as Clare – Boland had got to Mulhaire.

"In your statement, you said that you did this job for Mr Boland in late summer."

"I said that, yes. Though, now I think of it, the job may have been as far back as June."

"And it didn't go through your books, did it? That's why there's no record."

"That's right. It was a favour."

"In fact, isn't it the case that the accused put pressure on you to do the work without keeping any record of it?"

"I suppose."

"As though he had a secret to keep?"

Mulhaire smiled.

"Hell, no. I knew he'd been banned from driving – that was why he couldn't do it on the insurance. All he was bothered about was not having to spend his own money!"

The jury laughed. Clare's heart sank.

19

To Clare's surprise, Boland didn't take the witness stand. The following morning, closing arguments were made, the judge summed up, and the jury were sent out. The three Coppolas sat in the grey upholstered seats outside the courtroom, waiting for the twelve men and women to return. They were still out at ten past two, when Neil showed up. He'd just come off duty and was in uniform. Clare told him what had happened.

"I wasn't much good yesterday," he said. "I'm sorry."

"You've no reason to be sorry," she told him. "The things you got caught out on weren't your fault. If anything, they were mine."

He squeezed her hand.

"Whatever happens," he said, "it'll be all over once the jury come back."

Clare stared at the floor as she mumbled her reply.

"Will it?"

The jury returned after deliberating for two hours. Clare could read nothing into their expressions. They didn't look at Boland as he was brought back in. But they didn't look away from him, either.

Boland had already pleaded guilty to driving under the influence of alcohol and driving while being banned. There was only one thing for the jury to decide.

"On the charge of causing death by reckless driving, how do you find?"

The forewoman spoke clearly.

"We find the defendant 'not guilty'."

As the judge thanked the jury, Mum began to cry. Clare put her arm around her. She felt numb. The jury, she noticed, were all studiously avoiding looking towards them. On the other side of

Mum, Dad stood up.

"This man murdered my son!" he shouted at the jury. "How can you let him go free?"

"Sit down, please," the judge told him. "I don't want to have you taken out."

Dad sat, as tears started streaming down his face. The judge turned to Boland.

"Mr Boland, do you have anything to say before I pass sentence?"

Boland shook his head slowly. The judge took a deep breath, then spoke.

"Brian Boland, you have been found guilty of driving while disqualified, and driving while under the influence of alcohol, the crime for which you were first disqualified. Although you have been found not guilty of the larger crime, causing death by reckless driving, it is undoubtedly the case that you put the lives of others at risk.

"You chose not to give evidence yourself. The jury were not allowed to read anything into this, but I am. You have had the opportunity to show some remorse for your actions, and have not taken it. You need to be warned, in the strongest terms, not to offend again.

"You will be disqualified from driving for a further three years when your current ban runs out. In addition to this, you will serve a prison sentence of nine months."

Boland's face showed no emotion.

"Nine months," Clare said to Neil as they made their way out of the court house. "That's something."

"Not really," Neil told her, apologetically. "Most people get out between half and two-thirds of the way through their sentences. Boland's been inside on remand for nearly five months. He'll be out within a week. A month at the most."

20

Clare was already waiting for Neil when he got to The Peacock. Three days had gone by since the trial and she looked happier, more alive. For a few moments, Neil felt optimistic. He'd given up on her, but sometimes the moment you gave up was precisely the moment you found what you were looking for.

"I've got something to tell you," Clare said. "It's why I agreed to meet you, really."

"I've got something to tell you, too," Neil said. "But it's not good news."

The barman arrived with their drinks, which Clare insisted on paying for.

"Shouldn't you have gone back to university?" Neil asked.

Clare shook her head.

"That was what I wanted to tell you about. I'm not going back."

"No?"

Neil's first thought was: she's met someone – she's getting married and she wants to let me down lightly before I hear it from someone else. Then she told him.

"I start at Ryton next month."

"Ryton?"

Clare nodded. Neil was incredulous.

"You're joining the police?"

Clare smiled.

"I had my second interview last week. I wanted you to hear it from me first."

Neil shook his head in disbelief. As he tried to picture Clare as a WPC he said the first words which came into his head.

"You'll look terrible in a uniform. They'll make you cut your hair. It won't suit you at all."

Clare gave him a half-quizzical, half-annoyed look.

"That's part of the reason I couldn't keep going out with you, Neil. You're more concerned about the way I look than what's in my mind. Do you really think that the uniform had anything to do with my decision?"

"No," he said. "I don't. But what did make you decide to join up? The last six months haven't exactly been a great advertisement for the police force, have they?"

Clare shook her head.

"But I did realize that I wanted to do something useful with my life. As an architect, I might earn a lot of money. I might get to design homes or churches – things I could be proud of. But I'm more likely to find myself drawing up office blocks and supermarkets, or extensions to people's homes. In the police force you make a real difference to people's lives."

"Do we?" Neil asked, bitterly. "Most of them seem to hate us. You go into court these days, and a jury's going to believe that you've made half your evidence up, because that's what they've seen on TV. And it's worse for women – the villains are less scared of them, so they're more likely to have a go at you."

Clare thought he'd finished, but, as it turned out, he'd only just started.

"Half the PCs will call you a 'plonk' or a 'relief bicycle'. They'll give you all kinds of grief, and you'll have to take it or be treated like a leper. The other half'll hate you for being around because it makes them feel more vulnerable. And women have real trouble getting promoted. Not surprising, since most of them leave after five years or so.

"Did I tell you about my sarge, Jan? She's off on maternity leave. It's only six months since she got promoted. She'll not be back, I'll bet. I'm not trying to put you off, Clare, but—"

"Aren't you?" Clare laughed. "Sounds like it to me, but you're too late. I've signed up, and it's partly your fault – you're the one who made the job sound really good in the first place."

Only because I was trying to impress you, Neil thought, but he didn't say this. He changed the subject.

"How are your parents taking the result of the trial?" he asked.

Clare's confident mood evaporated.

"Mum's been really depressed. She hardly says anything. The doctor's prescribed tranquillizers but I don't think she's been taking them. Friends call round and she won't talk to them. Dad does his best, but he's had to go back to work. The firm's in a rough state at the moment."

"And how's he taking it himself?"

Clare turned the corners of her mouth down.

"Better than I expected. But he keeps getting calls from people in the community, which don't help. They've heard about it through the paper or on the news, and you can imagine what they're like – goading him to do some damage to Boland, or offering to do it themselves. 'A matter of honour' – that's what they say. They've seen too many 'Godfather' movies. As though hurting that slime could avenge Angelo! All it would do is put my dad in prison."

Neil was concerned.

"Do you think he'll do anything rash?"

"I don't," Clare said. "I mean, Boland had a fair trial, and Dad respects that. He keeps repeating: *Vengeance is mine; I will repay, saith the Lord*. Boland was found 'not guilty'. I guess that means there was a reasonable doubt about whether he did it or not. I mean, maybe – just maybe – he is innocent."

"But you don't really believe that, do you?" Neil asked.

"No," Clare replied. "I don't."

Neil was lost for conversation. He supposed that he ought to congratulate Clare on joining the force. She'd make a good officer, he thought. With her education, she was bound to do better than him, despite being a woman. But he would rather that she wasn't always going to be around, working on the same patch as him. If he was going to get over her, it wouldn't be any easier when there was always a chance of them running into each other at work.

"Anyway," said Clare, more cheerfully, "what was your news?"

"I'm afraid it's about Boland," Neil told her, in his most sober voice. "They're releasing him from prison tomorrow."

21

Clare woke late on Saturday. The night before, when she'd told Mum and Dad about Boland's release, had been an awful one. Dad demolished a litre bottle of *chianti classico* on his own. He kept cursing in Italian. Mum closed up on herself and refused to speak. Clare was stuck in the middle, unable to help and increasingly angry.

She looked at her watch. Ten. Downstairs, Mum was sitting behind the kitchen table, pasty faced. She was wearing her best cashmere sweater with a scruffy apron over it. Everything in the kitchen was spotless. It looked as though she'd been cleaning since dawn. Clare went over and put her arm around her.

"Are you OK, Mum?"

Mum gave Clare a weak smile.

"I'm all right now. It'll take me a while to get over things. But I'm OK."

"Did Dad go off to work?"

"Yes. An hour ago."

"I'll bet he had a bad head."

Clare smiled. Mum didn't smile back.

"Yes. He did have a headache, now that you mention it."

It was as though Mum had forgotten the previous night. Clare put the kettle on.

"I think I'll make myself a coffee and take it back to bed with the paper."

Mum stood up as though Clare had given her an urgent mission.

"I'll make you some proper coffee. It'll only take a second."

"No, really," Clare said. "Instant is fine. Do you want some?"

Mum shook her head.

"Why don't you go back to bed, Mum? You look shattered."

"I'm fine. Just a little tired."

As Clare poured boiling water on to coffee granules, Mum asked: "Will he be out now, do you think?"

"Boland? I expect so," Clare told her. "I think they release them early in the morning."

"And will there be lots of reporters there, like at the inquest?"

"I doubt it," Clare said. "He's not big enough news."

"He ought to be," Mum said.

"Yes," Clare agreed. "He ought to be."

There was nothing in the paper that interested Clare. A time would come, she thought, when world events would seem relevant to her again. But not yet. Downstairs, she heard electrical noises. Mum must have found some kitchen jobs that she hadn't already done. Clare supposed that it was good therapy. Then the noises stopped.

A minute later, Clare heard the front door slam. She sat up. Mum hadn't left the house since the trial. Something was wrong. Hurriedly, she pulled some clothes on and rushed downstairs. I'm being silly, she tried to tell herself. Mum's just gone out for milk or sugar.

The first thing she saw was the electric knife sharpener, still plugged in on the kitchen table. She looked over to the block next to the sink. One knife was missing – the biggest one.

"God, no!" she said aloud. "No, no, no, no, no!"

Clare wasn't conscious of deciding what to do, but she acted with great speed. She pulled on her coat, took the spare key off the hook and went out in to the back yard. There was no time for a cycle helmet, no time for gloves. She pushed the bike out through the narrow back passageway on to the street. She had no cycle clips, so she tucked her jeans into her socks, then mounted her bike.

At least Mum couldn't drive. That was something. She would have to catch a bus, or hail a taxi on Alfreton Road. Clare hoped it was the bus. On a good day, on a bicycle, you could overtake a bus, because it had to keep stopping.

She got to the bottom of the road. There was no one waiting at the bus stop, which meant that one had probably just gone. The traffic lights were changing. She cycled quickly across as cars began to thunder towards her.

Clare cycled as fast as she could, away from the junction where Angelo had been knocked down. After all her searches for garages, she knew this area like the back of her hand. There was a short cut across the Whitemoor Estate, where Mark Crowston lived, which would save her a little time. She could get to Boland's house before Mum did – if Mum was in a bus, not a taxi. Taking deep breaths, Clare cycled even faster.

Without gloves, her hands were cold. Soon her fingers were so numb that it was hard to change gears, but she kept going. She kept thinking about what Mum had in mind to do. Part of Clare badly wanted Mum to get there before she did, she wanted to wound, or even kill, Boland. After all, he deserved it. And any jury in the country would see that Mum wasn't in her right mind. They'd let her off. Wouldn't they?

At the corner of Western Boulevard was a big, complicated junction which was just too dangerous to navigate on a bike. Reluctantly, Clare got off, waited, and crossed at two sets of pedestrian lights. Then she cycled like crazy down a footpath into the Whitemoor Estate.

Here, the roads were quiet, almost empty. There had been a frost in the night and most of the cars were iced up, going nowhere. Clare nearly skidded a couple of times, as she hurtled towards the other side of the estate. She was going so fast that she nearly didn't notice the car which shot out of a side road, far too quickly. It parked a little way in front of her, honking its horn.

Clare recognized two of the lads who got out of this car, an old Ford Escort. They were the friends of Crowston who'd harassed her when she was out cycling in September. Normally, she would have taken a detour, anything to avoid them. But today they were in her way.

As it turned out, the youths didn't seem to notice Clare. The joyriders were preoccupied by a thin boy, with a tousle of red hair, who had opened the door to them. Clare thought she recognized him. He had been round to the Coppola house once or twice, a friend of Angelo's: Steven … she couldn't remember his surname, but something made her slow down as she passed his house. She heard a snatch of the lads' conversation from the doorway.

"I'm not coming out."

"Come on. It's Saturday. We'll have a laugh."

"I told you, I'm not coming out."

Then she was out of earshot. Before accelerating again, Clare glanced behind her. The boy who had remained in the car was leaning out of the passenger window. He yelled:

"Don't be a coward. Come out for a run, Blaze!"

"I told you never to call me that!" the red-haired boy snapped back.

A deathly cold ran down Clare's spine. She looked back, then cycled, cycled even faster, cycled faster than she'd known it was possible to cycle. She had to prevent her mother from committing murder.

22

The yellow Yakimoto Blaze which hadn't run over Clare's brother stood in front of the Boland house. There was no sign of Mum. For a moment it seemed to Clare that the whole thing was a dream. If this car hadn't killed Angelo, then Angelo couldn't be dead. How could he have been run over by one of his own schoolmates?

Clare dropped her bike on the pavement outside the house and ran up the path. She pounded on the front door.

"Hold on!"

A woman's voice.

"Hurry!" Clare shouted.

Mrs Boland answered the door.

"Yes?"

"Is your husband back?"

Mrs Boland gave Clare an angry, impatient look.

"Back? Yes, like I told the woman who just came. He's gone to his office, and that's where you should go if you've got any business with him."

"You say 'just came'," Clare said, urgently. "How long ago?"

"Five, ten minutes … hold on, I saw you in court, didn't I? Aren't you…"

"Call the police," Clare said, firmly. "Tell them that your husband's life is in danger. I'm sorry, I haven't time to explain. But do it *now*, please."

Before Mrs Boland could respond Clare was down the path, clambering on to her bicycle.

Boland's office was only five minutes' cycle ride away at the most. Clare should be able to beat Mum there, unless Mum was running. Clare had never known her mother to run anywhere in her life. But this morning, if Mum could sharpen a knife and take it out to harm someone, then anything was possible.

Clare turned on to another road. Still no sign of Mum. She was almost at Nuthall Road now. Maybe the police had got to her already. But they wouldn't have done. Even in the most urgent cases, average response time was five minutes, unless a police car happened to be in the right place at the right time.

There was ice on the road and a vehicle was approaching from a side road. Its side windows hadn't had the ice scraped off, Clare saw. The driver didn't notice her. He kept driving, straight in front of her, as though she wasn't there. Clare braked sharply, but she was going too fast, and skidded. Her bike hit the car side on.

"Silly cow! What do you think you're playing at?"

Clare picked herself up off the ground. Her head ached. There was a muddy stain all the way down her jeans which she knew would translate into a black bruise on her leg. She was too shocked to be angry.

The driver got out.

"Look! You've scratched my car!"

Clare got up. Her bike was lying in the middle of the road. The frame had buckled. It was useless.

"You drove straight into me," she said to the man. "It was your fault. You've destroyed my bike."

The driver sneered.

"You know where you can go," he told her, getting back into the car.

"Wait!"

The man made an obscene gesture and drove off, at speed. He hadn't even asked if she was all right. Clare picked up her bike and moved it to the side of the road, irrationally blaming herself. If she'd been wearing a helmet, her head wouldn't hurt so much. Angrily, she realized that she hadn't taken note of the car's registration number. Then she remembered why she'd been in such a hurry in the first place.

Nuthall Road was less than a hundred metres away, but every step cost Clare a gnawing pain in her leg and side. Even so, she ran or, rather, stumbled, a short pace at a time. She knew that she was almost certainly going to be too late, but continued all the same. By the time she reached the corner of the main road, the whole right side of her body was in agony.

A police car was coming down Nuthall Road, its siren bellowing. Clare looked up to Boland's office. There, at that very moment, was her mother, at the top of the steps leading to the insurance agent's door.

"Mum!" Clare screamed. "No!"

But the traffic noise was too high. She continued shouting as she forced her body to take her to the steps.

The police car pulled up alongside Clare. She was at the foot of the steps now. There was a railing, which she could use to pull herself up the staircase. Maybe, if she was lucky, there was still time.

"Clare?"

It was Neil. Of course it would be Neil.

"It's my mum," Clare panted, as she yanked herself up another step. "I've got to stop her."

"Let me by. I'll help her."

Neil was behind her now. There was another officer with him.

"No," Clare insisted. "It's not her who needs helping."

Clare could see over the top of the stairs. As she pulled herself up the last two steps she saw Boland, behind his desk, recognition slowly spreading across his face. Next, he looked beyond Mum. He must have seen Clare, with two police officers standing behind her. His face betrayed confusion, nothing more. Then he turned back to Clare's mother. That was when he saw the knife coming towards him. Sat in his chair, legs beneath the desk, Boland was temporarily trapped, unable to move out of the way quickly enough. His face turned white.

"Mum, no!"

Clare was through the door as Mum raised the knife. She was too far away for Clare to grab her.

"It wasn't him, Mum! He didn't kill Angelo. It wasn't him, I swear. It was someone else!"

The hesitation was enough for Brian Boland to pull his chair back and get out of the way. The two police officers ran into the room, between Boland and Maria Coppola.

"Drop the knife, Mum."

"Are you sure?" Mum asked, in a hollow voice.

"I'm sure. Someone else did it. I've found out who it was."

Clare's mother did as her daughter asked. Clare picked the knife up and handed it to Neil. Then she hugged her mother, who was crying.

"I'm sorry," Mum was saying. "I couldn't do it. I couldn't take him being alive and free while Angelo is … dust and ashes. I couldn't…"

"It's all right," Clare said. "It's over now. It's all right."

She turned to the three men facing her.

"Nothing happened here," she said. "It was just a misunderstanding."

No one spoke.

"Please." She looked at Neil this time. "Take me and my mother home. Then I have some information for you. I don't know if you can prove it, but I think I've found out who really ran over my brother."

In the corner of the office, Boland was pouring himself a drink. Clare held on to Maria. It was hard to tell which of them was holding the other up. The two police officers looked at each other.

"You're right," Neil said to Clare. "Nothing happened here. Or, if it did, it was over before we arrived. But something happened to you. What?"

"I'll tell you all about it," Clare sighed, as the pain rushed back into her body. "Later."

The four of them left the small office, Clare stumbling as she tried to keep up. Her mother held on to her arm, helping her to walk down the narrow stairs.

23

Clare was laid out on the settee. Her legs were exposed, padding and plaster covering the cuts and bruises she had sustained that morning. Her legs were far too fat, she'd always thought. It annoyed her that Neil was seeing her like this, without make-up and nice clothes. But he didn't seem to mind.

"The boy's name is Stephen Baker," Neil told her. "He's in the year above Angelo at Greencoat. He denied everything at first, but we eventually got him to admit to being in the car. He used to be in the Crowston gang. I guess that's where he learnt to take cars. I suspect Crowston knew it was him all along. He was laughing at us.

"Anyway, Stephen claims he wasn't driving, but won't say who else was with him. Evidently, he – or they – saw Angelo turning on to Bobbers Mill Road and decided to give him a bit of a scare. But there was a mother and child crossing the road, too, and they had to swerve at the last minute to avoid them. That's how they came to knock over Angelo."

"What'll happen to him?" Mum asked.

"I'm not sure," Neil said, apologetically. "He's only fifteen, but he could still be charged with causing death by reckless driving and do up to five years. Trouble is, we've only got Stephen's word for it that he was in the car at all. Angelo's deathbed identification isn't much use, I'm afraid. Evidently the car was burnt out the same day – it was a new blue GTI according to Stephen – so we're unlikely to get any evidence there, even if we're able to trace it. We'll get him, all right, but on a lesser charge."

"How will he be punished?" Dad wanted to know.

"A year or two in a youth detention centre, plus a driving ban from when he's old enough to drive."

"He should be banned for life," Mum said, angrily.

"Maybe," Neil told her, "but magistrates don't like to do that. If the offender knows that he'll never have a licence it gives him no incentive to keep within the law."

"I remember Stephen," Mum said, bitter tears falling down her face. "We gave him a meal once. Angelo was proud to have a friend who was older than him."

"He's just a stupid, frightened kid," Neil told her. "He says he hasn't been near a car since, that he's broken off with his old cronies. For what it's worth, I believe him."

"At least it's resolved," Dad said, quietly. "Now we can begin to pick up the pieces."

"There is one other thing," Neil said to Clare. "The car that knocked you over this morning. I want you to make a statement about it."

"What for?" Clare said.

"We might be able to catch him."

Clare shook her head.

"I don't know the registration number or the make of the car. I don't even think I'd recognize the driver again. I was in shock at the time, remember? So even if you managed to find him, all you'd have to go on would be the scratch on his car."

"That might be enough," Neil said. "And we might find another witness."

"I doubt it," Clare said. "Most probably, what it would come down to is my word against his. Forget it."

"That's not like you," Neil told her.

Clare smiled ruefully.

"Sometimes you need to recognize when you're fighting a lost cause. Then you can save your energy for a fight you have a chance of winning."

"Maybe you're right," Neil told her, getting up to go. "But I had you down as someone who didn't think there was such a thing as a lost cause."

Clare nodded her head abstractedly. Was it right to ignore some injustices and concentrate on others? She didn't know. But she was going to be a policewoman. She was going to find out.

Spring
Epilogue

Clare looked in the mirror. Neil was right – the uniform didn't suit her. It flattened her figure, making her look big rather than just tall. Then there was her hair. Most of it had been chopped off the previous day, immediately after they'd fitted her uniform at Sherwood Lodge. Now that it was shorter and thinner, it was less curly, more … ordinary. The way it finished, in a short, straight bob around her neck, made Clare's face seem bigger, too. She looked like a different person.

She had become a different person from the one she'd been nine months before. Clare realized that. Her brother was dead and things would never be the same again. She wondered what Angelo would feel if he knew what she was doing now. Pride? Or embarrassment, at a sister who had taken her quest for justice so seriously?

Someone called her name and Clare remembered where she was. She brushed a hair from her shoulder and walked down into the hall of Epperstone Training College. There was no swearing-in for this job, no graduation ceremony, nothing grand: only a stern-faced sergeant waiting to inspect the appearance of the new intake.

There were fifteen of them: twelve men and three women. Awkwardly, they formed a line, wanting to look each other over, knowing that they shouldn't. They had a week of what was called "familiarization" before they moved on to the regional training college at Ryton, where the real work began.

Clare stood upright, with her hands behind her back, wondering if she looked like a policewoman, wondering what she'd let herself in for. One of the others coughed. Clare began to worry about all this standing still. What if one of her feet went to sleep? Was she allowed to stamp on it? Things started going through her head, things that Neil had told her. Sixty per cent of the job is admin, he insisted. Most of the rest is just standing, or, if you're lucky, sitting around. You can tell the ones who come into the job for idealistic reasons, he warned her. They're the cynical ones with the huge chips on their shoulders.

She'd teased Neil about this when they went out for a drink last night, reminding him of what he'd said to her about lost causes the last time they met, two months before.

"You're the idealistic one," she told him, "not me."

"In that case," he answered, "why are you joining the police force?"

Had Clare given him an answer? No, she had kissed him instead. It had taken her more than six months to kiss him properly, and afterwards he looked like someone who had just experienced a minor earthquake.

"Does this mean you might…?"

Then Clare kissed him again and he got the message. She liked him a lot, though it had taken her a while to realize this, given the tragic circumstances under which they'd met. It was too early for either of them to guess how long they would last. What worried Clare most at this moment was the possibility that she'd confused her interest in Neil with her interest in the job he did.

Why was it that she wanted to do this, of all jobs, more than anything else? Police work, Neil told her last night, had little to do with detection, and even less to do with justice. When he said it, Clare hadn't believed him. However, at this moment, she wasn't so sure. A new chapter in her life was beginning and her head filled with questions, none of which she knew the answer to.

Was Clare ready to change her life so drastically? Would she have been better off finishing her degree first? Would Neil stay keen on her, now that she was keen on him, too? Was it a good idea to have the same job as your boyfriend? Was she good enough?

The inspection began.

DEADLY INHERITANCE

For Rod and Lizzie

1

"I ought to warn you," Vicki told Andrew as they turned a corner and saw the dark, near derelict house for the first time, "my family are *murder*. It's not too late to turn back."

"Come on," Andrew tried to tease her. "They can't be *that* bad."

Vicki didn't reply. As she slowed the car down, a dark cloud gathered overhead, casting the building before them into an even deeper gloom. It was a huge house, set in the crest between two hills. Dense, deep green ivy covered more than half of its front. There were a few run-down smaller buildings over to one side of it, and what appeared to be a small chapel on the other. Few visitors would expect to find so big a place in the middle of nowhere.

Vicki pulled up outside this vast, grey building.

"Welcome to Hetherington Hall," she said.

"It looks like a stately home," Andrew told her.

"A very small, insignificant one," Vicki assured him.

"Do you get tourists wanting a look inside?" Andrew enquired.

Vicki shook her head.

"We're too remote."

They were at the centre of the Cheviot hills, in Northumberland, near the border between Scotland and England.

"Is it haunted?" Andrew asked, as the big front doors opened.

"Don't be daft," Vicki told him.

A small, mustachioed man in a dark suit came out. He reminded Andrew of an undertaker.

"You must be Miss Victoria." There was a rich Scots lilt to the butler's voice.

"Yes," Vicki said. "And you must be McFadyen. This is my guest, Andrew Wakefield."

The butler met Andrew's eyes with a fake but friendly smile.

"Hallo, sir. Welcome home, miss. How was your journey from West Yorkshire?"

"Slow," Vicki told the butler before he picked up their bags and led the way inside.

"How come he wasn't sure who you were?" Andrew asked, as they climbed the steps into the hall.

"Our old butler died a few weeks ago," Vicki explained. "This is the first time I've met his replacement."

Satisfied, Andrew let himself be led into the deep, dingy hallway. Wide corridors with tiled floors were lined with heavy wooden panels. There was old furniture everywhere, with dark, ornately carved wood. Everything smelt musty. Andrew half expected to see suits of armour and weapons on the walls, but there were only mirrors and dark, dirt-ridden paintings. He wondered why they'd been allowed to get into such a state.

The three of them climbed a winding staircase, then walked along another passage. The butler paused at the end of it before opening the door to a long, narrow room.

"This is where you'll be staying, Mr Wakefield." He put Andrew's rucksack down inside the door.

"The bathroom's down that corridor, off the main landing," the butler pointed out.

"I'll dump my stuff, have a wash, then come back and find you before we meet Mummy," Vicki said.

"Fine," Andrew muttered, as Vicki followed McFadyen to the end of the passage. They went around a corner and out of sight.

Andrew unpacked in a gloomy mood. He hadn't expected to be allowed to stay in the same room as Vicki, but they weren't even going to be in the same part of the house. Not only that, but this room looked like it hadn't been used for at least a century. The smell of damp filled his nostrils. Despite it being sunny and warm outside, the house was chilly. The antique, bronze-coloured radiator in the bedroom gave out no heat whatsoever.

He found the bathroom and was relieved to find that the plumbing worked. The water was hot. There was an old-fashioned, single-bar electric heater on the ceiling. Andrew turned it on with the pull switch by the door and it warmed the room quickly. Feeling more comfortable, Andrew took his time freshening up. He wanted to be at his best when he met Vicki's family.

Back in the bedroom, Andrew hung his one smart jacket in the wardrobe, hoping that the creases would fall out before he needed to wear it again. When he closed the wardrobe door, a large chunk of plaster fell from the ceiling on to the bed. Andrew cursed and looked for a bin to put it in. There wasn't one. He tried to open the window, which looked out on to a steep, Cheviot hill. He meant to throw the plaster out, rather than start on the wrong foot by owning up to the damage, which wasn't his fault. But the window was jammed.

There was a noise on the landing. It sounded like a footstep on creaking floorboards, directly outside the room. Andrew kicked the lump of plaster under the bed, then opened his door. He stepped into the corridor, expecting to see Vicki. Instead, he saw the back of a tall woman with long, dark hair and a full-length dress, walking down the passage, away from him.

Andrew checked his watch. It had been nearly half an hour since McFadyen left him there. Vicki was meant to have come back for him. Where was she?

Andrew walked down the corridor and turned a corner, into darkness. After a moment, his eyes became accustomed to the lack of light caused by the absence of windows. There were rooms to the right, and another, narrow stairway, leading upwards. He continued down the corridor, turned a corner and found a second stairway, going down this time. He took it. The steep stairs twisted and turned. He remembered what Vicki had said about the house, on holiday.

"It's a bit of a ruin. Half of it's not in use. There are doors and stairways which were once important but now don't lead anywhere."

Andrew began to regret going after Vicki. After all, he had no idea where he was, and she would be turning up at his door any moment, wanting to introduce him to her parents.

At the bottom of the stairway, Andrew found himself in a large cellar with a high ceiling and pale stone walls. A passageway trailed off into darkness. There were several doors, all but one of which was closed. Andrew let his curiosity get the better of him. He pulled open the one door which was ajar, and peeked inside.

It was the kitchen. He walked into a well-lit room which smelt of mushy peas and boiled beef. Andrew felt like he'd stepped out of a bad dream into a cosy, picture-postcard past.

"You must be Miss Vicki's friend. Are you lost?"

The woman who'd spoken was small – even smaller than Vicki, who didn't reach Andrew's shoulders – and approaching middle age.

"I was looking for Vicki," Andrew admitted.

"I'm Moira," the woman said. "If you take this stairway over here, you'll find Vicki's room on the second left outside the first door you come to. But don't let her mother or Mr McFadyen catch you using the servants' stairs. They don't like that kind of thing."

When Andrew knocked on Vicki's door, her voice came back quavering and fragile.

"Mummy? I'll only be a moment."

When Vicki opened the door, her hair had been pinned back and she, like the woman he'd seen earlier, was wearing a long dress. Andrew hadn't seen his girlfriend in a dress before. With the change in her hair, it made Vicki seem a different person.

"It's you," she said, relieved, and kissed him. "I'm sorry I've taken so long. I popped down to see Moira in the kitchen."

"I just met her," Andrew said. "She told me where to find you. You never mentioned that you had servants. Is Moira the cook?"

"Sort of," Vicki said. "Moira's been with the family since she was in her teens. At first, she was the parlour maid. We had lots of servants then. Now she's kind of cook and housekeeper combined. We only have three servants these days. There's a maid who lives out and the butler." She paused, then added, nervously, "I know all this probably seems awfully grand to you, but it's a big house. No one could manage it without staff."

She sounded embarrassed, as well she might. At Bretton, the only sign that Vicki had any money was that she could afford to drive a car – and only a rusty old Mini, at that.

"You could have warned me before we came," Andrew complained.

"I know. But I was glad you wanted to come with me. I thought you might change your mind if I told you too much about … all this. I didn't want to come home alone."

"It's all right." He stroked her bare neck. When her voice went all vulnerable that way, it was hard to deny her anything.

"You're not alone," he whispered. They were about to kiss again when the door behind them opened.

"Victoria!" said a loud, haughty voice. "What *have* you done to your hair?"

Vicki flinched and didn't reply. The voice's owner stepped into the room. She was a tall, wide-shouldered woman, with electric eyes. Andrew had been wondering why Vicki hadn't gone to see her mother as soon as she got home. Now he began to understand. Taking a deep breath, Andrew took a step forward and faced the gorgon.

"I think her hair looks nice long," he said, holding out his hand. "By the way, I'm Andrew."

Nervously, he met her eyes. Vicki's mother frowned for a moment, then, without shaking his hand, looked again at Vicki. Andrew couldn't understand the fuss. He'd encouraged Vicki to let her hair grow over the summer, but, pinned back the way it was, you could hardly tell that it was any longer than it had been when they first met, back in June. The gorgon spoke.

"Make sure you have it cut before your father comes home."

Vicki didn't reply directly.

"Where *is* Daddy?" she asked.

"Abroad. He should get back by the weekend. I phoned to tell him that you were coming, though I didn't mention your ... guest." Now Vicki's mother gave Andrew the smallest possible glance of acknowledgement.

"Why don't you go up and see Cassandra before dinner?" she suggested to Vicki, before departing as abruptly as she'd arrived.

Vicki sat down on her bed, closed her eyes and groaned. Andrew thought of making a comment, but decided against it. Vicki might dislike her mother, but it wasn't done to criticize people's parents. Families were always a sensitive subject.

"Is Cassandra your elder sister?" he asked, when she opened her eyes again. Vicki nodded.

"I saw this woman walking down the passage earlier. She had long dark hair. Would that be her?"

"Yes," Vicki said.

"Should we go and see her?"

"No," Vicki said. "Sandra hates strangers, and I've left you alone long enough. We'll see Sandra if she comes down to dinner." She reached out to him and he sat down next to her on the single bed. They embraced.

"What did you think of my mother?" Vicki asked, when they broke apart.

Andrew tried to think of something tactful to say.

"She's … er, different."

"She's a dragon. It's the only way that she knows how to cope with people. She drives me up the wall."

Andrew said nothing and Vicki sighed.

"Sometimes," she added, "I feel like killing her."

2

Andrew and Vicki were still in her bedroom an hour later when there was a resonant, clanging sound.

"It's time for dinner," Vicki said. "We'd better go down."

Andrew felt more comfortable walking through the gloomy, draughty house now that he had Vicki's hand in his. They descended the main staircase. As they walked, their reflection appeared in endless antique mirrors: a tall boy in his late teens, with long, curly hair, accompanied by his petite, shy-looking companion.

A large golden gong stood in the hallway, still quietly vibrating. Opposite the bottom of the staircase was the dining-room. If Andrew had been expecting a huge room, capable of hosting a ball, he was disappointed. The dining-room was only the size of a badminton court. There was a grand fireplace opposite the dinner table, but there was no fire in it. The oak table was capable of seating ten or twelve. The room's grey walls were covered in portraits with heavy gilt frames. A few centimetres separated each from the other. Pride of place went to a crystal chandelier which hung over the centre of the table. The room, being in the centre of the house, had no windows. It was very cold.

Only four places were set. Vicki's mother occupied one. A thin boy of eight or nine sat in another.

"Cassandra is eating in her room tonight," Vicki's mother said. "She's disappointed that you haven't been up to see her yet. Paul, this is Andy, Victoria's friend. Andy, my son, Paul." The boy held out his pale, white hand and Andrew shook it. He didn't like being called Andy, but it seemed petty to object.

"Pleased to meet you," he said to Paul.

Vicki's brother was a blue-eyed, blond-fringed boy, with narrow ears and a spaced-out expression.

"Likewise," he replied.

"How's school?" Vicki asked her brother.

"Brilliant. I'm in the hockey team. I can't wait to go back." Paul stopped, apparently aware that his mother might be insulted. If she was at all hurt, she didn't show it.

"His first report was excellent," she boasted to Vicki. "Much better than yours at his age." As she spoke, Moira brought in the soup and placed it on the table beside Vicki's mother.

"Would you like me to serve, milady?"

"No, no, I'll do it. I wouldn't want you to have an excuse for spoiling the main course."

Moira muttered a patient "Yes, ma'am" as she retreated. Andrew wondered if he was expected to call Vicki's mother "ma'am" or "milady" too. He wondered whether she treated all of the servants as badly as she'd just treated Moira.

Vicki's mother slopped soup into the shallow bowls, complaining about the quality of servants these days as she did so.

"I've tried so many agencies, but you just can't get the staff. Today's Alice's night off, but I asked her to come in because you were coming home, Victoria. And would she? *Terribly* apologetic, of *course*, but she'd made 'other arrangements'."

"How's McFadyen working out?" Vicki asked.

There was a brief, cool pause. Vicki's eyes met her mother's. Andrew gathered that the butler was within earshot.

"Very well," Vicki's mother replied.

The pea and ham soup was delicious. Andrew had a second helping and stopped noticing the cold. As they were finishing, the butler came in.

"Do you require wine with the main course, milady?"

"No wine with dinner until my husband returns," Vicki's mother said. "I won't have anyone disturbing the cellar when he's away, no matter who comes to stay."

The way she said it implied that having guests to dinner was an unusual and disagreeable experience.

"Cellar?" Andrew asked Vicki.

"We have a wine cellar," Vicki explained. "Daddy keeps a lot of rare vintages down there."

"I see."

After Moira had cleared the plates away, there was an awkward gap in the conversation. To fill it, Andrew asked Paul if he was interested in football. Luckily, he was. The new season had just started and the two of them managed to fill the next five minutes discussing various teams' chances of winning the Premier League.

When the meal was over, and Paul was gone, the interrogation began. Vicki's mother swooped like a bird of prey. Andrew half expected to be asked what his "intentions" were towards Vicki. It was nearly that bad. Within five minutes, she'd got more out of Andrew than he had told Vicki in the three months they'd known each other.

"An orphan, you say? You were brought up in an orphanage?"

"No. A boarding school, most of the time."

"Your parents – how did they die?"

"In a car crash."

"And you had no other relatives?"

"Only an aunt. My mother's older sister."

"I see. And this *aunt*, why did she not bring you up?"

"*Mummy!*" Vicki complained. "You shouldn't ask that sort of thing!"

Vicki's mother gave her a glare which made it clear why Vicki didn't stand up to her mother more often.

"It's all right," Andrew said, with a glance at Vicki. "My aunt's much older than my mother … I mean, than my mother would have been. Her health's not good. She couldn't manage it."

"And what do you live on?"

"There's money – in trust – from my parents' will. The interest paid for my school fees and still gives me some pocket money, but I can't touch the capital until I'm twenty-one."

Vicki gave Andrew a look of surprise. He'd never discussed money with her. But then, she'd never told him that she came from a house like this.

"You must have had a hard life," her mother went on. The words were sympathetic but the tone which Vicki's mother said them in wasn't. She continued the interrogation.

"What course are you on?"

"I'm training to be an art teacher."

"Why?" she said, in a tone which suggested that Andrew's ambitions were hopelessly mediocre.

Before he could reply, Moira came in and cleared the coffee cups away.

"Will there be anything else, milady?"

"No, Moira," her mistress said. "That's all. Goodnight." Vicki's mother got up to go. She was very much taller than Vicki, Andrew realized, and had a hooked nose which was prominent in profile. She left the room with a regal nod in her daughter's direction. Vicki and Andrew were alone in the draughty dining-room.

"What's all this 'milady' stuff?" Andrew asked. "Is your father *Sir* Hetherington or something?"

Vicki looked embarrassed.

"It's worse than that, I'm afraid. He's a Lord."

"A *Lord*? What does that make you? Lady Victoria?"

Vicki shook her head.

"Mummy's a 'Lady'. I'm not. There are five different types of Lord. Daughters are only called 'Lady' if their father's in the top three: a duke, marquess or earl. With the other two, viscount and baron, sons and daughters are called 'The Honourable'. Daddy's a baron, the lowest kind."

"So he's Baron Hetherington?"

"Only on correspondence and a few official things. Otherwise, he's always referred to as Lord Hetherington."

"And you're the Right Honourable Victoria Hetherington?"

"Just *Honourable*. Not *Right*. I don't use it though. Never have. I'm not even sure I agree with people having titles. Do you?"

"I don't know," Andrew said. "It's not something I've really thought about."

He was still finding the house's atmosphere very oppressive. When he leant forward on the table, something creaked alarmingly. Every time that Andrew touched something, he felt like it was about to break. It would be easier to have this conversation somewhere else – anywhere else.

"I don't suppose there's a pub nearby?" he asked.

"There is one, but it's a twenty mile round journey. You have to be pretty desperate for a pint to go there. We'll go down and see Moira later. She'll find us something to drink."

Vicki stood.

"We'd better go up and meet Sandra. I don't want her to think that we're ignoring her."

Yet isn't she ignoring us, Andrew thought, by not coming down to dinner? But he said nothing. They left the dining-room through a different door and climbed the winding staircase in the centre of the house.

"Sandra has the second floor of the house to herself," Vicki explained. "Has done since I was eight or nine. I used to resent it. I had a room and she had a whole floor. But Sandra's not a person you can envy for long..."

"Why's Sandra like that?" Andrew asked.

"She once had a big disappointment," Vicki explained, in a cautious voice, "and she never got over it."

Before Andrew could ask what the disappointment was, they came out on to the second floor. The landing was even dingier than the floor below, if that was possible. It smelt of mildew.

"Most of this part of the house is closed up," Vicki explained, then pointed at the four doors off the landing. "These used to be guest rooms, but I don't recall us ever having guests in them. The rest of the floor was designed as servants' quarters, but Moira and McFadyen have more comfortable rooms on the first floor." She knocked on one of the doors.

"Sandra, it's me. Sandra?"

There was no reply. But the second floor wasn't silent. Andrew could hear a creaking noise from farther along the landing.

"Do you hear that?" he asked Vicki.

His girlfriend listened.

"Sandra must be doing her exercises," Vicki said. "Please, Andrew, be nice to her. She'll seem strange at first. She's ... unusual."

They walked to the end of the landing and turned on to a corridor. This was the front of the house. Through the grimy windows, Andrew could make out a brilliant sunset, shedding its crimson light over the Cheviot hills. The creaking noise grew louder. Vicki knocked on the next door they came to.

"Sandra, it's me."

The creaking stopped. Vicki opened the door. A tall, well-built woman sat on a mat on the floor, wearing a purple leotard. She was using some kind of rowing device and her pale skin glistened with sweat. Her body was that of an athlete. Her long, dark hair must have been like that of Vicki's mother, when she was young. There was a resemblance between mother and daughter. Sandra had a trace of the hooked nose and the aristocratic bearing. But there was a big difference between them, too. Sandra was stunning to look at.

Vicki's sister got up. She gave Vicki a strange, half smile, then she stared at Andrew.

"So," she said. "You found yourself a man."

"This is Andrew."

"A very good-looking one, too."

Andrew mumbled an embarrassed "hallo", and matched Sandra's firm handshake with his own. Sandra addressed her words to both of them, but didn't take her eyes off Andrew.

"As you can see," she said, "I'm halfway through my exercise routine. Why don't I join you when I've finished and showered? Then we can have a chat."

"Great," Vicki said. "We'll be in my room."

"She seems OK," Andrew said, choosing his words carefully as they walked back downstairs. "Not even unusual."

"That's because we caught her exercising, when she's at her most focused," Vicki said. "She's not always so … relaxed."

"Does she have a job?" Andrew asked.

Vicki shook her head.

"She went to university, but never graduated."

"Why?"

Vicki stopped, faced Andrew, and smiled gently.

"Don't ask me to tell you all our family history at once. Can't you take people as you find them?"

"Of course I can," Andrew said, defensively. "Sandra seems nice."

"She is."

Vicki looked away. During all their conversations over the previous three months, she had barely mentioned Sandra. Andrew was sure that there was a great deal which his girlfriend wasn't telling him. Not for the first time, it occurred to him that he didn't yet know Vicki very well at all.

3

Vicki's room was large but full. There were things everywhere, from furry animals to books and brightly-coloured pottery, making the room a cosy, intimate place. She had a good hi-fi and they listened to music for a while. Then Vicki looked at her watch. It was eight-thirty.

"Moira should have finished her chores for tonight. I'll pop down and visit her, see if she can rustle up a couple of cans of lager for us."

"Fine."

She left Andrew alone in the room. While she was gone, Andrew thought about their relationship. They had been constantly in each other's company for the last three months. So how come now that he was in her home, she felt like a stranger?

His thoughts were interrupted by a knock on the door.

"Come in."

It was Vicki's sister, Sandra. She was dressed casually and had brushed her hair back. Again, Andrew observed that she was a very striking woman.

"Vicki's gone down to see Moira," Andrew explained.

"I'll wait," Sandra said. "If that's all right with you." Sandra's manner was shy, as though she were embarrassed to be alone with Andrew. Yet her eyes examined Andrew so brazenly that he felt he was being appraised, like cattle at an auction.

"How did you and Vicki meet?" Sandra asked.

"We go to the same college," Andrew explained, glad to be on safe ground. "We met back in June. There was an exhibition of Henry Moore sculptures at the West Yorkshire Sculpture Park. It's near the college. I expect you know it?"

Sandra shook her head.

"I don't get out much."

"Anyway, Vicki and I were both looking at one of the pieces and we got talking. One thing led to another. We started going out and, after the exams, went on holiday together. The Greek Islands."

"It sounds idyllic," Sandra said.

"It was."

"And now you're here?"

"Yes."

"And where are you from yourself?"

Andrew took a deep breath, preparing to be asked the questions which he had already covered with Sandra's mother. However, just then, Vicki returned with the drinks.

"Hi, Sandra," she said, with forced cheerfulness.

Vicki had only brought two cans, so Andrew offered to give Sandra his and go for another one. Sandra insisted that she didn't drink. Then the two sisters began talking. At first, Andrew tried to participate, but Vicki and Sandra didn't make much effort to include him. In fact, they behaved as though Andrew wasn't there at all. He watched as the sisters held a detailed, but strained discussion about the family.

Vicki was his girlfriend, but Andrew found it hard to keep his eyes off Sandra. It wasn't that he fancied her, not exactly. Despite her jet black hair and all the exercise she took, the older sister's skin was surprisingly pale, like that of an albino, or a vampire.

Vicki and Sandra talked about their brother, Paul. Sandra felt that, since going away to school, he had changed. He had an unhealthy obsession with what she referred to as "his collection".

"He'll be better once Daddy comes home," Vicki said. "You know how he dotes on Daddy."

"But that's another thing," Sandra said, lowering her voice, though it was still easy for Andrew to hear every word. "Daddy's up to something."

The conversation continued, but Andrew found it hard to follow. The two sisters weren't speaking in code, not exactly, but all of the conversation's meaning seemed to take place between the lines. It was full of references to events which meant nothing to Andrew, yet everything to them. One thing was clear: both sisters loved their father.

After a while, Andrew had finished his lager.

"Would you like another?" Vicki asked.

"I wouldn't mind," Andrew said, "but I'll go for it myself. Unless there's a bell I can ring for some servant to magically appear with one."

"We do have a bell system," Vicki told him. "But we don't use it in the evening, unless there's an emergency. Both McFadyen and Moira go off duty when they've cleared up after dinner."

"Are you sure that you can find your way to the kitchen?" Sandra asked, with a faint teasing quality to her voice.

"I'll shout if I get lost," Andrew said. "Can I get you something?"

Sandra wanted orange juice, Vicki a coffee. Andrew took the servants' staircase to the kitchen, although he knew he wasn't meant to. He might easily lose his way if he took the other route. Lady Hetherington would be in bed by now, Vicki had said, so she wouldn't object.

The kitchen was no longer brightly lit. A single lamp burned in an alcove near the fridge. Andrew found the orange juice, a jug of milk and the last remaining can of lager. It didn't look like the Hetheringtons were big drinkers. Or eaters: the fridge was practically empty.

Andrew found an electric kettle and put some water on. As the water heated up, he heard a noise, coming from the far end of the kitchen. At first he thought it was a radio. But when the kettle clicked off, he could clearly make out voices. One belonged to Moira:

"You don't know what you're talking about. You've only been here five minutes."

The other was McFadyen's.

"Can't you see what's going on? They're…"

He couldn't make out the rest of the sentence. Moira said something like, "Now that Miss Vicki's home things will be…"

"Never mind Victoria," the butler was saying. "She's not…"

"I've seen this happen before," Moira interrupted, her voice getting louder. "His lordship will work it…" Then there was the sound of a door being shut and the voices became muffled. Andrew put milk into the coffee and walked back up the narrow, winding stairway. Hands full, he pushed open the door which took him on to Vicki's landing.

"Naughty, naughty."

Andrew almost jumped out of his skin. But it was only Sandra.

"You shouldn't use those stairs. They're only for servants. Vicki used to get into an awful lot of trouble going places where she wasn't meant to go when she was younger. I'm surprised she showed you."

"She didn't..." Andrew wouldn't let himself finish the sentence. He didn't want to land Moira in it.

"I've brought you your orange juice," he said, instead.

"Thanks," Sandra said. "I'll take it up to bed with me."

Andrew was carrying Vicki's mug of coffee in his left hand, and had the can of lager and glass of orange juice balanced on top of each other in his right. Sandra carefully removed both items from his right hand, then returned the can, letting her cool fingers linger against his.

"Nice to meet you, Andrew," she said. "Sleep well."

Andrew watched as she drifted down the corridor. He was disturbed that he found her so attractive, even though Vicki was on the other side of the door.

"You're very honoured," his girlfriend said, as he walked in with the drinks. "Sandra likes you. Sandra hardly ever likes anyone. Mind you, she hardly ever meets anyone."

Was now the time to ask Vicki about the secrets in her elder sister's past? Before Andrew could work out how to phrase his question, she was kissing him. Vicki apologized for being distant earlier.

"Coming home always makes me go a bit weird. I was sent off to school when I was Paul's age, and I've always hated having to come home in the holidays. Isn't that weird? For most people, it's the other way round."

"Not me," Andrew said. "I either had to stay in school or visit an aunt who wasn't really interested in me."

"I'm sorry," Vicki said, holding him tight. "You know, we have a lot in common."

"Yes," Andrew said. "I guess we do."

4

Vicki woke Andrew the next morning with breakfast in bed. "What time is it?" he asked.

It was just after ten, his usual waking time, provided he didn't have a lecture or seminar to go to.

"I always get up earlier at home," Vicki explained. "I forgot to mention – we have breakfast downstairs at eight-thirty. Anyway, look, I got Moira to make you your favourite."

She lifted the cover on his plate to reveal scrambled eggs on wholewheat toast. Andrew was barely awake, and not yet hungry, but he ate it anyway. The eggs were delicious: creamy and almost firm, just the way he liked them. He complimented the cook. While he ate, Vicki talked about all the places they could visit later on.

"You seem in a good mood today," Andrew told her, when he was on to his second cup of tea.

"Daddy rang half an hour ago," Vicki explained. "He'll be home tomorrow morning. I haven't seen him since Easter."

She hadn't seen her mother for the same period of time, Andrew noted, but had spent less than an hour with her since yesterday afternoon.

"So what do you want to do today?" Vicki asked.

"Why don't we start exploring the area straight away, since you say there're so many places to see?"

"Fine," Vicki said. "I'll give you a guided tour. Do you mind if I ask Paul to come along? He could do with the company."

"Not at all," Andrew said. "I'd like to get to know him."

Vicki went for her brother while Andrew dressed. He had a T-shirt around his head when there was a knock on the door. Before he could answer, it opened. The maid came in. She was a slim, pretty girl with a straight blonde bob.

"I'm sorry," she said, backing out of the room. "I came for your breakfast things. I thought..."

"It's all right," Andrew assured her. "Come in. You must be Alice."

The maid nodded.

"I'm Andrew."

"Pleased to meet you," she said, as he fumbled on his socks.

"Have you been with the family long?"

Alice shook her head.

"Since the beginning of summer."

There was no deference or shyness in her voice, Andrew noted. He'd half expected the maid to be a shy, giggly girl, the way they always were in movies. But there was an assurance about Alice. Apart from her uniform, she could have been one of the girls he knew at college.

"Are you local?" Andrew asked, as Alice picked up the tray.

"My family have a farm a few miles away."

"Vicki and I are going for a drive around the area today," Andrew told her, wanting to keep the conversation going. "Is there anywhere that you'd recommend I see?"

"Not today," Alice told him, as she backed out of the room. "It's going to pour with rain in the next half hour. And it'll turn cold. I'd put a sweater on over that T-shirt, if I were you."

Alice was right. By the time Andrew got downstairs, the sky had gone from blue to black. He was waiting for Vicki when Lady Hetherington swept into the hallway.

"I hope you'll be joining us for breakfast in the future," she said, in her irritatingly haughty voice. "We do expect our guests to fit in with the family routine."

"I'm ... sorry," Andrew stuttered. "I didn't know."

Vicki appeared.

"I can't find Paul anywhere," she said to her mother. "Have you seen him?"

"Paul seems to spend most of his time avoiding me this summer," Lady Hetherington moaned. "As you probably gathered last night, he can't wait to go back to school next week. Now you'll excuse me. I have to see McFadyen about the arrangements for your father's return."

She went into one of the rooms off the hallway. Andrew heard a distant bell ringing. As McFadyen scuttled across the hallway, Andrew and Vicki exchanged glances.

"You have to make allowances for Mummy," Vicki said, in a low voice, when the butler was inside the room. "She gets frustrated, being at home all the time. She likes to be in complete control, but there's no one much to be in control of. Daddy's often away. Paul's at school. I'm at college. And Sandra has weeks when she doesn't venture below the second floor."

Andrew nodded understandingly, remembering Vicki's outburst the day before about wanting to kill Lady Hetherington. Probably most people had these contradictory feelings about their parents: sorry for them one minute, wanting to kill them the next. Andrew wouldn't know. Some days, he found it hard even to remember his own parents.

"Uh oh," Vicki said, as thunder sounded from outside. "Maybe that drive isn't such a good idea."

Heavy rain followed a few seconds later. A minute after that, the front door opened and Paul ran in, wearing only shorts and a T-shirt. He was soaked.

"Where've you been?" Vicki asked.

Paul didn't reply.

"Need to go and get changed," he said, brusquely.

"Would you like us to come and play a game with you?" Vicki suggested, generously. "Monopoly, perhaps. Or Cluedo?"

"Not today," Paul told her. "I'm in the middle of mounting the new additions to my butterfly collection." He went upstairs.

"Butterflies?" Andrew asked Vicki.

"The hobby runs in the family. My father. His father. I don't know how far back."

There was a sudden noise behind her and Alice appeared from nowhere. She was carrying a tray with a pot of tea for two on it. Andrew smiled and Vicki spun round. Alice gave her the slightest of nods.

"Oh, Andrew, this is Alice."

"We've met," Andrew said. He smiled at Alice. "You were right about the rain."

Alice smiled back. Earlier her smile had been friendly. Now the look she gave Andrew was unmistakably flirtatious.

"Farmer's daughter," Alice said, before taking the tray into the room where Lady Hetherington was meeting with McFadyen.

"We should never have taken her on," Vicki said, even though the door was still half open. There was jealousy in her voice.

"Why?" Andrew asked.

Vicki didn't reply. Had she caught him looking admiringly at the maid? Most people would think that Alice was prettier than she was. Did Vicki think that Andrew fancied Alice? Was she that insecure? As far as Andrew knew, he was her first boyfriend.

Or maybe it was a class thing. Maybe, Andrew realized, it wasn't done for him to chat freely with the servants. But Vicki was on close terms with Moira, wasn't she? He might be a guest in Vicki's home, but that didn't mean that he had to adopt all the double standards of the English upper classes.

The rain didn't let up all day. Andrew's girlfriend stayed in a frosty mood, without explaining the reason why. Andrew wanted to look around the Hall, but Vicki wasn't keen to show him.

"Not while Mummy's home," she said. "Mummy doesn't like people nosing around. Daddy once suggested opening the place to the public, just for a few days a year. Mummy freaked out."

"But I'm not the public. I'm your boyfriend."

"Mummy's always hated my friends coming to visit. She did everything she could to discourage it."

"So how come she's let me stay now?" Andrew asked.

"I didn't give her a choice," Vicki explained. "I didn't ask her whether you could come. I simply wrote a letter home saying that I was bringing you. After all," she added, reaching forward and hugging him, "we've just spent the entire summer together. It's about time you met my family. I'm sure that you and Daddy will get on famously."

"Yes," said Andrew. "I'm sure we will."

Dinner was an even glummer affair than the night before. Andrew asked Lady Hetherington a bland question about what the neighbours were like.

"There are no *families* around here," Lady Hetherington complained. "No one of note. For years, I tried to persuade Victoria's father to build a place in Hexham – he is Lord Hetherington of Hexham, you know – but he wouldn't hear of it. He prefers to be here, in the wilderness."

But he isn't here at the moment, Andrew thought.

Alice began to serve the main course, a roast dinner. Lady Hetherington put her finger to the gravy boat.

"This gravy is barely lukewarm," she complained. "Take it down to the kitchen and have Moira heat it properly."

Alice gave a bland apology and left the room. Steam rose from the other dishes. Alice took her time. Andrew watched as the rest of the food went cold.

After dinner, Paul hurried upstairs to continue work on his collection. He said that he wanted his new butterflies mounted in time to show to Lord Hetherington on his return the next day. Lady Hetherington rang the bell for Alice to clear the coffee cups.

"And run me a bath before you go home," she ordered the maid. "It's been a very wearing day."

As far as Andrew could tell, Vicki's mother had done no work of any kind whatsoever.

"Remember," she said to Andrew before going upstairs. "Breakfast is at eight-thirty sharp."

"Want to watch some telly?" Vicki asked, when her mother was gone.

"Sounds like a good idea to me."

"I'll just pop upstairs and see how Sandra is. God knows when she ever eats. Do you mind if I try to persuade her to join us?"

"No. Fine."

While Vicki was gone, Andrew decided to go upstairs and put on a warmer sweater. The Hall was even colder at night, but the radiators still weren't on. He took the main stairway. The sound of running water could be heard through the wooden panels on the walls. Then it stopped. Andrew nearly bumped into Alice on the landing.

"Does this house ever get warm?" he asked her.

"I thought you'd got Miss Victoria to keep you warm," Alice teased. "Isn't she doing a good enough job?"

Andrew blushed. He had been around enough girls to know when someone fancied him. Until this moment, he hadn't really thought of the maid in a sexual way. But, now, he and Alice stood next to each other on the landing, close enough to feel the heat from each other's bodies. He wanted to touch her. There were also questions which Andrew wanted to ask, but he didn't know the right way to begin. Then there was the sound of a car hooting outside.

"That'll be my father, come to pick me up," Alice told him.

"I'll see you again," Andrew said, trying to keep his voice warm, but not too warm. Alice didn't reply. She skipped down the stairs, as though she was ecstatically happy to be getting out of Hetherington Hall.

"This is the TV room," Vicki told Andrew, a few minutes later. "Sandra was exercising, but she said that she might come down to join us, later."

At last, Andrew felt like he was back at the turn of the twenty-first century, not the twentieth. The room had a wide-screen TV with surround sound speakers, a stereo video and a satellite decoder. There were two comfy-looking sofas. There was even a small gas fire, which Andrew switched on.

"Daddy likes his comforts," Vicki said. "What do you want to watch?"

"Why don't we see what's on?" Andrew suggested.

Vicki pressed a button on the TV and immediately, before the picture appeared, there was a loud, ear-piercing scream which seemed to come from the back of the room.

"Amazing sound," Andrew said.

"That wasn't the TV!" Vicki shouted, rushing to the door. "That was my mother!"

5

The bathroom was in the middle of the second floor, close to the landing. Vicki and Andrew got to the door just as Sandra came hurtling down the stairs. McFadyen almost collided with Vicki's sister as he reached the landing. Moira followed behind. All five of them converged on the bathroom door, which was locked.

"Mummy!" Vicki called, shaking the door handle. "Mummy, are you all right?"

No answer.

"Stand aside," McFadyen said. He barged the door twice with his shoulder, but it didn't budge.

"Help me," he asked, and Andrew stepped forward. Between them, they managed to kick the door in.

"Oh, God!"

The voice was McFadyen's. Sandra followed him into the bathroom, and promptly fainted. As the butler leant down to help Sandra up, Andrew saw what they had seen. Lady Hetherington lay in the bath. The infra-red heater fitting floated beside her body, sizzling. Wires trailed from the ceiling. Andrew reached for the heater's pull switch and turned the lethal contraption off. It was too late though. Lady Hetherington's body had turned a horrible colour.

She was dead.

Vicki finally got in, saw what Andrew had seen, and screamed. He guided her back on to the landing and held her. On the floor, Sandra was coming round.

"Is she? Is she?"

"I'm afraid so," McFadyen said.

Moira was the last into the bathroom. She came out, shaking her head, then shut the door behind her.

"I always said those electric heaters on the ceiling were dangerous," she said to McFadyen. "Especially in an old house like this. Will I call for an ambulance?"

"Yes," the butler told her. "Better call the police, too. If we don't, the ambulance people will."

The housekeeper left. Sandra and Vicki were still sitting next to each other on the floor, in tears.

Andrew sat down and held Vicki, who was shaking. When Moira returned from calling the emergency services, he asked the housekeeper if she'd make some hot, sweet tea.

"I was about to suggest the same thing," Moira said.

A few minutes later, they were drinking tea in the dining-room, speechless from the shock. It was only when they were on their second cup that Vicki thought of something they'd all forgotten.

"Little Paul!" she said. "Where is he? Suppose he stumbles into the bathroom and finds Mummy like, like … that?"

"I'll find him," McFadyen said.

"No," Vicki said. "I'd better do it."

"Are you sure you're all right to?" Andrew asked her.

"I will be if you come with me," she said. "I know where he is."

Andrew followed willingly as Vicki climbed two flights of stairs.

"He uses the attic because it's a good place to dry out his butterflies before he preserves them," she told Andrew, as they walked across the dusty second storey of the building. The floorboards creaked and spiders' webs criss-crossed the ceiling. Andrew could almost believe that the webs were holding the ceiling up.

The attic was reached from a black, wrought-iron spiral staircase at the back of the second floor. Andrew's head brushed more cobwebs as they made their way up to the dark, dusty attic. Andrew found the place creepy and threatening. Whatever Vicki said, he thought that an attic was an odd place for a young boy to spend a lot of his time. Vicki gripped his hand as they clambered into it.

"This is going to be difficult," she said. "Help me."

"Paul?" Andrew called. He could make out a light off to their right, beneath the high rafters.

"Who's there?" Paul replied, nervously. "What do you want?"

"It's Andrew and Vicki," Vicki called. "We need to talk to you."

"Can't it wait?" Paul asked, impatiently. "I'm in the middle of something."

Andrew approached Paul, surprised to find him so assertive. There was a horrible smell coming from his direction. Andrew thought that he knew what it was: formaldehyde, the chemical used for preserving dead bodies. Paul was standing over a huge sink, surrounded by chemicals. Dozens of butterflies were laid out on paper beside it. A large, old-fashioned metal lamp was clamped to the sink, illuminating the jars of chemicals which surrounded Paul.

"Aren't some of those chemicals rather dangerous?" Andrew asked.

"Daddy showed me how to use them."

Andrew trod cautiously on the shadowy floor, wary of holes in the boards. Then he nearly tripped on an electric wire as he got nearer to the boy. Beside Paul, pale butterflies were laid out on brown parcel paper.

"How do you catch them?" Andrew asked Paul. "With a net?"

Paul gave him a condescending nod.

"And then?"

Paul frowned.

"Then I kill them, of course."

"Of course."

Vicki leant forward and put a hand on Paul's shoulder.

"Paul, can you come downstairs with us? We've got something to tell you."

"I can't leave this. Tell me up here."

"This isn't the right place," Andrew tried to explain. "I think you'll want to be downstairs."

"What is it?" Paul said, impatiently. "Are you two getting married? Congratulations and everything, but I really don't see..."

"It's nothing like that," Vicki replied, abruptly. Then she put on a pleading voice which Andrew hadn't heard her use before. "Please come downstairs with us, Paul. You can come back to this later."

Paul continued mixing chemicals.

"Give me two minutes," he said. "You can wait for me on the landing."

Andrew was glad to get out of the dusty attic, with its threatening shadows.

"How does Paul stand it up there?" he asked Vicki. "At his age, it would have given me nightmares."

"He's been going up there with Daddy since he was five," Vicki explained. "Daddy can't manage the stairs himself any more. He wanted Paul to carry on the work. But since he went away to school, he's had a lot to do in the holidays. His being up there might seem odd to us, but it's normal to Paul, I guess. I wish he'd hurry up."

Her brother took nearly ten minutes to come down. Andrew began to worry that the police would show up before he appeared. While they waited, Vicki brushed the cobwebs from his hair. For someone whose mother had just died in a terrible accident, she was remarkably calm. Maybe, Andrew thought, it was because she had to be responsible for Paul. Any other explanation was too cruel to countenance.

Eventually, the boy came out on to the landing, entering the dank air like an astronaut reluctantly returning to Earth.

"Well?" he said. "What is it?"

"It's Mummy," Vicki told him, in a quiet voice. "She's had an accident."

"What kind of accident?"

"A very bad one."

Paul looked from Vicki to Andrew and back again. A boy his age should be able to understand death, Andrew thought, especially one who caught butterflies. But Vicki couldn't bring herself to say the words.

"Your mother had an accident in the bath," Andrew told Paul in his gentlest voice. "I'm afraid that she's dead."

Paul's reaction wasn't one of pain or sorrow. In fact, for a moment, Andrew thought he saw the hint of a smile crossing the boy's lips. But his expression remained as distant as ever.

"I'm sorry to hear that," he said. "Can I go back to mounting my butterflies now?"

Vicki burst into tears. Andrew didn't know what to say. Paul stared at them, politely waiting for permission.

"Can I go?" he repeated.

"Go," Andrew told him. The boy scurried off. Vicki wept on to Andrew's shoulder.

"He's too young to really understand," he tried to explain. "The grief'll hit him later, the way it's hitting you now."

"Is this grief?" Vicki asked. "I don't know what it is. I'm not crying for her, I'm crying for me. Paul's reaction was more honest than mine. I'm crying because she never loved me, and I never loved her. Do you understand?"

Andrew wasn't sure that he did, but couldn't say that.

"I think so."

"Do you?" Vicki demanded, her voice becoming harder. "I'm crying because I'm glad that she's dead."

The emergency services took a long time coming. After a while, everyone congregated in the sitting-room, a vast room at the front of the house where Lady Hetherington had had her conference with McFadyen earlier in the day.

The sitting-room contained several ancient sofas, upholstered in velvet and heavily padded. There was also a chaise longue and numerous armchairs. Andrew thought it was the pleasantest room in the Hall. There was a feeling of space in it. The cream walls were recently painted, and less crowded with pictures than elsewhere in Hetherington Hall. The ornate plasterwork was in relatively good condition. A real fire burnt in the hearth so that, despite the high ceiling, it was warm. At any other time, it would have been a cheerful room.

"They've probably lost their way," Moira said. "It's easily done, after dark."

Andrew went to the window. Since this was the ground floor, the windows were clean on the inside as well as out, but he could make out no headlights in the distance.

"I'll ring them again," McFadyen said, leaving the room.

Everyone else sat in silence. Moira had her arms around Paul, who looked vulnerable but bored. Sandra wore a dress now – though not the one Andrew had seen her in the day before. It was a summer dress, but the style was very old-fashioned. It didn't fit her well either, being far too tight around the shoulders and upper arms. She must have bought it before she began her body-building exercises.

Andrew felt uneasy. He didn't belong with the Hetheringtons at a time like this. What made everything even more awkward was the way none of them seemed very upset by Lady Hetherington's death.

"They should be here any minute," McFadyen said as he came back into the room. Andrew got up.

"I think I'll take a look from an upstairs window, see if I can see them coming."

No one argued, so Andrew went up the side staircase and found his way to one of the front windows on the first floor. It was hard to see much beyond the shape of the hills in the night sky. Still, Andrew didn't relish rejoining the others in the sitting-room for a while, so he went up to the next floor. There were no lights to be seen from this height, either, but he waited there anyway.

Lady Hetherington's death bothered Andrew. He'd never seen death at close hand before, but that wasn't the reason. Everyone assumed that what happened was an accident. It seemed an unlikely one to him. What made the heater fall down? He wanted to take a look, before the police got there and – presumably – sealed the room off. How did you get to the bathroom from here? Andrew went back towards the main staircase, hoping that he wouldn't take a wrong turn. He stopped outside a room which he figured should be above the bathroom, and opened the door.

The room turned out to be Sandra's exercise room. Andrew had an idea. He turned the light on. If he was right, beneath these bare floorboards must be the hole in the ceiling where the wall heater had fallen. He might be able to work out what caused the accident to happen.

The floorboards were long and went from one end of the big room to the other. There was no way of lifting them. Luckily, however, some of them were cut into sections. He lifted one. Only darkness below. He lifted another. There was a chink of light to one side. Had the bathroom light been left on? Andrew couldn't remember anyone turning it off. If it was the bathroom beneath, then he only had to go a little to one side. Andrew moved Sandra's rowing machine and lifted the mat. Sure enough, sections of board had been cut, maybe to install the heater, years ago. He removed one of the sections.

Beneath the beams, Andrew could see where the plaster had given way. The wires were clipped along the beams, but the last two clips were missing. Enough wire had been freed for the heater to reach the bath and remain live. It was possible to see where the heater had been mounted, to one side of the bath. But the electric wires came in over the bath. When the heater came loose and fell, the pressure from the wires would cause it to swing in, on to and into the bath.

The cause of the accident was obvious. Moisture from the bathroom had weakened the plaster on the ceiling, causing it to crumble. At the same time, vibrations from the rowing machine above must have weakened the screws which attached the heater to a joist in the ceiling. The only mystery was where the clips which attached the wires to the beams had gone. Andrew guessed that pressure from the falling heater had caused them to spring out. They must be on the bathroom floor. He had no intention of going into the bathroom to make sure. Andrew already knew all he wanted to know. It was an accident – an easily preventable one, but an accident nevertheless.

He returned the mat and the rowing machine, then went back to the window at the front of the house. In the distance, he could make out small pinpricks of light, moving. Help was on its way.

6

The doctor quickly pronounced Lady Hetherington dead and an ambulance took her body away. The police stayed longer. The investigating officer, Detective Sergeant Sinclair, spoke to everyone. He asked Andrew a few cursory questions, then, finally, addressed Sandra, as she was the senior member of the family present.

"There'll have to be an inquest, but the result is a foregone conclusion: accidental death."

"What caused the accident?" Moira asked.

"The heater shouldn't have been placed so close to the bath in the first place," the sergeant told her. "I've examined the ceiling. The plaster was weak because of the moisture, but the actual cause of the accident was that the heater had worked itself loose over the years. Does anyone know when it was installed?"

"It was here when I arrived, twenty years ago," Moira said.

"Has the house been rewired, or have there been safety checks in that time?"

"Not to my knowledge," McFadyen told him, "but I've only been with the family for a few months. I could check the house records."

"Who is responsible for maintenance?"

McFadyen looked embarrassed.

"There used to be a handyman," Moira said. "But that position has been vacant for some time."

McFadyen coughed.

"Technically, it's my responsibility. When things about the house break, I get them repaired. There was, as far as I know, no indication that the heater was about to fall. Otherwise… The servants, naturally, use a different bathroom."

"Naturally," the sergeant agreed, in a sardonic tone. "I won't trouble you any further."

He turned to face the others.

"Again, my commiserations for your loss. A police photographer will be along in the morning. Until then, please stay out of the bathroom."

It was nearly ten when the police left. Vicki tried to ring her father in South Africa, but he was already on the plane home. Vicki left a message at the Gatwick Hotel where he usually stayed after a long flight.

"I think," McFadyen said, "that this is an appropriate time for us to retire."

The butler left. Moira followed him, after some whispered words of sympathy to Vicki and Paul. She didn't, Andrew noticed, say anything to Sandra. He went over to Vicki, thinking that there was now nothing to stop them spending the night together. He was wrong.

"Would you share my room?" Sandra asked Vicki. "I don't want to be alone tonight."

"Of course," Vicki said. "Paul, would you like Andrew to sleep in your room?"

"I'm OK," Paul said.

"I think it would be better if he did," Sandra said. "You know how you wake in the night sometimes, Paul."

Paul looked embarrassed and annoyed in equal measures, but agreed to let Andrew share his room. Vicki gave her boyfriend a small squeeze goodnight, then she was gone.

Paul's room seemed to belong to another world. One wall was covered with football posters, the others with pictures of wildlife, predominantly butterflies. There were plenty of toys and comic books. It was a comfortable, warm place. The same couldn't be said for the pre-war camp bed which Sandra gave Andrew to sleep on. Parts of it dug into his back so sharply that he ended up folding away the bed and sleeping on the floor.

Andrew tried to make more light conversation with Paul, but the boy wouldn't talk. Soon, he seemed to be asleep. Andrew was exhausted, but couldn't get off himself. The events of the day kept running through his mind. He wondered if the Detective Sergeant had gone up and checked out the exercise room. Had the police realized that the rowing machine was directly above the bath? Andrew decided that they probably had. They wouldn't mention it to the Hetheringtons because it might upset Sandra when she realized that she was partly responsible for the accident.

Andrew finally started drifting off to sleep at around midnight. He wasn't, however, completely under when a noise disturbed him. At first, he thought it came from someone moving about above his head. But that couldn't be. The rooms above were disused servants' quarters. Then the door creaked open.

Andrew was sleeping on the floor at the foot of Paul's bed and couldn't see very well. He wriggled his head around the bed, in case it was Vicki and she needed him. But it wasn't. The shadow in the doorway was taller: Sandra. She closed the door behind her, then leant down over Paul's bed.

"Are you all right?" she said in a low voice.

Andrew was about to say something when, to his surprise, Paul replied immediately.

"I'm fine. Andrew's sleeping in my room tonight," he whispered. "Don't wake him up."

"OK. I was worried about you. Sleep well. One day, all of this will seem like a bad dream."

She kissed him on the forehead and left. Andrew tried to get back to sleep, but was confused by this nocturnal visit. On the one hand, he found it touching that Sandra was so caring about her brother. But it was odd that she seemed to have forgotten that Andrew was in Paul's room. Unless...

What if Sandra hadn't expected Paul to be awake, but had been addressing her question to Andrew? What if...? But no, that was ridiculous. Andrew was years younger than Sandra, and he was Vicki's boyfriend. She wouldn't try to ... would she?

When Andrew woke in the morning, Paul was already gone. It was twenty to nine. Andrew dressed in the clothes he'd worn the night before and went looking for a bathroom. There must be at least one other bathroom on this floor. But if there was, he couldn't find it. Andrew couldn't even find his own room, where the rest of his clothes were. There would be a bathroom, he guessed, on Sandra's floor, but that was the last place he wanted to go that morning.

On the ground floor, Andrew found a toilet, and washed his face in the hand basin outside it. Then he went to the gloomy dining-room. It was empty and cold. No one had eaten there that morning. Andrew was about to leave the room to continue looking for Vicki, when he noticed a bell pull. He couldn't resist the temptation, and tugged it. There was no sound, so he tugged it again. Probably broken for decades, he decided.

Suddenly, out of nowhere, McFadyen appeared.

"You rang, Mr Andrew?"

It took Andrew a moment or two to recover his composure.

"I'm sorry, yes. Where is everyone? I mean, where do I get a breakfast?"

"Miss Victoria is in the breakfast room with Miss Cassandra. I'll take you there."

The breakfast room was on the other side of the hall from the dining-room. It had its own dumb waiter, through which food was brought up from the kitchen in the basement. Sandra was already gone. Vicki had almost cleared her plate.

"Andrew! There's plenty of kedgeree left in the dish. Shall I send it down to be heated up? Or would you like something different?"

He inspected the lukewarm fish and rice dish. It smelt delicious.

"This'll be fine as it is," he said. "Is there any tea?"

Vicki asked McFadyen to make a fresh pot.

"How did you sleep?" she asked Andrew.

"Fine," he lied.

"I didn't want to disturb you. Is Paul still in bed, too?"

"No," Andrew told her. "He was gone when I got up. Hasn't he been down for breakfast?"

Vicki shook her head.

"He's behaving very strangely at the moment."

"Surely, his mum dying..."

"I know, but before that – last night at dinner – and then, when we went up to see him in the attic, how did he seem to you?"

"Odd," Andrew admitted. "Spaced out, like he was short on sleep, or ill. But I assumed that he was always that way."

"No," Vicki said. "He used to be a normal, healthy, cheerful, affectionate boy. He's changed."

"Perhaps it's to do with being away at school," Andrew said, remembering Vicki's discussion with Sandra two nights before. "We covered it in my first year B.Ed. lectures. Kids often cope with separation from their parents by distancing themselves. That way, they don't have to acknowledge how much they're hurt by being sent away."

"Maybe that's it," Vicki said, as Andrew began to eat his kedgeree. "Adjusting to boarding school is difficult at first. Though I think Mummy and Daddy were right to send us all there. It's so isolated here. You can't learn to make friends unless you mix with other people your own age."

"I guess not."

Alice brought in a fresh pot of tea. She was followed by McFadyen.

"The police photographers have arrived," he said. "I can't find Miss Cassandra. Do you want to deal with them, Miss Victoria?"

"I'll do it," Vicki said, and left the room with the butler.

Andrew was glad to find himself left alone with Alice. The maid seemed to be lingering in the breakfast room. As she brushed crumbs from the table, her body rubbed briefly against his. Andrew pretended not to notice, but began a conversation.

"You must have been shocked when you came in this morning."

"I think her ladyship was the one who got the shock," Alice replied, curtly, as she collected more of the breakfast dishes.

"Sorry," Andrew told her. "Accidental pun."

"Some families have more accidents than others," Alice said, with a mysterious smile. He wanted to keep talking to her, but she walked out of the room before he could think of a reply. He abandoned his kedgeree and went up to the first-floor landing. The police were packing away.

"You can have the ceiling fixed now," the sergeant was saying.

"McFadyen will organize it," Vicki told him. "Though, personally, I don't think I'll ever be able to use this room again."

Andrew looked into the bathroom. The water had been drained from the bath, and the wall heater removed. There was still some plaster on the floor, but nothing to suggest that a tragedy had occurred there.

"Have you taken anything away?" he asked the sergeant.

"Only the wall heater. A report will have to be done on it."

Andrew thought of mentioning the clips which were missing,

the ones which should have held the electric wires to the joist. If they had held, the accident needn't have happened. But if he remarked their absence, it would be obvious he'd been in Sandra's room, looking for clues. Andrew didn't want to draw attention to his own morbid curiosity.

He and Vicki saw the police officers to the door. As their car pulled away, another came up the driveway. McFadyen hurried out to the front doors and opened them fully as a Bentley parked in the drive. A portly man in late middle age got out of the car.

"At last," Vicki said, before she ran over to greet him. "It's my father."

7

"Need a stiff drink," Vicki's father said, after greeting his younger daughter and butler. McFadyen brought him a tumbler containing two inches of pale whisky, which the Baron downed in two gulps. The butler stood to attention while Vicki and her father sat in the easy chairs of the drawing-room. Andrew stood uneasily at their side.

"Another," Lord Hetherington commanded.

McFadyen returned with the bottle, a twenty-seven-year-old single malt. It was only as he sipped this second drink that his lordship seemed to notice Andrew.

"Who the hell are you?" he asked. "New groundsman? I don't remember telling McFadyen to take on another servant."

"This is Andrew," Vicki told her father. "He's my boyfriend." Lord Hetherington blinked twice, then held out his hand.

"Any friend of Vicki's is a friend of mine."

"I'm sorry we aren't meeting under happier circumstances," Andrew told him, not sure whether he ought to be adding "m'lord" to the end of each sentence. Lord Hetherington gave him an abrupt nod of acknowledgement then proffered the whisky bottle.

"Drink?"

"A bit early in the day for me."

"What's your name again? Where are your family from?"

Andrew answered the first question quickly, ducking the second.

"Wakefield. Andrew Wakefield."

"Wakefield. That's where Vicki's at college. Local boy, eh?"

"I'm at the college, too. Training to be an art teacher."

This seemed to satisfy Lord Hetherington's curiosity for the moment.

"Where's my Paul?"

"He had breakfast early," Vicki told her father. "He's probably in the attic, with his butterflies. Shall I get him?"

"No, no. Let him keep at it. And Sandra?"

"Gone for a walk, I think."

"Is she...?"

There was some kind of secret communication passing between father and daughter, Andrew saw. Vicki replied in a tone which made it sound like she was speaking of an invalid, or a very small child.

"Better than normal, I'd say. I think with Andrew here, and the police, she's been on her best behaviour."

"Good, good."

His drink finished, Lord Hetherington got up from his easy chair. He showed no sign of the alcohol having affected him.

"Family meeting later tonight. A lot to discuss. Till then, arrangements to be made. I'll be in my study. McFadyen, make sure Paul comes to see me when he emerges, won't you?"

"Yes, m'lord."

He fondly kissed Vicki on the forehead.

"Good to have you home, my dear."

"Good to have *you* home."

Vicki and Andrew were alone again.

"How are you?" he asked, coming over to sit on the arm of her chair.

"I'm fine. I'm glad Daddy's back. He spends a lot of time away. I thought he might be gone for days."

"What does he do?" Andrew wanted to know.

"He has ... business interests. I think part of the reason he stays away so much is that he and Mummy don't ... didn't get on. Not for a long time. That's also one reason why she was ... the way she was."

Andrew waited to see if Vicki added anything to this. She got up.

"Why don't we go for a walk?" Vicki suggested. "There are all those wonderful walks I told you about yesterday. And I need to get outside, clear my head."

"Good idea," Andrew agreed enthusiastically.

The sky was a brilliant blue. It was the first week of September, but felt more like high summer. The landscape was a blizzard of purples, browns and different shades of green.

"You must get a lot of walkers around here," Andrew commented.

"Surprisingly few," Vicki told him. "You see, there's so much beautiful countryside here and in Scotland, but the population's tiny. Also, we're right in the middle of the Cheviots. Unless you know your way around, there's no way you can drive somewhere and do a short, scenic, circular walk. So only the most intrepid hikers tend to make it this far in."

"You're very lucky to have so much beauty to yourselves."

They held hands and followed a sheep path along the edge of a tree-lined hill. A little later, they came to a small pool filled with water lilies and sat by it. On the banks of the pool were some wooden huts, partly concealed by the long grass and bracken which had begun to turn brown.

"What are they?" Andrew asked Vicki.

"Can't you tell?"

He examined one. The huts had no roof and were open on one side. Each had a wooden seat built into it. Andrew was mystified until he got in and spotted some red plastic casings, littering the ground.

"Shooting."

"Yes. They hide themselves in there, then pop up and shoot when the birds fly overhead. Grouse mostly, and pheasants. Daddy used to have big parties over every summer, but lately his health hasn't been so good. They're hardly used now."

They stood there, looking at the rolling hills, purple with heather. This must be paradise, Andrew thought to himself. For a few moments, he forgot Lady Hetherington's death. He put aside his attraction to Alice, and stopped thinking about the maid's enigmatic words that morning. Instead, Andrew looked at Vicki and she looked at him.

"This place is wonderful," he said. "I love it."

"I knew you would," she said, hugging him. "I knew it."

As they walked back to the Hall, dark clouds began to sail in from the south. Their gentle walk became a mad dash to avoid the rain.

8

Lord Hetherington met Andrew and Vicki at the front door. "Did you see Sandra on your walk?" he asked.

"No," Vicki told him.

Andrew hadn't given Vicki's sister a moment's thought while they were out.

"Has Paul come down?" Vicki asked.

"Yes. We've been looking at his butterflies. How do you think he's taken it?"

"I'm not sure," Vicki said. "He's not really himself."

Her father agreed.

"I shouldn't have stayed away so long. Couldn't be helped, but there it is."

Vicki smiled sympathetically.

"No one's blaming you, Daddy."

"Thing is, I am to blame in a way. If the house had been properly maintained ... place should have been rewired back in the seventies ... sixties even ... always putting things off, your grandfather was. And I'm the same. Can't be helped. She's gone now. Maybe it's for the best. She had a miserable life, poor old bird."

Vicki didn't reply. A telephone rang nearby. Andrew looked around and saw a black Bakelite phone in a nest under the stairwell.

"Isn't one of you going to answer that?" he asked.

Lord Hetherington looked at Andrew as though he'd made an impertinent remark.

"It's normally the butler's job," Vicki explained.

"McFadyen's driven to Kelso to buy some supplies," Lord Hetherington said, as the phone continued ringing.

"Why don't I answer it?" Andrew suggested. Unanswered

telephones got on his nerves almost as much as unnecessary etiquette. He picked up the phone before Vicki or her father could reply.

"Hetherington Hall," he said, into the crackly mouthpiece.

"May I speak to Lord Hetherington?" a female, professional-sounding voice asked.

"Who shall I say is calling?"

"My name's Mary Rutherford, Doctor Mary Rutherford."

Andrew covered the mouthpiece. "A Doctor Mary Rutherford for you," he said to his lordship.

"Ask her what she wants."

"Could I ask you what the call's about, Doctor?"

"No. I do need to speak to Lord Hetherington in person."

Andrew covered the mouthpiece again and passed this information on. Reluctantly, Lord Hetherington went to the phone.

"Hallo, hallo? What can I do for you, Doctor? Hallo? Anyone there? Hallo?" He put the phone down. "Woman must have hung up."

Andrew picked up the phone again and listened. There was no dialling tone.

"It's completely dead."

"Nuisance," Lord Hetherington complained. "McFadyen can sort it out later. What are you two up to now? Got any plans?"

"Nothing much," Vicki said.

"No studying to do?"

Andrew hadn't brought a single book with him, but Vicki made a pretence of having some work which needed doing.

"Then go and do it, child. Why don't I show you the library, my boy? Are you interested in our family's history?"

"Yes. Of course I am."

"Daddy!" Vicki complained. "You'll bore Andrew senseless."

"Nonsense. You go and get your work done. I'll return Andrew in time for afternoon tea."

They walked across the house. Andrew liked Lord Hetherington more than he had expected to. He seemed to be old-fashioned but, etiquette aside, not stuffy or stuck up. As they walked, he and the old man talked first about South Africa, then about Vicki.

"She seems very happy, Andrew. I think I must have you to thank for that."

Andrew stuttered something in reply. Talk of happiness the day after Lady Hetherington's death seemed misplaced, somehow.

The library was a grand, dark room at the back of the house. It was full of bookcases with glass doors. Inside them were endless hardbacked books, the majority bound in leather. There were some more modern books: a complete *Oxford English Dictionary* and the current volume of *Debrett's Peerage*, but no paperbacks whatsoever. The majority of the volumes seemed to be chronicles of Northumberland. Others were bound scrapbooks, of a sort. They were called "house" books, and detailed visitors, expenses, births, deaths, employment of servants and so on, handwritten by the Lord Hetherington of the time.

The present Lord Hetherington showed these to Andrew. Some of the photographs were of his ancestors with members of the royal family and other famous people. But none were recent. Andrew got the impression that the family no longer moved in those circles.

He was hoping to see some early pictures of Vicki, but these weren't on offer. The nearest he got was the family's entry in *Debrett's*. His host was, the book confirmed, Lord Hetherington of Hexham – Hexham being a market town south of the Cheviots. He was a "baron by writ" whose family was ennobled in the Middle Ages. The family built Hetherington Hall in the second half of the nineteenth century.

"Do you have any pictures of Vicki when she was young?" Andrew asked, as her father put down the book covering the years between the First and Second World Wars.

Before he could answer, Lord Hetherington had a coughing fit. Andrew stood back, waiting for it to end. The fit went on and on, alarming him. Lord Hetherington was turning blue in the face.

What to do? Andrew knew next to nothing about first aid. The only thing he could think to do was to run out of the library in search of help. Then, in a corner of the room, he noticed the bell pull and hurried to it. Within moments of his call, McFadyen was in the room with them. His lordship was sitting on the floor, coughing blood.

"He's been like this for a couple of minutes. Can you get him some water, quickly?" Andrew pleaded.

The butler ignored him. He darted forward, reached into one of

Lord Hetherington's pockets and produced a small blue pill. Then he performed a delicate manoeuvre which involved tilting his lordship's head back and inserting the pill under his tongue. Lord Hetherington stopped coughing.

McFadyen went to one of the bookcases, which, when pulled out, became a drinks cabinet. There was a decanter filled with water. McFadyen poured some of it into a heavy crystal glass and passed it to Lord Hetherington. When Vicki's father failed to take the glass McFadyen tipped the water into his mouth, a little at a time.

"His lordship needs to rest," McFadyen told Andrew when he'd finished. "Alice will be serving afternoon tea in the sitting-room in a few minutes. You can join Miss Victoria there."

Andrew did as he was told. Vicki was waiting for him on one of the big sofas.

"I hope Daddy hasn't been boring you to death," she said.

"It was quite ... interesting," Andrew replied. "But your father had a bit of a funny turn."

He told her about the coughing fit and McFadyen administering the pill. Before he could finish, Vicki ran off to see her father.

"Daddy has a heart condition," Vicki explained, when she returned, a few minutes later. "And a bad chest. He probably talked too much when he was with you. Don't worry. The doctors say that he's good for years and years yet if he takes it easy. He'll join us when he's had a little rest."

She poured some tea, then asked, "Did you come across Sandra?"

"No."

"She's not upstairs," Vicki said. "I don't know where she could have got to."

Before they could discuss Sandra further, Alice came in with a large poppy seed cake which Moira had made earlier. While the maid was in the room, she twice caught Andrew's eye. He felt flattered that this attractive girl fancied him. But he was also embarrassed, in case Vicki noticed them exchanging glances. And he was concerned, remembering Alice's remark about "accidents" that morning. The next time that they were alone together, he must ask her what she meant by it.

Paul joined them and they sat, making conversation, drinking tea and eating cake. After a while, Lord Hetherington came down, apologized to Andrew for giving him a scare and assured the others that he was well. He even played a game of chess with Paul.

Sandra didn't appear, however, and Vicki's father was feeling tired, so he suggested that they postpone their family meeting until the next day.

It was a cosy domestic scene. The Hetheringtons looked like a perfectly normal family, Andrew thought, who were coping well with their bereavement.

Too well.

9

At breakfast the next day, Andrew and Alice exchanged friendly smiles, but Vicki was there throughout, and seemed in an odd mood, so Andrew thought it best not to make conversation with the maid.

"Don't you find it odd?" he said to Vicki later that morning. "Having servants who are practically the same age as you?"

"Who? Alice? I'm not used to her yet, I must admit," Vicki said, confusing him. "I expect that you find the whole concept of having servants odd. For me, it's the other way round – I've only just got used to cooking and cleaning for myself in the flat at college. The other girls think I'm a terrible slob."

Sandra hadn't shown up for breakfast. Andrew gathered that she rarely did. No one seemed terribly worried.

"She wasn't around when I looked for her earlier," Vicki said, "but her bed was slept in last night. I checked."

"Does she often behave like this?"

"She sometimes stays on the second floor for days on end," Vicki admitted. "You hear her creaking about at night, but if you go and seek her out she's liable to fly into a rage. She sneaks into the kitchen. Once she ate an entire family picnic Moira had prepared the night before. After her midnight feasts she goes back upstairs and makes herself sick."

"But she looks so healthy at the moment."

"That's because she's on one of her exercise binges. They last up to a month. She has them once or twice a year." Vicki sighed. "Hopefully, she'll be normal enough to go to Mummy's funeral."

"Isn't it about time you told me what … happened to Sandra?" Before Vicki could answer this question, McFadyen appeared.

"Excuse me, Mr Andrew, Miss Victoria. Have you seen Alice? She's meant to be helping Moira."

"Not since we finished breakfast," Andrew told McFadyen.

"I'll remind her if we do," Vicki said.

As McFadyen went out, Lord Hetherington came in.

"I was wondering if you'd seen Sandra," he said, "so that we can have the family conference we were meant to have last night."

"I'm sorry, no," Vicki said. "I could go up and look for her."

"Best not," her father said. "Best not. Incidentally, if one of you should happen to answer the phone and it's that doctor again, get me straight away, whatever I'm doing."

"I didn't know the phones were working," Vicki replied.

"According to McFadyen, there's nothing wrong with them."

Andrew was about to ask why Lord Hetherington didn't just ring the doctor back. But then Vicki's father spoke again, in a softer voice.

"By the way," he said, "I spoke to the undertaker this morning. Funeral's on Friday."

"Doesn't there have to be an inquest first?" Andrew asked.

"Yes. Tomorrow." Lord Hetherington looked at Vicki. "No need for you to come, my dear, but if Sandra shows up, remind her about the meeting, won't you?"

Vicki agreed that she would and Lord Hetherington went off to do whatever it was he did. Vicki's father seemed recovered from the attack he'd had the previous day, but he also gave the impression of a man with a lot on his mind.

Sandra didn't show up during the day. Nor did Alice, as far as Andrew could tell, though the maid's absence wasn't remarked on again. Vicki and her father seemed concerned about Sandra, but not in a big way. After dinner, Andrew, Vicki, Paul and Lord Hetherington watched a video: an interminable war film whose name Andrew never caught. Paul and his lordship were thoroughly absorbed. Andrew and Vicki held hands and watched politely.

The next day, Lord Hetherington went to Kelso for the inquest. Vicki and Andrew decided to explore the area by car. They drove to the coast, having a fish and chip lunch at Seahouses. It was too windy to walk on the beach, so they decided to leave the Farne Islands and Lindisfarne for another day.

On the way back they stopped off in Wooler, where they poked around an antique shop for half an hour. It was a relief to be away from Hetherington Hall. When they returned, both of them felt tired, but relaxed.

Andrew went up to his room. It was clear that Alice was still gone. She hadn't been there at breakfast and his bed hadn't been made. Funny how quickly you got used to having things done for you. He told Vicki, but she was more concerned about Sandra. She went up to the second floor after dinner, called her sister's name a few times and opened a couple of doors.

"If she's prone to odd behaviour, her mother dying can't have helped," Andrew said.

"I know," Vicki agreed. "Sandra was the only one of us who was really close to Mummy. It must have hit her harder than appeared at first." Her voice trailed off. "But I need to tell her about the funeral tomorrow," she added.

Andrew found it odd that somebody could just vanish in a house, even one of this size. Yet Vicki assured him that the second floor, in particular, was like a rabbit warren.

"If Sandra doesn't want to see anyone, she won't."

"Maybe we should go down to the kitchen at night, keep watch for her."

"No," Vicki said. "We'll let Sandra be. But let's go down to the kitchen and see Moira, anyway."

Moira was sitting by the stove, still wearing an apron, soaking her feet in an enamelled basin full of hot water.

"You poor thing," Vicki said. "Are you exhausted?"

"I'm not, but my feet are. Bring the sherry from the butler's pantry, dear. I've not had that Alice to fetch and carry for me today and I deserve a bonus."

"What do you think happened to Alice?" Vicki asked Moira.

"Now that's a mystery. She was always such a reliable girl."

Andrew found this answer odd, as Alice had told him that she'd only been working for the Hetheringtons for a couple of months. Why did Moira use the word "always"? But he said nothing. Vicki and Moira obviously had plenty to talk about.

At first, Vicki and Moira tried to include Andrew in their conversation. He, however, said little. Soon, the two women began to forget that he was there. As they drank the sweet sherry, Vicki and Moira began to discuss the old days, when Vicki was growing up in the hall.

It was interesting for Andrew to hear Vicki talking about her childhood, which she rarely discussed with him. She and Moira reminisced about the eccentricities of servants who used to work in the house. Several, he gathered, had been sacked because they didn't come up to Lady Hetherington's high standards. No direct words of criticism were uttered, but Andrew began to get a clearer picture of Vicki's parents: her father as an easygoing, affectionate father, but none too successful businessman; her mother as an ambitious, neurotic tyrant.

Not for the first time, he couldn't help wondering if someone had wanted her dead.

10

The funeral was a small family affair in a chapel a hundred metres from Hetherington Hall. The tiny chapel was even more badly in need of repair than the hall itself. Vicki told Andrew that the chapel used to host a weekly service for the family and servants, but the last one was before the Second World War.

The Hall's other outbuildings stood empty now, and, apart from the stables, which had been converted into a garage, were ramshackle and potentially dangerous. Next to the chapel was a cemetery which housed generations of Hetheringtons. A marble slab stood by the place where Vicki's mother was to be buried. It marked the graves of Vicki's grandfather and grandmother. Lord Hetherington was their only child.

Sandra didn't come to the funeral. Apart from the vicar, Paul, Vicki, her father and Andrew, there was only Moira, McFadyen and Mr Gallagher, the family solicitor. The friends of Lady Hetherington's débutante days had either deserted her, or not been informed of her ladyship's death. The service was over very quickly.

Afterwards, everyone hurried back to the Hall, but Andrew lingered. He felt out of place on this intimate family occasion. That was how he came to spot someone new approaching the cemetery after everyone else was out of sight. A woman with dark, familiar hair stood by Lady Hetherington's graveside with a strange smile on her face. Sandra had made it to the funeral after all.

Having stood outside watching, Andrew was the last person back into the house. He walked into the hallway unheard, and was about to go into the sitting-room when he heard Lord Hetherington's voice. Andrew stopped, thinking for a moment that his lordship's words might be addressed to him.

"You're sure you won't stay for a drink and something to eat?"

"No. Thank you. I have a lot of other business to attend to. Here are the papers you asked for," Mr Gallagher's voice replied.

"Thanks, Henry. I'll go over them and return everything next week. We'll discuss whatever alterations need making then."

"I must admit, Percy, that I'm nervous about all these documents being out of the office safe. If you would only allow me to make photocopies..."

"No. No copies. Once a copy exists, another can easily be made, then another. You understand?"

"Of course. You realize, though, that your will is among these documents. In essence, your wife's death doesn't change any of its provisions. Therefore I don't see the need..."

His lordship brushed these arguments aside.

"I'll see you next week, Henry. We'll sort it all out then." He began to usher the solicitor out. They walked straight past Andrew, too busy talking to notice him.

"By the way," Mr Gallagher said. "I've had Doctor Rutherford on the phone, asking after you. She said it's urgent that she talk to you, but there's been some fault on your line."

"How the deuce did she get your number?" Vicki's father asked, in an irritated voice. "She's meant to contact me directly. In fact, she rang here the other day, but we were cut off."

"If you remember, when..." They went outside and Andrew couldn't hear the rest.

Andrew joined Vicki and Moira, his head buzzing. As he sat down, Paul left the room.

"Where are you going?" Vicki asked.

"To look at my butterflies," Paul said.

"Poor lamb," Moira said when he'd gone, "spending all his time with dead butterflies."

"He'll be back at school next week," Vicki said.

"And you think he's happy there?"

"I don't know," Vicki said. "I was."

Moira shook her head.

"Eventually you were, my dear, when you were twelve, or thirteen. Until then you were miserable. Why, when you came home, you used to come down to the kitchen and cry your little eyes out on my pinny."

Vicki didn't comment on this. Instead, she asked, "Does Paul have many friends at school, do you know?"

"I don't, dear. Why don't you ask him? I must be going." Moira left and Vicki took the hint she'd given.

"Have you seen the butterfly collection yet?" Vicki asked Andrew.

"No. Where's it kept?"

"In a special room in the cellar. The cold down there helps to keep them in perfect condition. I'm sure that Paul would love to show the collection to you."

Instead of going down by the servants' stairs, Vicki took Andrew down a staircase at the back of the house, the one he'd used on his first evening at the hall. This time, as they walked away from the kitchen, into the dark reaches of the cellar, Andrew was conscious of a loud, throbbing noise.

"What's that whirring?" he asked.

Vicki opened a door, revealing a massive metal contraption.

"The generator. We're too far out to have our own power lines."

"What powers the generator?"

"Oil. A tanker comes once a month. They pump the stuff in from the back of the house. The central heating boiler's in there, too."

"Perhaps we could turn it on," Andrew said.

Vicki smiled.

"It wouldn't make a lot of difference. Hetherington Hall is like a lot of old country houses. The family spent a fortune putting in central heating when it had only just been invented. Now it's completely out of date. The thing consumes gallons and gallons of oil and hardly has any effect on how hot the house is. But, needless to say, we can't afford to have it replaced. Come winter, we spend our entire lives wearing thick sweaters."

They went further into the cellars. Vicki showed Andrew the wine cellar, which was locked. Then they turned a corner and found themselves facing an iron door with an even more impressive lock.

"Better knock," Vicki said. "This is Paul's territory."

Andrew knocked. A couple of moments later, the door opened, slowly. Paul was still wearing the slightly too tight suit he'd put on for the funeral.

"Hi, Paul," Andrew said. "I was wondering if you'd show me the family butterfly collection."

The miserable expression on the boy's face seemed to dissolve, although he kept his voice flat and bored.

"OK," he said. "You may as well come in."

The room was square with a low ceiling. On every wall, from the floor to the very top, were wooden drawers, hundreds of them. In the centre of the room was a glass-topped table with a lamp above it. On closer examination, the top turned out to be backlit and the surface was a vast magnifying glass.

"My grandfather had this room made," Paul said.

"Are all the drawers full?"

"Nearly. Do you want to see?"

There are – Paul informed Andrew – about three hundred and eight species of butterfly in Europe alone. All of them were represented in the Hetherington collection. Each drawer held a species. Paul slid out glass trays which contained numerous sub-species of each butterfly. Andrew pulled out a drawer at random.

"What's this one?" He pointed at a butterfly whose label indicated it had been captured in Northumberland the year before. Its upperside was dark brown with silver-blue scales, while the underside was pale grey, with a kind of blue tint to it, and small white-ringed spots.

"It's a *Cupido Minimus*."

"Does it have an English name?"

"Do you mean proper name or a translation?"

"A proper name."

"They're called 'Little Blue', though the one you're pointing at isn't so little. Its forewing is nearly fourteen millimetres long. You only get them that size high up. I caught it in my summer holidays last year. Daddy said he'd never seen a bigger one. But they're very common. Let me show you something much rarer."

Paul produced an Andalusian Anomalous Blue, which he and his father had found on a holiday in Spain two years before.

"This one was only discovered in 1979 and it's very rare. Most collections don't have one. You can tell it mainly by the white stripe on the underwing."

They'd spent nearly an hour in the butterfly room before they were interrupted. Paul explained all of the parts of the butterfly to

Andrew, then showed him what he thought of as the collection's highlights. From Vicki's bored yawn, Andrew gathered that she had never spent so long in here before. He was beginning to tire himself when, to their surprise, Lord Hetherington came in.

"Ah, I was beginning to wonder where you three were. You'll forgive me for deserting you earlier. I've been preoccupied with clearing up your mother's affairs. Most rude of me. Have you showed them our *Agrodiaetus Violetae*, eh, Paul?"

"The Andalusian Blue. Yes, Daddy."

"Good, good. You know, I've always meant to write a book about butterflies. Maybe it's something Paul and I can do together, when he's older." He smiled, a man at ease with his family. "Time for lunch," he added.

The four of them went upstairs. Despite the cake an hour before, everyone was hungry. The morning's funeral already seemed forgotten.

11

"Is there any word about Alice?" Andrew asked Lord Hetherington as they were finishing lunch.

Vicki's father grunted a negative and started a conversation with Paul about butterfly hunting. Andrew said nothing, but his opinion of Lord Hetherington began to fall. How could Vicki's father care more for butterflies than for a human being?

The more he thought about it, what kind of person collected butterflies, anyway? He could understand why someone collected things which they could use, like books or CDs. He could almost understand why people might collect things which they could only look at, like postcards, or postage stamps. But butterflies? Beautiful creatures which have once been alive and which you have to kill to preserve? After an hour looking at them in that cold, catalogued room, Andrew found the idea more and more repugnant.

When he and Vicki were finally on their own in her bedroom, he told her his feelings. His girlfriend agreed with him.

"I can happily watch butterflies in the air outside, fluttering over the heather. Looking at them under glass gives me the creeps. It was clever of you to show such interest, though. It got you into Paul and Daddy's good books. They like having you around."

"It wasn't as calculated as all that."

"No," Vicki said, kissing him. "Of course it wasn't."

Later, Vicki told Andrew some more about Paul – how when he was younger he was very sickly and spent a lot of time in hospital. At one point, he wasn't expected to survive.

"I'd like to see some pictures of you and Paul when you were younger," Andrew said. "Your father showed me stuff from generations back, but nothing recent."

"I don't remember very many photos being taken," Vicki said.

"I'd still like to see them," Andrew pressed her.

"There ... might be some more in the library."

"Why don't we go and look now?"

Vicki seemed reluctant. Andrew remembered that Lord Hetherington had used a key to get into the library. Maybe Vicki wasn't allowed in there. But, if so, why?

"Come on," he pressed. "We've got nothing better to do."

"Oh, all right," Vicki said.

He followed her down to the butler's pantry. McFadyen wasn't around, and Moira was absorbed in preparing dinner, so Vicki took the library key from one of the hooks on the inside of the pantry door.

"Why's it kept locked?" Andrew asked, as Vicki let them into the room. She didn't reply. Andrew went over and began looking through the leather-bound house books. They were roughly in order, but weren't indexed or labelled on the outside, so it was hard to find the newest ones. The most recent ones he found were from the early sixties.

"I don't know where the rest are," Vicki said.

Andrew had a good look round. There were some books of a similar shape and size pushed back on one of the very top shelves. He pointed.

"Could they be them?"

"I'll take a look." Vicki got some wooden steps to stand on and reached to the back of the shelf, which stood nearly three metres off the ground.

"Ow! What is that?" Vicki hurried down the steps holding a broken whisky glass. Blood was dripping from her hand.

"How did that get up there?" she asked. "Oh, God, I hope I haven't got blood on any of the books."

"Never mind the books," Andrew told her. "What about you? That's a nasty cut on your palm."

"You're right," Vicki said. "It hurts."

She was, Andrew saw now, losing a lot of blood. He pulled a handkerchief from his pocket to stem the flow. As he was giving it to her, Vicki's body crumpled. She'd fainted.

Andrew caught her and laid her on the wooden floor.

"Vicki! Wake up, Vicki!"

Blood dripped into the cracks between the boards. Vicki murmured something, but didn't wake. Andrew tied the handkerchief round her hand to close the cut the best he could, then rang for McFadyen. He sat on the floor by Vicki and waited for the butler to come, cradling her head on his thigh. Nothing happened. Andrew got up and rang the bell again. This time, when he went back to Vicki, she came round.

"I'm OK," she said. "It wasn't the pain. It was the sight of the blood."

"I've rung the bell twice to get McFadyen to bandage you up, but nobody's come."

"I guess we'll have to go and find some bandages ourselves."

They walked slowly down to the kitchen, where Moira fussed over Vicki and bandaged her hand.

"You have a little rest before dinner, dear. You've lost some blood and you'll be tired. I'm sure Andrew can find something to occupy himself."

"I'll be fine," Andrew said. "By the way, the blood's left a bit of a mess in the library. If you give me a cloth, I'll..."

"Don't you worry," Moira stopped him. "I'll clean that later. You take Vicki up to her room."

Andrew walked Vicki up by the servants' stairway. She looked done in. He put her to bed and she fell instantly asleep.

Andrew went to his own room. Another lump of plaster had fallen from the ceiling on to his bed. He brushed it off and did some thinking. Where was Alice? Why were the house books for the last thirty-odd years missing? And what was the cause of Lady Hetherington's death?

The more he thought about it, the more suspicious Vicki's mother's death seemed. Even with the rowing machine above, a fitting didn't suddenly fall like that. It would work its way loose over a long period. Somebody would notice and fix it. Unless...

Unless somebody went into the bathroom, loosened the screws to within a millimetre of the end of their thread, then went into Sandra's exercise room, took up the floorboards and removed the clips which held the wire.

No. It was more likely that they'd do it the other way round. Then they'd actually test the fall of the bar heater, making sure that it would land in the bath, making contact with water. Finally, they'd put it back up, just before Lady Hetherington took her bath.

There was a flaw in the argument, however. For it to work, the murderer would have to know that Sandra would do her rowing exercises at precisely the same time as her mother took her bath. Unless, that is, Sandra was the murderer…

Vicki's sister *could* have done it. Shortly after the "accident", she vanished. Why? In remorse, or shock, or because she was afraid of being arrested? But there was a problem with this theory. Of all the members of the family, Sandra was the only one who seemed to get on with Lady Hetherington. If it was murder, why did she do it?

Sandra might be strange, but she still had to have some kind of motive. No matter how messed up Sandra was, on the brief occasions when Andrew had met her, she seemed rational enough. She would only do something for a reason. Perhaps the motive lay in the problems of her past, which Vicki had hinted at. Or perhaps they lay in the missing house books in the library.

Andrew went back to Vicki's room to check that she was all right. She was still fast asleep. It was gone seven, but the dinner gong hadn't rung. Moira must be running late. He decided to risk going back to the library on his own.

Andrew hoped not to run into Lord Hetherington. Andrew was a guest in the house. No one had actually told him that there were certain rooms he could go into and certain ones he couldn't. Yet it seemed implicit that he was only meant to enter particular rooms by invitation, and the library was one of them. He half expected it to be locked, but the door remained open, as Vicky and he had left it two hours before.

Vicki's blood still stained the floor. Moira would find it hard to get out. Andrew climbed the wooden steps as she'd done earlier. He was taller than Vicki and could see the remains of the broken glass on the top shelf. Gingerly, he reached around them, pulling out the leather-bound volumes. The books were dusty, he realized, as he slid them into his hand. Yet no dust had gathered on the broken glass. Who had left it there? And when? And why?

Expectantly, Andrew took the house books to the big oak table in the centre of the library, and opened the first one. It was dated thirty years ago. He found a wedding photograph of Lord and Lady Hetherington. It was true: Vicki's mother was once a beauty. There were various clippings from newspapers, and a list of the friends and relatives who attended the wedding. Again he wondered why none of these people had turned up for her funeral.

Andrew turned the pages and realized, suddenly, that the book had been badly mutilated. A lot of things were still there – he found, for instance, Vicki's first school report, and an account of Lord Hetherington employing Moira "after a satisfactory interview with her ladyship" – but a lot of things weren't. There were glue marks where clippings or photographs had been removed. As the book went on, whole pages had been torn out. He could find no trace of Vicki's birth, nor that of her elder sister. The last section of the book had been removed completely.

Andrew turned to the next book, the one which should have documented the last ten years.

Its pages were completely blank.

12

"I hadn't realized how tired I was," Vicki said when she came down for dinner at eight. "I've been sleeping badly," she explained. "I keep waking in the night, thinking I hear noises."

Lord Hetherington was quiet during dinner, a rabbit stew, which Moira served on her own. It must have been McFadyen's night off, Andrew decided. They drank the Châteauneuf-du-Pape which his lordship had brought up from the wine cellar, finishing the bottle before Moira produced the meal's crowning glory, a bread and butter pudding.

"Is tonight a good time for our family meeting?" Vicki asked, as they drained their coffees.

Lord Hetherington looked awkward.

"Are you recovered from your accident, earlier?" he asked, in a tone which suggested that this wasn't the real reason for his reluctance. Andrew felt they wanted him out of the way. He had yet to tell anyone about the mutilated books in the library, but now didn't seem like a good time.

"If you'd like me to leave," he said, "I'd quite understand."

"I'm sure you do understand, Andrew," Vicki's father said slowly, "that some matters are best kept private. What I want to discuss, however, can only be broached when Sandra is here. After all, she's … the eldest."

"Does that mean I can leave the table?" Paul asked.

"Of course, old chap, if that's what you want."

Paul got up and started rummaging in a corner. Lord Hetherington started up a forced conversation about Andrew's art course. Then Andrew managed to get in a question about the missing maid.

"Have you rung her home?" he enquired of Lord Hetherington.

"I think McFadyen did the day she disappeared," his lordship replied, in an off-hand manner. "They didn't know what had happened to her. But the phones are still on the blink and her family are farmers – you can only catch them in at certain times. I'm sure there's nothing to be concerned about."

Andrew wasn't so sure, but it was clear that Lord Hetherington didn't want to discuss the matter further.

"You must be concerned about Sandra, though?" he commented. Lord Hetherington nodded.

"Yes. But it's not the first time she's behaved in this way."

Andrew decided that it was time to broach the question which Vicki had refused to answer earlier in the week.

"How did it happen?" he asked. "What made Sandra the way she is?"

"She was supposed to marry," Lord Hetherington said, in a cold voice. "But it went tragically wrong." He paused, but his chilly expression told Andrew not to attempt any more questions.

"I think," Lord Hetherington went on, "that I ought to go up and find Sandra now. I shall try to persuade her to come down for a family meeting, tomorrow afternoon. If she won't come, we will hold the meeting without her, at two. There are things we have to discuss which won't wait any longer."

Paul put down his Nintendo and helped his father out of the room.

"He suddenly looks very old," Vicki said.

"What do you think he wants to talk to you about?" Andrew asked, now they were alone. From her awkward responses earlier, he judged it safest not to ask any more questions about Sandra's wedding for a while.

"Money, I suppose. He's been strapped for cash for years. Paul's school fees can't be helping. You know, Daddy only does the most essential repairs to the house, but even so, as you can imagine, it costs a fortune to run."

"Aren't there things that he can sell?"

Vicki shrugged.

"Some furniture, maybe. The wine cellar. All the good paintings went years ago. The only ones left are portraits which are worth less than they'd cost to restore."

"So what is there to discuss?"

Vicki measured her words carefully.

"Daddy always expected to die before Mummy did. Now all that's changed. Paul is the heir, because he's male, but he can't manage the Hall until he's twenty-one."

"That's not fair, is it?" Andrew commented. "Why should it be the boy who inherits, succeeds to the title?"

"It's just the way things are," Vicky said. "It makes no difference to me, anyway. If it was the eldest who inherited, I'd still miss out. What I care about is us keeping the Hall, and the land around it. Does that sound awful to you? Do you believe in inherited wealth?"

"Not really. But if I'd grown up in a place like this…" Vicki didn't let Andrew finish the thought.

"You see, I might not end up working round here, or even living here, but I want to always be able to come back when I feel like it. I want my own children to have what I had."

"You think there's a risk of your father selling up completely?" Andrew asked.

Vicki nodded.

"Daddy's made some bad investments over the years. I guess a lot depends on what he was doing in South Africa. He's bound to tell us about that at the meeting tomorrow."

"About Sandra…" Andrew began.

"I don't want to talk about Sandra now," Vicki said. "That was tactless of you, to bring it up at the dinner table, when Paul was still in the room. Daddy was embarrassed."

Taken aback by the anger in her voice, Andrew waited before telling Vicki about what he'd found in the house books while she slept. When he did, Vicki shrugged and said it didn't make sense. She didn't seem interested. Andrew could tell that his girlfriend was holding something back, but she was in a bad mood, so he didn't challenge her. They played an endless game of Trivial Pursuit.

Later, going back to his room at midnight, Andrew thought he heard steps on the stairway. Perhaps, he thought, Sandra was sneaking down to the kitchen, getting herself something to eat. He stood on the landing, hoping to get a glimpse of her.

But it wasn't Sandra. It was Paul, in pyjamas and bare feet. He nearly bumped into Andrew as he hurried on to the landing on the way back to his bedroom. The boy scurried off without speaking.

13

The next day it turned cold, but the heating wasn't switched on. Andrew found it hard to get out of bed. Eventually, though, he put on his one warm sweater and went down for breakfast, very late. Vicki was waiting for him. She hadn't eaten yet, either. Andrew rang the bell, but McFadyen didn't appear.

"I hope he hasn't vanished too," Andrew quipped to Vicki. The look on Vicki's face told him that she didn't appreciate the joke. They went to the kitchen and got some muesli and orange juice. The stove had been on and it was warmer there than in the breakfast room, so they decided to stay in the kitchen while they ate.

Moira wasn't around either, so Vicki made a pot of tea herself.

"I often had breakfast down here with Moira when I was home from school," she said.

"Why not with your parents?"

"Daddy was away a lot. Mummy and I were never that close. She always spent a lot more time with Sandra than with me."

Andrew finished his muesli, which was dry and rather stale.

"Where do you think Moira is?"

"Probably cleaning somewhere."

"I've been thinking," Andrew said, "about Alice. Has there been any word from her?"

"I only know what Daddy said at dinner last night," Vicki told him. "He deals with matters to do with the servants."

"But suppose something's happened to her?"

"Then her parents would have called, or the police. Why are you so bothered about her?"

Andrew didn't reply at once. He didn't know how much Vicki had noticed the undercurrent of desire between him and the maid.

But that wasn't the only reason for his concern. Alice's absence on its own might not have worried him, but following so soon after Lady Hetherington's violent death, it seemed ominous. Without answering Vicki's question, he pressed his point.

"The phones here keep going out of action. Someone could have been trying to call. Where does she live? Nearby?"

"Her family farm's about five miles away."

"Why don't we go and visit her?"

"I don't see the..."

"Just for a minute or two, to set my mind at rest. Then you could show me some more of the area." Andrew gave Vicki a warm smile, to show that he wasn't getting at her. Reluctantly, she conceded.

"If we're going to go, we'd better get a move on, or we won't be back in time for lunch."

It was nearly eleven. They took the servants' stairs up to the main hall. Vicki was right. Moira had been cleaning. The doors to nearly all of the rooms off the hall were open and a vacuum cleaner stood outside the sitting-room. But it wasn't switched on. Andrew could hear Moira's voice, coming from the one room whose door wasn't open.

"Which room is that?" he asked Vicki.

"My father's study."

While Vicki went to get the car, Andrew stood in the hall, listening.

"...finished," Moira said, angrily. "I don't blame him. I've been a fool to stay all these years, haven't I? And now it's all crumbling down around you."

Vicki's father replied in a softer, placatory tone. The only words which Andrew could make out were "all right".

"No," Moira replied. "It won't be all right. That's what I'm trying to tell you. All you can think about is your plans for Paul. It's too late for Sandra, but what about Vicki?"

Andrew couldn't hear the reply, but what Moira said next sent a chill down his neck.

"That's all very well, but there's her boyfriend, too. He's not all he seems. Have you taken a close look at him?"

Andrew heard the sound of a car horn. He waited to hear what Moira said next, but Lord Hetherington was talking about McFadyen and something to do with money. The car horn sounded again and Andrew went out to join Vicki.

Andrew was relieved to be out of the house at last. It was a chilly, windy day, but an attractive one. Clouds scudded across the sky and the cotton grass bent in the stiff breeze. Despite her bandaged hand, Vicki insisted on driving. As they got away from the Hall, she seemed to relax a little.

"If we're going to her house," Vicki said, "I suppose I ought to tell you about me and Alice, before she does."

"What do you mean?"

"There was a time," Vicki said, without taking her eyes off the road, "when I used to play with Alice. She's eighteen months younger than me, but she was the only girl anywhere near my age for twenty miles or so. Daddy used to send the Bentley and have her brought up to the house."

Andrew was surprised that Vicki hadn't mentioned this before.

"Did you get on well?"

Vicki shook her head.

"Towards the end I used to bully her terribly. Not let her use my toys, insist that she did all the tidying up, that sort of thing. I don't know why. When I was Paul's age, I turned into a pretty horrible child. I'd grown out of it by the time I was a teenager, but, by then, the age difference mattered too much. Alice and I never made it up."

"She must have been very cheesed off with you."

Vicki looked embarrassed.

"Alice used to let me boss her about. She didn't have friends outside school either, the family farm being very remote. So she tried to hang on to me until I dropped her." She paused, then asked, "Do you hate me?"

"Of course not," Andrew said. "But I can see why Alice might. How long has she worked in the Hall?"

"Only since the summer. Mummy took her on, knowing full well how uncomfortable it would make me."

"Have you spoken to her much since we've been here?"

"Are you kidding?" Vicki pulled up outside a small stone farmhouse.

"You remembered the way," Andrew said.

"Of course I did. This used to be part of the Hetherington estate," Vicki explained. "I suspect Dad sold it to Alice's father because he needed the money for my school fees."

As they got out, Vicki put her bandaged hand on Andrew's arm.

"Can you do the talking?"

A woman in dungarees came to the door. She eyed Vicki and Andrew suspiciously.

"And what can I do for you?"

Andrew suddenly realized the delicacy of the situation they were in. If Alice's mother didn't know that she had disappeared, he might throw her into a panic.

"It's about Alice," he said.

The woman shook her head angrily.

"She's not coming back, if that's what you're after. Not even if..." She was interrupted by her daughter. Andrew was relieved to hear Alice's voice.

"It's OK, Mum. I'm a big girl now. I'll talk to them."

"All right," Alice's mother said. "But don't you let that Victoria talk you into anything. I've got to see to the pigs." Alice's mother pushed past them. Alice stared calmly at Vicki and Andrew.

"You'd better come in," she said.

The room was small but cosy. There was a wood fire burning in the grate. Alice motioned them to sit on the sofa while she stood by the fire. Vicki stayed standing.

"We were worried about you," Andrew said. "Vanishing like that."

"Who said I vanished?"

"Everyone," Andrew told her. "Moira. McFadyen."

"McFadyen knew why I went. He won't have said anything in front of you for fear of upsetting the apple cart. After all, he was in the same boat as me – at least that's what he said. Did you ask his lordship?"

"Well..."

Alice looked at Vicki.

"He's a slippery old sod, isn't he, your father? There are some stories I could tell."

"How dare you?" Vicki said, testily. "You've no right."

"This is my house which my family own," Alice snapped. "I've got every right to say what I want to in it."

"Then I'm not listening to you." Vicki walked out of the room without a backward glance.

"We didn't come to argue," Andrew said, standing up slowly. "We were both worried about what had happened to you."

"Have you come to pay her?" Alice's mother had come back into the room.

"Pay?" Andrew said, weakly. He was working out what should have been clear to him days ago.

"She's owed six weeks' wages. That's why she's left. That new butler kept making excuses, so she went to see his lordship as soon as he got home. Fat lot of good it did her. He claimed to be broke, told her he'd have plenty of money by next week. Have you brought the money?"

"I'm afraid..."

"I'm not surprised. You'd better get out before your girlfriend drives off without you."

Alice defended Andrew.

"This has nothing to do with him, Mum. It's not his fault his girlfriend treated me like muck when I was a kid, or that her father gave me the only job I could get then treated me like muck, too. Leave him be."

"Thanks for defending me," Andrew said to Alice. "But I'd better go."

The girl gave him a tender, admiring look.

"You seem like a nice bloke," she said. "I don't know what you're doing with *Miss* Victoria, I really don't."

"Maybe she's changed since you knew her," Andrew muttered, then added: "What will you do if you're not going back to the Hall?"

"Work on the farm," Alice said. "There's plenty of work – just no money to pay me with. But it's experience, I suppose. I've applied to go to Sutton Bonnington Agricultural College next year." She smiled at Andrew as if to say, "You see, I'm not just a maid." Andrew went to the door, then turned back.

"You said you had some stories to tell. Were any of them about Vicki's sister, Sandra?"

Alice smiled.

"The crazy sisters," she said.

Andrew ignored the jibe against Vicki.

"Do you know who Sandra was supposed to marry?"

"They keep that quiet, do they?" Alice's mother said, coming back into the room. "I'm not surprised. I'll tell you who Sandra was going to marry: Charles Partington. Have you heard of him?"

"Was he from round here?" Andrew asked.

"He was. You ask Lord Hetherington what happened to Charles Partington. Go on, ask him."

Andrew wanted to question her further but, at that moment, Vicki sounded the horn on the car. Reluctantly, he went out to join her.

14

"Damn!" Vicki said, a couple of minutes after they'd left Alice.

"What's wrong?" Andrew asked. Then the spluttering noise made by the engine rendered his question redundant.

"I meant to get some petrol in Wooler the other day, but I forgot."

The engine spluttered again and died.

"How far are we from the Hall?" Andrew asked.

"At least seven miles by car. Maybe five over the fields."

"We could go back to Alice's farm," he suggested, "scrounge some petrol from them."

"You're kidding, aren't you?" Vicki said. "After the way they treated me?"

"Oh, come on," Andrew said. "From what you told me, Alice has every reason to dislike you and your family. I'll go alone, if you like."

"No!" Vicki said. "I'd rather walk."

"All right," Andrew said. "We'll walk back to the Hall. It'll only take a couple of hours. McFadyen can come back in the Bentley and bring some petrol."

As he said this last sentence, it occurred to Andrew that he hadn't seen McFadyen since the funeral. Alice said he hadn't been paid. Suppose he, too, had walked out?

"I'll be late for the family meeting," Vicki said.

"They won't start without you," Andrew assured her. "It can't be helped." He got out of the car, then went round to her side.

"Take the hand brake off. You steer, and I'll push the car into the side of the road so that tractors can get by."

They moved the car then set off over the fields. The day was cold and windy. They weren't dressed for the open air, but there was no choice. Vicki seemed preoccupied. Andrew decided not to tell her that he'd discovered who Sandra was meant to marry. It could wait.

"Is this your land?" he asked Vicki, as they made their way through the purple heather.

"Some of it is," she replied, shivering a little. "I don't know the precise boundaries – anyway, we wouldn't be trespassing. There's a public right of way through all of it. Some agreement with the National Trust."

Andrew looked around at the rolling hills and the vast, unpeopled places beneath. Yes, he thought, this land ought to belong to everyone.

They walked mostly in the valleys, passing a few sheep, a river, a tree plantation, but no people. Andrew had read somewhere that Northumberland was the last wild place in England. Maybe it was true. He and Vicki walked in silence, holding hands except where it was too steep to keep their balance. They had been walking for an hour when Andrew spotted a trail snaking around a hill.

"What's that?" he asked Vicki.

"What does it look like?"

"A road."

"That's what it is."

"Where does it lead?"

Vicki paused.

"A family called the Partingtons used to live there. That road leads to their house."

"I'd like to see it."

"It's not on our way home," Vicki said, tetchily.

"A few minutes won't make any difference."

"It'd take more than a few minutes," Vicki said, "and, anyway, it's a ruin. There's nothing to see."

"I like ruins."

"Well, I don't want to go there."

"Why not?"

"If you must know," Vicki said, looking away from him, "the place gives me the creeps. There was a bad accident there. People died."

"How did it happen, the accident?" Andrew asked.

Vicki's voice became impatient.

"An electrical fault. Look, if you really want to go there, let's make it another day. OK?"

"OK." Andrew was about to ask another question when Vicki remembered something. She swore.

"What is it?"

"I left the keys in the car."

"Not too many car thieves round here, I'd have thought."

"I guess not," Vicki said. "Who'd want my old Mini anyway? We'll go straight back for it after lunch."

The weather had turned colder and the only way to stay warm was to walk quickly. Andrew began to feel very hungry. As the Hall came into sight, all he could think about was how a bowl of Moira's pea and ham soup would warm them both up.

They walked into the Hall through the front door. Everything was the way they'd left it. The vacuum cleaner stood exactly where it had been three hours before. A two-day-old copy of *The Scotsman* sat on the table by the phone. Vicki went into the sitting-room and rang the bell. Then, when no one came, she went to her father's study, knocked on the door and, when there was no reply, went in. Andrew waited a moment, then followed her. The study was an untidy room, with two filing cabinets and loose papers everywhere. It was empty.

"Where is everybody?" Vicki asked, aloud.

Andrew picked up the phone on Lord Hetherington's desk. The line was dead.

"Let's go down to the kitchen," he suggested.

If they were expecting to find Moira there, they were disappointed. Andrew looked in the pantry, and found them a banana each. They ate hungrily.

"What do you think's going on?" Vicki asked, as Andrew put the skins into the bin.

"I've no idea. They can't all be out. Where shall we look?"

"The first floor, I guess."

They took the servants' stairs up to the first floor, then walked around shouting.

"Hallo. Is anybody there? Hallo?"

There was no reply. They got to Paul's room. There was no sign of him. Next, they went to Lord Hetherington's bedroom, which Andrew hadn't been in before. It was a large, ornate room, with a four poster bed and a coal fire in the grate, unlit. It was also empty.

"What are we going to do?" Vicki asked.

Andrew had to admit that he had no idea.

"This is freaky," Vicki said. "I've never, ever been in the house on my own before."

"You're not alone now," he told her.

They hugged. Vicki was still shivering.

"I'm afraid," she said. "Aren't you?"

"Not yet," Andrew said.

What was making her afraid? Andrew hadn't told Vicki his suspicions that her mother had been murdered. He hoped that he was wrong about that. After all, Alice's disappearance turned out to have a simple, if depressing, explanation.

Vicki broke away from him.

"I think we should get out of here," she said. "I know where Daddy keeps the spare set of keys for the Bentley."

There was a bureau in the corner of the bedroom. Vicki opened one of the drawers and pulled out the keys.

"But where should we go?" Andrew asked.

"The police."

"Isn't that overreacting? What's the crime?"

"I don't know. Daddy's solicitor, then: Mr Gallagher."

Andrew tried to calm Vicki down.

"Maybe we're panicking too quickly. There's probably a perfectly simple explanation. Where's the garage?"

"The old stables round the back. There's a door near the library."

They hurried out. Andrew glanced into the library as they left. No one was in there. Vicki's blood – dry, now – still stained the wooden floor.

"Here," Vicki said, handing him the key to the garage. "Can you open this? My hands are shaking."

Andrew took the key, but when they got to the garage, he didn't need it. The stable doors, like the rest of the doors in the house, had been left wide open. There was no car inside.

"Now are you afraid?" Vicki asked.

15

Storm clouds gathered overhead. The nearest building was Alice's farm, a good three hours' walk away. Andrew told Vicki that her father and brother were bound to come back, but she wasn't convinced.

"He's gone," she said, her voice rising anxiously. "The servants have walked out and Daddy's taken Paul and left. Paul's the only one he really cared about – the male heir he waited so long for. Daddy must have gone bust. That was what the family meeting was going to be about."

Vicki seemed on the verge of hysteria. Andrew remembered what Alice had said about the "mad sisters". Was Vicki secretly as unstable as Sandra? Andrew couldn't believe it. He tried to calm her down.

"There's bound to be a simple explanation."

"Sure," said Vicki. "Maybe Daddy's creditors are about to seize the house and he's done a runner. I'll be penniless."

"Would that be so bad?" Andrew asked, trying to comfort her. "Look at the other people at college. They haven't got money behind them. They have to get by on their wits, on their qualifications."

"It's not the money I'm bothered about," Vicki said. "We've always been short of money. It's my home. How can you let somebody take away your home?"

"You can even get used to not having a home," Andrew told her.

"I'm sorry," Vicki said, more tenderly. "I was so wrapped up in myself that I forgot. But what are we going to do now?"

Andrew thought for a moment. "I think we ought to search the house from top to bottom."

"What are we looking for?"

"Something. Anything that'll give us a clue as to what happened to the others."

"You know what gets me?" Vicki said.

"What?"

"Moira not being here. I can understand McFadyen walking out. He's only been with the family for a few months. But Moira's been with us for more than half her life – for all of mine. Even if she hadn't been paid for weeks, like Alice, I can't believe that she'd just walk out like that. We were ... are close."

"Maybe she's with Sandra."

"I doubt it. Sandra and her never got on that well."

"Why don't we check her room? That'll tell us if she's left."

"I guess," Vicki said. "Yes. We'll start there."

"Where are the servants' rooms? I've never seen them."

"No," Vicki told him. "You wouldn't have."

In the mid-nineteenth century, Vicki explained, when Hetherington Hall was built, the fashion among the highest gentry was for servants to be seen as little as possible. Therefore, separate passageways were created for the servants to use when they moved from one part of the house to another.

"So the house is full of secret passages?"

"They're not secret if you know what you're looking for. The doorways are concealed behind some of the wooden panels in the corridors. There are also two staircases meant for servants: the one we've just used, which leads from the main part of the house into the kitchen, and another one, which goes up from the back of the butler's pantry. We haven't used that before because the only place it goes to is the servants' living quarters."

They walked down to the kitchen and into the butler's pantry. At the side of this recess was the board where the bells rang. It looked like a complex kind of board game or early pin table, and bore the name: Edmunson's Electricity Corporation, Westminster. Most of the bedrooms were numbered. Andrew couldn't tell which was which. There were bells for the "boudoir" and the "white dressing-room", amongst others. Andrew wondered how many of these rooms were still used at all.

"Come on."

They climbed the staircase behind the pantry. Andrew realized that this was where he'd heard voices coming from on his first night in the Hall. McFadyen and Moira would have been talking to each other in their private quarters. He and Vicki walked up to the first floor, where there were just two rooms leading off the stairway: one to the left and one to the right. A third door was up a few more steps. It was locked.

"Where does this one lead?" Andrew asked Vicki.

"To the next floor. In the old days, most of the servants would have lived in the small rooms up there. Only the two most senior servants – the butler and his wife in those days – would get the bigger rooms on this floor. There never used to be any heating on the top floor, either. I guess the door's been locked for years."

Andrew tried the door to his right. It opened.

"This is McFadyen's room," Vicki told him.

"Not any more."

The room was empty. It had been meticulously cleaned out. No traces of the butler remained.

"It looks like he's done a bunk," Andrew said. "Presumably for the same reason as Alice."

Vicki nodded agreement. She tried the remaining door. It opened.

"This is Moira's room," she said.

Moira's room was bigger than the butler's, and crammed with things: a chest, a dressing table, a wardrobe, a TV set, and a small desk. There was no need to open any of the drawers to see if Moira had cleared them. They were overflowing. The room told a story of a full life lived in a small space. On the desk was a photo of Vicki, when she was maybe five years old, the only early picture of her which Andrew had seen. She was sitting on the housekeeper's lap, a smiling, innocent child.

"Fancy Moira having this," Vicki said, picking it up. "I've never seen it before. I don't remember her ever having her hair that way. Doesn't she look pretty?"

"So do you," Andrew said. "Anyway, your fears must be groundless. Moira hasn't cleared off, like Alice, or McFadyen. Though I suppose she could be with McFadyen."

"I don't give a stuff about McFadyen," Vicki said.

"But maybe Moira does," Andrew suggested. "Think about it. She's fortyish, and single. He must be about the same age, and I didn't see a wedding ring. It would be natural if…"

"I don't think so," Vicki said. "Let's brave the second floor, shall we?"

They went back through the kitchen and up the servants' stairway to the second floor. Vicki began calling out names.

"Paul?"

"Sandra?"

"Daddy?"

"Moira?"

There was no response. Next, they began opening doors. The last time Andrew saw Lord Hetherington, he was climbing up to this floor, looking for his eldest daughter. Andrew wondered if he'd found her.

They looked first in the exercise room. It was empty, the equipment unmoved since the last time Andrew had been in there.

"Let's try her bedroom," Vicki said.

Andrew would never have thought that the next room they went into was a bedroom. True, it had a single mattress on the floor. The rest of the floor was uncarpeted and covered with cheap, faded women's magazines, many of them cut or torn up. Amongst the copies of *Hello* and *Cosmopolitan* he spotted issues of *The Bride* and *Wedding World* with cover dates ten years old. Andrew was about to leave when he spotted a door, leading off from the bedroom.

"What's through there?"

"It's Sandra's dressing-room. I've never been allowed in it."

"Come on."

They went into the dark, narrow room. Andrew fumbled for a light switch.

"I feel like I'm breaking her trust, coming in these rooms," Vicki said. "She never lets anyone in here, not even Mummy."

"I'm surprised she's got so many clothes," Andrew said, opening one wardrobe, then another. "You said she hardly ever goes out."

"Most of these are ancient," Vicki pointed out. "Look at the styles."

Andrew was about to open the final wardrobe when there was what sounded like an enormous explosion.

"Only thunder," Vicki said. "The storm must have started." There was no window they could go to in the dressing-room, but Vicki was right. There was another loud thunderclap, followed by the sound of heavy rain. In the next moment, Andrew could have sworn that he heard something running across the floor above them. He immediately thought of Vicki's brother, preserving butterflies.

"Is that Paul, do you think?"

"I doubt it," Vicki said. "Probably a mouse, running from the rain. The roof leaks."

As Andrew opened the third wardrobe, he smelt something sickly, and sweet, something almost rotten. Then, before he could see what it was, the lights went out.

16

"A power failure," Vicki said. "That's all. It happens all the time."

"What do we do?"

"Wait for it to come back on. But let's get to some light." They felt their way out into the bedroom. Andrew could see the dark sky through dirty windows. A bolt of lightning struck the chapel, illuminating the gravestones around it.

"Look!" he said. "There's someone there."

But the light had gone and Vicki missed it.

"Either it's a fuse, or the generator's turned itself off," she told Andrew.

"Does it often do that?"

"Sometimes. It's an old system. I know how to work it. We'll wait for the storm to pass, then I'll go down and start it up. I'll put the heating on at the same time. I'm freezing."

"Me too."

They huddled together in the creepy room.

"Who did it look like?" Vicki asked Andrew. "In the cemetery?"

"I'm not sure," he replied. "It was only for a second or two. It might have been Paul."

"What would Paul be doing out there?"

"What would *anyone* be doing out there?"

"I don't like it up here," Vicki said. "I want to go downstairs. There's a fire in my room. We could light it."

"Sounds like a good idea to me."

They stumbled down the stairs at the side of the house and found their way to Vicki's dark room. Vicki lit a candle. Andrew watched as she made up the fire, a ghostly figure in the half light, adding wood to the tight coils of newspaper which were already in the grate.

"We'll be in trouble if the storm goes on for too long," she said, as deep red flames filled the room with an eerie light. "There's only enough wood to last an hour or so."

But the storm went on and on. They sat by the fire, not wanting to put voice to the dark thoughts going through their heads. At least the crackling and spluttering of the fire blocked out whatever other noises filled the old house. Andrew didn't believe in ghosts, but Hetherington Hall was the sort of place which could change anyone's mind. The fire waned, and the wood ran out. The room became cold again. They got under the covers of Vicki's bed to keep warm. Then, tired from their long walk earlier, they fell asleep.

When they woke, hours later, the storm had passed. It was evening. The sky was nearly clear, but what little light there was had already begun to drain from it.

"We'd better go downstairs," Vicki said, "sort out the power before the house is completely dark."

They made their way down to the cellar, carrying candles. By now, they'd given up expecting to meet anyone else in the house, so no longer called out names as they walked downstairs. The cellar was cold and dark. Andrew was glad that they didn't have to go too deeply into it. Vicki changed a fuse, but nothing happened. Then she played about with the pilot light and pulled a lever. There was a cranking noise and a shuddering and the generator whirred back into life. The light in the room came on.

"Now all I have to do is switch on the heating," Vicki said. She went over to the thermostat and paused. "That can't be right."

"What is it?"

She pointed at the fuel gauge. It was touching "empty".

"It never goes down this low."

"When does the oil tanker come?"

"At the end of every month, but the fuel never goes below a quarter full, not even in the winter. The tanker can't have been for at least two months, probably three." She paused and shook her head. "The money situation must be even worse than I thought. No wonder Daddy hasn't had the heating on. The fuel could run out at any moment. Then we won't have any lights or power of any kind. We'd better hurry upstairs, turn off as many things as possible. That way, we can make what little there is left last a bit longer."

As they hurried up the stairs back into the house, Andrew thought he heard something: a distant shout, or scream. He stopped and listened, but all that he could make out was the loud whirring of the generator. Still, as he walked back into the now brightly lit Hall, he couldn't help feeling that someone, somewhere, was calling for help.

They walked around the ground floor, candles in hand, turning off lights. Andrew tried the phone. It was still dead. Vicki joined him in the hallway.

"What do we do now?" she said.

Andrew didn't hesitate to say what he really thought.

"Every instinct tells me to get out of here."

"I can't do that," Vicki said. "This place is my home. It's my inheritance. I need to find out what's going on."

"All right," Andrew responded. "Where do we start looking?"

Vicki thought for a moment.

"Daddy's study," she said. "That's where he keeps all the financial papers."

Andrew remembered something else – how Mr Gallagher had given Lord Hetherington various papers, including the will, straight after the funeral. Would they be in his study, too? And why had Vicki's father wanted them?

He didn't, however, tell Vicki about this, in case it worried her further. She'd just gone on about her "inheritance". What if her father had decided to cut her out of his will? Or what if there was nothing left for him to leave?

The study didn't look as though it had been tidied recently. Nor did it look like anyone had left it in a hurry, which Andrew found strange. There was a green wire tray, marked "pending". It contained Lord Hetherington's unopened mail: mostly bills, by the look of it. There was also a yellow tray, marked "current", containing correspondence that he was working on, and a third, blue tray, "out-going", which contained letters waiting to be posted. Vicki went through the trays while Andrew searched the drawers of his desk, looking for something to shed light upon her predicament.

Lord Hetherington was the kind of person who kept everything. There were bank statements going back thirty years and numerous insurance documents. None of this stuff was in order, either. Eventually, Andrew managed to find the most recent – the insurance policies were all up to date, but his bank account was badly overdrawn. Credit card statements showed that Lord Hetherington was like his daughter – over his credit limit – only he had four cards and the limit on each was ten times the size of Vicki's.

Andrew looked in vain for his lordship's will or any other legal documents. Maybe they were in the trays which Vicki was searching. Nor did he find anything which might have been removed from the house books in the library. The biggest drawer, however, contained a lot of family papers, the sort of things which would have found their way into the house book had Lord and Lady Hetherington been keeping them up to date. There was, for instance, McFadyen's letter of application for the post of butler, and the reference provided by his previous employer, a churchman called Cardinal Chambers. The butler might have been better off if he'd stayed where he was.

Vicki blew her nose and Andrew turned round. She was, he saw, in tears.

"What's wrong?" he asked, going over to her. "Tell me what's wrong."

"This." She handed him a letter, postmarked South Africa, which was where Lord Hetherington had just come back from.

"It arrived this morning," Vicki told Andrew. "It's the only piece of mail he's opened since he got home."

The letter said that Hetherington Hall and all attendant lands were being bought, for a seven figure sum, by a Mr Pik Brickell of Capetown. It seemed that Lord Hetherington had told Alice the truth when he said that he would soon have plenty of money.

"Does it say when he'll get the money?" Andrew asked Vicki. She shook her head.

"All that's here is bills, bills and more bills. The oil company. The Council tax. The bank, threatening to take him to court. American Express. Even the butcher's in Kelso."

Andrew told Vicki what he'd found about the overdraft and credit card bills.

"Where do you think he's gone?" he asked, when he'd finished.

"I suppose that Daddy's lying low somewhere until the money arrives and he can spend it. He must have taken Paul. Maybe Sandra too. I don't know about Moira. Maybe she's gone with him."

"In that case," Andrew wanted to know, "why was all her stuff left behind?"

"I don't know," Vicki said. "Maybe you're right, and she did leave with McFadyen, not realizing that the money really was coming this time."

"I don't think so," Andrew said. "She was still here this morning, whereas McFadyen was gone yesterday. Tell me, was the Bentley in the garage when you got the Mini out this morning?"

"Yes," Vicki said.

"So it must have been your father who took it, not McFadyen. But I still don't see why he'd have cleared off like that."

Vicki shrugged.

"He walked out on my mother enough times," she revealed.

"You never said."

Vicki shrugged despairingly.

"Nobody likes to tell tales on their own father. But there were affairs, when I was younger. And there've always been money troubles. I nearly had to leave school once because the bills hadn't been paid." She held up an envelope. "There's a letter from Paul's school here, 'reminding' Daddy that he still owes for last term."

"Why did things get so bad?" Andrew asked.

Vicki sighed.

"Daddy's never had a proper job. He's always lived on investments. And betting. But, as far as I can see, he's never been terribly good at either. Mummy had some money, I think, and inherited more when her parents died. But it's all gone now." She burst into tears again. "I can't believe he'd do that. I can't believe that he'd sell the roof from over our heads."

Andrew tried to comfort her.

"Maybe he had no choice."

"He didn't even consult us."

"I guess you were right earlier – that's what the family meeting was going to be about."

"I'm sure it was," Vicki said. "But if Daddy'd already decided what he was going to do, what difference would a meeting make?"

"Is the house definitely sold?"

Vicki looked at the letter from South Africa again.

"I don't know. It says here that there are some forms which he has to sign and take to his solicitor. I suppose that Daddy's taken them with him."

"Did you find any other papers?" Andrew asked.

"Like what?"

"His will, for instance."

"That's kept at the solicitor's."

"I don't think so." Andrew explained what he'd overheard after the funeral the other day. Vicki thought about it.

"If he's selling the house and land, Daddy won't have anything to leave to anyone, except his title."

"There's the money from the house."

"He'll get through that in no time. He must owe half of it."

By now it was dark and too late to do anything else. The phone was still dead. They slept in the same room that night. At least, Vicki slept. Andrew lay awake, listening for noises and worrying about what was happening. What kind of family was this, which took death in its stride, then deserted their youngest daughter?

The house remained quiet. Still unable to sleep, Andrew decided to set aside his fears and go downstairs. He sat in the kitchen with a glass of milk, thinking. So many people were missing: Moira, Paul, Sandra, Vicki's father. He knew none of them well, yet found it hard to believe that they had all simply deserted the house. But what were the alternatives? All he could think of was this: *if they didn't leave of their own free will, someone must have got rid of them.*

How would they do that? They could have been scared away. Or...

Or he and Vicki were in great danger. He'd made a mistake. He should never have left Vicki alone, not for a minute.

Andrew hurried back upstairs to her room, slowing his footsteps down as he got nearer and treading gently so as not to wake her. He opened the door slowly, intending to sneak in without switching the light on. But when Andrew got inside, he saw that the bedside lamp was already lit. Vicki's bed was empty.

She was gone.

17

Andrew tried to think. It was just after midnight. He had been out of the room less than ten minutes. He told himself that Vicki could have gone to the bathroom, or downstairs, looking for him. But he didn't believe either idea. She was sleeping too heavily when he left her.

He waited for a minute, listening, making up his mind what to do before it was too late. Then he went upstairs.

"Vicki?"

No reply. Andrew turned on the landing light. Something shot down the corridor. A mouse, or a spider. Nothing sinister.

"Vicki?"

Andrew was beginning to get spooked. The house had swallowed up everybody but him. He tried to cling on to rational thought. It was the only tool he had left. Above him, he thought he heard a noise.

"Vicki?"

No sound. Why would she have gone up to the attic? Andrew could think of no reason, but there was no reason for her to have gone into any of the other rooms, either. He walked down the corridor, trying to remember where the entrance to the attic was concealed.

The first door he opened was Sandra's bedroom. The room had a foul, fetid smell, he noticed, which hadn't been there earlier. Everything else about the room was exactly as they had left it.

"Vicki?"

They'd forgotten to turn off the light, which Andrew did now. If the power ran out in the middle of the night, he'd never find Vicki. The next room he came to was the one he was looking for: a small servants' foyer with a door leading up to the attic. Or so Andrew thought. When he opened it, the passage led downwards, rather than up. He was confused, then remembered what Vicki had told him about the secret servants' passages which ran through the house. This one must lead down to McFadyen and Moira's rooms. The door at the bottom, locked this afternoon, was now ajar.

Andrew was about to open the opposite door, which must lead upwards, into the attic, when he heard a noise to his right, where there was no visible door. He pulled at the wooden panelling. It swung open and, sure enough, there was a concealed passage. Andrew poked his head into a narrow, unlit corridor. Someone was in there, holding a candle, which illuminated their face in a sickly, pale light. He couldn't make her out properly.

"Vicki?"

The figure shrieked, dropped the candle, and disappeared around a corner, but not until after Andrew had recognized her. It wasn't Vicki. It was her sister.

Sandra was gone before Andrew could register what was going on. He thought about following her, but the candle had gone out when it fell. He had no light. Sandra might know her way around these dark, narrow corridors, but Andrew didn't. And if Vicki's sister were still alive and living there, the chances were that she was responsible for at least some of what was going on in the house. Andrew already suspected her of having killed her mother. What if she had done the same to her father, sister and brother? It didn't bear thinking about.

Vicki had a torch in her room. Andrew went back down for it. If he was going to explore those dark, secret corridors again, he needed a light. He also needed a weapon. Having taken the torch from Vicki's dresser, Andrew hurried back down to the kitchen and looked for a sharp knife. His glass of milk was on the table where he'd left it earlier, empty. Andrew glanced at it, then opened a drawer, looking for something sharp.

He found table knives, forks, wooden spoons and three different whisks. In the next drawer he found a garlic press, a potato masher, two sieves and a rolling pin. Andrew was about to open the next drawer when he thought about the milk. He hadn't finished his glass of milk earlier. But someone had.

Andrew opened the next drawer. Tea towels. He looked at the

wooden surfaces next to the cooker. There, to the left of the bread bin, was a wooden knife block. He walked casually to the bread bin and took a medium-sized knife from the middle of the block. He brushed his thumb against the blade, to make sure that it was sharp. Then, very slowly, he turned round. A figure stood in the shadows by the butler's pantry, a burnt-out candle by its side.

"Sandra?" Andrew murmured.

The figure didn't move. Knife in hand, Andrew stepped forward, whispering gently.

"I won't hurt you. Talk to me, please."

The figure cowered in the darkness. Andrew didn't dare move too quickly. She could rush back up the stairway she had come down and instantly lose him in the darkness. His torch was on the table. He was five metres away from her and didn't have time to grab it. Also, from the way she was hunched over, Sandra might easily be carrying some kind of weapon. But Andrew needed to get to her. He needed to find out what she'd done with Vicki.

"Please come here," he said. "I promise I won't hurt you." The figure half turned, getting ready to make a run for it.

"Don't leave," he pleaded. "Look. I'm moving away." Andrew took two steps to his side and the figure stopped moving.

"Let's talk," he said, taking another step to the right and reaching his hand out. He was hoping that he was groping in the right place. His hands fumbled along the wall. Then they hit the switch and another light came on.

The figure in the corner flinched. It wasn't hunched over, as Andrew had thought, and it wasn't Sandra.

It was Paul. His face, Andrew suddenly realized, was remarkably similar to his eldest sister's.

"Paul!" he said, heartily. "You scared me! I thought you were Sandra! Where've you been? Vicki and I have been worried about you."

"Upstairs," Paul said, in a quiet voice.

"We thought that you and your father had left."

"I hid in the attic." His small voice was trembling.

"Why?" Andrew said. "What's wrong? What are you afraid of?" The boy stared at Andrew, his timid, rabbit's eyes coming into focus as Andrew walked towards him.

"'Fraid of *you*."

Andrew stopped walking.

"Why?" he said. "What have I done to scare you?"

"Moira said."

"What did Moira say?"

Paul trembled.

"She told Daddy that he shouldn't trust you."

"Why did she say that?"

Andrew wanted to know what, if anything, Moira had against him. However, if Paul knew, he wasn't telling.

"Moira was wrong," Andrew said, softly. "You can trust me. I'd never do anything to hurt her, or you."

Paul didn't reply. His clothes, Andrew saw now, were filthy. His eyes were even more sunken and spaced out than they had been before.

"Do you know where Vicki is?" he asked, unable to hide some of the urgency in his voice.

Paul glanced up the stairway. He was thinking of making a run for it.

"Not telling," he said.

Andrew put the knife down and took another step towards Paul.

"Listen," he said in his kindest voice. "Moira's not here. I think that she and McFadyen left."

"Moira wouldn't do that. She wouldn't leave Vicki and me."

"OK," Andrew said. "Maybe you're right. But, whatever's happened to her, she's not around. There's only you, me and Vicki. But I've lost Vicki. I need to find her. Do you know where she is?" Paul shook his head. Andrew tried another question.

"Do you know where Sandra is?"

He shook his head again.

"Why were you hiding in the attic?"

Paul didn't answer. Instead, he said:

"I'm hungry."

"I'll get you some food in a minute," Andrew promised, though he knew that there wasn't much of anything left. "What made you come downstairs again?"

"I heard something."

"What?"

"I heard Vicki, walking about beneath me, calling out."

"Why did you come down then? You didn't come when we called

you earlier."

Paul's eyes narrowed.

"She wasn't calling me. She was calling you."

"I see. Then what happened?"

"I heard her open a door, close another. Then I heard her scream, and a banging noise. I was worried. I thought you'd hurt her."

The look on his face showed that he still suspected Andrew of having attacked his sister.

"When?" Andrew asked, urgently. "How long ago?"

"About five minutes before you came upstairs."

"Come on!" Andrew said, picking up the knife again. "We've got to find her."

"This way's quicker." Paul pointed up the dark staircase.

Andrew hurried after the boy, his torch ineffectually scattering its pale beam in Paul's wake. But Paul didn't need light, not even the candle he'd been holding before. He was, Andrew realized, used to moving about in the dark. They came out in the foyer which Andrew had entered a few minutes earlier.

"I think I know which one she might be in," he told Paul. They turned left. Why had Vicki screamed? If Andrew hadn't been so far down, in the kitchen, he would have heard her too. If anything had happened to Vicki, he would never forgive himself.

"Which room?" Paul asked.

"Sandra's bedroom," Andrew guessed. "There was a light on in there earlier which shouldn't have been. Come on."

They went into the bedroom where he'd turned off the light a few minutes before. But, this time, Andrew noticed another light, seeping out of the dressing-room. He switched on the main light and saw that the dressing-room door was ajar. He was about to go in there when something stopped him.

A bloodstained arm pushed the door fully open. Vicki staggered into the bedroom, pale as a ghost. One side of her nightdress was speckled with blood. Andrew rushed to her arms.

"You're bleeding!"

"It … it's all right," Vicki stuttered. "It's not my blood."

"What happened?"

"A noise woke me up and you weren't there. I called your name. Then I thought I heard something moving about upstairs. I … I guessed you couldn't sleep. I thought you must have decided to finish searching the house. But I didn't want to be alone, so I came up after you."

"I should never have left you," Andrew told her. "I'm sorry."

"Someone was moving about upstairs," Vicki repeated. Her voice was a dazed monotone. She seemed to be suffering from shock.

"It was Paul."

"I came into this room. I remembered this was the last room we came to before the power failed. The bedroom light wasn't on, but the dressing-room light was. I thought you might be in there, so I went in and ... and..."

"What?"

"There was one wardrobe door, half open."

"What? What?"

Vicki stared at him helplessly.

"Don't let Paul see it."

Andrew let go of her. Paul came over, sheepishly. Brother and sister held hands. Andrew opened the dressing-room door again and looked to his right, at the wardrobe. He'd been about to check it when the lights went out in the storm: the wardrobe with the sweet, sickly smell. There, hanging in the middle, was a blood-stained wedding dress. Vicki's sister Sandra was wearing it, with a dagger twisted into her heart. Judging by the smell coming from her, she had been dead for days.

18

Back in the bedroom, Paul and Vicki stood exactly where he'd left them.

"Come on," Andrew said. "Let's go downstairs."

Vicki began to cough. Andrew didn't know whether she'd told Paul what had happened to his elder sister, and he didn't ask.

"I'm cold," Paul said.

Andrew turned off the lights behind them.

"We're nearly out of fuel for the generator," he told Paul. "We have to conserve power."

"There might be some wood in Daddy's bedroom," Vicki said, in her half-asleep voice. "We could go there."

"Good idea."

While Andrew made the fire, Vicki talked to Paul. He told her what he'd told Andrew earlier, but in more detail.

"You don't know where Daddy's gone?" she asked when he'd finished.

"No."

"He didn't say anything about going away?"

"No."

"Do you know if Daddy ever found Sandra?"

"I don't think so."

"And what about you, Paul. Did you see Sandra?"

He shook his head.

"Is she? Is she?"

"Like Mummy. I'm afraid so."

As the fire flickered into life, Paul burst into tears.

"I never wanted any of this to happen. Never!"

Vicki cuddled him.

"Course you didn't. No one did."

She was wrong, Andrew knew. Someone had wanted Sandra and her mother dead. Someone very close to home.

As brother and sister huddled in front of the fire, Andrew tried to work out what was going on. The main suspect for Lady Hetherington's death, Sandra, had been murdered herself. That left four more people who had both means and motive to murder mother and daughter: Vicki's father, McFadyen, Moira and Paul.

Or maybe it should be five. Vicki could have caused the accident, could have killed her sister, too, but it seemed highly unlikely. She'd only been back in the house for a day when her mother died. As for Sandra, there were times when Vicki could have stabbed her, but Sandra was bigger and stronger than Vicki was. Whoever had put Sandra in that wedding dress, then hung her in the wardrobe like a slab of meat, was either a strong person, or had an accomplice. No. Not Vicki. Andrew might as well suspect Alice, all those miles away on her family farm.

Could Lord Hetherington have killed his wife? He was out of the country at the time. Or so he had led them to believe. When Vicki phoned him in South Africa, he had already left. However, Andrew doubted that he was strong enough to do what had been done to Sandra, either. Which left the two servants. Andrew was inclined to discount Moira. She had been with the family nearly twenty years, and was clearly loyal to them. He was beginning to worry about what had happened to her. Both Paul and Vicki felt that she wouldn't walk out on them. In which case…

That only left McFadyen. Andrew knew little about the butler. He was quiet, and seemingly efficient, despite a shortage of staff to help him. Andrew had assumed that he walked out for the same reason as Alice – not being paid. But maybe the butler wasn't all he seemed. Andrew decided to talk it over with Vicki.

"I've been thinking…"

"Ssssh…" Vicki pointed at Paul, who had nodded off to sleep. "Help me put him in Daddy's bed. Then we'll talk."

They carefully laid Paul in his father's double bed, dirty clothes and all. Then they sat down by the fire.

"What do we do next?" Andrew asked, in a low voice.

"I reckon that, first thing in the morning, we get out of here. As soon as it's light, walk to the nearest place with a phone, and call the police."

"Sounds sensible to me," Andrew said. "Who do you think did it?"

"I don't know," Vicki told him. "I've been thinking about Mummy – maybe her death wasn't an accident. Do you think that Sandra could have killed Mummy, then stabbed herself?"

"Hanging from the coat rail like that? I don't think so."

"In that case," Vicki said, "it could be anyone: an escaped lunatic, a serial killer."

Andrew yawned. It had been a very long day. Fear and adrenalin had kept him going, but now he was exhausted.

"I can't see an escaped lunatic serial killer coming all the way to the Cheviots, can you? Whoever it is, I think we'll find the solution in this house. This isn't random. This is connected to the history of the Hetherington family. I'm sure of it."

Vicki was silent.

"Any ideas?" Andrew asked.

"I'll think about it," Vicki assured him. "Let's talk about it in the morning, when we're both more awake."

Andrew was too tired to take it any further.

"Listen," Vicki went on. "I think that one of us should stay awake all the time, just in case. I've had more sleep than you, so I'll do the first shift. You get down near the fire and I'll do until three. You can do three till five, then I'll keep watch until daybreak. OK?"

"OK."

The fire was warm and the heat from it began to cloud Andrew's head. He quickly fell asleep. At three, Vicki woke him and he did the next two hours in a sleepy haze. Nothing happened. Then Vicki did another turn. When Andrew woke again at seven, she was sat on the hearthrug, staring blankly at the fire's embers. Paul slept on. Vicki and Andrew hugged.

"What's that noise?" Vicki said, breaking away. It was coming from outside the house. He snapped fully awake.

"Sounds like an engine."

"Please, let it be the police," Vicki said.

They went to the window. Through the dirty glass, Andrew could make out something red, parking outside the front door.

"It's the post," he said.

"I forgot about the post," Vicki said. "Brilliant! We can get a lift to the phone. Come on."

Andrew tried to open the window and call out.

"It's stuck."

"It's always been stuck. Come downstairs. Quickly."

As Paul blinked awake, Vicki and Andrew hurried down to the ground floor. Two envelopes lay on the mat in the hall. Andrew kicked them aside as Vicki fumbled with the lock on the front door. Then she pulled it open. As they rushed out into the damp, overcast day, Vicki still in her blood-splattered nightdress, they saw the Post Office van turning round in the drive.

"Hey!" Vicki yelled. "Wait!"

The van finished turning and slowly set off.

"Wait!" they both shouted.

Vicki and Andrew began to run up the drive. Surely the driver could hear them? But the van was old and its engine noisy.

"Wait!"

As they got closer to it, the van began to accelerate. They ran after it for a long time, waving their arms madly. All it would take was for the driver to look once into her rear view mirror. But it didn't happen. The van disappeared into the distance. Disappointed, the couple walked back to the Hall. It began to drizzle.

"We'll have to walk it later on," Vicki said.

Andrew agreed. The rain became heavier. When they got back to the Hall, the front door still hung open. It was scarcely any warmer inside than it was out.

"You'd better get dressed," Andrew said to Vicki. "Is there any more wood around that I could collect for a fire?"

"You could start smashing up the furniture," she said. He wasn't sure if she was being serious.

Andrew picked up the mail from the floor and handed it to Vicki. One letter was addressed to Vicki, airmail from Israel, and she tucked it into the pocket of her nightgown. The other was for her father. It was postmarked Kelso, the previous day.

"I think it's from Mr Gallagher," Vicki said. "I'd better open it."

She was right. The name at the top of the heavy, cream paper was "C. Gallagher, Solicitor." The letter read as follows:

My Lord,

I have, in accordance with your wishes, prepared the contracts and deed of sale, transferring ownership of Hetherington Hall to Mr Brickell. Mr Brickell's solicitor informs me that the deposit is ready for transfer.

You may recall that we had an appointment at four this afternoon for you to sign the contract and endorse any alterations which you have decided to make to your will. When you did not arrive, I telephoned the Hall repeatedly, but could not get through. British Telecom inform me that there appears to be a fault on the line, but they cannot deal with it until you complain in person.

I have received several faxes from Mr Brickell's solicitors wishing to confirm our exchange of contracts. I would be grateful if you would contact me and arrange a fresh appointment to deal with these matters as quickly as possible. I would, of course, be willing to come to the Hall if you are indisposed.

I have the honour to remain,

My Lord,

Your Lordship's obedient servant,
Charles Gallagher.

Vicki put the letter down.

"So Daddy meant to go straight from our family meeting to signing the contracts which sold off the Hall."

"It looks like it," Andrew replied. "But he didn't get there. Why?"

"That," said Vicki, "is something I'd really like to know."

"You don't think that someone here might..."

Vicki's voice became angry.

"If I'd known that Daddy was about to sell off the house," she said, "I might even have killed him myself."

"Don't talk like that," Andrew said. "Let's try the phone."

"To get the police?"

"Yes. But I'd like to talk to Gallagher first. It seems to me that he might be the one person who knows what's going on."

But the phone was still dead.

Paul, Vicki and Andrew dressed, then ate breakfast in the kitchen. They had stale muesli soaked in long-life orange juice, washed down by tea made with powdered milk, the remaining dairy milk having gone sour. While they ate, Vicki read her letter from Israel.

"Interesting?" Andrew asked, surprised that she could do something so normal as read a letter.

"Just kibbutz gossip. I'm not really taking it in."

Andrew stared into space, thinking. He was fairly sure now that Lord Hetherington was dead. He expected that Vicki had worked this out, too, but didn't discuss it with her. He was no nearer to working out who had killed Lord Hetherington's wife and eldest daughter, or why.

When they'd eaten, they went up to the hall and tried the phone again. No change. Andrew decided to question Paul some more before they went.

"Is there anything you've seen in the house while you were hiding, Paul? Anyone in places where they shouldn't be?"

The boy shook his head apathetically. Andrew pressed him.

"Think, *please*. You spent all that time up in the attic. Who came up to see you? Who was on the second floor apart from Sandra?"

Paul spoke slowly.

"Daddy came to see me."

"What about the servants: Moira, McFadyen?"

"No."

Andrew dredged his mind for other ideas.

"How about someone who used to work here? Alice, for instance?"

"No."

"This is getting us nowhere," Vicki said. "The rain's over. Let's go."

Andrew was stubborn.

"I wonder whether we should search the house one more time before we leave," he suggested. "We haven't looked through all of the servants' passages you told me about, or the cellar. We might find..."

"No," Vicki asserted, bluntly. "We'll leave that to the police. I want to get Paul out of here. I want to get out of here myself."

Andrew had to admit she had a point.

"All right," he said.

"Paul, go and get your coat."

"He knows something," Andrew told Vicki when Paul was out of the room. "Why did he hide away in the attic like that? It doesn't make sense. He knows something he's not telling us."

"Maybe," Vicki said, in a pointed voice, avoiding Andrew's gaze. "It's pretty hard to know what goes on in other people's minds, isn't it?"

She gave Andrew a hard, peculiar look. He judged it best not to ask what she meant by her remark.

19

Outside, the sky was still dark and threatened to rain again. They took the route which Vicki and Andrew had travelled the day before, but in reverse. Alice's farm was, it seemed, the nearest occupied building with a phone.

The three of them moved more slowly than the day before. Paul was small for his age and found it hard to keep up. Both he and Vicki seemed preoccupied and didn't talk. Andrew tried to take his mind back through the events of the last few days, looking for loose ends which might mean something. Could the South African who was buying the house be behind the deaths? What did Doctor Rutherford want with Lord Hetherington? Could McFadyen or Moira have a motive for the murders?

He came up with no answers at all.

"We ought to go this way," Paul said, when they came to two paths at the end of a field. "It's quicker."

"I prefer this one," Vicki said.

"Why?" Paul moaned. "I thought you said we were in a hurry."

"What is it?" Andrew asked, gently. "Why can't we go the way that Paul suggests?"

"Oh, very well," Vicki agreed, reluctantly.

The path came up through woods, then led down again, into a valley. They crossed a drystone wall in a bad state of disrepair.

"Are we still in Hetherington land?" Andrew asked Vicki.

"I don't think so."

Then Andrew saw what Vicki had wanted to avoid. They were in a valley. Ahead of them, a track snaked through the hills. Before them were the ruins of a big house. Only the low outline of its ground floor was still standing.

"Partington House?" Andrew asked Vicki.

She nodded.

"Have you been here before?" he asked Paul.

"It's a great place to play. Look!"

"Not now, Paul."

Ignoring his sister, Paul hurried on towards the house. Andrew found his behaviour bizarre. He was acting like a child on holiday.

"I'd better go after him," Andrew said. He followed Paul into the ruin, while Vicki trudged on towards the track ahead.

Partington House had once been the size of Hetherington Hall, or bigger. The little of it left standing gave the impression that it was a more airy, less claustrophobic building. In the middle of it, Andrew walked through what was once one of the main rooms. Then his foot slipped.

Andrew grabbed on to the wall and levered his foot out from where it was trapped. He'd mildly twisted his ankle, but realized that he'd been in danger of much worse. Below Andrew was the cellar. In places, the floorboard had been burnt away, or collapsed. Here, grass had grown over it, but the boards beneath were loose and rotten, decayed by fire and ten years of hard Northumberland weather. If they had given way, he could have had a nasty fall.

"This place is a deathtrap," he told Paul. "They should put up notices."

"No one ever comes here," Paul replied. "Except me, and I'm not meant to. But I know the safe way round. You should follow me more closely. Come on, I'll show you the best bit."

"Let's just get out of here," Andrew protested, but Paul was on his way.

Gingerly, because he was two or three times Paul's weight, Andrew followed Paul along one of the main foundation walls, then round a corner where he could make out what was once a big window, looking out on to the wood behind.

"Very nice," he told Paul. "But now we'd better catch Vicki up."

"Look at this first."

Paul charged on. It was odd, the way he was behaving, like a little boy playing games. He was, Andrew decided, too young to really take in the deaths of his sister and mother. Paul wanted to show Andrew this place that he loved, failing to realize that several people must have died in the fire here. Andrew humoured him.

"Where are you, Paul? I've lost you."

"Over here."

He was two rooms away, at the edge of the house.

"Is it safe?"

"Just go straight ahead."

Andrew did as he suggested. Gorse was growing through the floorboards. He dodged the prickliest sections. In the distance, he could see Vicki, walking up the hill. Then he looked around and could no longer see Paul.

"Paul!"

The boy was behind him.

"Sorry, Andy," Paul said, pushing him. "She told me to."

Before Andrew knew what was happening, he lost his balance. Paul pushed him harder. Andrew was suddenly terrified. The ground beneath him was anything but safe. He was falling into a black hole.

He grabbed at the gorse. It tore his hands, and began to come away. His body slammed against one of the cellar's side walls. As the gorse gave way, he slid down the wall.

Andrew landed with a thud. If he had fallen straight down, in the middle of the cellar, he would have been killed, or done himself a severe injury. As it was, all he got was a mighty jolt. He had cut his hand. His skin was cut, bruised and scraped in several places.

What had Paul meant to do? Andrew tried to piece together the meaning of his last words. *She told me to*. He could only be referring to Vicki or Moira. Why would Vicki wish such an accident on him? She had, Andrew remembered, been behaving strangely. Alice's words about the "mad sisters" echoed in his brain. Yet, even if Vicki was unbalanced in some way, why had she chosen to have Paul attack him, now? Nothing added up.

The cellar was very dark and cold, but Andrew was in no hurry to get out of it. He was in a quandary. Should he go after Vicki, and attempt to protect her? Or should he lie low, letting Vicki and Paul think that he'd been knocked out, or worse? He no longer knew if he should be trying to protect his girlfriend or hiding from her.

Andrew moved slowly, partly because of his bruises and partly because he didn't want to attract attention from above. He had to find the cellar steps. He prayed that they were made of stone. For, if they were wood, and had been burnt away in the fire ten years ago, he could be trapped here for ever.

Andrew felt his way along the walls. There was the odd glint of light from above, but barely enough to see by. He might have passed the steps, for all he knew. There could be any kind of trap waiting for him. He remembered how, the last time he was in the cellars of Hetherington Hall, he'd thought he heard someone screaming. This time, the person screaming would be him.

Andrew edged his way along. Something moved under his feet and, for a horrible moment, he thought that the ground was going to give way beneath him again. But it was only a lizard, darting out of danger. Andrew stumbled on, realizing that he had no sense of geography. Which way to go? At one end of the ruined house, the cellar was completely exposed. There would be light. He could see, but he could be seen from above, too. The question was: seen by who?

It didn't make sense. If Vicki wanted to kill him, why would she get Paul to do it? If the deaths were all to do with the Hetherington inheritance, Vicki had nothing to gain by Andrew's death. Unless she thought that he… Another idea occurred to Andrew. Maybe Vicki's behaviour today was connected to the letter that morning – not the one to her father, but the other one, to her, from Israel. What was in it?

Andrew decided that he had to chance it. He had to get out of the cellar and go to her. For, if Vicki was innocent, she must be in enormous danger.

Andrew was distracted by a noise: a gentle moan, or whimper. There was someone else in this section of the cellar with him. Where? Andrew didn't know whether to run from the noise or go to it. He saw a gap in the floorboards over to the side of him. A small shaft of light poked through it. Cautiously, Andrew made his way to where the noise was coming from, using the light to guide him. Whoever it was, they might need help.

The noise stopped. Andrew stumbled on. There was a louder moan as he nearly fell over a body. Pulling himself upright, Andrew could make him out: face sunken, one eye open, more dead than alive. It was Vicki's father.

"What happened to you?" Andrew asked. "How did you get here?"

Lord Hetherington gasped for words. Close up, his lungs sounded bad. His breathing was shallow and raspy.

"She … lured … me … here," he said. "Y-yesterday."

"Who?"

"Broke … both … my … legs."

He opened his eyes briefly, and managed two full sentences.

"I … know who … you are. It's … up to … you, now."

"I'll help you," Andrew said. "I'll go for help. Just tell me who did this. Please."

Lord Hetherington's eyes were closed. Andrew could tell that he was fading fast. He had only just got here in time.

"Please, Lord Hetherington. Stay awake a moment longer, please. Tell me who brought you here."

His mouth opened and closed.

"My … daugh … ter."

"Vicki? Do you mean that Vicki's behind this?"

The sound he made next was merely a whisper, and Andrew wasn't even sure that he'd heard it.

"Sh…"

"What? Please tell me. I don't understand."

The mouth opened and closed again.

"…"

Andrew took Lord Hetherington's pulse. He was dead.

20

Before leaving Lord Hetherington, Andrew searched his pockets. He took his wallet from a trouser pocket and a large manila envelope from the breast pocket of his jacket, then put them into his borrowed Barbour. He also found a cigarette lighter, and used it to make his way to the stairs which, thankfully, were made of stone. Andrew clambered safely into daylight just as it began to rain.

There was no sign of Paul or Vicki, for which Andrew was grateful. Which way to go? He hadn't come by this route before. He might easily overshoot Alice's farm, and there wasn't another dwelling for miles. The wind was getting up and the rain was becoming stronger. Not only that, but he'd twisted his ankle earlier and the fall into the cellar had badly shaken him up. There was no way he could walk for miles and miles in this condition, even if he knew the route to Alice's farm. There was only one thing for it. He would have to make the short walk back to Hetherington Hall.

Andrew calculated that he had a small advantage. No one knew that he was alive. He would probably have the house to himself, at least until the police came. That was, presuming Vicki and Paul went for the police. What story would they tell? That their sister was dead and their father had vanished? Perhaps they would blame Andrew for the murders. Perhaps the whole thing had been planned from the start. Vicki had lured Andrew to the Hall in order to make him the scapegoat. It was a frightening thought.

By the time Andrew reached Hetherington Hall, he was soaked and, though it was only early afternoon, the sky was dark as night. There were no lights on in the building. It was almost certainly empty. But Andrew took no chances, going in by the back door, next to the garage. The stable doors, he noticed, had been closed. He didn't remember Vicki doing that.

Which room to go into? Safest, he thought, to choose one where the light would not be seen from outside the house. Andrew went to Lord Hetherington's study, treading quietly in case Paul or Vicki had returned. Once inside the study, he put on the desk lamp, adjusting the light carefully so that it couldn't be seen through the bottom of the door. Keeping his Barbour on, for the house was very cold, he took out Lord Hetherington's wallet and the large brown envelope.

Before he could open them, Andrew heard someone coming in through the front door. Hurriedly, he stuffed the envelope and wallet back into his pockets. To be on the safe side, he turned out the desk lamp. Then he heard two sets of footsteps, coming towards him. It sounded like Vicki and Paul. Andrew stood behind the door in case one of them came into the room.

But the people weren't coming towards him. They were going upstairs. Cautiously, Andrew slid the door open. It was too late to see anything, but he heard part of a conversation.

"...can't have got far. She's probably sheltering somewhere, or looking for her precious boyfriend. We'll wait till the rain stops, then go out for her again in the car."

"Why did you try to run her over?" Paul asked.

"I explained," the voice said. "She pretends to be your friend, but she isn't. You won't be safe while she's around." Andrew trembled. Although the woman's voice was familiar, he couldn't work out who it belonged to. It was a Hetherington voice, yet it wasn't Vicki's. Then the voice became more tender.

"Are you all right? Can you go through with this?"

"Yes," Paul's voice replied.

"You're sure?"

"I'm sure, Mummy."

Then they were out of earshot. Andrew was dumbfounded. He had seen Lady Hetherington's body in the bath. He had been at her funeral. Yet ... right now, he was prepared to believe anything. Had Lady Hetherington somehow faked her own death, in order to take revenge on the family who didn't love her?

Andrew sneaked upstairs, not by the main staircase, but by the servants' one. He now had a pretty good idea of how the hidden passages in the house worked. However, when he peeked out on the first floor, there was no sign of Paul or his "mother". It was deadly quiet.

Andrew was about to go up to the second floor when he heard a door open. He snatched a look down the corridor, then quickly withdrew his head. They were coming towards him. Both were in shadows, so Andrew couldn't properly see the woman with Paul. She could be anyone. But he could see which room they'd come from. It was Vicki's.

The woman's voice was saying:

"I knew it, I knew it! I thought he came to marry her, but it was more than that! He came for revenge, Paul! Moira was right." Paul's small voice came next.

"I liked him. He was nice to me. I didn't want to..."

"You have to be strong, Paul. We'll go back later, make sure he's dead. When we call the police, I don't want them to find their murderer still alive and denying everything."

"What about Vicki?" Paul asked.

"She's probably back there, looking for him."

"Even after she got that letter?"

There was a pause before the woman spoke again.

"Maybe you're right. But Vicki doesn't know the full story, so I doubt that she's ready to desert him yet. Now, before we look for her, can you reconnect the phone? I need to call Doctor Rutherford."

"I'll do it now, Mummy," Paul said.

Paul went downstairs, while his companion went up. As Andrew came out into the corridor, he could hear Paul going into the cellar. It had been him all along, disconnecting the phones whenever he was told to. Before Andrew found out anything else, he wanted to know what was in the letter which Vicki received that morning. As quietly as he could, Andrew made his way to her room.

The letter lay open on her desk. It was from one of Vicki's friends, Freya. She was taking a year out in Israel, on a kibbutz. The letter began by thanking Vicki for her postcard from Greece.

Glad you're having a great time. Can't wait to meet your new guy. I wish you'd told me more about him. Is he from Bretton or did you meet him on holiday? What does he look like? What does he do?

Then there was a load of stuff about the kibbutz and Freya's sex life, which Andrew skipped. Before he knew it, the letter was over. Andrew was mystified as to what had had such a big effect on Vicki. Then he turned the last page over and found a PS.

By the way, I meant to tell you at the end of term, but never found you. You were probably working on your exhibit for the Summer Show. Thing is, there was this guy at Bretton, asking lots of questions about you: where were you from, who were your family, what kinds of things did you like, did you have a boyfriend, all that kind of stuff. He was very good-looking: tall, thin, brown curly hair – your type, really – but there was something a bit creepy about the way he was acting. I didn't tell him much. His name was Andrew something. If I were you, I'd watch out for him when you go back.

Andrew put the letter down. It could have been worse. All it meant was that Vicki knew that they hadn't bumped into each other by accident at the Henry Moore exhibition in June. Andrew had known that Vicki often visited the sculptures, and used them to get the opportunity to strike up a conversation with her. He could understand her being upset when she discovered this deception. But he had his reasons. She would see that. He could explain it to her.

Andrew had to get to Vicki before Paul and the woman he called "Mummy" did. Would Vicki still trust Andrew? She had to give him the benefit of the doubt. Earlier, he'd heard "Mummy" talk about going out in the car. She must have been using the Bentley, "borrowing" it from Lord Hetherington after his fall. Andrew needed the car. Vicki, he remembered, had picked up the spare set of keys earlier. Where would she have put them? He looked around her room, praying that she hadn't taken them with her.

Andrew didn't have far to look. The keys were amongst the mess of stuff on Vicki's desk. He picked them up and edged back into the corridor. He had to get out to the back door without being seen. This meant that he had to go down the main staircase. Andrew didn't know where Paul was. He prayed that he wouldn't bump into him as he sneaked out of Hetherington Hall.

Andrew crept down the stairs. Every creak sounded like a death threat, yet no one came. He got to the main hall and was halfway to the back door when the place seemed to explode.

Andrew nearly jumped out of his skin, but it was only the phone ringing. Heavy feet hurried down the stairs. At first, Andrew was going to hide in Lord Hetherington's study, but there was a phone in there, too. So, instead, Andrew ducked into the breakfast room, where he could just make out the telephone table by the staircase.

The phone kept ringing. Andrew hoped that it wouldn't stop before whoever it was got there. It didn't. From the breakfast room, Andrew saw a slim arm reach out to pick the receiver up. When Andrew saw the arm's owner, his heart nearly stopped. He was looking at a dead woman.

It was Sandra.

21

She had lost a little weight, it seemed. From where Andrew was standing, Sandra looked more like her neurotic mother than a body builder. He guessed that this was because she had been starving herself, hiding out in thc house's attics and secret passageways for days. Maybe it was her whom he had seen in the passage yesterday, not Paul. Her voice sounded different, too. Not like when he'd first met her, nor like the voice he'd heard that afternoon. Sandra seemed to be putting on a kind of forced jollity for the telephone.

"Doctor Rutherford. I was about to call you myself. Yes, the phone has been out of order. BT have only just repaired it. My father wanted to get back to you, but he's not been well. I see … yes. No, I'm Sandra, her sister … I'm afraid he can't come to the phone. He's still ill. You know that my mother died last week? We're all terribly upset. If you could be brief…"

There was a long pause while Sandra listened. Then she spoke again.

"No. Not at all. No contact since … it happened. The family completely cut her off. The baby was adopted. I don't know the details. She wouldn't be able to trace … no, good, of course not. I expect that she'll want to start a new life, a long way away. It was good of you to call us, though. I'll tell my father what you've told me… There's no need to get in touch again. We can contact you if anything comes up. All right. Thank you. Goodbye."

She put the phone down. As Andrew watched, a look of triumph spread across her face. She said "yes" to herself in a kind of hiss. Then she walked quickly back up the stairs, skipping every other step.

Andrew got out of the house as quickly as he could. He opened the garage doors to find that he was right: the Bentley had been returned. He got into it and examined the controls, praying that he could get the car to work. He had to find Vicki before Sandra did.

The Bentley started first time. Luckily, the car was an automatic and easy to operate. The engine purred as Andrew drove out of the garage, on to the long driveway, hoping that whatever Sandra and Paul were doing inside was noisy enough for them not to hear him leave.

It seemed an age before he was out of sight of the house, but it was probably only a minute. Which way to go? Andrew tried to remember the way to Alice's farm, where there was a phone, but knew he'd get lost on the winding minor roads. His best hope was to make it to Partington House, which was where he'd last seen Vicki. Where was she? And if she saw the car, what would she think? Did she know that Sandra was still alive, and probably wanted to kill her?

How come Sandra was alive? Andrew thought about the body in the wardrobe. It looked real, and smelt disgusting. But neither he, nor Vicki, had examined it closely. And Paul, who didn't look at it, hardly seemed shocked at all. Maybe he knew it was a mannequin, smeared with real blood – say, from an animal, whose carcass had been left in the wardrobe to create a convincing smell. Yes, that made sense. But why would Paul and Sandra put it there?

Maybe the faked death wasn't aimed at Vicki, but at Sandra's father. Lord Hetherington had a weak heart. Sandra must have known that he would go looking for his eldest daughter eventually. When he found the mannequin in the wardrobe, she hoped that he would do more than faint – he would have a heart attack, and die.

But what would be the point of killing him? And why did Paul call Sandra "Mummy"?

Of course. Everything made sense if Sandra really was Paul's mother. Lady Hetherington was younger than her husband, but not substantially so. She was in her early to mid-fifties when she died. She would have been at least forty-three when Paul was born. That wasn't an impossible age to have a child, especially these days, but it was still pretty late in life.

Sandra, on the other hand, would have been nineteen or twenty when Paul was born. She was due to have married, but it was called off. Suppose that part of the reason for her deep distress was that she was already pregnant? Suppose Paul was her son, by Charles Partington. That would make Paul...

Andrew stopped himself from jumping to conclusions and tried to recall the details of the phone call he'd overheard between Sandra and Dr Mary Rutherford. Adoption had been discussed then. Sandra said something about there being no contact, but she talked about the mother in the third person, about her wanting to start a new life. He couldn't figure it out.

Yet if Sandra were Paul's mother, it would explain the strong resemblance between them. And Vicki had told him, more than once, that Lord Hetherington had always wanted a son. So, of course, he and Lady Hetherington would have adopted Paul. But could an adopted son inherit a title? Andrew didn't know.

Absorbed in these questions, Andrew nearly missed the turning which would take him in the direction of Partington House. He prayed that Vicki was still somewhere nearby. A few cows grazed to his right. There was no sign of Vicki.

Andrew took a turning and found himself on the narrow track which went round a hill, then down into the valley which contained the ruins of Partington House. As he passed the brow of the hill he saw someone. Vicki was walking slowly along a footpath not far from the road. He'd found her.

Andrew braked sharply. Before he could get out of the car, Vicki ran off, over the fields. Andrew got out of the car and ran after her, yelling.

"Vicki, wait! Vicki, I've come to help you. Stop."

But it did no good. She just ran all the faster, towards the ruined house, where four people had already died for no good reason that Andrew knew of. He didn't want Vicki to be the fifth.

Andrew followed. His body was bruised and battered from the fall earlier, but Vicki, too, seemed tired. He began to catch her up. At least, he thought, she could hear what he was calling.

"Vicki, don't go into the ruins. They're dangerous."

But his words seemed to have the opposite effect. Vicki ran straight into the shell of Partington House, towards the very area where Andrew had fallen earlier.

"Vicki, stop! You'll fall!"

Too late. One moment, she was there. The next, she was gone. Andrew reached the edge of the house himself, but couldn't see her.

He had to go after her. Cautiously clinging to the remains of the walls, he edged his way around the ruin, searching for her.

"Vicki, where are you?"

She didn't answer. Then, for a moment, the wind dropped, and Andrew could hear her anxious breathing, her involuntary whimpering, only feet away from him.

"Vicki, it's all right. I'll help you."

Her voice, when she spoke, was bitter and full of recriminations.

"Stay away from me!"

"I've never done anything to hurt you, Vicki."

"I'll jump!"

"Don't. You could kill yourself."

"Why do you care? You've already tried to kill me once today."

"What do you mean? How?"

"In the Bentley. You tried to run me over."

"Just now? I didn't see you. I wasn't trying to..."

"No. Earlier. When I was walking to Alice's and you and Paul deserted me."

Andrew saw that Vicki was clinging to a piece of wall. As she spoke to him, she was trying to pull herself up, but her efforts were having the opposite effect to the one she intended. The ground around her was falling away, and the stones in the wall were working loose.

"Vicki, you have to believe this: it wasn't me in the Bentley earlier. I was trapped in the cellar that you're about to fall into. Let me help you."

"No."

"Vicki, your father's already down there. He's dead. Please let me help you."

"Daddy? No. I don't believe ... no, get off!"

As Andrew was speaking, he'd got nearer to her, and now he grabbed Vicki's arm, pulling her out.

"Let me help! You can kill yourself later if you want!" The bit of wall which Andrew was holding on to gave way.

They both fell head first into the darkness.

22

Andrew came round to the taste of Vicki's lips against his.

"Please wake up, Andrew, please."

"I am awake," he mumbled.

"I guess," she said, as his eyes blinked open and she came into focus, "this means that you really do love me."

Andrew's mind was hazy. He had no idea how long he'd been unconscious.

"Why? What did I do?"

"You tried to stop me falling and nearly killed yourself. You broke my fall. Are you all right? Can you stand up?"

"Sure I'm all right. My head aches. That's all."

She helped him to his feet. It wasn't just his head, Andrew realized. Everything ached.

"How long was I out for?"

"Ten, fifteen minutes," Vicki said. "You don't look too good to me. Do you think we can get out of here?"

"No problem," he assured her. "I've already done it once today."

They moved away from the hole they'd fallen through and the little light it cast, into blackness.

"It's awfully dark," Vicki said.

Andrew reached into his pocket.

"*Voilà!*"

Vicki gripped his hand.

"That's Daddy's lighter."

"I'm afraid so."

"Is what you said earlier true? Is he…?"

"Yes." Andrew kept talking to Vicki as she cried. "He told me that his daughter lured him here. I thought that he meant you, but actually, he meant Sandra."

"Sandra's dead!" Vicki exclaimed.

"She isn't. I've seen her."

"And I've seen her body. Where's Daddy?"

"Over there."

Vicki took the lighter and sat quietly with her father. Andrew watched as she said a prayer over his limp body.

"I took something from his pocket," Andrew said, after a while. "I think it's the will."

Vicki nodded and stood up.

"We'd better get out of here," Andrew said. "Paul and Sandra will come looking for us. They want to kill both of us."

"Why?"

"I don't know," he said. "Maybe Sandra wants to inherit the house, the money..."

Vicki joined him.

"Another thing," Andrew said, as they walked towards the steps.

"What?"

"From what I heard Paul and Sandra saying, I don't think that your mother was Paul's mother. I think that Sandra was. It explains a lot."

Andrew couldn't see Vicki's expression, but her voice was full of disdain.

"It might explain a lot," Vicki said, "but it isn't true. I was with Sandra when Mummy went away to have the baby. Sandra wasn't pregnant. She was depressed, manic even. But not pregnant."

"If it's not Sandra, then who...?"

"I was beginning to think that you were the person behind all this. The letter I got from Freya this morning freaked me out."

They emerged into the overcast day. The rain had stopped, but it was hard to tell, because the trees, heavy with water, were letting it fall in a soft, steady flow of droplets. Vicki looked at Andrew with a sceptical, weary face.

"Who *are* you?" she asked.

It was time to tell her everything.

23

"Andrew Wakefield's my real name. The aunt, the one I told you about, she adopted me. Wakefield's her ex-husband's name."

"I thought you didn't get on with her."

"I didn't. They sent me away to schools. When I came home in the holidays, we argued so much that I begged to leave. I ended up boarding full-time from when I was thirteen. I haven't seen them for years."

"And your real parents. Who were they?"

Andrew hesitated.

"You've probably worked that out already."

"The Partingtons?"

He nodded.

"I was away at school when the house burnt down. I haven't been back since. They wouldn't let me go to the funeral. My aunt never told me how it really happened. She made up a story about a car crash – because she thought it would be less upsetting, I guess – but I always knew that there was something mysterious which I hadn't been told.

"You know, I looked through the microfiche at college, and it wasn't even in the papers. Now and then, I'd hear my aunt talking about what happened when I wasn't meant to be listening. They used your family's name. Then, when I went to Bretton, I heard someone mention you. I asked people about you. When I found out where you were from, I knew that I had to get to know you, to find out what happened to my family."

"And have you found out?" Vicki asked.

Andrew shook his head.

"Not completely. I know that Sandra was supposed to marry my older brother, Charles. He'd graduated from university the summer before the fire. But I don't know what happened then. Did he jilt Sandra? Or did he die in the fire before the marriage could take place?"

Andrew looked back at the ruin.

"It must have been quite a fire, to destroy the building so badly. The entire side section is missing."

"That's where they kept the oil tank and the generator," Vicki explained.

"Aah."

Vicki stood on the edge of the ruins, thinking.

"We must have met," she said, "when we were children."

"Yes."

"Why did you lie to me?" she asked. "Why couldn't you have been honest?"

"Would you have told me the truth?"

Vicki looked away.

"I don't know," she said. "But if I'd known who you were, I wouldn't have allowed myself to fall in love with you."

"I fell in love with you, too," Andrew said. "It wasn't part of a plan."

Now Vicki turned to him. This wasn't the time to talk about love.

"Are you sure Daddy said that Sandra lured him here?"

Andrew tried to recollect Lord Hetherington's final words precisely.

"He said 'my daughter'. At the time, I thought he was talking about you. I asked him again. The last thing he said sounded like 'Sh…' I assumed he was trying to say 'Sandra'."

Vicki's face turned terribly pale. She slowly shook her head.

"Have you worked something out?"

"I don't know. It's impossible. Unless…" She didn't finish the sentence.

"Look," Andrew said. "We'd better get out of here. Paul and Sandra could come looking for us at any minute. The car's over there. We have to get to the police."

"I guess you're right," Vicki said.

They walked towards the car.

"Your brother," Vicki said. "What was he like?"

Andrew thought for a moment. There was no point in being tactful about someone who'd been dead for ten years.

"I don't really remember. I didn't like him, I remember that. He was tall, with dark hair and a very square chin. I thought he was cruel. He was ten years older than me. My parents doted on me – before I was born, they'd been told that my mother could never have another child – and Charles resented that. He used to pick on me all the time. When he died, I felt guilty for not liking him. I tried to forget about him."

"I don't remember him at all," Vicki said. "All I remember are the arguments. I'd be in my room, but I could hear them shouting at one another. Sandra and..."

"Your mother?"

Vicki looked embarrassed.

"I'll tell you later. You're not the only one who's been keeping a secret. Isn't that someone in the car? Who did you come with?"

Andrew turned around in alarm.

"No one."

"Have you got the keys?"

"They're in the ignition."

Andrew heard the Bentley start. Then there was a shout.

"Andrew, Vicki, get off the road. She wants to kill you!" The shouter was Paul, standing on the hillside. Before they could react, the engine ignited and the Bentley accelerated towards them. Andrew and Vicki began to run down the hill.

"Not that way!" Paul called. "She'll try to run you over!"

Andrew ran after Vicki, who was quicker than him. He glanced back. The Bentley had turned round and driven up the hill, out of sight. Maybe Sandra had realized that the game was up. She was trying to make her escape. Andrew wanted to catch Vicki up, but his body ached badly from the two falls he'd had earlier. Vicki stopped for him. They were both panting, and out of breath.

"I can't run any further," he told her.

"Why did Paul warn us?" Vicki asked.

"I don't know. Shouldn't we go and ask him?"

"No," Vicki said. "It might be a trap."

They looked around. Paul was running towards them.

"Let's go to the house," Vicki said. "She can't run us over there."

Vicki was right, but Andrew didn't really want to go near the house again. He didn't want to go anywhere. Then Paul shouted.

"She's coming back!"

"Let me help you," Vicki said.

On Vicki's arm, he limped towards the building where he had grown up, the house where his family had died. Behind them, the Bentley's engine stopped purring and began to roar.

"This way!" Vicki insisted. "Quick, by that wall!"

Andrew went where she said, glancing round as he did. The Bentley had left the road and was heading towards them. Paul ran behind it, yelling.

"Mummy, stop! Mummy!"

"Just there," Vicki said, pointing to a spot to the left of them. "That's where Daddy fell in, isn't it?"

"Yes. I think so."

"All right. Get out of the way. Behind that wall, quickly!" As the car hurtled towards them, Vicki hurried to one side, so that the driver had to choose either her or Andrew to aim at. Andrew was behind a wall, so she turned, driving the Bentley straight into Vicki. Vicki clung to one of the foundation walls. A foot in the wrong place and she would fall into the cellar. The Bentley was a well-constructed car. It would kill Vicki while the driver hardly felt a thing.

And it was coming awfully fast.

At the last moment, Vicki jumped aside, clearing the Bentley's path by centimetres. Andrew grabbed Vicki's trembling body as the Bentley smashed into the foundation wall. They both turned to look at it. The wall shuddered and held. The driver turned to face them with a menacing, death's head stare.

"That's not Sandra," Andrew suddenly realized. "That's someone else."

The ground began to give way on the side nearest to them. As the driver undid her seat belt and grappled with the door, her side of the car tilted down until it was at a ninety-degree angle. Then the whole floor gave way. The car toppled and crashed into the cellar.

They stared down after it. Andrew could see the driver clearly. Her eyes seemed to stare into his soul with an unnatural piercing glare.

"She's not moving," Vicki said.

"That's because her neck's broken," Andrew told her.

24

Paul came running to them. He looked down at the smouldering wreck.

"Is she?"

"Yes," Vicki told him. "She is. Do you know who she was?"

Paul nodded.

"She told me her name was Sh-Charlotte," he stuttered. "She said that she was Sandra's twin sister, and my real mother. She looked like me … and Sandra. Was she telling the truth?"

"Yes," Vicki said. "She was."

Paul turned to Andrew.

"I really didn't want to hurt you," he said. "But she told me I had to. She said that you were really Andrew Partington, and your brother had done terrible things to her and Sandra and you'd do the same thing to Vicki if I didn't make you fall into the cellar. She said you deserved it. I'm sorry. She told me if I didn't she'd…" He was in tears.

"It's all right," Andrew told Paul. "I shouldn't have lied about who I was. And you helped us in the end. What made you change your mind?"

"I helped her fix the phone junction box so that she could listen in and cut it off when she wanted. She said that we had to kill Vicki, and Moira, because then we'd be safe. She'd pretend to be Sandra and look after me. I'd be the new Lord Hetherington."

"Moira?" Vicki said, urgently. "Is Moira still alive?"

"She is," Paul told them. "She's locked up in the butterfly room. Charlotte went down there just before we came after you. She said she had to do something with the generator."

"Oh, God," Vicki said. "We've got to get back there."

"What is it?" Andrew said to her. "What's wrong?"

"Don't you see? She wants to destroy the evidence. She's going to destroy the Hall the same way that she destroyed Partington House. She doesn't care about the Hall, only about the title for Paul."

"Is she really Sandra's twin?"

"Yes. I was going to tell you, but ... there's no time to explain now. She'll have set the generator to overload and removed the safety valve."

"How do you know all this?" Andrew asked.

"Because that's what she did before – to your family. I'm sorry. I thought she was dead. Daddy said she'd killed herself, not long after it happened. He made us all promise not to talk about her, for Paul's sake, he said. If I'd known..." She stopped speaking. Paul was tugging at her sleeve.

"Come on," he said, "we've got to go!"

"Wait!" Andrew said. "I can hardly walk. Surely it's all right. There's hardly any oil left."

"There doesn't have to be that much fuel," Vicki said.

Behind them, there was a loud bang. For a moment, Andrew thought it was Hetherington Hall. Then he turned round and saw that it was the Bentley. Flames poured out of the hole in the ground. Thick black smoke filled the air.

"Like I said," Vicki repeated. "It doesn't need that much fuel."

"You and Paul will have to go without me," Andrew told her.

"I don't want to leave you."

"I'll be all right. Take care."

Paul and Vicki left, no longer brother and sister, but aunt and nephew.

Andrew sat on the driveway to what had once been his family home, trying to think. He seemed to have discovered what he had set out to find: Vicki's elder sister, Charlotte, had caused the death of his father, mother and brother. He still didn't know why. But he was nearly there. Vicki, it seemed, knew the answer. Maybe, if he had told the truth from the start, she wouldn't have kept back the story of Sandra's twin sister. By now, four more people were dead and, unless Vicki was very swift, a fifth would die too. What could have happened ten years ago to set these terrible events in motion?

A car hooted and he looked up. It was Vicki's brown Mini, driving down the winding road into the valley. The car drove up to where he sat and the driver got out, smiling cheerfully. It was Alice, her blonde hair blowing in the breeze. She looked so lovely that Andrew thought she was a mirage. Alice smiled at him, then stared at the smoke. Finally, her eyes rested on Andrew's tattered clothes.

"I saw the smoke," she said. "What's going on?"

"Over now," he muttered. Aching and exhausted, Andrew couldn't get any more words out. Alice pointed at the car.

"I found this parked on the side of the road a mile from our house with the keys left in it. Your stuck-up girlfriend ran out of petrol, did she?"

Andrew nodded.

"When she didn't come back for it, I put a couple of gallons in and decided to drive it over. Then I saw the smoke and made a detour."

She took a breath, and looked around.

"What happened?" she asked.

"Can I tell you later?" Andrew asked. "It's a big relief to see you."

"You look like you need some help."

"I can hardly walk," Andrew admitted.

"I'll get you into the car."

Alice put her arms beneath his shoulders and helped him up. For someone so slender, she was surprisingly strong.

"Lean on me," she said, and he did. Then she added, "Where's Vicki? She didn't start that fire over there, did she?"

Andrew's brain suddenly came back to life.

"We have to drive to Hetherington Hall now, as quickly as possible," he insisted. "There's someone there in terrible danger."

Alice looked at him as though he was mad.

"Please," Andrew said. "Trust me."

Alice stared at him for a few seconds, weighing the situation up.

"All right," she said, as Andrew squirmed uncomfortably into the passenger seat, "let's go."

Andrew hardly said a word to Alice once he was in the car. She was driving – and talking – very quickly indeed.

"You're Andrew Partington, aren't you? My mum recognized you when you came round on Friday. She used to clean at your house."

"Did she?"

"She said you wouldn't remember. But Mum couldn't understand why you didn't know that Sandra Hetherington was going to marry your brother."

"I was away at school when it all happened."

Alice nodded. She was keeping her eyes on the road, and didn't turn round to see the fascination with which Andrew received the information she was giving him.

"It was terrible," Alice said. "You must have had an awful time. People still talk about it. What happened to the sister?"

"Which sister?"

"Charlotte. The one they say did it. 'The mad twins', my mum used to call Sandra and Charlotte. They were both in love with the same bloke – your brother. But presumably you know all this already?"

Andrew bit his tongue.

"Not all of it. I never came back here, not even for the funeral. The aunt who looked after me thought that I was too young to understand."

"Everyone round here reckons that Charlotte burnt your old house down. But it was covered up, wasn't it? They put Charlotte in some loony bin – that's what people say – though some reckon that Sandra's the really loopy one. Is all that true?"

"I don't know," Andrew told Alice. "But I think so."

They were coming up to the hall. Andrew checked his watch. Vicki and Paul were coming the shorter way, over the fields, but they wouldn't have had time to get here yet.

"Don't park too close," Andrew told Alice. "There might be danger."

"Danger?" she said, getting out of the car. "Look, Andrew, I like you. I want to help you. But you're acting as though you're in shock or something. What's going on?"

"The Hall might be about to catch fire. I'm going in."

Alice looked at him, presumably to check if he was frothing at the mouth. Then she helped him out of his seat.

"Why are you going in, if it's dangerous?"

"Because Moira's trapped down in the cellar."

Alice gave him another hard look.

"If she's really in the cellar, than I'd better go for her. You can barely walk."

"I'm going in too."

"Come on then, if you can."

Andrew could hardly object to Alice helping him. He didn't want to put her life at risk, but he couldn't save Moira on his own, either. Alice rushed ahead. He could barely keep up with her.

"Where in the cellar?" she asked, as they went into the hall.

"The butterfly room. A right turn at the end."

She got to the top of the cellar steps and opened the door. There was a deafening clanking noise.

"It's hot," she shouted, before going down. "You know, I wouldn't do this if it was anyone other than Moira. She's the only person here who ever treated me decently."

Andrew followed as closely as he could. There were sparks coming from the generator. The key to the butterfly room was, thankfully, in the lock. He heard Alice going into the room. She came out again just as he was getting to the bottom of the steps.

"I need your help," she told him. "Moira's really weak and dehydrated. She can hardly walk."

Andrew joined Alice in the butterfly room. It smelt rank and airless. Moira was panting. She had lost a lot of weight. Andrew worked out that she must have been in there for three days.

"Wait," Moira whispered as they lifted her between them. She pointed to one of the wooden drawers on the table.

"There's no time to save butterflies," Andrew said.

"Not butterflies," she whispered.

He reached for the drawer and looked in it. There were clippings and torn pages. The drawer concealed the pages which had been torn from the house books – the hidden history of Hetherington Hall. Andrew picked them up and stuffed them into his jacket.

"Come on," Alice said.

The buzzing noise from the generator intensified as they carried Moira along the corridor. Andrew could hardly climb the steps himself, never mind help Moira. Somehow, with Alice pushing from behind, they all got into the hall.

The noise from below grew louder as the pressure in the oil drum mounted. Andrew realized that what he was hearing now would have been the last sound which his parents and brother heard before they died.

"Move!" Alice exhorted. "Move!"

They burst through the door into sudden sunshine. As they stumbled down the steps, Andrew saw Vicki and Paul running across the fields towards them.

"Stay back! Stay back!" Alice shouted.

The explosion blew out all of the windows on all three floors. Dirty glass showered Andrew, Alice and Moira, cutting what skin they had exposed. Andrew kept moving until they got to the car. Then, as flames engulfed the house, they sheltered behind it. Paul and Vicki joined them.

"Are you all right?" Vicki asked the housekeeper, hugging her.

"I am now, my dear. I am now."

25

Mr Gallagher, the Hetherington family solicitor, met Andrew, Alice, Vicki, Moira and Paul at the police station. He spoke to Andrew.

"I knew your parents," he said. "They were good people."

Andrew reached into one of his pockets and handed the solicitor the envelope containing the will.

"Have you read this?" the solicitor asked.

Andrew shook his head. Mr Gallagher got out the papers and looked through them for several minutes.

"I see. I see," he muttered to himself.

A Detective Inspector came in and spoke to Mr Gallagher.

"I spoke to Dr Rutherford, as you suggested. She confirmed that Charlotte Hetherington was released into the community last month. When Charlotte didn't get in touch with her social worker, Dr Rutherford contacted Hetherington Hall, with some difficulty. She says that she has spoken to you and to Charlotte's sister."

"Did she tell you that Charlotte had been released?" Andrew asked Mr Gallagher.

"Yes," he admitted. "The Doctor said that Charlotte was mentally stable, showed no interest in returning to her family, and had been found a placement in the south of England. I told Lord Hetherington this and, as a result, he made a small provision for her in his new will."

Then the solicitor picked up the document and read from it.

"And to my eldest daughter, Charlotte, I leave £10,000, on condition that she does not seek to have contact with the new Lord Hetherington."

He put the papers down.

"However, the new will has no legal weight, because Lord Hetherington died before it could be witnessed. Moreover, this will assumes that Lord Hetherington has the proceeds from the sale of Hetherington Hall. He intended to make adequate provision for each of his daughters. He meant to pay off his debts, buy a modest house, and live off the interest from his capital. When he died, the capital would have been divided equally between Paul, Sandra and Victoria, apart from bequests to Charlotte and Moira." He turned to the housekeeper.

"There is a bequest to you in the old will, Moira, but I don't know if there'll be the cash to cover it. Does anyone know if his insurance policies were up to date?"

"They were," Andrew told them.

"In that case, there should be enough to pay off the debts. You might have some money to see you through college, Vicki. Things will be more difficult for Paul."

"I'll look after Paul," Vicki promised.

"I'll help you, dear," Moira said.

"I'm sure that Andrew will help as well," Mr Gallagher told the others. "After all, he is Paul's uncle."

Andrew had already worked most of this out, but the situation still felt very strange. Only this morning, his nephew had tried to kill him. Mr Gallagher turned to Andrew again.

"Do you know the full story of what happened?"

"Nearly. It all started with my brother, Charles, I think."

The solicitor nodded.

"Charles was a feckless young man. Officially, he was Sandra's boyfriend, but he was secretly seeing Charlotte, too. The girls were near identical twins, but had very different personalities. Finally, Charles decided to marry Sandra, but still slept with Charlotte from time to time. Sandra suspected, and complained, but Charlotte was the dominant of the twins, and a convincing liar. Shortly before the marriage was due to take place, Charlotte discovered that she was pregnant. She must have told Charles, but no one knows how he reacted. My guess is that he told Charlotte that he wanted nothing further to do with her. The following night, Charlotte tampered with the generator at the Partington house, causing it to explode.

"Charlotte was found to be unfit to stand trial. The case was kept out of the papers, but the story was common knowledge, and the

Hetheringtons stopped moving in society from that date. They had Charlotte committed to a home, where her pregnancy was kept a close secret. Shortly after her committal, Sandra and Vicki were told that Charlotte had killed herself. They had no reason to disbelieve their parents."

He lowered his voice.

"I was – against my better judgement – drawn into the secret. After the twins, Lady Hetherington could bear no more children. Lord Hetherington longed for a male heir. When a scan showed that Charlotte was carrying a male child, he determined to pass it off as his own. Lady Hetherington went away, claiming to be pregnant. When the baby was born, Charlotte was told that it was being adopted. In fact, a friendly doctor falsified a birth certificate, describing Lord and Lady Hetherington as the parents.

"Unfortunately, it now seems that Charlotte realized what had been done. On her release from hospital, she came straight to Hetherington Hall, and set about getting revenge for herself and assuring her son of his inheritance. She must have sabotaged the heater in the bathroom – it didn't matter who was killed, she wanted to get everyone, except her son Paul, whom she warned."

"She came into my room at night," Paul interrupted, in a shrill voice. "At first, I thought she was Sandra. She was really nice to me. I'd get her food and stuff. You saw her, Andrew, the night when you stayed in my room."

He started crying again.

"I never wanted to hurt anyone, but she said we had to. We had to."

"It's all right," Vicki hugged him. "It's all right."

The solicitor continued.

"We don't know how Charlotte killed Sandra. I suspect that she forced her to put on the wedding dress, then stabbed her. Sandra was physically strong, but frequently deranged since Charles died. And Charlotte could always twist Sandra around her little finger.

"The other deaths you know about. I surmise that, by killing Lord Hetherington, Charlotte hoped to ensure that her son became the next Lord Hetherington. She would pose as Sandra and, between them, they would inherit everything. But her actions had the opposite effect. The house, having burnt down, cannot be sold. It was, I'm sad to say, badly underinsured. And the deception about

Paul's parentage has to end here, too. There's bound to be publicity. As a bastard grandson, he cannot inherit."

Vicki looked perturbed.

"It's me, then," she said, with a grimace. "I'm the only one left."

"What does that make her?" Andrew asked. "A baroness?"

"I'm afraid not," Mr Gallagher told her. "This will be a shock, Victoria, but you, too, are illegitimate. Lady Hetherington was not your mother."

Vicki's eyes nearly popped out of their sockets. Mr Gallagher continued.

"As I explained earlier – after the birth of the twins, Lady Hetherington could bear no more children. Your father was – as I'm sure you're aware – a promiscuous man. Your mother was one of his mistresses. He and Lady Hetherington did formally adopt you, but, as I'm sure you're aware, adopted children cannot inherit a title." He paused, then added, "I'm sorry."

Vicki was in shock.

"I never wanted a title," she said. "But you say, my mother … wasn't my real mother?"

"No."

"Then … who is?"

The Detective Inspector came back in.

"We're ready to take the statements now."

Mr Gallagher got up.

"If I could have a brief word outside first, Inspector. There are one or two things I'd like to clear up."

The solicitor went out with the policeman. When Andrew looked back at Vicki, she and Moira were holding each other's hands.

"Why do you think I stayed with the family all those years?" Moira was asking. "I told your mother that they could only adopt you if I was allowed to stay. She didn't like it, but she put up with it. Then, when they found you were a girl … she never loved you like I did. I couldn't leave."

Mother and daughter sobbed in each other's arms.

Andrew, Alice and Paul left the room quietly, giving the two women some privacy.

"The ambulance has arrived," Mr Gallagher told Andrew. "Is there anything else you want me to tell you before they take you to hospital?"

"I think I know the full story," Andrew told him. "But there is one thing I'm curious about. What happens to the title now?"

Mr Gallagher frowned.

"If Charlotte had lived, it would have been hers, no matter what her crimes, because she would have been Lord Hetherington's only surviving legitimate child. As it is, the title falls into abeyance. If no legitimate heir can be found, then..." The solicitor made a gesture like a puff of smoke disappearing.

"Perhaps," he added, "that would be the most appropriate ending."

FINAL
CUT

For Mike Russell

March

Prologue

The moment she walked through the door, every eye in the building turned to Sarah. Someone wolf-whistled. She let herself be ushered to the appropriate place. She was used to attention.

Sarah was nearly six feet tall, and dressed to the nines. She was the model who the Princess of Wales had recently referred to as "breathtaking". She had long, blonde hair and a thin but perfectly proportioned figure. Her face had something harder to define: character, maybe, or charisma, whatever – she didn't know. It was the secret ingredient which people said made her more than very good looking – it made her a great beauty.

Still, Sarah found something unnerving about getting so much attention, here of all places. Then someone said something. The production line started up again. Every eye in the building, including Sarah's, turned to watch it.

From where she was standing, Sarah could see the entire process of assembly. It started at the other end of the factory, with an engine being put on to a conveyor belt. The belt moved on. Robots attached the chassis to the engine: a grey shell, full of gaping holes. At this point, you could hardly tell what it was. Then the body sailed through a shower of red paint and began to resemble what it was to become.

Next, a hundred fans dried the paint. The chassis moved on down the line. Hydraulic arms inserted seats and upholstery. Wheels were added, automatically. Tyres were put on and blown up to the correct pressure. Headlights, tail lights and number-plates were fixed in place as the robotic arms scuttled to and fro. Finally, windows were lowered into position, polished and sealed. The completed car was lowered on to the ground and there was a spontaneous round of applause, which Sarah joined in. The whole process had taken barely two minutes.

A man in a white laboratory coat walked up to the car, beaming in the direction of the camera.

"Omega are *proud* to present the *Excelsior*, a car so perfect, so ahead of its time, that the first human hands to touch it could well be *yours*."

There was a noise behind him. One of the car doors – the front passenger one – opened. Sarah gasped. She was seeing something which was impossible, something which made no sense at all. Before her eyes, a young man in jeans and a T-shirt fell out of the car, on to the concrete floor. There was a small red hole in the centre of his forehead, from which blood began to gush. The man's body jerked spasmodically for a second or two, then stopped.

He was dead.

1

"Cut!" Leo Fitzgerald got down from his director's chair and strolled across to the steadicam operator.

"It looked fine from the monitor. Any problems your end?" The woman shook her head.

Fitzgerald spoke into his megaphone. "All right everybody, that's a take. We're done here."

Suddenly the set, which had been so quiet, sprang into life. At least a hundred people appeared, then vanished almost as quickly. The director walked over to Sarah and extended his hand. Sarah shook it.

"Thanks for fitting me into your schedule. Enjoy the show?" he asked. Sarah grasped for words.

"It was ... impressive. How did you do that, with the body?" Fitzgerald tapped his nose.

"Professional secret. Maybe when we get to know each other a little better, I'll tell you."

Several people came up to the director, but he motioned them away with the slightest movement of his hand. Then he put his arm around Sarah's bare shoulders, and guided her out of the lot, talking all the time.

"Have you met Brett?"

"No. I'm really looking forward to..."

Fitzgerald didn't wait to hear her reply, but kept talking. Like most men, he assumed she was an airhead.

"You might have the look I'm after. How old are you: nineteen? twenty?"

"Seventeen," Sarah admitted.

"You're kidding? You made the cover of *Vogue* at *seventeen*? Way to go! Done any acting?"

Sarah thought about exaggerating her small parts in school plays, then decided against.

"Only a few commercials, when I was younger."

They got into a small buggy, rather like a golf cart, and Fitzgerald began to drive. They crossed the studio complex at a leisurely pace, hardly seeing anybody. It was like being in a ghost town, full of vast, silent warehouses. As he drove, Leo talked. His voice had the usual mid-western lilt, with occasional hints of London.

"There's nothing wrong with doing TV commercials," he told her. "That's where I started. Commercials, rock videos, TV movies – finally a music film, which grossed twenty times what it cost to make. So for the next one – *This Year's Model* – the studio have given me final cut. Know what that means?"

"No."

"It means that what I say goes. When I finish the picture, no one can change a single frame. It means I'm not a hack any longer. I'm an artist. An *auteur.* There aren't many of us left."

"I see."

Sarah wondered if Fitzgerald showed off like this all the time, or was just doing it to impress her. If it was the latter, he needn't have bothered. Since her career had catapulted, barely twelve months ago, Sarah had had every conceivable pick-up technique tried out on her: fashion photographers filled her room with flowers, TV personalities offered her slots in their shows, pop stars promised to produce hit records for her.

So here was a film director, offering to make Sarah a star. She had flown to LA today because Sally, her agent, insisted she had to. A major movie would take Sarah right to the top of the supermodel league. But Sarah suspected that Leo Fitzgerald was like all the other men she encountered in the beauty business: sadly shallow.

The director wasn't her type at all. He was thirtyish, with dark, curly hair and a high forehead. He was very thin, and his skin was unnaturally pale for someone who lived in Los Angeles. Sarah was supposed to be flattered when intelligent, mature men were interested in her. She didn't know what she wanted, but it wasn't the men she met. Maybe she needed someone around her own age, someone who didn't make her feel like her teenage years were being snatched away from her.

"Here we are."

They pulled up outside another, newer building. Fitzgerald took Sarah's arm to help her out of the cart, then they walked inside. It was smaller than the huge sound stage she had just left, and so crowded with cameras and sets that it felt claustrophobic.

"What are they making here?" Sarah asked.

"A mini-series. Studios mostly make TV these days. Movies are made on location."

Sarah hadn't realized this. She wondered where *This Year's Model* would be filmed. If the film even existed. Fitzgerald had promised to send Sally a script, but it had never arrived.

"Brett! I hope we haven't kept you waiting."

A tanned, mustachioed actor walked out from between two cameras, smiling over-enthusiastically. Fleetingly, he looked Sarah up and down, then turned to Fitzgerald. Sarah continued to stare at the actor, remembering all the stories and rumours she'd read about him. The star looked synthetic somehow, as though he'd just stepped out of the screen. Sarah had seen him in a lot of films, and though he hadn't made one for years, he didn't seem to have aged at all.

"She's too young," Johnson told Fitzgerald tersely. "I had my agent check her out. She's seventeen."

"Nearly eighteen," Fitzgerald replied, which wasn't true. "And she looks a lot older. Ask anyone."

"I've got a daughter, twenty-five. How do I look in this picture if I marry a seventeen-year-old?"

Marry? This was the first time Sarah had heard that she was supposed to marry Brett Johnson. She'd thought her role would be a small cameo. According to her agent, Sarah would be playing herself.

"Brett," Fitzgerald coaxed, "believe me: the age gap is sexy. It's dangerous. This is your comeback. You need to reinvent yourself."

Johnson didn't look convinced.

"We've brought her all the way over from England," Fitzgerald went on. "Give the test your best shot."

Johnson nodded. As Fitzgerald told the technicians what to do, the star turned to Sarah and gave her his famous reassuring smile.

"Nothing personal," he said. "Have you read the script?"

"Not yet."

"Don't. It stinks. They're doing a complete rewrite on the third act. No one's got any idea how to end the thing."

"Are you ready?" Fitzgerald asked. "I'll go over the lines."

"Do you think that you could tell me the story?" Sarah asked the director. "I was under the impression that this was quite a small role."

"It keeps getting bigger," Fitzgerald told her, with an evasive look. "But basically, it's very simple. The two of you meet, start to fall in love. Brett's a kind of father-figure to you. But he's got a dangerous edge. That's all your character needs to know for this scene. Here. You're Melissa Vine. Brett's Matthew Harper."

Sarah read the page.

INTERIOR. NIGHT. HARPER'S APARTMENT. MATTHEW HANDS MELISSA A COCKTAIL. THEY SIT DOWN ON A SOFA.
HARPER: You were magnificent today.
MELISSA: All I did was dress and undress, pace up and down a catwalk.
HARPER: *Catwalk*. I like that word. It suits you somehow. You're very … feline.
MELISSA LOOKS AWAY: People have warned me about you.
HARPER: But you came back with me anyway. Why?
MELISSA: I don't know. Curiosity, I guess.
HARPER: And we all know what curiosity did to the cat.
THEY KISS.

Sarah put the page down.

"You want us to actually do the kiss?"

"Please. It's important."

She glanced at Johnson. He grinned and pulled a tiny aerosol out of his trouser pocket, then squeezed the breath-freshener into his mouth. Sarah read the script again, not sure if she was meant to learn the lines.

"Let's do it," Fitzgerald said. "And Sarah, don't worry. Just be natural."

Sarah adjusted her make-up, wondering how she was expected to be natural playing a romantic scene opposite a very famous actor who was older than her own father. But she did as she was asked.

She sat on the sofa next to Brett, closer to him than felt comfortable. The lights were very bright and surprisingly hot. Somehow, when she spoke, the words in the script seemed to have etched themselves on to her memory. When Johnson got to the bit about being feline, he began to stroke her neck. His voice purred. Before she knew it, they were kissing. It was a proper kiss, like the ones boys had given her before she was famous. After a few seconds, Johnson pulled away.

"Thank you," Fitzgerald said.

Johnson stood up and offered Sarah his hand.

"Nice meeting you," he said.

Fitzgerald joined him. It seemed to Sarah as though she no longer existed.

"We'll let you know," the director said.

The two men walked out, leaving Sarah alone in front of the bright lights. Sweat ran down her face. She wondered whether she had just been given the Hollywood brush-off. She had been playing it so cool, yet she was aware now that she had taken an important test, and all kinds of things could depend upon it. She felt exposed and very alone.

Then, without warning, the lights went out.

Sarah blinked. The studio was very dark. There were distorted, threatening shadows everywhere. Sarah had no idea how to get out. She shivered. Moments ago it had been stiflingly hot, but now it felt like England in winter. Then she heard a noise, a movement.

"Hello?"

No reply. Sarah began to curse herself. Why had she come here? She'd just got one career going. She didn't need another one. Before her eyes could adjust to the light, footsteps approached. A silhouette stepped out of the shadows.

"Who?" Sarah stuttered anxiously. "What?"

A hidden hand flicked on a light switch. Standing by the door was a girl, a little older than Sarah.

"Hi. I'm Stacey, Mr Fitzgerald's assistant," she said. "He asked me to drive you back to your hotel."

2

Jonathon Wood often wished that his sister was older than him. Somehow, he felt, it would make things easier. Here he was at eighteen, spending all his time preparing for exams, hoping that he'd got good enough grades to get into university. Meanwhile, seventeen-year-old Sarah was earning thousands and thousands of pounds, travelling all over the world.

It had been this way as long as he could remember. Sarah had started appearing in TV commercials when she was three. After that, she kept getting offers. Things had gone a little quiet between her ninth and thirteenth birthdays – the occasional catalogue job – and Jon thought that she was settling into an ordinary life. His sister even talked about becoming a journalist or something in television.

But then the work picked up, even though she was still at school. It seemed that Sarah's looks (she was the same height as Jon and very thin, with high cheekbones and innocent, enigmatic eyes) were suddenly in fashion. Jon hoped that this fad for child-women would fizzle out, but instead it boomed. In the last year, Sarah Wood had become a household name. Her picture was everywhere.

It even affected his friendships. Jon was never sure whether people really liked him, or were sucking up to him because they wanted a chance to get close to his glamorous sister. He promised himself that when (if) he got to university, he would deny any relationship with Sarah. Wood was a common name, after all. He would make a fresh start.

Jon loved his sister. He didn't envy her, exactly, but he couldn't help resenting her, especially when she rang just after breakfast and told him that she was on the beach at Malibu.

"I thought you were in Paris."

"I *was*. Something came up. That's why I'm ringing. I'm having dinner tonight with this film director, Leo Fitzgerald, and I need some conversation points. Do you know anything about him?"

Jon was a film buff. He spent a lot of his spare time watching videos, or crossing the city on the Underground, seeking out obscure, crackly prints of minor masterpieces.

"Leo Fitzgerald. Sure. The one who made *Grunge Plunge*?"

"That's right."

"He's a real character. Spent most of his twenties working in a video shop on the King's Road, making rock videos and experimental films in his spare time. He's got this reputation for working really fast and cheap. I think *Grunge Plunge* cost less than a million to make."

"Have you seen it?"

"I saw it at the cinema, yeah. It's a comedy about the Seattle music scene – kind of a beach movie – lots of loud, distorted guitars with indecipherable lyrics. And no story. You'd hate it."

"What else has he done?" Sarah asked.

"I think he did some TV commercials in this country. Then he went to Hollywood, made a couple of TV movies. Do you remember that one about the phantom hitch-hiker and the serial killer? We watched it together at Christmas. That was him."

"Really? It was gruesome."

Jon felt another nugget of information nestling in the back of his mind and tried to dig it out. This was something his friends teased him about: his obsessive appetite for movie trivia.

"Why are you having dinner with him, anyway?" he asked.

"It's a working meal. Sally's coming. I did this audition yesterday. He might have a part in a film for me."

"A part?" Jon laughed incredulously. "I remember you in *Little Red Riding Hood* at primary school. You were dreadful. You're a model, sis, not an actress."

"That was a long time ago," Sarah insisted. "Anyway, thanks for your help. I've got to go. My sunblock's wearing off. If I spend any longer on the beach, I'll start to tan."

As soon as she'd hung up, Jon remembered what he'd read recently about Fitzgerald. It was in the NME's movie news section. Fitzgerald was directing a comeback picture for Brett Johnson.

The star had won Oscars in the past, but when his career slid, he'd developed a big drink and drugs problem. There'd been a car crash where a passenger was killed. After that, he'd disappeared from view.

Jon wondered why Leo Fitzgerald really wanted to have dinner with his sister. To talk about a part in the film was probably a bluff, he decided. Fitzgerald simply wanted to go out with her, like every other man she met. His sister, an actress? Even she wasn't stupid enough to fall for that one.

"I'm not an actress," Sarah told Fitzgerald, sipping her Chardonnay and trying to be cool when she was really very excited. "Why me?"

Fitzgerald grinned.

"Why not? Be yourself. This isn't Shakespeare. You're young. You're sexy. You're on the cover of *Vogue*."

Sarah felt out of her depth. She glanced at Sally, who smiled reassuringly.

"I might be comfortable playing myself if this weren't such a big part."

"Other models have gone straight into acting: Lauren Hutton, Brooke Shields, Rene Russo..."

"Who?" Sarah wrinkled her nose. These were names she only knew vaguely, names from before she was born. Fitzgerald shrugged.

"I guess they were before your time," he muttered. He leant forward and made intense eye contact.

"Look, if it makes you feel more comfortable, say we're using you for your publicity value. The business these days is all about generating pre-publicity, a buzz. The big movies do most of their business the weekend they open. The hype is everything. You're big news at the moment. The papers are bound to suggest that you're having an affair with the co-star. We'll get lots of mileage out of the denials and no comments."

"Co-star?" Sarah said, trying to hide the distaste in her voice. "You mean Brett?"

"No." Fitzgerald had a twinkle in his eye. "Didn't I tell you? The other major part is Brett's son: Aidan. He falls in love with Melissa and tries to warn her about his father."

"Who plays Aidan?"

"We've only just got him under contract. Luke Kelly."

"*Luke Kelly?*"

Sarah's heart leapt. Luke Kelly was an Irish-American actor with looks to kill for. A year ago, before Sarah's career really took off, he had been her heart-throb. Her wardrobe at home was covered with photographs of the young movie star with deep brown eyes which matched the colour of his long, curly hair.

"That's right. Luke Kelly." Fitzgerald smiled anxiously, uncertain of Sarah's reaction. "Don't believe the stories you've heard about Luke being difficult. He's a pro. And he guarantees millions of extra teenage girls at the box office."

Sarah ate her meal, barely tasting it. Any doubts she had evaporated. She was going to be in a film with Luke Kelly. She must remain cool. Sometimes, it was hard work being sophisticated and successful when you were only seventeen. You couldn't show that anything impressed you. She tried to think of more conversation, but she had already used up all her questions about serial killers and rock videos. Then she thought of one.

"The sequence you were filming today. The dead body in the car. Was it for this film?"

"No," Fitzgerald said. "We're still in pre-production. That was a trailer for a film they're having difficulty promoting. They got me in because it's a bio-flick about a British director."

"So how does the complicated murder fit in with the plot?"

Fitzgerald shrugged. "The plot? Who cares? Like I told you, all that counts in movies these days is getting big numbers at the box office. Ever see *The Big Sleep*? A classic, but the plot had more holes in it than a golf course. You want the plot to make sense? Read a book."

Sarah smiled, not sure if he was joking.

"Where's *This Year's Model* being made?" she asked.

"England. Originally it was going to be New England, but we're on a tight budget and the pound's weak at the moment. So we're filming the entire thing on location in the Home Counties. That's one of the reasons we have to find a British model."

Sarah went to the restroom, in two minds over whether to accept. She'd hoped that she would be working somewhere more exotic than England, where everyone was contemptuous of success and the weather was drab and unreliable. She could think of better places to spend six weeks of the summer. But when she got back to the table, it seemed that a deal had been done. Sally was all enthusiasm, predicting great things for Sarah's future.

"This film will change your life," she told her.

Sarah wondered whether her life hadn't changed enough already. Leo offered his hand. That was the way deals were done in this town. One handshake, and she was committed.

"Are you happy?" he asked, seeing her hesitate.

Sarah thought for a moment, then had an idea. "Could I ask you a favour?"

"Shoot."

"My elder brother, Jon, he's a big movie buff. He's hoping to do Media Studies at university. But he hasn't got a job this summer and he could really use the experience, and some money. Is there any chance you could find him a job on the film?"

Fitzgerald smiled reassuringly. "There are union restrictions, but I'm sure I can work something out."

They shook hands and Sarah's doubts dissolved. It would be good to have her brother along. She hadn't seen enough of Jon in the last year. She didn't want to grow apart from him. And she wanted to share her good fortune. Sarah couldn't believe it. She was going to be in a feature film. She was going to work with Luke Kelly. She could hardly wait.

July

3

The village of Bradlington was small. It was full of old-fashioned shops and chintzy, restored period cottages. The place had a dull, safe air about it which reminded Jon of a hundred other villages his family had driven through on Sunday afternoon outings. He got off the bus at seven in the evening and asked for directions to the hotel.

"There's only one," he was told.

The late Victorian building didn't look big enough to house a whole film crew, but Jon dragged his suitcase into the small lobby.

"I'm with the film," he said at reception.

"What film?"

Half an hour, and an expensive taxi ride later, he found himself at a large, faceless hotel just off a main road, five minutes' drive from Bradlington New Town. Reception told him that his sister hadn't arrived yet. Nor had his room been allocated.

"I've been told to report to the lighting director."

"You'd better wait over there."

Jon sat down on a red sofa, hoping that the evening wasn't going to be an anti-climax. He'd been so excited about the prospect of working on the film this summer that it had been hard to concentrate on his A-levels. Now they were over, he had no idea how well he had done and, for the moment, he didn't care.

Jon's job, the production assistant explained on the phone, was as a runner, or gofer, as in "go for this, go for that". He should be prepared to do anything, at any time. He sat on the sofa nervously, wondering whether he ought to be seeking out his supervisor. It was late and he was hungry. No one else seemed to be checking in.

Maybe he'd made a big mistake by not arriving earlier. This was a cut-throat business; everybody said that. Maybe somebody else had already taken his job. Sarah had assured him that everything was OK, but she'd been out of the country for most of the last four months. They'd hardly spoken.

"Jon?"

A young woman in jeans with closely cropped black hair and a *This Year's Model* T-shirt was standing over him.

"I'm Karen. Nice to meet you."

Jon stood up to shake her hand. Karen's head only came up to his chest.

"Have you eaten?" she asked.

It was hard to tell how old she was – not much more than him. Jon was instantly attracted to her.

"No."

"If I were you, I'd get a sandwich on room service and an early night. You need to be up at five in the morning." She turned to reception and got Jon a key.

"You're sharing with Todd, one of the camera operators."

"Thanks, er..."

Jon wondered what Karen's job was: some kind of production assistant, he guessed, but she was not the one he'd spoken to on the phone.

"Actually, I was told to report to the lighting director."

"I know," she said, matter of factly. "That's me."

Jon blushed.

"Get an early night," she told him. "Once this thing gets going, no one'll get much sleep."

But Jon slept badly, too excited to doze off before midnight, when Todd blundered into the room. The shaggy-haired, overweight American had clearly had too much to drink. In the morning, though, he was up first, with no trace of a hangover. He greeted Jon cheerily and regaled him with anecdotes and advice culled from films he'd worked on as they made their way to Bradlington Hall.

By ten, Jon was exhausted and starving. He'd been up since six and he felt like he'd done a full day already. The crew were on a ten-minute break and he was grabbing some coffee and a bacon roll. Karen came into the trailer. Earlier, Ruth Greenwood, the assistant director, had formally introduced them.

"Think of Karen as your adoptive mother," Ruth told Jon.

"Jon, we need some more gaffer tape," his adoptive mother told him now, in a stern voice.

Jon went for it. Todd had warned him – you didn't argue about length of breaks in the movie business. Every second was phenomenally expensive. This was a cheap movie, but the budget was still for several million dollars.

The first scene to be filmed was one where Matthew (Brett Johnson) and Melissa (Sarah) met for the first time. It was an outdoor scene. Melissa was being photographed modelling the English country look. Matthew was staying with the family whose country mansion, Bradlington Hall, provided the backdrop for the shoot. Already, a gaggle of locals had gathered on the edge of the set, watching the crew's preparations.

"Hey, Luke!" someone called.

Jon looked around. A long-haired youth in a parka was pointing towards him.

"That's Luke Kelly," the youth said, and a child standing by him came running over to Jon.

"Luke, Luke, can I have your autograph?"

Jon shook his head.

"I'm not Luke Kelly. He hasn't arrived yet."

The boy looked bitterly disappointed. He walked back towards the onlookers. Jon hurried to Karen with the tape.

"What was that about?" she asked.

Jon shrugged. "Here I am, worried everyone will work out I got the job because I'm Sarah's brother. Instead, people mix me up with Luke Kelly."

Karen examined Jon's looks with an appraising eye. Jon had grown his hair over the summer. Until recently he'd kept it short, and wore glasses a lot, even though he was only a little long-sighted. He didn't like people to comment on his resemblance to Sarah. But all that was about to be changed. He was going to make a new start and wanted a new image to go with it.

Karen's scrutiny embarrassed Jon. She was at least five years older than him, he realized now, and she made him feel like a small boy.

"You do look a little like Luke," Karen said. "Same colour hair.

Same build. But your eyes are much kinder than his. I've worked on films with him before. He's ... in the States, we'd call him a jerk. You know what it means: arrogant, immature, a pain..."

"A bit of a prat," Jon translated.

"A prat. Precisely."

"Thanks for the warning," Jon told her, and Karen continued securing the equipment.

It started to rain and everyone retreated to the trailers. Sarah had her own trailer. She had arrived not long before – her flight from the Seychelles had been delayed, and Jon hadn't seen her yet. The crew crammed into the trailer where food was served. The director, Jon was impressed to see, stayed with the crew.

"If this rain doesn't let up," Fitzgerald was saying, "we'll have to move on to the indoor stuff. You'd never think that this was August. Why didn't someone remind me about English summers?"

In a corner of the trailer sat three models, each wearing long, Laura Ashley-style dresses. Why was it that Jon's sister was starring in a film and these women – all older than her – weren't? What did she have that they didn't? Jon expected that they were asking the same question.

The assistant director came into the trailer.

"There's a break in the cloud," Ruth said. "I reckon we've got about ten, fifteen minutes before the skies open up again."

"All right," said Fitzgerald, "let's go for it."

The models were supposed to be being photographed lolling about in front of the mansion. Jon's sister came out of her trailer, long hair flowing around a flimsy, white lace camisole. Beneath it was a long, pleated floral skirt. She walked straight past Jon without acknowledging his presence, taking up her position amongst the models. Jon felt insulted.

"Jon, Leo's monitor needs moving," Karen shouted.

Jon ran for it. There was no time for ego games on a shoot like this, he figured. He'd have time to catch up with his sister later.

Sarah heard someone call her brother's name but she didn't notice him. She was too on edge to take in anything other than the spot where she was meant to be standing. This was an establishing shot of the models on the lawn. For this first scene, Sarah was doing almost exactly what she did every day of her working life – posing.

Chronologically, the scene after this one took place indoors, where Brett Johnson was watching the models. It would be filmed later. For economic reasons, all the scenes in one setting were shot at the same time. So the next to be filmed would be the most important scene, where Matthew and Melissa meet for the first time.

The first scene was over before Sarah really knew it. She began to get nervous. It was easy for Leo to say that all she had to do was play herself. Sarah found it hard enough to be herself when she was with one other person. What did you do when you were surrounded by actors, a crew and cameras which picked up the smallest false note in your performance?

They began the meeting scene. As soon as Brett had been filmed walking over towards Sarah, it started raining again.

"I can't believe it!" Fitzgerald announced over the tannoy. "First day of shooting and we're behind schedule. OK, let's improvise."

Leo called Brett and Sarah over. He began pointing and speaking very quickly. Then it was the technicians' turn. The group came charging back and began rapidly moving equipment in the rain. Sarah saw her brother, but still didn't get a chance to speak to him. He was too busy.

"Don't worry," Brett Johnson said to her, seeming to sense Sarah's unease. "It's always a little crazy on the first day. Everyone will settle down. And you'll be fine. I promise."

"Thank you," Sarah replied. "I hope you're right."

"We're going to do a quick set-up in the summerhouse," Karen explained to Jon. "Melissa will run in there to get out of the rain and Matthew will be waiting for her. It might make a better scene. Come on, give me a hand with this."

Moving the equipment took fifteen minutes. It was a big risk. If the rain stopped, then not only would the move be wasted, but all the equipment would be in the wrong place. But the rain kept coming. The crew didn't have time to secure all the equipment properly. Karen had to stand just off-camera holding a light, so that the actors wouldn't be in shadow. Then, as they were about to start shooting, Leo Fitzgerald had an idea.

"I want to try an overhead shot," he announced.

"We haven't got time to erect scaffolding," Ruth told him.

"Doesn't matter. Quick as you can," he ordered the technicians, "while we're rehearsing the movements. Mount a camera on the tree."

The summerhouse was nearly all glass and an oak tree hung over it.

"I'm not going to sit up there on a branch," the camera operator complained. "Suppose it breaks on me?"

"Just mount the thing somehow," Fitzgerald said. "We'll operate it by remote control."

Jon was summoned to help get the camera up the tree. He carried ladders while other runners brought ropes. Soon they had a pulley in position to lift the camera.

"We should be using scaffolding," the camera operator complained to Jon. "A more experienced director would know that. But Leo insists on doing everything: director, producer, director of photography ... he thinks he knows it all, but he doesn't. We'll never get a steady shot with this set-up."

Somehow they got the camera into position, held in place by rope and tape. When it was done, the camera operator refused to climb the tree and crawl along the branch to get the lens pointing in precisely the right direction.

"I'll do it," Jon offered. He was thin and weighed less than ten stone. Heights didn't scare him.

"All right," said Leo. It was the first time he had spoken to Jon. "But be careful. That camera cost a fortune."

Jon climbed five metres up the ladder, then moved across the tree. As children, he and Sarah used to climb trees all the time. It was second nature to him. The branch to which the camera was attached hardly sagged at all. He was sure that it would take his weight easily. But he edged along cautiously, in case the camera wasn't tied on as securely as it should be. The branch moved around a little under his weight, but not much. He felt safe.

The camera wobbled as Jon adjusted its position. Soon, he had it pointing through the appropriate window of the summerhouse. Glancing down the viewfinder, he could see his sister talking to Johnson. Karen's light went on. They had started filming. The image zoomed in. Whoever was operating the remote control focused tightly on Brett and Sarah's faces. Jon's sister was wearing her most childish, innocent expression. Brett reminded Jon of

Clark Gable, smiling smugly in *Gone With The Wind*.

The rope attaching the camera to the branch was tight, but Jon put another roll of tape around the camera, just to be on the safe side. Then he inched his way back off the branch. Rain was still pouring heavily. He was soaked through.

"Good job," called the director.

The crew were between takes and Jon headed for the shelter of the summerhouse. Rain pounded on to the glass.

"We're going to do it once more," Fitzgerald announced, "for the overhead shot."

He went over and looked at the monitor, then called to Karen. "You're in shot. Shift to the left a little. Hold the light a bit higher. That's better. Don't move an inch."

Karen, at full stretch, smiled resignedly as Fitzgerald called out, "Action!"

Melissa ran into the summerhouse, almost bumping into Matthew. Her hair, which had been so perfect earlier, was now lank and had darkened with the damp. Her camisole looked like someone had thrown a bucketful of water over it.

"Hello," said Matthew.

"I'm sorry," Melissa responded. "I didn't know there was anybody in here. I'm with..."

"Don't apologize," Matthew told her in his honeyed voice. "I came in here to get out of the rain, the same as you. I'm only a visitor here myself. Let me introduce myself. I'm..."

Watching them, Jon was surprised by how calm his sister was, how natural. Maybe she *could* act, after all. It annoyed him. Didn't she have enough going for her already?

Fitzgerald didn't make them finish the scene.

"Cut!" he called out. "We've got enough. Let's move into the house."

What happened next seemed to take place in slow motion. The lights went off. Outside, the rain suddenly became even stronger and the summerhouse turned darker. Jon felt as though he was under water.

His sister and Brett Johnson started to walk off the set. Behind them, Karen relaxed, put down the light she'd been holding, and followed them. When she reached the precise spot where Jon's sister had been standing a moment before, there was a crashing noise. Shards of glass filled the air. Karen looked up, as did Jon. A huge camera was falling from the broken window, trailing gaffa tape and rope. Karen tried to move, but wasn't quick enough. The camera smashed into her head, knocking the small woman to the ground.

Brett was the first to get to her. Jon wasn't far behind. He looked up at the hole in the ceiling, where rain was beginning to pour through. He thought he saw a shadow moving, but couldn't be sure. Then he turned his attention to Karen.

"How is she?" Jon asked Brett.

The actor shook his head and called to a crew member. "Get an ambulance. And get something to cover her up with."

Sarah came and stood by Jon. It was the first time they'd met in four months, but Sarah said nothing. Members of the crew tried to lift the camera off Karen's body. Brett stood up and turned to Sarah.

"Don't look," he said. "The camera smashed her face in. It's not a pretty sight."

Sarah turned to Jon.

"That could have been me," she told him.

Immediately, people surrounded Sarah, comforting her. Jon edged away. It was as though Sarah was the one who had died, not Karen. The lighting director's lifeless body lay sprawled across the summerhouse floor. Jon stared at it in horror. He'd never seen a dead person before. Karen's face was turned away from him. She didn't look dead at all. She looked like she would get up at any moment and tease him for being so worried, then order him to put the broken camera away.

Jon left his sister with Brett Johnson and the others, and ran outside into the heavy rain. Had there been someone in the tree? If there had been, there wasn't now. There were no longer any by-standers either, though there had been a dozen watching the filming earlier. Everyone but Jon was under cover. He stayed out in the rain, trying to take in what had happened. Only minutes before, Karen had been flirting with him. Now she was dead. How could life end so quickly, so meaninglessly? Jon stood by the tree as water splashed down his face, watching shadows in the rain.

4

"You can't blame yourself," Sarah told Jon. They were sitting together in her trailer, waiting for the police. It wasn't a joyous reunion. Sarah had apologized for not greeting him earlier. There hadn't been a spare moment, she said.

"I feel responsible," Jon told her.

"It wasn't your job to attach the camera to the tree."

"But I was up there."

"Yes, and you put some extra tape on to secure it. I watched you. If it hadn't been for that, the thing might have given way before. Ten seconds earlier and that camera would have landed directly on me!"

"There's something else," Jon told her. "I thought I saw someone, or something, up there in the tree."

Sarah frowned. "It must have been your imagination."

Jon shook his head.

"Or a squirrel," Sarah said.

"That camera was secure. I know," Jon insisted.

"That camera weighed half a tonne. And the rain suddenly got heavier. The weight was too much. It was an accident."

"I'm not sure."

They were joined by Leo Fitzgerald, who looked unnaturally calm. He spoke to Jon.

"The police are on their way. Please don't blame yourself in any way. It was a tragic, freak accident. If anyone's to blame, it was me. We should have used scaffolding." He turned to Sarah. "We're going to suspend filming for a while. I'll get someone to drive you back to the hotel."

"Do you want me to stay with you?" Sarah asked her brother.

"No. I'll be OK."

While he was waiting for the police, Jon walked over to the camera in the summerhouse. Karen's body had been taken away by the ambulance workers, but there was a tiny patch of blood on the floor by the camera. Jon looked at the black masking tape, trying to work out where it had split, and why. Despite what his sister had said, the camera didn't weigh that much, probably less than he did.

And then there was the rope ... it hadn't torn, as you would have expected, but seemed to have unravelled. Yet Jon was sure that the knots had been tight. He'd had trouble moving the camera around. Had he loosened them somehow? Was Karen's death his fault? What if her death wasn't an accident? No, that was absurd. What else could it be?

"Mr Wood?"

"Yes."

"Detective Sergeant Wilson. Can I have a word?"

Jon answered the policewoman's questions about what had happened. At first the questions were gentle, but as they went on, the interview turned into a grilling.

"Are you trained in safety procedures for such circumstances?"

"No."

"What qualifications did you have for operating the camera?"

"None. But I wasn't operating it, I was securing it. They asked me to do it because I'm light and good at climbing trees."

" 'Good at climbing trees'," the sergeant said aloud as she wrote it down in her notebook. "I'm sure that will impress the jury at the inquest."

"But look," Jon said, "I'm not sure that the camera falling *was* an accident. I thought I saw someone moving in the tree just after it fell. And if you examine the way the tape's been torn..."

"That's enough," the policewoman said, like a teacher silencing an impertinent pupil. Jon shut up.

"Listen," the sergeant went on, more kindly. "I expect you blame yourself for what happened. You shouldn't. I blame the people who were supposed to be in charge. But don't start making up stories about sabotage. The dead woman has a family. Silly stories at the inquest would upset them. Do you follow me?"

"Yes," said Jon. "But the tape..."

"Forensic will look at it. You can go now."

* * *

Jon slunk away. Most of the crew had gone back to the hotel. He should join them there and await instructions, but he didn't feel like being around film people at the moment. He felt like being alone. The rain was easing off. He walked towards the woodland on the edge of the estate.

"Hey!"

He had bumped into a figure in a hooded anorak, coming out of the woods. "Sorry," he told the youth. "I was miles away."

The youth gave him a sullen look.

"I saw you earlier. You're not Luke Kelly, are you?"

Jon shook his head.

"You look like him."

"If you say so."

The youth removed his hood. He had long, straggly, fair hair and a pallid, spotty face.

"You're working on the film though?"

"That's right."

"What was that big crash an hour ago? I was sheltering from the rain. When I came out of the woods an ambulance was leaving and the police were arriving."

"There was an accident. A camera fell on someone and she got killed."

"She?"

"One of the crew."

The youth shook his head. "Bummer! That's why everyone's leaving, huh?"

"That's right."

"Dangerous business, the movies. Look, I hope you don't mind me asking, but, like, is there any chance of me getting a job on the film? Extra, runner, cook – I'd do anything. What did this woman do?"

Jon shrugged. Karen had been dead less than an hour and already someone was trying to get her job.

"I'm not the one to ask," he told the youth. "It's my first day in the business. I'm the lowest of the low."

"How did you get your job?" the youth asked.

Jon evaded answering precisely. "Favour from a friend."

The boy nodded. "Connections. It's all about connections." He started to walk away. "Thanks anyway."

"Hold on," said Jon, not sure whether to be suspicious of the guy or sorry for him. "What's your name? If I hear anything..."

"People call me 'Slacker'," the youth said. "Call me that if you like."

"And where do you live?"

"I'll be around," Slacker told him. "You'll see me."

"I'll see you around, then. My name's Jon."

"See you, Jon."

That guy could be me, Jon thought as he walked away. Nothing to do all summer, hanging around pathetically for a taste of the action. Maybe Jon would be able to put in a word for Slacker. That was if he still had a job himself, after what had happened today.

By the next day, at the hotel, nobody was discussing the accident, as though talking about it might bring on further bad luck. Karen's body would be flown home, Jon learned. A replacement for her had been hired already. The studio would probably be fined for breaking safety procedures. Karen's family would get an out-of-court settlement. It seemed that Slacker was right: this sort of thing happened all the time.

Jon went to the bar. There, all the talk centred on Luke Kelly. The teen idol was due to arrive the next day. He wouldn't be on location for the whole shoot, as he was booked to star in another movie in five weeks' time.

"What's he like?" Jon asked Todd, his room-mate, remembering what Karen had told him earlier.

Todd grinned salaciously. "Luke likes to party, in every sense of the word. But he's not ... you know, one of those brat-pack types. He's a loner. Never keeps a girlfriend longer than it takes to make a picture. Doesn't have any friends outside the business. He's a little weird, I guess, but a lot of people get that way when they make it early."

Jon nodded, thinking about his sister. How was she handling fame? He'd seen so little of her over the last year that it was hard to be sure.

"How old is Kelly?" he asked.

"Twenty-two, three, something like that. Made his first film five years ago, playing one of the Beach Boys. *Surf's Up*. See it?"

Jon shook his head.

"Lousy movie. Even the cover versions of the songs were dreadful. But Luke took his shirt off a lot, and it was a hit with teenage girls. He got the lead role in the first *Cool College* feature and he had it made. He's been taking his shirt off ever since."

Jon laughed.

"There is one thing about Luke," Todd went on. "He's big on practical jokes. You wake up in the morning and there's a horse's head on your pillow, or you get in your car and find someone's filled it with sand, that'll be Luke."

"He sounds like a fun kind of guy," Jon said sarcastically.

Todd looked like he was going to say something, then glanced downwards instead. One of the other actors must have come into the room. You didn't badmouth actors in front of their colleagues – that was something which Jon had already learned. All actors were notoriously insecure, and would assume that you were saying similar things about them. Jon turned round to see who had walked into the room.

"Hi," said his sister.

"Hi," Jon mumbled.

Sarah was wearing jeans and a T-shirt. She looked like a normal person for once. Some of the colour had returned to her face since the day before. They gave each other a hug.

"You eaten yet?" Sarah asked him.

"Not hungry."

"Come to the restaurant with me. I could use some company."

Jon gave Todd a reluctant shrug, and joined Sarah. He could hardly not go with his sister. She had got him the job, after all, and the accident yesterday must have been as big a shock for her as it was for him. But he couldn't help resenting the way she had asked him.

Several of the other actors and the director were in the restaurant. There was a kind of pecking order, Jon realized. The talent ate first. The crew came later. He shouldn't be here.

Fitzgerald nodded at Sarah.

"Chef tells me the chicken's very good," he said.

"Maybe," Sarah said, "but I'm a vegetarian."

They sat at a table on their own. Jon ordered the chicken, Sarah asked for stuffed peppers.

"What have you been doing?" she asked him.

He told her about the set he'd been working on at Bradlington Hall.

"How about you?" he asked when he'd finished.

"I've been reading the script, or what they've given me of it. They won't explain the ending – Leo says they've got someone in Hollywood working on a rewrite."

"What's the script like?"

Sarah shrugged. "I'm no judge. I've never read one before. Come up to my room later. I'd like your opinion."

"In other words", Jon said, "you don't like it."

"There are one or two things I'm not..."

She looked up. Three waiters were bringing in large silver salvers, which had covers on to keep the chicken hot. Ceremoniously, they deposited each of the salvers on the film entourage's tables at precisely the same moment. Jon hadn't realized that this was so posh a hotel. From the kitchen came a loud, stagey voice, speaking in a mock English accent.

"*Dinner is served.*"

On the last word, each of the waiters whipped off the covers to the salvers. Three chickens began to hurtle across the tables, their feathers flying everywhere. Blood spattered the tablecloth. Jon saw that the chickens' heads had been cut off.

Someone screamed. Sarah flinched and grabbed Jon's arm in shock. He looked around. In the entrance to the dining area, various members of the crew were looking on, laughing hysterically.

The chickens were dead within seconds.

"Who's that?" Sarah asked.

A man in a white coat and a huge chef's hat came out of the kitchen, grinning demoniacally. When he whipped the hat off his head, Jon recognized him at once. It was Luke Kelly.

5

Sarah recognized the film star when he took his hat off. She felt sickened, humiliated. There was blood on her T-shirt. Across the table from her, Jon looked angry. At the entrance to the dining-room, members of the crew were laughing, as though this was a huge joke. The director and the people sitting around him started to laugh awkwardly too. They didn't want to offend the big American star. Only Brett Johnson remained stony-faced. Jon stood up, his face brittle with anger.

"Let's go and eat somewhere else."

Sarah pulled her brother back towards his seat.

"No, we'd better stay. I've got to work with him, even if he is a jerk. Would you hold our table while I change my T-shirt?"

Jon nodded, sitting down reluctantly. Sarah had to walk past Kelly and the crew to get upstairs. She avoided looking at the American actor.

"Hey!"

Luke Kelly grabbed Sarah by the forearm as she passed him. She turned to face him. In the flesh he was even better looking than on the pictures she'd pinned to her wardrobe door. Somehow, this made her feel even angrier.

"Let go of me!"

Kelly smirked his famous smirk.

"A woman with a temper. I like that. Leo tells me that we're going to fall in love."

Sarah almost blushed. For the last four months, she'd been having day-dreams about Luke Kelly. In them, he would ask her out while they were making the film. Had Fitzgerald somehow guessed this?

"Pardon?" she said to the actor.

"We fall in love in the movie. I steal you from my daddy."

"Is that right?" Sarah snapped. "I haven't got that far in my copy of the script. I'll take a look at it now, when I'm upstairs, getting rid of my bloodstained clothes."

Kelly looked a little sheepish.

"Sorry about that. I didn't mean to make you scream, either. It was just my little way of introducing myself."

"It was infantile," Sarah told him. "And cruel. Oh, and that wasn't me screaming. It was one of the waitresses. If you're so sorry about it, why don't you go over and apologize to her?"

"Calm down, Sarah," Leo said. "It was only a little joke."

"No," said Kelly. "She's right." He got up and walked over to the waitress, who was busy removing chicken feathers from the floor.

Sarah didn't watch any further. She went up to her room. Maybe she'd order some dinner on room service, read the rest of the script there. She felt dirty, defiled. She needed a shower.

In her room, Sarah undressed, throwing the cotton T-shirt into a bin. It wasn't worth saving. The blood would never come out properly. In the shower booth, she turned the water onto hot, then tucked her hair into a shower cap and increased the pressure so that it pounded her body. Maybe she wouldn't eat at all. She'd have an early night. She had to be on set at six in the morning.

The shower refreshed her. She'd get that script read before she went to bed. She turned off the water, and was about to get out of the booth when she thought she heard a noise. She listened carefully. Water still dripped from the shower nozzle, but she heard what sounded like a door opening and closing. Then there was a voice. Sarah couldn't distinguish the words. It must be next door, she told herself. She was nervous for no reason. Pulling the shower curtain aside, she reached for her towel. Then she heard footsteps.

Sarah stepped back into the shower booth and pulled the curtain to, concealing herself. Who was in her room? What did they want? She stood stock still in the shower, hoping that whoever it was would go away. She felt rattled. The lighting director's death had unsettled her. Jon's suggestion that it wasn't an accident was even more unnerving. What if...? But no, that was too preposterous.

Who was at the door? It couldn't be the maid, not at this time of the evening. Suppose it was Luke Kelly, playing another practical joke? The footsteps were coming towards her. Someone was calling her name, but she couldn't hear the voice properly because of the dripping shower nozzle.

"Sarah?"

If it was Kelly, she wanted a towel around her. Sarah told herself not to be nervous. She wasn't in any danger here, not in a hotel in the Home Counties. She pushed the shower curtain aside and reached to the rail for the large white bath towel that was hanging there.

"Sis!"

Sarah jumped as her brother poked his head into the bathroom.

"There you are. I was worried about you. You said you'd come straight back down."

Sarah stepped out of the shower, relieved.

"I'm sorry," she said. "I forgot. I just..."

Jon began to laugh.

"You're white as a sheet," he said, "and you look really silly in that shower cap."

Sarah laughed too.

"Let's get some supper on room service," she said. "And we can look at the script together. Is that OK?"

"Fine by me," Jon said. "The atmosphere in that dining-room's turned poisonous."

Sarah dressed in the bathroom while Jonathon ordered food. Then he kicked off his shoes and they sat on the bed reading the loose pages of the script. Sarah picked up from where she had left off earlier. The script wasn't complete, but there was enough of it for her to see that Luke Kelly had been telling the truth. She had two passionate love scenes with him. Now that she'd found out he was so obnoxious, how was she going to handle them?

When Jon got to the love scene pages, he burst out laughing. "I see you get to undress Luke Kelly. That should be fun."

Sarah frowned. "He's the one with the sense of humour."

"You used to like him," Jon said. "Didn't you?"

Sarah cringed. There were some things you didn't need an older brother around to remind you about.

"You won't tell anyone, will you?"

"Now would I do a thing like that?" Jon replied, teasing her.

Sarah thumped her brother with a pillow.

"You'd better not, or I'll ... I'll..."

Jon grabbed the other pillow and held it over her head. "You'll what?"

As they swung pillows at each other there was a knock on the door. Sarah burst into a fit of giggling. There was another knock.

"Yes?" Jon said, finally recovering himself.

"Room service."

They kept reading as they ate their food, getting the script greasy.

"What do you think?" Sarah asked, when her brother had got to the last page.

Jon was diplomatic.

"You've certainly got a big part. Are they paying you enough?"

"My agent will sort that out. What do you think of the story?"

Jon shrugged. "It reminds me of that old Hitchcock movie, *Suspicion,* with Brett Johnson in the role that Cary Grant played. Is he a wife-killer, or is he perfectly innocent? You're never sure if the wife's in danger or not. In this screenplay, the writer doesn't seem to have made up his mind."

"Was Cary Grant guilty in the end?" Sarah asked.

Jon shook his head. "Hitchcock meant him to be, but the studio made him go for a typical Hollywood compromise ending. Anyhow, the twist in this script is the Luke Kelly character. Is he what his father says he is: a no-good, scrounging waster? Or does he really have the lowdown on the father, who marries models then murders them? I think the current ending's a bit weak."

"Maybe you think they should make me into the villain?"

"Interesting idea," Jon said, "but I don't think it'd fit. Anyway, the film's got to finish with you in the arms of the hero."

"That's a relief," Sarah said. "At least you don't think that I'm going to get killed."

Jon smiled. "You're kidding. How many films have you seen? They never kill the beautiful girl. She's got to kiss the hero in the final scene."

Sarah looked at her watch. It was nearly ten.

"We'd better get to bed. Early start in the morning."

Jon nodded. "I have to be on set an hour before you do."

He paused, deciding whether to say something.

"You know, I thought – from what I saw before the accident – you were good today. I was impressed."

Sarah was impressed too. She couldn't remember the last time her brother had praised her.

"Thanks," she said. "That means a lot to me. G'night."

"G'night."

A moment after he had gone, there was a knock on the door. Sarah noticed that her brother's trainers were still on the floor. He might be able to walk around the hotel barefoot, but he'd need them in the morning.

"Come in, stupid!"

The door opened.

"How did you know I was stupid?"

Sarah looked up to see the grinning face of Luke Kelly.

"What do you want?" she snapped.

"Aw, come on," Kelly gave her his famous "who, me?" smile. "Please don't bite my head off. I came to apologize. I was waiting for you to come back downstairs. Then, when you didn't, I found out which room was yours. I've been standing round the corner. I didn't want to embarrass you by walking in on you and your boyfriend."

"Who told you that he's my boyfriend? He's..."

Kelly grinned. Already, she realized with irritation, he had her on the defensive.

"Hey," he said, "I don't want to pry into your private life. Who you hang around with is your concern. Right?"

"Right."

Let him think that Jon's my boyfriend, Sarah decided. What does it matter?

"But I hope we can be friends," Luke went on. "We got off on the wrong foot. I'm sorry."

He offered her his hand, smiling sheepishly. "Apology accepted?"

"Apology accepted, I guess."

His hands were surprisingly soft and warm. There was a twinkle in his eyes as he said goodnight. He's awfully good-looking, Sarah thought, as she shut the door on him, and locked it; but he's far too fond of himself for his own good.

She got into bed, but, although she was tired, found it hard to sleep. Her mind kept going over the last two tumultuous days. One thought stuck with her. Suppose Jon's earlier suspicions were right? Suppose the lighting director's death wasn't an accident?

When she finally slept, Sarah's dreams were filled with odd images. Grinning gargoyles in chef's hats fell from trees. Then, before they could hit the ground, the gargoyles turned into smiling, seductive film stars. At one point she dreamt that she woke, and that somebody was in the room with her. Each dream was punctuated by a dead, dark-haired body, sometimes on the summerhouse floor, sometimes falling from a car. And all the while, in every dream, Sarah had the sense that she was being watched. But why, and by whom, she couldn't say.

6

Melissa gazed into Matthew's eyes. They had just spent a wonderful afternoon together, boating on the lake. But now it was time for her to go.

"I love you," Matthew said. "Don't leave me."

Melissa stroked his hand.

"You're a wonderful man, but I've only known you for a few days. You've got a past that I know nothing about. And you're so much older than I am."

"None of that counts. All that matters is the future, *our* future. I can make you happy, Melissa. No one else can make you as happy as I can. If you think I'm wrong, tell me."

He was holding her tightly now. The script called for him to get back in the boat in a moment. But they were in the wrong positions. Sarah tried not to think about this as she said her lines.

"I think I love you, Matthew. But I'm scared..."

"Don't be scared, my darling. Be brave. Marry me."

"Oh, Matthew..."

The actor relinquished her now and took a step backwards.

"Don't answer me now. I'll come back tonight. Tell me your decision the—"

As he was speaking, Brett took another step backwards and lost his footing. He slid, landing on his bottom in the motor boat.

"Cut!"

Everybody was laughing, except Brett.

"Are you all right?" Sarah asked, getting into the boat with him. "That was a nasty fall."

Brett sat up. "I think only my dignity is hurt." He called to the director. "What went wrong there?"

"You got carried away," Fitzgerald called. "Moved out of position. We'll rehearse it again before the next take. Do you remember how to start the boat?"

"Good question," Brett replied. He smiled at Sarah. "I'm not the world's most practical man."

He reached for the cord coming out of the engine. "I pull this, don't I?"

"That's right."

Brett pulled it, and the engine roared into life.

"At least it works," Brett said. The boat pulled away from the quay.

"How do I stop it?" Brett called over the engine noise, as the boat strained the rope holding it.

"Try pulling the cord again."

Brett did, but the cord gave way in his hands. The actor cursed. As he spoke, the small speedboat snapped its line to the quay, and hurtled off into the lake. Brett swore again.

"Any idea how to steer this thing?" he asked Sarah, who was sitting at the end farthest from the engine. As the boat picked up speed, Sarah shook her head and clambered towards him. Brett reached for the steering wheel. Sarah tried to stay calm, but the boat was going faster still. She had to work out how to switch the engine off.

On the quay, members of the crew began gesticulating at them. Then Sarah saw the reason why. Blue flames were starting to streak around the engine. Black smoke poured into the air as the flames grew bigger. They were on fire. Sarah turned to Brett.

"Jump off!" she called.

"I can't."

"We're on fire. You have to."

"I can't. I'm afraid of water. I can't swim!"

Sarah pulled out the one lifejacket attached to the deck. "Then take this, before it's too late. Now!"

Brett let Sarah put the yellow jacket round his neck. Then, quickly, without looking back, she dived into the water.

The lake was dirty and deep. As Sarah surfaced, several metres away from the boat, she heard an enormous bang. Looking over, as her eyes cleared, she saw that the engine had exploded. The whole boat was aflame. Noxious, oily smoke drifted over to her, making it difficult to breathe. She dipped underwater again, trying to swim back towards the quay, hoping that Brett had jumped off in time.

Sarah surfaced again, unable to see Brett or the shore through the smoke. Did the crew have a lifeboat? She had no idea. She went under once more in order to avoid the smoke which was starting to suffocate her. Her clothes were too heavy. They were dragging her down. She managed to kick off her shoes, then swam away from the smoke, surfacing again in cleaner air.

She took a few gulps of air and looked around. She still couldn't see the shore.

It amazed her that Brett couldn't swim. But Sarah wasn't that good a swimmer herself. A handful of lengths was usually her limit, and she didn't like to linger in the deep end. What made it worse now was that she didn't know in which direction she was going. The quay could be anywhere. Maybe it was hidden by the smoke. She could see some green land, a hundred metres or so away. It could be the shore, or it could be the little island in the middle of the lake. Either way, she would be safe there. Sarah swam towards it.

A hundred metres wasn't far. But in cold, clammy water, with a soaked summer dress, she couldn't move quickly. And the smoke from the burning engine must have got into her lungs, too. She was finding it hard to breathe properly. Where was everybody? She was getting nearer to land. She could make out detail. But she was slowing down. She could see grass, trees. There was someone standing in the trees, watching her. Why didn't he come and help her? Sarah's legs were tired. She couldn't go much further. And her head ached. How it ached!

She relaxed for a moment and took in a mouthful of water. Summoning all her strength, she lifted her head up and spluttered the water out. But then she was coughing and going under again. It wasn't fair. She was so close. It wasn't...

"Here. Grab on to me."

Strong arms reached around her shoulders.

"Just let your body relax. Let me swim you to the shore."

Sarah felt herself moving more quickly. Then she began to lose consciousness.

"Don't pass out," said the familiar, reassuring voice. "You've got to keep breathing. It's not far now."

Somehow, Sarah managed to keep her head above water.

The next thing she knew, she was on dry land, being given mouth-to-mouth resuscitation by the crew nurse. Her body convulsed for a moment, then she vomited up the rest of the putrid water she had swallowed.

"She'll be all right now," Sarah heard the nurse saying. Then her brother was standing over her.

"How do you feel?" he asked, tenderly.

"I'll live. How's Brett?"

"They're just bringing him in now. But he'll be all right. He had a lifejacket on but you had to swim all that way. You nearly made it."

"Was it you," Sarah asked, gratefully, "who brought me in?"

Jon shook his head.

"I wasn't here. They sent to the house for me. It was him." He pointed to the figure sitting on the lawn in wet boxer shorts, talking to the director. Sarah's heart pounded heavily. Her life had been saved by Luke Kelly.

"Come on," said the nurse. "We're going to get you back to the hotel and into a hot shower and a warm bed for a while."

"I need to thank..."

"You can do that later. Help me with her, would you, Jon?"

Jon and the nurse lifted her into a waiting Land Rover. Her brother offered to go with her but Sarah refused.

"Speak to Luke for me, would you?" she asked him. "Say..."

"I know what to say. Take care of yourself."

"OK."

The Land Rover started off, then slowed down again by the quay. The nurse got out and returned with Brett Johnson. He looked pale.

"You showed great presence of mind there," he told Sarah. "If you hadn't put that lifejacket on me, I might..."

"Don't be silly," Sarah told him. "But I'm surprised at a big grown man like you, never learning to swim."

"It's a phobia," Brett told her. "My shrink reckons I must have been thrown into deep water somewhere when I was a child, and never recovered. She can't cure me of it. I used to keep it secret, but the scandal sheets 'exposed my weakness' when they were dumping on me a few years back."

"That's a nasty thing to do," Sarah told him, sleepily. Then her head became woozy again and she passed out.

When his sister had gone, Jon walked over to the young American. Someone had given Luke a towel and he was drying himself off.

"Sarah asked me to thank you for what you did."

Kelly nodded brusquely. "It was nothing. Anybody would have done it. I just happened to be nearest."

A girl from Costume came over. "We've got some substitute clothes lined up. If you'd like to come to the trailer..."

"In a minute." He smiled at Jon. "The show goes on. They're going to film my first scene. I stand by the shore, watching my father, jealous of his lusty young fiancée. Why did I agree to do this junk?"

Jon felt no need to be diplomatic. "Because it's got more class than *Cool College 5*?"

Luke raised his hands in mock surrender. "True, that's the film I'm making next. But the only class in this film comes from your girlfriend."

"Girlfriend?" Jon asked, awkwardly. "You mean Sarah?"

"You're a lucky guy. She's something special."

"That's as may be, but she's not my girlfriend."

"Oh, come on," said Luke, with a glint in his eye. "What were you doing in her room late last night? Why did Leo send for you when she nearly drowned?"

"Because," Jon explained slowly, "she's my sister."

Luke blinked. "You're kidding?" he said. He looked closely at Jon's face. "No, I can see you're not."

"You're right. I'm not."

Kelly smiled. "In that case," he said, "I hope the two of us can be friends."

He offered Jon his hand. Jon was reluctant to take it but, after all, Kelly had just saved his sister's life ... maybe. They shook hands.

"Gotta go," Luke told him. "Clothes to wear, scenes to shoot. Maybe we can have a drink together in the bar tonight."

"Yes," said Jon. "Maybe."

When Luke had gone, Jon tried to work out what Luke meant when he said "in that case". He thought he knew. Luke had planned to take Jon's girlfriend away from him. Now that he knew she wasn't his girlfriend, the two of them could be friends. If that was the way Hollywood stars acted, Jon wanted no part of it.

Jon walked back towards the lake where the remains of the boat had been dragged on to the shore. As he turned out of sight of the crew, a familiar long-haired figure came out of the woodland.

"Hi, Jon! How are you?"

"I'm OK," Jon replied, reluctant to call the youth Slacker, which he thought was a stupid name. "But I haven't had an opportunity to ask about a job for you. There's been too much going on."

"That's all right," Slacker said. "I know it's a long shot. Was that Luke Kelly I saw you talking to just now?"

"That's right," said Jon, wondering why the youth was so interested in Kelly.

"What's he like?"

"About as funny as a headless chicken," Jon replied, listlessly.

Slacker looked confused. "People say he's a bit of a brat. How's he getting on with Brett Johnson?"

"I wouldn't know," Jon replied.

He was suddenly suspicious. Suppose Slacker was a stringer for one of the newspapers? He seemed very inquisitive, for a fan. The crew were under strict instructions not to let out any gossip from the set.

"Why do you hang around here all the time?" Jon asked the youth.

"I'm just after a job, like yours, you know? I'm on the dole. I'd like to get into a film school, but I haven't got the qualifications. If I could get some experience..."

"If I were you," Jonn said, in a cordial but distanced voice, "I'd try and talk to the casting director or the location manager."

"I'd be willing to work for free..."

"The most they can do is say 'no'," Jon told him. "Everyone'll be moving over to the house after they shoot a short scene with Luke in it. Maybe you can catch them then."

"Thanks," said the youth. "I appreciate it."

"You're welcome."

When Slacker had gone, Jon examined the boat. What remained of the engine was a charred ruin. The hulk of the boat was intact, but badly burnt. Could someone have sabotaged it in some way? There was no way for Jon to tell. One accident proved nothing. Even two could still be a coincidence. A third would prove sabotage. But what happened if the culprit was third time lucky?

Back at the hotel, Sarah collapsed on to her bed.

"Just an accident," Leo had insisted. "There was no real danger."

Not to Brett, perhaps, in his lifejacket, but she had never felt more scared. Sarah resolved not to put herself near any risky situations for the rest of the film.

Although she felt knocked out by her ordeal, she couldn't sleep. Finally, she sat up. She would read the script again, making sure that she could insist on safety precautions for every possibility. There was a fire scene, for instance: she wanted lots of extinguishers, a doctor – you name it. And she'd better ask about the ending. If there was going to be some kind of chase across the roof of Bradlington Hall, as Leo was considering, then she wanted a stunt double.

Sarah leant down to pick up her script where she'd left it that morning, beside the bed. It wasn't there. She felt under the bed. Nothing but the sneakers Jon had left the night before. Where was the script? She must have taken it with her this morning. But no, she had learnt her lines. There'd been no need. Maybe a maid had been in, tidied it away. Sarah was too tired to get up and look for it now. Anyway, who would want a script? It had no financial value.

Suddenly, she felt very tired. She'd find the script when she woke up. And, if she'd mislaid it, she could always get another one. Her mind drifted off into shallow, dreamless sleep.

7

Film-making, Jon decided, was another world, where the normal rules no longer applied. Whatever disasters occurred, however little sleep you got, the demands of the moment swept you along. When Sarah and Brett returned to the set the next day, both looking only a little the worse for wear, there was a spontaneous round of applause from the crew and the rest of the cast. But then it was straight into work. They were filming the ballroom scene.

Extras flooded the house. Jon noticed Slacker, with his hair tied back, dressed as a waiter. He must have talked his way into a job, after Jon's advice that morning. That was good, because it would get him off Jon's back. Slacker couldn't be in Equity, the actors' union, but then, neither was Jon. Leo bent rules, or simply ignored them, all the time. He was short of extras, so everyone pitched in.

Jon was dressed in a tuxedo, the first time he'd ever worn one, and paired with a glamorous girl who had played one of the models the day before.

"How many movies have you been in?" she asked.

"None. This is the first."

"Mine too. I'm Mary."

"Jon."

"You must have done some acting … on the stage?"

Jon shook his head. "I'm not an actor. I'm just a … general dogsbody. I'm doing this for the experience, before I go to university."

"Film school?"

"Hardly. Media Studies and Humanities. How about you?"

"I get by," Mary said, casually. "I had a walk-on in *Casualty* recently. I've got some auditions coming up." She glanced over Jon's shoulder. "You know what makes me really sick?"

"What?"

"People like her." Mary pointed at Jon's sister. "She's got a career already, modelling. Fitzgerald has half a dozen hot actresses audition for the role, then goes and hires some tramp who's never acted in her life. I'll bet they're an item."

"I don't think so," said Jon, diplomatically. "Maybe she got lucky. It's the way of the world – those who have, get more."

"Isn't it just!"

"Action!" the director called.

Matthew and Melissa were in the middle of the ballroom, dancing, when suddenly Matthew stopped.

"What is it?" Melissa asked, concerned.

"Somebody I didn't expect to see."

"You want to leave?"

Slowly, Matthew shook his head. "It's all right. He's seen us now."

The steadicam tracked Aidan, walking across the crowded dance floor towards Melissa and Matthew. Aidan's face was sombre, emotionless. The two men faced up to each other in silence. Finally, as the music ended, Matthew spoke.

"Melissa, this is my son, Aidan."

"Your *son*?"

"Aidan, this is my fiancée, Melissa."

"*Fiancée?* Again?"

Melissa gave a small start when Aidan said the word *again*. Jon's sister and Luke Kelly looked at each other with their eyes on fire. Was that acting, Jon wondered? Or was it a result of what had happened the day before, when Luke rescued Sarah?

"Perhaps," Aidan said, "I could have this dance with my stepmother-to-be?"

The band struck up a waltz. Matthew held on to Melissa.

"Not today, Aidan. Maybe at the wedding … *if* you're invited."

Aidan bowed curtly and walked off, straight in front of Jon and Mary.

"Cut!"

"Oh, that was brilliant!" said Mary.

"Did you think so?" Jon asked her. He'd thought Sarah's acting was OK, but not brilliant.

"Yes. The way he walked past us. There's no way they can cut us out of that scene now. We're bound to be in the finished film."

The extras were moved away while Fitzgerald shot the next scene, where Matthew and Melissa had their first argument. Jon watched as his sister did a convincing job of losing her temper.

"Is there anything else you're keeping from me? Are you sure that you don't have any *grandchildren* I should know about?"

"Aidan's my only child."

"What did he mean when he said *again*? How many times have you been married?"

"I don't like to talk about my marriages."

"Why not? I love you, Matthew. But we can't make a life together if you keep secrets from me."

"I promise, darling. I'll tell you everything, in time."

"I'm not sure if I can wait that long."

Melissa, her eyes artificially watering with nitroglycerine, walked away.

Sarah was exhilarated. She hadn't realized how much fun acting would be, compared to modelling. Some things were the same: the waiting around; the constant attention; the endless make-up and wardrobe sessions. Preparation took up more time than anything else. But what Sarah enjoyed was *performing.* They did three takes of the scene where she argued with Brett and each one was different. It was the excitement of never knowing exactly what was going to happen next which made the job so exciting.

One thing disturbed her. As Sarah walked off, she passed an actor who looked naggingly familiar. He was tall and thin, with his hair tied back, because he was dressed as a waiter. Sarah tried to figure out where she had seen him before, but wasn't sure.

Luke caught up with her as she was going into her trailer to get changed. He was still in his tuxedo. His curly brown hair was tousled. He looked just like he did in the first film she had seen him in: *Cool College*.

She stopped on the steps of the trailer.

"I didn't get the chance to thank you properly for what you did yesterday," she told him. She had slept most of the time since then. Luke shrugged.

"It was nothing. Anyone else would have done the same. I just happened to get there first."

"It didn't feel like nothing to me."

Luke gave her a sincere smile. "Maybe I offset the lousy impression I made the other night, at least."

"I already forgave you for that."

"Good." His smile became more raffish. "Then let me take a chance on our getting to know each other better. I've heard about a little restaurant about five miles from here. Good food, very quiet. We could go there tonight."

Sarah hesitated long enough to make it seem like she had to think about it. "I'm busy tonight," she lied.

"Tomorrow then. The day after's a rest day. We could stay out as late as we wanted."

Sarah continued to hesitate. "Do you promise to be on your best behaviour?" she asked.

"I promise."

"Then I guess I owe you a date."

Back in her room, Sarah got changed slowly, thinking about what she should wear the next evening – which dress, which perfume. Or maybe it would be more cool to put on casual clothes, make it look like she went out with big Hollywood movie stars every day of the week.

Every so often, Sarah had moments where her life stopped seeming real to her. This was one of them. A year ago, she was taking her GCSEs. A date with Luke Kelly was the kind of day-dream that she and her friends confessed to in giggly, girly conversations. All sorts of men had asked Sarah out over the last year, but she'd turned them all down. There hadn't been one of them that she really liked, who had made her feel the way she felt this minute.

There was a knock on her door. Sarah put down the dress she was holding.

"Who is it?"

"Jon."

She let her brother in.

"They sent me with some new pages from the script."

Sarah finished brushing her hair. She remembered that she still hadn't found the script she misplaced earlier.

"What are they like?"

"I haven't read them. I'm not meant to."

Sarah turned round. "I wouldn't have minded. Leave them on the bed. I'll look at them later."

Jon stared at her, then glanced at the bed. "Nice dress. Going out somewhere?"

"Luke's taking me to a restaurant tomorrow."

Jon looked uncomfortable. "How could you date him, after what he did the other night?"

Sarah wished she hadn't told her brother. Jon was overprotective when it came to boyfriends. He didn't think anyone was good enough for his sister and this made her angry.

"It isn't really up to you who I go out with, is it? Remember how you kept trying to put me off your friend Gareth, and Steve Mackay too, when he asked me out?"

"That was years ago. They were…"

Sarah interrupted. "This is my life, Jon. Get your own. You seemed to get on well with that extra, Mary, today. Why don't you see what she's up to?"

"I just can't understand you going out with someone who cuts the heads off chickens."

"He didn't do it himself," Sarah retorted. "And what's the big deal about it? The chickens were going to die anyway. You were going to eat one of them. Or have you become a vegetarian overnight, like me? If I can let it go, why can't you?"

Jon threw his hands in the air and walked out, leaving the new script pages on the bed. Sarah felt upset for a while, but managed to talk herself out of it. He was a little jealous, that was all. It was understandable. Jon might deny it to himself, but he couldn't help being jealous of her success. Sarah's getting into films made it all worse. Films were the one thing Jon knew about and she didn't.

Now Sarah had discovered that she could act. If she was in Jon's shoes, she'd probably feel a bit sick about it, too. But she'd make it right. Jon ought to see that her movie career was an opportunity for him, not a problem. And if he thought she was going to turn down a date with Luke Kelly, who had saved her life, because of one silly practical joke, he had another think coming.

8

Heads turned as Luke and Sarah walked towards their secluded corner table.

"You're being recognized," Sarah told Luke.

"Nonsense," the film star replied. "You're the one they're interested in."

"I'm not that well known."

"Maybe. Maybe not. But the way you look tonight, every guy in the room wants to know you better, and every woman in the room wishes that she was you."

He sat down opposite her, wearing his T-shirt and jeans. Maybe that was what people were really looking at, Sarah thought: a scruffy young man in a restaurant which normally required a jacket and tie. She had opted for a white linen dress with box pleats, the kind of classic which was neither formal nor casual. To her delight, Luke couldn't keep his eyes off her.

"I want to know all about you," he said, after ordering the wine. "Your full life story."

Sarah gave him an edited version. Her first sixteen years took about two minutes to recount.

"Then, in the last year, things started to change."

Luke raised his eyebrows. "Whoa! Hold on! Are you telling me that you're only seventeen?"

"That's right."

He shook his head, brown curls floating over his eyebrows. "You're incredible, you know that? You're going to be huge. Only seventeen. I thought that I made it when I was young."

"How old were you when you made your first picture?"

"Eighteen. Nineteen when it came out, but I claimed to be

twenty. You know how it is with guys. We always want to be older than we really are." He paused. "But we're still talking about you. How did it happen? One minute you're – what did you call it? A *catalogue girl*. The next you're all over fashion magazines, on the cover of *Vogue*, practically a supermodel..."

"Just like that."

"Just like that. How?" Luke asked, as he poured champagne.

Sarah shrugged. "I got lucky. I guess... I was in the right place at the right time. I thought I'd grown too tall, too gawky. I didn't have a big enough chest. But then older girls with a similar kind of look started to make it, and everyone was looking round for younger, new faces with the same kind of appeal. There I was. It was very exciting, but kind of unnerving, too. You dream about something like that happening to you, but when it does, you're too busy to appreciate how glamorous it all is. It just feels like hard work."

"I know what you mean."

"Sometimes I get jealous of my friends. They're at college, they have normal lives, boyfriends ... no pressure. Most of them haven't even thought about a job yet. While here I am, constantly making career moves, like this movie. We can't relate to each other any more. I go back and see them, but it's not the same. I know I've lost them."

Luke nodded sympathetically. "Some people take time out, go to college, pick up their career again later. Jodie Foster did it."

"Yes, and look what happened to her," Sarah replied. "She got stalked by some weirdo who ended up shooting a president. You can't go back, can you? You can't have fame and wealth and then pretend that it never happened."

Luke looked wistful. "I guess you're right," he said thoughtfully. "But I sure as hell keep trying."

"You must have had to grow up quickly too," she said, as their vichyssoise arrived.

"At first I loved it," he said. "I was hanging out with all these cool people. Women started throwing themselves at me. You know, I was a Chicago meat-packer's son, not one of the Hollywood brat pack. I thought I'd arrived in the land of plenty..." He sighed. "But the girls weren't so much interested in me as the guy on the silver screen. Then, after a while, the attention gets real wearing.

You just want to hide. These days, the only women I date are actresses. The only friends I have are the people on whatever movie I'm working on at the time. Sometimes it gets a little lonely and I do crazy things, like the other night."

"Why don't you stop," Sarah suggested, "take a rest for a while?"

Luke leant forward and stroked her hand. "I wouldn't know what to do with myself."

Sarah withdrew her hand and ate some more of her chilled soup. "You're being silly. You'd find things to do."

"Maybe if I had someone like you with me."

Sarah smiled sympathetically. She was on the verge of being bowled over by Luke, yet part of her remained cynical. She might be falling for his standard lonely movie star chat-up line, so she gazed into his clear blue eyes and tried to sound sensible.

"Maybe you need to get away on your own first – find yourself – before you're ready to get into a real relationship."

Luke nodded. "Maybe you're right. When I've finished the film I've got lined up after this one, maybe I'll do just that."

They finished their soup in silence. As soon as the waiter had taken their plates away, a middle-aged woman came over to the table holding a menu.

"I hope you don't mind," she said to Luke, "but my teenage daughter is such a big fan of yours. She'll be so excited when we tell her we saw you. Would you sign this?"

Luke's eyes narrowed. "Don't you know *anything*?" he snapped. "You *never* interrupt stars for autographs until they've finished their meal. Aren't I entitled to a little privacy?"

The woman blushed a deep scarlet and turned away. Sarah felt embarrassed and angry with Luke.

"If you don't go after that woman this moment and apologize," she hissed at him, "I'm walking out of this restaurant right now!"

Luke looked shocked. Without speaking, he got up and went after the woman. Sarah could hear him grovelling, asking for the name of the woman's daughter. He came back.

"It wasn't for her daughter, you know. I could tell. It was for her."

"Who cares?" Sarah said, trying not to raise her voice. "And how can you possibly know? You're so arrogant it amazes me. Two years ago, if my mother had seen you in a restaurant, I'd have killed her if she hadn't tried to get your autograph for me."

"Really?" Luke said. "You were a fan?"

Sarah blushed. "Sort of. There's nothing wrong with being a fan."

"You're right," Luke said. "You know something?"

"What?"

"You're the most real person I've met in years."

He leant forward, nearly singeing his long hair over the flame from the candle. Then he moved the candlestick aside and kissed her, full on the lips. Sarah hesitated for a moment, then kissed him back. It was a long, heavy kiss, which lasted until the food came. Sarah sensed the presence of the waiter, discreetly keeping his distance with their next course in his hands. She pulled gently away and Luke smiled sweetly. No one had ever kissed Sarah that way before. Somehow, she knew that nothing would ever be the same again.

9

Jon walked up to the director's trailer. He was about to knock when he heard the argument going on inside.

"You've ruined the whole thing! What did you think you were doing?"

"It's my call. There's nothing you can do about it."

"You don't think so? Suppose I go to the studio, tell them what you're doing? You think they'll like it if you end up killing the girl?"

"Like I told you, I haven't made my mind up yet."

"What's to make up? Either you..."

A voice spoke in Jon's ear.

"Interesting conversation?" Luke Kelly asked.

Jon was embarrassed. "I ... er ... had a message for Mr Fitzgerald. Now doesn't seem to be a good time."

Kelly nodded. "Sounds like you're right. I had a meeting arranged with Leo, but, heck! Want to go get a beer?"

"Sure."

Jon joined the American in the hospitality trailer. A week had passed since the incident in the dining-room, and there had been no more bad jokes. Luke had been out with Jon's sister twice. Jon wasn't happy about it, but so far the actor seemed to be treating Sarah well.

"Are you enjoying the shoot?" Luke asked Jon, passing him a chilled bottle of Rolling Rock.

"It's hard work," Jon said, "but it's interesting. Leo's fascinating to watch. A lot of the time, he seems to be making it up as he goes along. It's exciting."

"That's right," Luke told him. "There aren't many like him left – none at all in Hollywood. They'll drop him soon."

"Is the business that cruel?" Jon asked.

"Crueller. A handful of directors and stars get big enough to do exactly what they want. But if they relax and have a few flops, the past counts for nothing. Same goes for actors."

"So what keeps you going?"

Luke shrugged. "I'm small fry, expendable. There's another like me along every summer – great pecs, fresh-faced. We have a life expectancy of about five years. Then you can try and go for bigger, more legit roles, like Tom Cruise, or you can take the James Dean route."

"'Live fast, die young, leave a pretty corpse'?"

"That's the one. I'm really hacked off with doing *Cool College* sequels. The film wasn't much good in the first place, but the last two really sucked."

"Why do you have to be in them, then? Couldn't you refuse?"

Luke shook his head. "I signed this stupid restrictive contract when I was eighteen. My agent keeps trying to renegotiate it, but..." He shrugged his shoulders. Jon saw the locations manager walking towards the trailer. It was time to get back to work.

As Jon walked past the director's trailer, a bearded man with dark hair and sunglasses walked out. He had to be from Hollywood, Jon figured. Who else wore shades on an overcast day? Jon decided to use this moment to deliver the message from the locations manager. However, before he could get over to the trailer, Sarah ran over, sheets of pink paper scrunched up in her hand. She didn't see Jon, but walked straight into Fitzgerald's trailer, without knocking.

Jon didn't want to eavesdrop, but he couldn't help hearing the first part of the conversation.

"How can you do this to me? We had a distinct verbal agreement. My agent assured me..."

"Come on, Sarah. You've revealed more than I'm asking on modelling jobs. Professionals think of their bodies as tools, not possessions..."

"Hold it right there!" Sarah interrupted the director. Jon was impressed by his sister's attitude, the way she was standing up to Fitzgerald. "Don't start throwing that *you're a professional and it's only a body* routine at me," Sarah shouted. "It's my body! I own it. I'm not doing this for you, or for anybody, ever! Got it?"

Jon didn't hear Fitzgerald's reply, but he did hear the obscenity his sister threw back at him before she walked out of Leo's trailer and stalked over to her own, oblivious to Jon's presence.

Jon knocked on Fitzgerald's door.

"What is it?"

"Urgent message."

"Come."

"Oh," said Fitzgerald, as Jon entered the room. "It's you." He took the note, read it, and threw it in the bin. Jon turned to go.

"Tell me," said Fitzgerald. "I have half a dozen up and coming American actresses begging me to play the girl torn between Brett Johnson and Luke Kelly, but I go for your sister, give her a big break. Even give her brother a job too."

"So?"

"So, how come she won't lose her clothes for a couple of scenes? Why can't I get her to understand that this isn't art, it's business? I have to sell this movie. And her body is what every hot-blooded American male over the age of thirteen will want to see."

"Was nudity in the script?" Jon asked, politely.

Fitzgerald looked angry. "We're not shooting the script. We're shooting the movie that I want to make."

"But if it's not the movie that Sarah thought she was making, then she's got a point, hasn't she?"

Fitzgerald became angry. "Your sister is a no-talent, minor model who got lucky because we happened to need someone who looked like her. And if she doesn't do whatever is necessary to get this picture made, then she's going to be on the scrap heap before she's old enough to vote!"

Jon didn't know what to say. He admired Fitzgerald, and had nothing against sex on the screen. It seemed hypocritical to him that films could show violence in gory detail but weren't allowed to portray the human body doing something much more natural. But Sarah was his sister. He didn't want to watch her cavorting with Luke Kelly on screen any more than he had to.

"Is there any reply to that message?" he asked, sullenly.

Fitzgerald growled. "Tell him we can discuss the fire scene after dinner tonight."

"OK. 'Bye."

Jon went over to Sarah's trailer. The door was half open. He'd go in and talk it over with her. Then he saw that Sarah wasn't alone.

Luke Kelly was with her.

"He told me I was a lousy actress," Sarah was moaning. "He told me he only hired me for my body."

"You know that's not true," Kelly comforted her. "Everyone says how natural you are, how convincing. He was trying to wind you up so that you'd do what he wants, that's all."

"Why should I have to strip off? It's not in my contract."

"Relax," Luke said. "I'll see him for you, sort it out. If the scene's necessary, he can always get a body double for you."

"Would you talk to him? I'd really appreciate that."

"Of course."

Kelly leant over and put his arms round Jon's sister. They began kissing. Jon backed off as quietly and as quickly as he could manage, bumping into someone as he did.

It was Mary, the actress who'd been his partner in the ballroom scene.

"What are you?" she asked him. "A detective or a pervert?"

Jon smiled awkwardly. He recognized the film dialogue which Mary was teasing him with.

"That's for me to know and you to find out," he replied.

"She's your sister, isn't she?" Mary said. "I'm sorry I bad-mouthed her the other day. I was wrong about her and Leo, anyhow."

"You were."

Mary grinned coquettishly. "She was saving herself for a bigger catch." She walked off, leaving Jon in embarrassed silence. He often found himself in situations like this – on the edge of things, observing. *Never eavesdrop*, his mother had once warned him. *You'll overhear things you're better off not knowing*. Maybe that applied to all three of the conversations he'd overheard this afternoon. Did Fitzgerald really think that Sarah couldn't act? Jon thought she was good, but he was hardly an objective witness, and neither was Luke. Did Luke really care about his sister? Or was he just using her? Would he drop her as soon as the shoot was over?

Jon was so wrapped up in his thoughts that he didn't notice Slacker until the scruffy youth was alongside him outside the canteen.

"How's it going?" Slacker asked. "Know if there are any more crowd scenes I could get a part in?"

"Just one," Jon told him. "They're filming the wedding tomorrow. If you go along to the casting director, they might be short of a body or two."

"Thanks. I appreciate your help. You're Sarah Wood's brother, aren't you?"

"How did you find that out?"

"I hear things. Is it true she's dating Luke Kelly?"

Jon replied curtly with a question of his own. "Are you working for the press?"

Slacker looked affronted. "No. I swear."

"Whatever," Jon said. "It's none of your business."

Jon walked away, thinking about the conversation he'd overheard between Leo and the bearded man – the one about the girl dying. What had it meant? Still, there was no point in getting obsessive about it. This was only a movie, after all. Then he thought about Karen and the exploding boat. He had to watch everything that was going on very carefully, very carefully indeed.

He walked up to the Hall to help prepare for his sister's wedding.

August
10

As the shoot went on, some of the tensions of the first few days seemed to dissolve. Sarah's agent, Sally, negotiated a compromise over the nude scenes the director wanted. A body double would be used for one of Sarah's love scenes with Luke, while she would remain partially clothed for the other. Jon was relieved.

Sarah was still going out with Luke. Jon had to get used to the fact that he wasn't going to see much of his sister any more. The closeness he thought they had was illusory, he now realized. It made him angry at first, but he'd learn to cope with it. Jon used to con himself that he was happy about Sarah's success. Now he knew that he'd been lying to himself because he didn't want to admit how alienated they were from each other. They didn't inhabit the same planet any more, and it was pointless to pretend otherwise.

Anyway, Sarah spent all her free time with Luke Kelly. As Melissa and Aidan's relationship developed onscreen, so the couple became inseparable offscreen. Sarah insisted that Luke was different when you got to know him, that being with her was changing him. Jon affected disinterest. After a few weeks, he avoided conversations with his sister. He spent a lot of time hanging out with Todd, picking up tricks of the trade, gossip, stories – anything that might be useful to him in the future.

Occasionally, Jon managed to slide into conversation with Leo Fitzgerald. You could learn a lot just by hanging around Leo. The director encouraged Jon a little. Now and then he would tease the boy over his curiosity about the unfinished script.

"You know who I learnt a lot from? Roger Corman – the master of the quickie. He could make a film in two days, using recycled sets from the film before. For him, a two-week shoot was a luxury and everyone doubled up their jobs. You know what he used to say about a script? '*What you need is a very good first reel, because people want to know what's going on. Then you need a very good last reel, because people want to know how it all turns out. Everything else doesn't matter.*'"

"You don't believe that?" Jon asked.

"It's probably the best sense I've ever heard in the movies."

Jon wasn't sure if the director was winding him up or not.

When he wasn't around Todd or the director, Jon spent some time with Mary. The actress had been half-promised a small speaking part which was being newly written into the screenplay.

"They're not paying me at the moment," she told Jon, "but I've got free bed and board. It's more fun than sharing a flat with four other actresses in Neasden."

Jon and Mary went out for pub lunches on rest days. At times, they seemed like a couple. Yet, somehow, they never progressed beyond parting pecks on the lips. Jon had never had a serious girlfriend. Mary seemed willing at times, but nothing ever came of it. Maybe it was her, not wanting to throw her pretty self away on a penurious student. Or maybe it was him, avoiding a relationship for reasons which he couldn't put words to, but had something to do with his sister and Luke Kelly.

Soon the final week of shooting approached. Leo was precisely on schedule. So far, all of the film had been shot on location, but the scene they were shooting today could only be done in the studio. Leo had hired Shepherd's Gate, an old studio on the edge of London, an hour's drive from Bradlington. Jon gathered that the director had got a cheap deal because the studio was about to be shut down and demolished.

The studio sound stage was shabby and decrepit. As the crew cleaned up over the weekend, they sneezed endlessly in the dust which had settled everywhere. By Sunday night, Jon felt like he'd crawled through a desert, but the set was in place and ready to be set on fire.

Leo had lived up to his half-promise. Mary had landed a speaking part as Jane, an old friend of Melissa's. Now the two of them were sitting in a replica of Melissa's room at Bradlington Hall. This scene was taking place just before the wedding, as Jane helped Melissa into her wedding dress.

"You look gorgeous," Jane said. "I'm so happy for you."

"Thanks for agreeing to be a bridesmaid at such short notice," Melissa told her. "You saved my life."

"Believe me," Jane said, "I wouldn't have missed this for anything."

Then she paused, noticing the tear which was dripping down onto Melissa's white dress.

"Melissa, what is it? What's wrong?"

Melissa turned her tear-stained eyes to Jane.

"I can't get it out of my mind. Suppose Aidan's been telling the truth? Suppose Matthew did murder all his other wives? Suppose I'm next?"

Jane gave her a hug, then handed her a tissue.

"You know you're being silly," she said. "Matthew's been unlucky, but all three of his wives died in accidents. They weren't murdered. And Aidan's been psychologically disturbed since he was a child. Matthew showed you the doctor's reports. That's why he didn't invite him to the wedding, in case he does something crazy."

"But maybe Aidan's right," Melissa protested. "Maybe I'm the one acting crazy, marrying someone thirty years older than me."

"Either you love him or you don't," Jane told her. "Age doesn't come into it."

Jon watched the monitor as the camera closed in on Sarah's face, showing the doubt in her eyes. How could anyone say that she couldn't act?

"Cut!" Leo Fitzgerald called. "OK, that's a wrap. Let's get on with setting up the fire scene."

Jon hurried into action. This was the most complicated set-up in the film. Minutes after Melissa and Matthew exchanged vows, his sister would be trapped in her room when the building caught fire. All of the other guests would get out. Then Aidan, after an argument with Matthew, would charge back into the building and save Melissa's life.

"Now do you believe me?" he would ask, once they were outside. But Melissa would still be uncertain, knowing that someone set the fire up, but not knowing whether it was the father or the son.

The actual wedding scene had been shot weeks earlier at the stately home. To keep location costs to a minimum, Fitzgerald arranged for the couple to marry in the mansion's chapel, then have the reception in the house. The set had been decorated to look like the house they were supposed to be in. Carpenters had built a mock-up of the west wing. Beyond Sarah's room were two corridors and a staircase. The shots of guests watching the fire from outside would be faked later, using visual overlays during the editing.

The trick with fire scenes, Leo Fitzgerald explained to the crew, was not to burn the actual sets, but to burn the plastic gunk which they had spread over the walls. Timing was crucial. If the first take went wrong, you were left with scorched walls. Two special effects people would have to put out the fires, repaint the walls, then wait for the paint to dry before spreading the flammable gunk all over them again. But the crew only had a day to shoot the whole thing, and it was already getting on for noon.

Sarah sat in the part of the set which was her dressing-room, looking calm. Mary, the extra who had landed the part of the bridesmaid, was on the edge of the set. She had a short scene with Luke Kelly, who was going to go into the fire himself. Fitzgerald had offered Kelly a stuntman double, but Luke wouldn't hear of it.

Jon got onto the crane which was holding the camera for the overhead shots. The previous day he'd been given a temporary promotion, to Camera Assistant, when the woman whose job it was had come down with appendicitis. Jon wouldn't get a credit for this, as he wasn't in the union, but he'd be able to tell people precisely which scenes he'd helped to shoot.

The job wasn't very difficult but Jon took it seriously. He was responsible for the safety of the camera and maintaining the level of film stock. He was tired, having stayed up late the night before, reading the manual, then arriving early this morning to make sure he was fully confident with the equipment.

As the crane lifted into the air, Jon saw Slacker, wearing technician's overalls, standing by a row of fire extinguishers. The youth must have talked his way into a job on the safety crew. Sarah had insisted on maximum safety for this scene and Leo had assured her that there was no risk. Near Slacker, Brett was getting into his position on one of the corridor sets. Who started the fire? Brett or Luke? No one knew. Fitzgerald still hadn't revealed how he intended to end the film. Jon wondered whether the director had even made up his own mind yet.

"We're going for everything in one take," Fitzgerald announced over the tannoy. "This scene's the fulcrum of the film. I want to do this in real time, and I expect you all to be covered in real sweat by the time it's over. I don't want anyone to panic, no matter how hairy things look down there. We've got all the safety angles covered. Now, help me get the shots I need to make this movie a masterpiece. I know we can do it.

"Ready?" the director went on, a little nervousness in his voice. "OK. Everybody into position. Action!"

11

Sarah waited patiently for the scene to begin. This was her most complicated scene, even though she didn't have to learn any lines for it. Mainly she had to react – to the smoke coming in through the door, to the flames surrounding her in the corridor. She had to look out of a window and consider whether to jump. Luke, meanwhile, would fight his way through the flames and carry her to safety, just as she seemed about to be overcome by the smoke.

Luke's part in the film was nearly over. He had to leave a week before the end of the shoot in order to start work on his next film, *Cool College 5*, which he wasn't looking forward to.

"Why don't you join me," he'd said to her last night, "as soon as this shoot is over? You could fly to LA, stay at my house in the valley. We'd have a great time."

"You'd be working," she protested.

"No one works that hard in LA. Making movies there isn't like it is here, with a slave-driver director. It's laid back."

"I'll think about it," Sarah told him, cautiously. "I do have some other assignments lined up. I'd have to talk to my agent."

"You don't want to carry on as a model after this," Luke insisted. "Come to LA with me. Stay as long as you like. I'll introduce you to people. You'll get lots of offers, I promise."

Sarah was so lost in her thoughts that she didn't hear Leo call "Action!" She noticed, though, when the walls were set alight, and she began to perform. Helped by a fan, smoke began to seep beneath the door in the room where Sarah sat. The crew filmed Sarah's reaction shots quickly. Then, when the flames had built up enough, the camera moved in to a medium close-up of her opening the door, seeing the flames, and being driven back by the heat.

The heat from the flames was real. It shocked Sarah. Never mind Luke being offered a stunt double, maybe she should have one for herself. She went to the window, opened it, and screamed for help. The actual sound of the scream didn't matter, as it would be re-dubbed later. She backed into the room. Now she just had to wait for Luke, coming to rescue her.

Off-stage, Sarah heard Luke being given his instruction to get into position. He had a conflict with Matthew first of all, which ended with Aidan knocking his father out in the middle of the flames. Sarah could barely make out their dialogue above the sound of the fire. It was hard to believe that the plastic stuff they'd been spreading on the walls could make so much noise.

The fire was very realistic. Flames were even beginning to lick their way across the front of the sound stage. No one had told Sarah that this was going to happen. Unless ... Sarah backed up against the wall ... suppose it was going wrong? But no, she was an actress. There was a camera crew a few metres away from her and Leo had gone over the stringent safety checks with her only minutes ago. She mustn't panic, mustn't spoil the take, or it would be hours before they could start again.

From above, it seemed to Jon that the fire was getting out of control. Fitzgerald kept on filming regardless. Sarah wasn't in any danger, but the fire in the corridors was way too strong – the actual sets were on fire and smoke was building up. Still, the camera kept rolling. Sarah continued to act, despite the fact that, at the edge of the set, Luke had walked off and was arguing with the director.

"I can't go through that! It's too hot!"

"Don't be a wimp," Fitzgerald told him. "Now, go!"

Luke moved back into camera shot. Brett was still lying on the floor where Luke had knocked him out earlier. In a moment he would be able to get up, as the camera followed Luke across the set.

But when the camera followed Luke, Brett didn't get up. The smoke must have got to him. And the fire was dangerously near, too. Flames were building up around the whole stage now. It was becoming an inferno. In her room at the side of the set, sweat poured down Sarah's wedding dress. Meanwhile, Luke was trying to make his way across the set. He climbed a burning staircase. Then he crossed the first corridor, starting as he burnt his arm by brushing it against a wall.

It was impossible to see what was going on in the final corridor. Smoke billowed through, flooding the room where Sarah waited.

"This is ridiculous," Jon shouted into the intercom. "Luke and Sarah are in danger! Get them out!"

But the little red light on the intercom didn't come on and Jon realized that the electrics were probably out, too. If this went on much longer, the entire studio would be ablaze.

The smoke was building up. Sarah knew that there were always delays, that time was certain to stretch out when you were stuck in a room with smoke pouring in at you, beginning to fear for your life. Yet she *must* be safe. There were people all around her – the crew. There were trained fire fighters. Or were there? She couldn't remember. She couldn't think. On a signal from Ruth, the assistant director, Sarah was meant to collapse. But she couldn't see Ruth any more and pretty soon she wouldn't have to fake collapsing. The room she was in didn't have a flammable coating, but it had started to burn. All the smoke and heat were getting to her. It was hard to stay upright.

Jon nudged Jo, the camera operator, in the back. She looked around saying, "What is it?"

"We've got to get down! My sister and Luke are in danger!"

Jo shook her head. "It just looks that way. It's meant to. If there's a problem, the people on the ground will sort it out. Leo'll kill me if I don't get all of this."

"But there's nothing to see! There's too much smoke."

"They're great atmospherics, that's all."

"Look, Jo, that's my sister down there..."

He reached for the lever which would lower the crane. Jo turned round, giving Jon the coldest stare he had ever received in his life.

"This is the movies, Jon. If you wreck a shot without permission from the director, you'll never work in the business again!"

Jon shook his head.

"Just keep filming," he said, as he pulled the lever. "I'll take the responsibility if Leo complains."

Smoke billowed out from beneath them. It was already unbearably hot. As the camera platform began to go down, Jon felt like he was descending into hell.

* * *

Luke didn't appear. Never had Sarah wanted to see someone so much in her life. Suppose he was in danger too? But she didn't have time to worry about him now. She had to worry about getting out of here.

"Help!" she called.

There was no response. Where was Luke? Where was her brother? She looked up for the camera on the crane. It was coming down towards her. If it came down close enough, she could climb onto the camera platform. They could whisk her out of here. But then the crane stopped, several metres above her head. What should she do? Perhaps the only thing for it was to run straight into the flames in front of her on the stage. Run for dear life to the safety of the crew. She could hear shouting off-stage. Somewhere, an alarm was sounding. Finally, they must have realized the risk.

There was movement now and for a moment Sarah thought that she was saved. She began to walk towards the sound. That was when she realized that she couldn't run anywhere, because her lungs were full of smoke. The moment she tried to walk in the direction of the sound, she fell to the floor, gagging for breath.

But it was better on the floor. There was less smoke. She could breathe a little. And there was someone coming towards her – only a shadow in the smoke, but it was getting nearer. She tried to make a noise, to call out. She hoped that whoever it was could see her. The shadow was getting closer, closer.

And then, with a gasp of horror, Sarah saw the shadow's face: it had long, singed, fair hair and wore a horrible yellow plastic mask. Reaching out for her, the shadowy figure seemed to wear a sickly, terrifying grin. Sarah tried to defend herself, but it was no good – she had no energy left to strike out or run away. He was going to get her.

She passed out.

Jo swung the camera platform back away from the set. They had got in close to Sarah, but then began to choke on the smoke. Flames licked the camera as the alarm sounded below. Finally, people were springing into action.

"We're getting out!" Jo told him. "Otherwise the heat will damage the film!"

"At least let me down," Jon insisted.

"OK, OK. We must have enough footage now."

Jon could see movement on the set as he jumped off the platform and ran towards it. People were using fire extinguishers, but the flames were too strong. A few metres from the fire, Ruth, the assistant director, was reviving Brett Johnson. Of Luke and Sarah there was no sign.

Jon ran towards the part of the set where his sister should be. It was a blazing inferno. Parts of the set were collapsing. Another part was burnt out. How could a competent director allow this to happen? Fitzgerald was nowhere to be seen. Then a figure began to crawl out of the flames, dragging something behind him. It was a tall, ghostly figure, with long, scorched hair and a yellow mask. Suddenly, Jon realized that it was Slacker, and the person he was dragging was Sarah. Jon ran forward to help him.

Slacker pulled the mask off as the nurse ran towards them. "She only just passed out," he said. "She was conscious when I got to her."

The nurse began to give Sarah oxygen. Slacker looked wrecked, even paler than usual, and scared. Jon put his arms around him.

"You did brilliantly. You saved her life."

The youth nodded distractedly. "I'd better get cleaned up," he said.

Jon returned to Sarah. Her eyes opened. "What happened?" she moaned.

"The fire got out of control," the nurse explained. "But you're all right now."

Sarah sat up and looked around. "Where's Luke?"

As she spoke, her boyfriend walked out of the burnt-out part of the set, supported by Leo Fitzgerald. His clothes and hair were scorched and his face was covered with black carbon, but he didn't look as bad as Sarah. She stood up.

"Thank God you're all right!" she said, hugging him close to her.

"You look like Miss Havisham," he told her.

"Save that for the camera," Leo told them. "I want to get you two straight back to the house, looking just the way you are now. We'll film Luke carrying you out of the west wing. It'll be really authentic."

"I think these two need checking at a hospital," the nurse warned. "The smoke may have damaged their lungs."

Fitzgerald looked at Luke and Sarah. "They can stand, can't they?" he asked. "Come on, the show must go on!"

While the nurse treated Sarah and Luke, Jon accosted the director. "You can't just walk away from this! Sarah nearly died. If it hadn't been for this guy here..." He looked for Slacker to point him out, but the long-haired youth had gone.

"Listen," said Fitzgerald. "The fire got out of control. I'm sorry. It's a risk we take. But don't exaggerate the danger. We got some great footage..."

He turned to Jo. "Everything all right your end, Jo? Your monitor lead burnt out."

"Fine," she said. "No thanks to my new assistant."

Leo turned back to Jon. In the distance, he could hear fire engines. Jon wanted to complain about Sarah being forced to drive to the hall and do the next scene, but he had stuck his neck out far enough already. Fitzgerald turned round.

"Here's the fire brigade. I thought we'd disconnected all the alarms, but we set off the ones in the next studio. Ruth can liaise with them. I have a film to finish."

The fire was starting to die down, mainly because everything that would burn was already burnt. It was odd, Jon thought, the way that the front of the sound stage had caught fire, almost as though someone had planned to trap the people inside.

As Jon looked closely at the fire, he thought he saw something, right at the back of the set, where it had been strongest: a large can, of the type used to hold petrol. But maybe it was meant to be there.

"Was all of this accidental?" he asked Ruth, who was watching the fire brigade trail a hose in. "It got strong awfully quickly."

The assistant director shrugged.

"I haven't seen one go up as quickly as that before," she said. "But all the wood in this place is ancient, and dry as a tinder box. It's a good thing they're demolishing it, or the rebuilding costs would be huge."

"Did you use petrol to light it?"

"You're kidding!" Ruth said. "That would make it burn too strong and way too fast."

"Isn't that exactly what happened?"

Ruth shook her head. "Leo may be headstrong and obsessive, but he isn't stupid enough to risk burning people to death deliberately."

*   *   *

The remains of the blaze were quickly put out. Jon watched with Sarah until Luke came and told her that it was time for them to drive to Bradlington Hall. When she'd gone, Jon followed the firefighters into the charred scenery, intending to point out the petrol can he'd seen earlier.

It was no longer there.

Had Jon imagined it, or had someone removed the can while he was talking to Ruth? What motive would anyone have for making the fire worse than it was? Jon didn't know. All he did know was that there had been too many accidents on this film shoot and this was one too many. Any two of the three could have been coincidence, but, taken together, they formed a pattern. Who was at the centre of it?

12

They had finished filming the rescue scene at Bradlington Hall and Sarah was exhausted. She couldn't believe that Leo had insisted on filming the brief shot of Luke carrying her out of the hall on the same day as she had nearly burnt to death. But he had done so, even though it meant filming in late afternoon, when the light was poor.

Now Sarah lay in Luke's arms on her bed. Luke had been less affected by the fire earlier. He kissed her passionately, but Sarah felt too wasted to respond. Seeing how frazzled she was, he began to massage her back.

"That's nice," Sarah murmured, "very nice."

"Why won't you come back to the States with me?" Luke asked after a while. This wasn't the first time he'd asked her the question but Sarah still wasn't sure how to reply.

"I've only known you for a month. How can I throw everything in and just come after you?"

"Why not?"

"I want you to respect me, Luke. I have a career. I'm independent. I'd like to come and visit you, but on my terms."

"Fine. I do respect you. What are your terms?"

"That you stop putting all this pressure on me and let me come in my own time. Also, I'd like you to meet my parents."

Luke turned over. "*Meet your parents?* Are you kidding? You make me feel like I'm fifteen years old."

Sarah explained. "I'm only seventeen. I still live at home, in a sense. I'm not there much, but my mum and dad like to know who I'm with. They feel more comfortable if they've met them. What's so odd about that?"

Luke shrugged. "Nothing, I guess. OK, anything you say. I'll meet your parents. But don't make me wait long. Come soon. Come quickly. I want to show you my beach house. I want to take you for moonlit walks on the beach at Malibu."

"I'd like that," Sarah whispered, kissing him softly on the lips. "You know I would."

"I've got some good news," Luke went on. "Leo has lent me his car for the rest day tomorrow. He's staying in the hotel and working on the end of the script."

"You mean he still hasn't worked it out?"

"No. The screenwriter came over with the rewrites but Leo threw half of them out. Thing is, he's only got me for three more days, so he has to get the ending worked out quickly or he'll end up paying a lot extra for pick-up shots back at Burbank."

"Pick-up shots?"

"They're bits that are filmed later to fill in gaps in the story, or because things didn't come out. The point is that he doesn't need his car tomorrow. Come for a drive with me."

"I'd love to."

"Good."

She kissed him again.

"I love you," he murmured into her ear.

"I love you too," she whispered back.

There was no point in holding out any longer. They had come through a fire together. Sarah had a feeling that they might just go through the rest of their lives together, too.

"Seen this?"

Todd handed Jon one of the tabloid Sunday newspapers as he was eating his breakfast. The front page headline was:

"SUPERMODEL AND SUPERBRAT!"

The sub-heading read, 'Romance flares up for model superstar Sarah Wood and teen heart-throb Luke Kelly after he saves her life twice!" The story beneath was salacious and inaccurate. It credited Luke, not Slacker, with pulling Sarah out of the fire, and made Luke's saving Sarah from drowning sound a lot more brave and dramatic than it had been. Maybe Luke *had* saved her life, Jon thought, but she was near land and there were a lot of other people just behind him.

"Suspicious, isn't it?" Todd said.

"How do you mean?"

"All those insider quotes, like 'Friends say they've never seen Luke so happy.' What friends? 'Close family confide that Luke is Sarah's first real love.' Have you been talking to the *News of the Screws*?"

Jon shook his head.

"Of course you haven't. It all comes out of the mouth of Kelly's publicist. He's given her the whole story, or Fitzgerald has." Todd scratched his head. "Makes you wonder though."

"What?"

"That fire yesterday. You were there. Did it look like an accident to you? Or do you think it was set up to make Kelly look like a hero?"

Jon was lost for words. He hadn't seen Sarah since Slacker pulled her out of the fire. She never left Luke's side these days and Jon chose not to hang around them. Sarah probably didn't know who had saved her. Could Luke have taken the credit?

"Makes you think, doesn't it?" Todd said.

"Yes," Jon said. "It certainly does."

He decided to visit his sister, taking the newspaper with him.

When Jon got to her door, he found it open. He knocked anyway.

"Come in," said Luke Kelly's voice.

Kelly was standing by the window, in a brown, crumpled leather jacket, while Jon's sister brushed her hair.

"Jon, how you doing?" Kelly said.

"I wanted a word with Sarah."

"She's sitting right there."

Sarah turned round and gave Jon one of her dazzling smiles, the fake one she reserved for distant relatives and remote family friends. "What is it, Jon?"

"Can I have a word with you on your own for a minute?"

"I haven't got any secrets from Luke. And we're just about to go out for the day. Can it wait?"

Jon shrugged. "I guess. But you might want to give Mum and Dad a ring before they read this." He handed Sarah the paper, then turned to go out. Sarah said nothing, but Luke followed him into the corridor. Jon ignored him. Luke grabbed Jon roughly by the arm.

"What is it with you?" he said in a low growl. "I thought we were friends. But you seem to be trying to get between me and your sister."

"Then it doesn't look like I've been very successful, does it?" Jon replied. "And if you like my sister so much, how come you planted that story in the papers?"

"*Me?*" Luke retorted, incredulously. "I need publicity like I need a hole in the head. If you want to know the source of the story, talk to our precious director. All he cares about is media coverage: hype, hype, hype, and it doesn't matter how he gets it. But don't try to screw things up between me and Sarah. I can be a nasty enemy."

"That, I can believe," Jon said, breaking loose of the actor and returning downstairs to the crew, where he belonged.

13

Leo Fitzgerald drove a red two-seater MGB. It was a meticulously restored, open-top, vintage sports car. Sarah and Luke walked out into the car park in the hot August sun. The director was chatting with Brett Johnson. Leo dangled the keys in front of Luke.

"You take care of her, all right? Not one scratch, no dents, or I'll write you out of this movie."

"You're lending him that beauty?" Brett said, in disbelief. "I hope it's fully insured."

"It is, and so is Luke."

"Shouldn't you be indoors," Luke suggested, caustically, "fixing the script?"

"It's all happening in here," Leo said, pointing to his head. "Anyway, Brett's been giving me some ideas. Do you have any suggestions to make, Luke? Or you, Sarah?"

"You're paid to work out the ending," Luke told him. "Sarah and I are paid to make people believe it. C'mon, Sarah."

He took her arm. Sarah had an opinion or two of her own, but didn't feel like she could say anything now without appearing to disagree with Luke, so she didn't.

"We got a nice publicity puff out of you two in one of today's papers," Fitzgerald said. "Did you see it?"

"Not yet," Luke said.

"I..." Sarah began, but before she could get the sentence out, Brett interrupted her.

"Who is that guy over there? I keep seeing him around. Is he an extra, or what?"

Sarah looked where Brett was pointing. It was a long-haired youth she thought she'd seen before.

"I've noticed him," Sarah said. "Wasn't he one of the fire guards yesterday?"

"I've not hired him for anything," Fitzgerald said.

"Wasn't he an extra in the party scene?" Luke asked.

"I don't think so."

"Usually," Brett said, "people come and hang out by a movie set for an hour, two at the most. Then they see how slow everything is, get bored and go away."

"Except fans," Luke told them. "Or should I say *fanatics.* I sometimes get that in the States: creeps who hang around the location every minute of the day. You know the type – they haven't got a life of their own."

"That's rather sad," Sarah said.

"You mean pathetic," Luke told her. "It's not like autograph hunters – one signature and they're out of your face. People like that can make your life a misery. There was this girl once ... aw, never mind. Let's frag him."

"What?"

"Get in the car."

Reluctantly, Sarah did as she was told. Luke started off the MG with a roar, then drove across the car park. The long-haired youth was walking away. He'd reached a deserted section at the far end of the car park. Luke sounded his horn and the youth glanced round.

"Now we'll have some fun," Luke told Sarah. He began to circle the youth with the MG, going faster and faster. The boy, who couldn't be much older than Sarah herself, looked frightened out of his wits. He tried to get out of the way of the car, but Luke kept widening and narrowing the circles.

"Stop it!" Sarah screamed. Luke ignored her.

"You're scaring him and you're scaring me!"

The youth's long, dirty-looking hair flew around his face, covering his eyes. If he was unlucky, he would run straight into the car.

"Stop it!" Sarah insisted. "This is horrible!"

Luke ignored her again. The boy froze, seeing that there was no point in trying to get away. Luke began to slow down. Leo Fitzgerald was running over.

"Hey!" Luke called out, cruising up to the youth, "what's your problem?"

The youth was very thin and pale. Sarah wondered where he'd slept the night before.

"What do you want?" he asked, sounding defensive and scared.

"I want to know why you're hanging around my place of work," Luke told him.

"I want to know the same thing," Leo broke in. "Who are you?"

"I ... I wanted to get a job on the film," the youth stuttered. "There weren't any going, but I kept turning up anyway."

"Where are you from?" Sarah asked, kindly.

"Ipswich."

"That's a long way to come."

"I think you'd better go back there," Fitzgerald told him, sternly. "This is a job of work we're doing, not a spectator sport. Come see the picture when it's released. Until then, go home. Otherwise I'll get security to throw you off the set any time you come near."

"I, I, uh..."

"Have you got any money?" Sarah asked.

The youth shook his head. She reached into her purse.

"Here," she said. "How much is the train fare?"

She'd been scared of the youth, but now she could see that he was just another loser. He'd done what people were supposed to do – travelled hundreds of kilometres in search of an opportunity, and found nothing.

"I ... I don't know," said the young man. "I hitched."

"Put your money away," Fitzgerald told Sarah. He turned to the youth. "OK, you had a go at getting work. I respect that. But there's nothing here for you. We've done all the crowd scenes. We'll be wrapping the picture up in a few days. Now I want you gone. Actors get superstitious about strangers on set. So wait here. I'll get security to drive you to the station, buy you a ticket, put you on a train. All right?"

"All right," said the youth. "Thank you."

Then he turned to Sarah. "Thank you, too."

"You're welcome."

Sarah heard Leo giving instructions to the head of security, who apologized, explaining that they thought Slacker was on the crew. Then Luke revved the engine and they drove off at speed.

"Why were you so horrible to him?" Sarah asked.

"Wait until you've been in as many movies as I have," Luke

lectured her. "You'll come to loathe cretins like that, too."

He put his foot down on the throttle. It bothered Sarah, the way Luke could call people "cretins". At times, he seemed to act as though he and people like him were on a different planet, where different rules applied. It wasn't right and she would tell him so. Over the last month, he seemed to have changed, to have become less callous. But suppose it was all an act put on for her behalf? Sarah tightened her safety belt.

"Where are we going?" she asked.

Luke turned to her and smiled. It was hard to be mad at him for long when it was a perfect summer's day and his brown, curly hair was blowing in the wind.

"Wait and see," he said, and pressed even further down on the accelerator.

Soon they had left the main road and were flying through country lanes. Despite the narrow, winding roads, Luke kept the speedometer hovering between fifty and sixty.

"Slow down," Sarah told him. "You're scaring me."

"This isn't fast," Luke insisted. "Wait till you see where I'm taking you."

Suddenly, he pressed hard on the brakes and they swung off the country lane into a dirt road. A hand-painted sign by the turning read "Private".

"Where...?"

"Mark, the locations manager, found this place. They couldn't use it, for one reason or another, but he told me about it."

The sports car bounced up and down, juddering uncomfortably on the rough track, which led up a steep hill. When they'd gone half a mile, they turned a corner and passed a sign which read *Danger! Proceed at your own risk.*

"Luke, I don't like this."

"If it's like Mark told me, you'll be amazed. Here we are."

Sarah stared at the spectacle below. They had arrived at the edge of a vast quarry. Winding paths were cut into sheer mountains of rock, latticed with caves. In places, the rock had crumbled away. In the middle of the quarry was a hollow filled with rubble, the result of occasional landslides.

"Leo was thinking of setting some kind of car chase here," Luke explained, "but the logistics were too difficult. You can't get into that hollow there. Let me show you what it would have been like."

He accelerated towards one of the cliffs.

"What did they used to mine here?" Sarah asked, trying to stay calm.

"Tin, maybe. Or copper. Or chalk. I dunno."

Dust blew around them as Luke drove onto a track carved into the side of the cliff. The car was small, but even so, the road was less than a metre wider.

"Do you know where this comes out?" Sarah asked.

"Don't worry. It'll come out somewhere. Mark said he drove down it."

"In a car like this?"

"No. A Land Rover."

Luke speeded up the MG. It shuddered and shook as it hurtled along the rocky, narrow road.

"Luke, this is dangerous!" Sarah told him as they approached a blind corner.

"Hey, I do my own stunt driving. Didn't you know that?"

"Let's go back," Sarah pleaded, holding onto his arm for safety.

Luke shook his head. "There's no turning back." He pointed at the road. "Look. There isn't room to turn around. We'll have to go wherever this takes us."

"Then slow down at least!"

Luke didn't seem to hear her. He kept driving, faster and faster, tightly cornering each hairpin bend. Sarah imagined herself in the film, *Thelma and Louise*, making a suicide run into the Grand Canyon. Fifty metres beneath them was the hollow full of rubble. It looked like a death pit.

"If you don't slow down," she yelled at Luke, "I'll, I'll..." Before she could work out what she meant to say, Sarah screamed, as the next bend revealed a huge rock blocking their path.

They were driving straight into it.

Luke did an emergency stop. For a moment, Sarah thought they were going to skid off the track. But the car came to a juddering halt against the rock instead. The bumper was bent, but the car's two occupants were unharmed.

"Damn!" Luke said. "We'll have to move it."

Tears flooded down Sarah's face. She was shocked and relieved to be safe.

"Don't..." she began to beat her fists against Luke's chest. "Don't ever do anything like that to me again."

Luke put his arm around her. "Calm down, baby, calm down. You were never in any danger. Trust me."

"I want to trust you!" Sarah yelled. "But you're making it really, really hard."

"Come on," said Luke, getting out of the car. "Let's shift this rock."

This was easier said than done. The rock was half Sarah's height and very heavy. Moreover, it was deeply embedded in the ground.

"Mark must have come down a different way," Luke muttered on their third attempt.

"Isn't there any way we can lever it? Does the car have a wheel brace?"

"One of those things that turns the jack? Let's look."

They found the wheel brace in the boot. After a lot of prodding and pushing, they managed to wedge it in a gap beneath the rock. Then the two of them put all their weight onto the metal rod. Slowly, the rock began to move.

"Back!" Luke yelled.

The rock picked up momentum, moving forward as the couple pressed their bodies against the cliff wall. The movement of the rock had started a small landslide, but nothing hit them. There was a huge crashing sound. When they looked over the edge, the rock was gone, smashed into smaller stones scattered around the rubble.

"Let's hope we don't get a puncture," Luke said, picking up the mangled wheel brace, which was even more badly bent than the bumper.

"Where do you want to go now?" he asked, as they set off again, this time at a more moderate speed.

"Just get us out of here," Sarah said, "and take me back to the hotel."

14

Brett Johnson was holding court by the hotel pool. He didn't like giving interviews, but Leo had insisted that he do some publicity for the film while he was in Britain. So the BBC's *Filmnight* was doing one of their "On Location" reports and a handful of journalists were getting a short press conference.

The TV people wanted the pool to look natural, so the director had asked members of the crew to hang around in their bathing costumes. Jon had nothing better to do. Neither had Mary. She was excited about having got the small part of the model/bridesmaid, which hadn't been in the original script, and hoped to get her picture in the TV report.

"*This Year's Model* is turning into my big break," she told Jon. "My agent says I'll get lots of offers if it's a hit."

"I'm sure you will."

"Tell me, Brett, why did you choose this picture for your comeback?" asked the *Filmnight* presenter.

"It was the script," Brett said with a twinkle in his eye. "It's an original variation on a strong theme. And the director, of course. I've been following Leo's work for a long time now."

The presenter leaned forward with a nervousness that implied he was going to ask a "difficult" question.

"You're working with Luke Kelly for the first time. Now, he's got the sort of reputation that you used to have: bit of a hell-raiser, demon with the ladies and – not to put it mildly – a nightmare to work with. How have you found him?"

Brett gave his sweetest smile. "Luke's a pussycat. I've heard those stories but, let me tell you, if he wants to get a reputation as bad as mine used to be, he's got one hell of a lot of work to do."

The presenter laughed sycophantically. "Now the one real

surprise in the casting for this movie was the choice of Sarah Wood as the leading actress. Without spoiling the plot, is it true that you get to marry her during the film?"

Brett raised his eyebrows slightly. "There are wedding bells, yes. But something gets in the way of the wedding night. I won't tell you what that is, but I will tell you one thing: Sarah's had no acting experience, but Leo knew exactly what he was doing when he cast her for this movie. She's a natural. It wouldn't surprise me if she won an Oscar before she's twenty-one."

"Praise indeed," the presenter said. "Let me finish with a ... sensitive question. It's ten years since you won your own Oscar for best actor and four since you last made a film. Do you think you can make it all the way back, to become as successful as you were before?"

Brett shrugged and smiled enigmatically. "Others have done it. Look at Richard Gere. Heck, look at Dennis Hopper. But, to be honest, I don't think about it much. I guess I just feel lucky to have survived. I've lost some friends along the way. I feel like I owe it to them, and to my fans, to do the best I can."

"Brett Johnson, thank you very much."

There was a screeching noise as a car pulled up in the car park.

"Mr Fitzgerald, can you come over here for your interview?" one of the BBC production assistants asked.

"Wait a minute."

Fitzgerald shot off towards the car park. Jon got out of the pool. He could see why Leo had hurried off the moment he saw the car – it was Fitzgerald's own. Sarah got out of it. Ignoring the director, she marched straight to the hotel entrance.

Fitzgerald pointed angrily at the bumper of the car, which was dented. He and Luke had a heated argument. Jon considered getting closer, finding out what was going on, but decided against. He walked back to the pool. Should he go to Sarah? No. She'd find him if she needed him. Jon wondered if, by showing her the newspaper article, he'd caused a row between her and Luke.

The BBC crew were getting some pool shots. Mary was preening herself enthusiastically. Jon jumped into the water, dive-bombing her. Why shouldn't he have some laughs for a change? Mary retaliated by throwing a beach ball at him. For a few minutes they managed to have some silly, childish fun.

"Jon!" Leo Fitzgerald had returned to the set. "The BBC are keen on getting a couple of minutes with your sister. Could you fetch her?"

"I'm wet," Jon told him. "Can't you phone her room?"

Fitzgerald shook his head. "She's not answering. I think she's in a bad mood. She might need some persuading. Get her down here, will you? What do you think I pay you for?"

Resentfully, Jon got out of the pool. He was an extra, a gofer, and, yesterday, a temporary camera assistant, but Fitzgerald wouldn't let him forget that he'd got the job because he was Sarah Wood's brother.

He knocked on her door.

"Who is it?"

"Jon."

"Go away. I don't want to see anybody."

"Leo sent me. They need you to answer a couple of questions for this BBC thing."

"I won't do it."

"Fine, I'll tell him. But Sarah, what's wrong?"

There was no reply, but as he pressed his ear to the door, Jon could make out a whimpering sound. She was crying.

"Sarah, please let me in. I want to help. Let me in."

A few moments later, the door opened. His sister's face was red and blotchy.

"He dumped you, did he?"

She shook her head. "No. I dumped him. But it feels just as bad as if he did it."

"What happened?"

Sitting on her bed, Sarah told Jon about her day.

"First there was that awful newspaper story. Then there was the horrible row with this pathetic boy in the car park."

As she told him the story, Jon felt a stab of recognition.

"That was Slacker."

"You know him?"

"Not really. I thought he actually had a job on the set. He must have been pretending."

"Pretending?"

"Yeah. He was desperate enough. First the kid pretended to be an extra, then he must have borrowed the fire guard equipment. That explains why he disappeared so quickly afterwards."

"Fire guard?" Sarah asked, confused.

"Yes," Jon told her. "Didn't you realize who he was?"

From the blankness in Sarah's face, it was obvious that she didn't. "What do you mean?"

"What I mean is, he's the guy who pulled you out of the fire yesterday. He might have saved your life."

"Oh, no!" Sarah said. "And I helped them get rid of him."

"It sounds to me like you tried to help him."

"But I should have helped him more. I should have..." Sarah looked mortified.

"What happened next?" Jon prompted.

Sarah told him about a horrifying drive around a dangerous, deserted quarry and an ice-cold, silent journey back. Then she became more tearful.

"And the nearer to the hotel I got the more I thought, *I can't go to America with this bloke. I can't introduce him to Mum and Dad.* He's six or seven years older than me, but he acts like a spoilt child and he treats me like I'm there purely for his amusement."

"At least you worked it out in time." Jon gave Sarah a big hug.

"But I fell in love with him," she cried. "I've never been in love before. I've had crushes, but they didn't mean any more than sticking some film star's picture on the wardrobe door."

"Mum took those pictures down," Jon told her. "They'd started to fade. The Sellotape was peeling."

Sarah laughed bitterly. Then she pulled away from Jon and looked him straight in the eye.

"I wasn't in love, was I?" she said. "I just wanted to be. I turned a blind eye to his faults. I was in love with the idea of being in love with Luke Kelly."

"But you're not any more."

"No, I'm not."

There was a knock at the door.

"Sarah, it's Leo. The BBC are waiting downstairs."

"I'll get rid of him," Jon told her.

"No. I've got a bone to pick with him."

She opened the door and raised her voice. "If you think I'm going anywhere near the press after that story this morning, you've got another think coming. Or maybe I will. Maybe I'll tell them the real story of how you nearly got me burnt to death yesterday!"

"Both those things were Luke's idea," Fitzgerald protested. His voice was urgent. "Please let me explain."

Reluctantly, Sarah left the door open.

"You think I want to publicize accidents on my set? Luke suggested that we let the thing build up a bit more before he went in. Maybe he added some petrol. If he did, I don't know where it came from or what happened to it. Anyway, I'm sorry. I guess we overdid the effects. Luke wanted to stage this dramatic rescue and persuaded me that it would make terrific publicity. But somehow the fire got out of control. I had to drag him out. You were never in any serious danger."

"It felt like it."

"Brett was the one who nearly suffocated."

"He didn't have to go straight on and film another scene an hour's drive away."

"OK," Leo admitted. "Maybe I was over-zealous about that, but we'd never have got that look with make-up, and Luke was keen."

"You're the director," Jon cut in. "You're responsible, not Luke."

"No one was hurt," Leo insisted. "We got the publicity. We got some magnificent footage. I looked at the rushes last night. We've got some terrific reaction shots on Sarah."

"So that's what this is all about," Sarah said. "You still think that I can't act, so you had to make it real."

Fitzgerald shook his head. "Brett was just telling the BBC you're a natural. And you get better the more we go on. But every actor needs a little goading now and then, a little danger. It's the way I work."

"Well I don't like it!" Sarah said, slamming the door on him.

"Just wait till I get my hands on Luke Kelly," Sarah said to Jon. "He'll wish he never left Hollywood."

"Do you think he set up that other thing as well?" Jon asked. "The exploding motor boat?"

"I don't know," Sarah said. "But I intend to find out. There's nothing I'd put past him."

15

The phone rang just after Jon had left the room. Sarah was trying to sleep, but couldn't get thoughts of Luke out of her mind. Half of her hoped that this would be him. But it wasn't. It was her agent, Sally.

"I've had Leo Fitzgerald on the phone. He says that you're refusing to do interviews and you're in a mess over Luke Kelly." Sally's voice softened. "I thought I'd better see if you were all right, Sarah. Are you?"

Sarah told her what had happened since they last spoke. Sally was sympathetic but business-like.

"Directors have to be dictatorial. They're in charge of huge budgets. But I'll relay your safety concerns to the studio. In the meantime, though, don't forget that Leo is giving you a big break. And your contract does specify that you'll be available for publicity whenever practicable."

"It's a rest day," Sarah argued.

"It's free publicity, for you as well as the film. Put on your prettiest frock. Put Luke Kelly to the back of your mind. Please."

"OK, Sally, but for you, not for Leo Fitzgerald."

"Thank you, dear."

Sarah put on her favourite white linen dress, made herself up, then chose a pair of blue sunglasses. Her eyes were still puffy from crying. As she was about to leave, the phone rang. She nearly didn't answer it. After all, if it was Luke, she had nothing to say to him. Once she made up her mind about something, she never changed it.

It was Luke. He sounded distraught.

"I just wanted to say..."

"Don't say anything," she interrupted. "It's over."

She hung up.

Acting in front of a camera was one thing. Being interviewed by a TV presenter whose show she always watched was another. Sarah wished that she was in the pool, not sitting by it in the bright sunshine. She tried to relax, but nearly froze up completely once the questions started.

"Sarah, you've had amazing success as a model just recently, but now you're starting a movie career. Why the sudden transition?"

Sarah smiled awkwardly at the presenter, trying to look glamorous and modest at the same time.

"Leo made me an offer I couldn't refuse. When I went to see him I thought that the part would be just a cameo, but he had amazing faith in me. And I couldn't turn down the opportunity to work with Brett, who's always been one of my favourite actors."

This wasn't strictly true. You had to varnish the facts in situations like this. But there was a limit. Sarah wasn't going to praise Luke if she could avoid it. The presenter asked her a question about her role, which she answered in detail.

"...so, in a sense, I'm playing myself, but I hope to take on more varied and challenging parts in the future."

"Does that mean your modelling days are over?"

Sarah gave him a big, bashful smile. "Oh, I'm not ready to give up my day job just yet. We'll see."

The presenter leant forward and brushed her arm in what was meant to be a sensitive gesture. "There's one other question which I have to ask you, because if I don't, the tabloid reporters who've been hanging around all day will. I don't mean to pry but ... are there real-life wedding bells for you and your co-star Luke Kelly?"

Sarah lost her cool.

"That's ridiculous! Who told you that? Was it Leo?"

The presenter prevaricated.

"Well, er ... there have been all these rumours ... the story about him rescuing you from a fire..."

Sarah spoke sternly.

"They're all rubbish. My relationship with Luke Kelly is purely professional. Any other story is just publicity."

The presenter laughed nervously.

"It sounds as though you don't like him very much."

"I don't know Luke Kelly very well," Sarah said straight into the TV camera, "but my impression of him so far is that he's mad, bad and dangerous to know. Does that answer your question?"

"It does. Sarah Wood, thank you very much for joining me."

"You're welcome. I'm sorry I kept you waiting."

As Sarah walked back to the hotel, half a dozen reporters ran up to her, blocking her path.

"Sarah, if we could have a comment or two."

She snapped back.

"Did you hear what I just told the BBC?"

"Yes, but..."

"Then I'm sorry, but I've got nothing to add."

"Aw, c'mon. Nothing?"

She marched into the lobby with the hacks following her.

"Luke! There you are," one of them called out. "Could we have a few words?"

Sarah looked round, just in time to see her brother saying, "I'm not Luke Kelly."

He walked over to Sarah. "How did it go?"

"All right. But I'd like to get away from these bloodsuckers."

"I've got my car," Jon told her. "We could drive somewhere."

"Why not? I don't want to spend any more time in my room."

As they walked back outside again, Sarah heard shouts.

"There they are! Get them!"

Cameras clicked. Jon and Sarah ignored them.

"I can see the stories now," Jon said. "*Sarah consoles herself with mystery Luke look-alike.*"

"With any luck," Sarah told him, "someone will tell them who you are and they'll figure that the rumours about me and Luke were the result of people confusing the two of you."

Jon shook his head.

"They'll print whatever suits them," he said, "whatever sells the most papers. You should know that by now."

"Yes," said Sarah. "I guess I should."

They drove out in the direction that Luke had taken Sarah before.

"There's a good pub in a village about fifteen kilometres away," Jon told her. "They do decent food and it's pretty quiet."

* * *

They had a peaceful lunch, sitting outside at a wooden table by a stream. No one recognized Sarah. No one confused Jon with Luke Kelly. Jon made light conversation, avoiding the subject of the American actor. Later, perhaps, they would confront Luke about the fire, about whether the time he saved Sarah's life had been faked, too. But that could wait. Now, the pair of them talked about family and old friends.

Sarah was aware that she had grown apart from her brother over the last few months. Her relationship with Luke hadn't helped either. But now the distance between them seemed to melt away. It was like old times. Sarah filled Jon in on films she'd seen in the States which hadn't reached Britain yet. Jon told Sarah about things on television that she'd missed.

By the time the pub was throwing out, Sarah had loosened up a lot.

"Will you make more films?" Jon asked her.

"I hope so. I've enjoyed this one a lot. Sally's already looking for another part for me, but she says that I probably won't get really good offers until *This Year's Model* comes out."

"If it's any good."

Sarah nodded. "A big *if.* How about you?" she added. "Has doing the film given you any ideas?"

Jon grinned. "I'd really like to make films," he said. "The life suits me. The work fascinates me. But I still want to go to university," he added. "I've learnt a lot these last few weeks and maybe the experience would help me get a job. But I don't want to go straight into a career just yet. I want time to think, mess around, maybe make a few experimental videos or films on Super-8. Of course I might not get into university..."

"When are the results out?"

"This Thursday. If I do get in, I'll probably concentrate on the Media side of the degree."

One of the bar staff started ostentatiously wiping down the table next to them.

"Come on," Jon said. "Let's go."

He drove Sarah back to the hotel by a different route, for variety. As they got nearer to the hotel, Sarah began to look disturbed.

"What is it?"

"Oh, nothing. This bit up ahead, I think it's where Luke took me earlier."

"Sorry."

"It doesn't matter."

As she spoke, they saw that the road ahead of them was blocked. There was already barely room for two cars to pass each other, but a police car appeared, braked sharply, and turned a narrow corner. There was an ambulance behind it. The white vehicle tried to follow the police car into the dirt road, but failed, getting one of its wheels stuck in a rut.

"We'd better help," Jon said.

He parked the Nova on the verge and he and Sarah walked over to the stranded ambulance.

"Need a hand?"

"Please," said the driver. "I hadn't realized how bad this track was."

With a bit of pushing they got the ambulance free and it backed on to the lane.

"Aren't you going up there?" Jon asked the driver.

"What? And risk that happening again? No. We'll wait here. It's just come over on the radio. There's very little chance of getting the body out."

"What happened?"

"There's an old quarry at the end of that track. It's meant to be sealed off but kids with motorbikes are always getting rid of the fences and going for a burn. Evidently someone went over the side."

"I see."

"Luke," Sarah said.

Jon turned round to see his sister looking distraught.

"I've got this feeling that it's Luke," she said.

"Why?" he asked her. "Is this the place he brought you to?"

"Yes. Jon, we must take a look."

Without another word, Jon went back to his car and drove it round the ambulance to the entrance.

"I'm sure you'll be wrong," he told Sarah as she got in. "It'll be some kid on a motorbike like the ambulance driver said."

"I expect you're right," Sarah said, looking distracted as they rattled along the road.

They drove in silence. There was a police car parked at the top of the road. Two police officers were talking to a youth with a motorbike. Presumably, he was the one who had reported the accident. Jon stopped his car and got out.

"What's going on?" he asked the first officer.

"There's been an accident. I'd rather you left, sir. This is private land and we don't need spectators."

"We're not spectators," Sarah said. "We came up here because we're worried about a … a colleague of ours. Who's been hurt?"

"Hard to tell," said the officer, pointing into the quarry. "Whoever it was is nearly covered up now."

Jon looked over the side. He could see nothing – just endless rubble, piled at the bottom of a sheer drop.

"There used to be a way through to there," the second officer told them, "but there've been so many landslides it would take a week to dig our way in."

"Not that there's any chance of the person in the car still being alive," the first officer said. "Not after that fall, and the fire."

"Car?" Sarah interrupted. "Did you say it wasn't a motorbike, it was a car?"

"I saw it go over," the lad in the motorbike jacket told her. "Whoever it was was driving like a maniac, really fast."

"What was he driving?" Jon asked.

The motorcyclist told him.

"It was one of them vintage sports cars – don't know the name," the motorcyclist said. "Red, it was. Just went flying off the road, landed with a big bang. Then the tank must have gone up because it caught fire. Probably died quickly. Better than the other way."

"What other way?"

"Buried alive. After the car crashed, what with all the vibrations, there was a big landslide. The wreckage must be fifteen metres under by now."

Sarah's face had turned a deathly pale.

"Do you know who was inside the car, Miss?" the first officer asked.

"Yes," said Sarah. "I was here with him earlier today. He's an American actor. His name's Luke Kelly."

16

The press conference was called for seven that evening. Leo wore a black suit. He also had black sunglasses on, even though the briefing was taking place in one of the hotel conference rooms. He spoke into a microphone.

"Luke Kelly died at between three and four this afternoon. His death was a tragic accident. I, the studio and everyone involved in the production of *This Year's Model* would like to pass on our deepest sympathy and condolences to his family." He paused. "And now the Detective Inspector and I will answer any questions you have."

"How exactly did it happen?" a reporter asked the Inspector.

"The information we have so far suggests that Mr Kelly drove off a narrow quarry road and his car – I should say the car that he borrowed from Mr Fitzgerald here – fell over fifty metres. In such circumstances, death would almost certainly have been instantaneous."

"Have you recovered the body?"

"That may take some time."

"Is there any chance that he's still alive?"

"None whatsoever."

"What about suicide?" a woman from the *Daily Mail* asked. "Could he have done it deliberately?"

The Inspector shook her head.

"We have an eyewitness. As far as the police are concerned at this stage, there are no suspicious circumstances."

"Mr Fitzgerald, would you care to comment on Luke's relationship with the model, Sarah Wood?"

Watching from the back of the room, Sarah flinched.

"No, I would not. And Miss Wood is not answering any questions today."

"Was Luke insured, Mr Fitzgerald?"

"We always insure our stars," Fitzgerald announced confidently, "but it's unlikely that we'll need to claim on our policy. Practically all of Luke's performance is already in the can."

Surely that can't be true, Sarah thought. As far as she knew, the film's ending still hadn't been definitively worked out, never mind shot. How could they have an ending without Luke?

"How long will you be suspending production for, Mr Fitzgerald?"

The director didn't pause for breath. "We won't. Luke was an important young actor, but I knew him well, and he wouldn't have wanted us to stop work for even one minute. We're on a tight schedule. We'll be completing the shoot this week and the film will be on general release by Christmas. It's the way I work. It's the way Luke would have wanted it. This is his last picture. We hope to make it his best." He stood up. "That's all, folks."

There was a barrage of questions, but Fitzgerald ignored them. Sarah slipped out quietly before the reporters' insatiable curiosity could be turned on her. She felt tormented. If she hadn't finished with Luke ... if she had just spoken to him on the phone, maybe he wouldn't have done something so reckless. Did he mean to kill himself? She would never know. But she would always feel directly responsible for his death.

"Jon, I want a word ... alone."

Jon followed Leo Fitzgerald up to his suite. It was a massive, luxurious room, with a computer and printer in one corner and a wide-screen TV and video in the other. There were multi-coloured sheets of paper everywhere. He had no idea what the director wanted.

"Drink?"

Leo opened the fridge, which was filled with bottled beers and wines. Jon asked for a Pilsner Urquell.

"You look like Luke," Fitzgerald said as he poured the beer into a glass.

"A little," Jon agreed.

"A lot," Fitzgerald insisted, "from a distance. We can make your hair identical. And if we shoot you in profile, in shadow, no one will be able to tell the difference."

Jon couldn't believe his ears. "You want me to be Luke Kelly? What about my voice? I'm not a mimic."

"Don't worry about that," Fitzgerald told him. "We'll get someone convincing to dub the voice when we're back in LA. Will you do it?"

Jon thought about it. "Didn't you just tell the press conference that practically all of Luke's part had already been shot?"

Fitzgerald smiled ruefully. "I was lying. The last thing we want is for the public to realize that they're not watching the real Luke Kelly. We've got a love scene and the climax to do. We'll need you for three days' shooting on a closed, high-security set. Are you in?"

It was obvious that Fitzgerald really needed Jon. It seemed a mercenary thing to do, but Jon decided to be hard-nosed about the deal.

"How much extra will you pay me?"

Fitzgerald smiled as though he'd been expecting the question.

"We can't do this through the books. The unions would have a fit. I'll put you down on incidental expenses. Two thousand pounds, in your back pocket."

"Five."

The director kept a poker face. "All right," he said finally, "three."

Jon shook his head. "Split it down the middle."

"OK, four." Fitzgerald sighed. "That's a lot of money for an eighteen-year-old."

Jon smiled and shook his hand. "Maybe I'll use it to finance my first film."

Fitzgerald laughed unconvincingly. "See Debbie, the production accountant. She'll give you half tomorrow and half when you've finished. Now remember, absolute secrecy on this. Only the people who are directly involved in the production need to know about it."

"OK," said Jon. They shook hands.

"You'd better learn this," Fitzgerald told him, thrusting a computer print-out into Jon's hands. "I've just rewritten it to avoid having to shoot any close-ups. Your lines are marked."

Jon went back to his room and read the pages. Who would die at the end? Brett, as in one version? Or Luke, as in another? At last he would get to find out.

* * *

Sarah looked at herself in the mirror. It was the morning after Luke's death and she felt haggard. At seventeen, she looked thirty-five. It would take Make-up a lot of time to get her halfway presentable. The show had to go on, Leo Fitzgerald said, and she had to fulfil her contract. But the last thing she felt like filming was a love scene, body double, or no body double.

There was a knock on her door. She hoped that it was Jon. He had comforted her the previous afternoon, but she hadn't spoken to him since the press conference to announce Luke's death. When she'd called his room, Todd had been evasive about Jon's whereabouts.

"Come in," she called.

Jon was an enigma to her. Until yesterday afternoon, he'd behaved so coldly during the shoot, Sarah had half suspected him of being behind one of the odd accidents which had plagued them. She hated the way he looked at her sometimes, like she wasn't his sister, but some kind of object.

No one opened the door, so Sarah got up and opened it herself. It wasn't Jon. He would have just barged in, not waiting for her to reply. It was Brett. The actor was holding a bunch of white lilies.

"I thought you might appreciate someone to talk to," he told her.

"Thanks," she said, taking the flowers. "It was nice of you to come."

"You've got a pretty bad press this morning," Brett said. "I thought someone ought to warn you."

"It's OK," Sarah said. "I'm expecting it."

"You think you are," Brett told her, "but when the vilification starts to hit you, it'll hurt. I know. I've been there."

Sarah remembered various rumours about Brett's past.

"I know what it's like to be responsible for someone's death," Brett told her.

"You do?"

He nodded. "A girl I was dating, not much older than you. I was a wreck at the time, out of my head on drugs and booze. I was driving her to the beach. I went off the road, turned the car over. I got out of the car without a scratch on me. She broke her neck. There isn't a day goes by that I don't think about that girl and her family."

"It's good of you to confide in me," Sarah told him, "but you're not making me feel any better."

Brett smiled sincerely. It was odd, being here alone with him. It didn't feel real. His expression was so familiar, Sarah felt like she was watching him in a movie.

"The point I'm trying to make," Brett said, "is that I was responsible for that girl's death. But you aren't responsible for Luke's. He killed himself, deliberately or otherwise."

"If it hadn't been for me..." Sarah began to say.

Brett shook his head. "It might still have happened the same way. Luke was a reckless young man who found it hard to handle fame. His career had hit a plateau and he knew that the only place for him to go from there on was down. Maybe he decided that it was better to be a dead legend than a live has-been."

"You think so?"

"I do. There've been times when I've considered that course myself." He leant forward. "Listen to me, Sarah. Luke was talented but, from what I've seen, you have the promise to be a more mature actor than he was. You're already a more mature person. Don't let his death drag you down too."

There was a call from outside.

"Sarah, are you ready?"

"Coming."

She stood up and kissed Brett on the forehead.

"Thanks," she told him. "You helped."

When Sarah walked onto the set, she thought she was seeing a ghost.

"...Luke?"

For a moment, she thought she was going to faint, but then she heard her brother's voice.

"Didn't anybody warn you?"

"You're pretending to be Luke?"

"That's right."

She turned to Leo Fitzgerald. "Does that mean we still have to do the love scene?"

"That's right."

"So where's my body double?"

Fitzgerald looked irritated. "What do you mean?"

"I told you before that I'm not going to take my clothes off. Sally said she'd sorted it out with you. I haven't changed my mind."

"We can't have both people in a love scene played by body doubles," Leo protested, "it wouldn't work."

"That's your problem," Sarah told him.

Fitzgerald threw his hands in the air. "All right, I give in. Let's drop it. Luke was the one who was really keen on the nudity anyway."

Sarah was flabbergasted. "It was *Luke's* idea?"

"That's right. He said that steamy sex scenes were important to his new image."

"Now are you convinced that he was a prat?" Jon whispered.

"Yes," Sarah muttered back. "I think I am."

"OK," said Fitzgerald. "Jon, get down to your shorts. Sarah, put your nightie on. Let's get on with this."

They both changed and got into bed. It felt ridiculous.

"Oh, Aidan," said Sarah. "How could I have been so wrong about you?"

"It's not your fault," Jon replied, in a flat monotone. "Anyway, we're together now. I love you."

"And I love you too…"

As Brett burst into the room, interrupting them *in flagrante*, both Jon and Sarah burst into hysterical laughter.

"Cut!"

"I'm sorry," said Sarah, still giggling, as she let out all the tension of the weekend. "This might take some time."

17

"Are the rumours true?" Mary asked Jon as he sat down for his lunch. "Are you doubling for Luke?"

"My lips are sealed."

"I'll bet they are!"

She planted a kiss on them. Suddenly, after flirting with Jon for nearly six weeks, she was making a play for him. Jon was flattered, but he wasn't interested. These days he was too concerned with acting and his sister's safety to get involved in a romance.

"What are you doing tonight?" she asked.

"I'm busy," he told her with a grin. "I've got lines to learn."

"Some other time maybe."

"Maybe."

She got up to go, looking hurt. She wasn't used to being given the brush-off.

"Oh," she said, trying to sound casual but with an edge to her voice. "Have you seen the papers?"

"Only *The Guardian*."

"Congratulations!" she said bitchily. "You made the front page of both the *Mirror* and *The Sun*."

Mary pulled a paper out of her bag, handed it to Jon, and walked off.

"THE GIRL WHO DROVE LUKE KELLY TO HIS DEATH" was the headline. Beneath it was a photograph of Sarah and Jon, walking into the hotel two days before. The caption said that the photo was of "*Luke with supermodel Sarah, only hours before his death. A few minutes after this photograph was taken, she dumped him.*"

"What?" Jon said aloud.

The story was worse.

> *Superstar Luke Kelly took his own life after being rejected by haughty supermodel Sarah Wood, friends believe. Luke had told them that Sarah was "the love of his life", but she dumped him after a tempestuous, month-long romance. "She was just playing with his affections," a close colleague said, "and when he got too serious she dropped him like a hot brick. Luke was heartbroken."*
>
> *The police will not say whether Luke's death was accidental or suicide, and the inquest may be delayed because of difficulties excavating the quarry where Luke met his tragic death. He and Sarah had visited it only hours before in the car which he would die in. Psychologists say that the manner of his death was almost certainly a message to Sarah. Miss Wood was unavailable for comment last night.*
>
> *Meanwhile, fans all over the world have been mourning the superstar's death.*

"It's unbelievable!" Jon said to Todd, who was sitting by him. "They're vilifying her!"

"That's just the press," Todd replied. "Wait until some of Luke's fans get anywhere near Sarah. They're bound to blame her for his death. If I were her, I'd get a bodyguard for the next year or two."

The days immediately after Luke's death were the worst. The production was constantly plagued by the press. Sarah couldn't see Jon, except on the closed set, in case his role leaked to the media. The story still hadn't died down. On the breakfast news, there had been an item about how police had had to abandon attempts to dig out Luke's body because of the danger. There'd been another landslide.

Sarah was upset about Luke's death and still blamed herself, but there was no one she could really talk to about it. Jon was too biased against Luke. Her parents were too far away. And her part in *This Year's Model*, which was meant to boost her career, was having the opposite effect. In the few days since his death, Luke's legend had grown and grown. Teenage girls held endless wakes. Actors who had refused to work with him in the past saluted his "great talent". There was talk of a posthumous Oscar. His death was romantic – attributed not to drink or drugs but to a broken heart. And Sarah was the one who broke it. She was Public Enemy Number One. She had no movie future and the papers now described her as an "ex-supermodel". Sally rang to say that there had been several cancellations.

"Adverts that are meant to appeal to young women, basically," Sally explained. "Obviously they can't risk alienating the Luke Kelly audience while you're cast as the villain of the piece."

"I see," Sarah replied. "Have there been any new offers?"

"Only the kind that you don't like me to pass on to you," Sally told her. "Men's magazines, that kind of thing. Don't worry. It'll all come out in the wash."

But Sarah knew it would take a long time to revamp her image. She'd had an incredibly successful year, but now it looked like it was all ending. Maybe it was for the best. Whatever talent she had wasn't worth the fantastic sums she earned. She was being paid for the way she looked, that was the sum of it.

And her looks were all that Luke Kelly had fallen for: a sexy waif with an English accent. Sarah wanted to be more than that. She wanted relationships that were more than skin deep. She wouldn't find what she was looking for in the fashion world, nor in motion pictures, that was for sure. Maybe she ought to welcome the end of her success. Maybe it was time for her to move on.

Since Luke's death, security had really tightened up. There was no chance of someone like Slacker hanging around the set now. Two of the guards even carried guns. The large men assured Sarah that this was to make her absolutely secure, but she wasn't convinced. Having guns around made her feel more at risk.

Every day there were reporters hanging around Bradlington Hall. Today, Sarah also noticed several young women, about her own age. They were wearing *Luke Kelly – the legend lives* T-shirts. When they saw Sarah coming, the women hissed. One of them shouted: "Murderess! Killer!"

Then there were other obscenities and threats. Sarah kept her head down. She felt terrible. In a way, she wanted to go over to them and explain, but anything she said would probably make things worse.

Sarah walked on to the set, script in hand, and greeted Jon. Finally the truth was to be revealed. Which of the men was the monster:

the father or the son? Sarah knew the answer which was in the script, but she wouldn't be surprised if Fitzgerald changed it at the last moment. As she prepared, she could see the director and Brett, talking intensely.

"You ready?" she asked her brother.

"Ready as I'll ever be."

"All right," called Fitzgerald. "Let's go for it."

Sarah stood in the doorway, just behind a full-length mirror. Melissa was watching Matthew prepare the poison which was to kill her. He had been evil all along, while Aidan was in the right. Now, Matthew thought that his son was out of the way, and so did Melissa. But Aidan had secretly returned. In a moment Melissa, eavesdropping on her husband, would accidentally make a noise. Matthew would see her and realize that the game was up.

"OK, Sarah," Leo called. "Prepare to react as though your heel's suddenly snapped."

Sarah was meant to fall forward, in front of the mirror, but as she did, there was a commotion at the edge of the set. A teenage girl, not much younger than her, came running across the room screaming obscenities, pursued by a security guard.

Suddenly there was pandemonium. Several more young women followed the screaming girl. There were reporters close behind. Sarah flinched as the girl threw something at her. It landed on her chest. Then there was a flash like lightning. Sarah dropped to the ground, a red stain spreading across her chest.

"It's all right," Brett told Sarah, helping her up. "It's only tomato ketchup. They were setting you up for a photograph."

As Sarah looked around she saw Leo, wrestling with a photographer. A security guard grabbed the man from behind and Leo opened his camera, removing the film. "Get him out!" he shouted.

A minute later the other security guard returned and began apologizing to Leo. "All of a sudden there were so many of them. I think they were goaded on by some of the reporters. They made a run for it, with the press following. It won't happen again."

"It'd better not," Fitzgerald said, angrily. "Is everything clear?"

"We've got them all out. We're doubling the security presence at both entrances to the house."

"All right," said Fitzgerald. "Let's get on with it." He turned to the wardrobe manager. "Have we got another dress like that? We have to have her in the same dress for continuity."

"I'll get one."

Sarah got changed, feeling shaken. Even the men with guns hadn't made her any safer. Nor had she had one word of sympathy from the director. As soon as the film is over, she thought to herself, I'm going to get out of all this for a while. I'm not going to let them break me. I'll show everybody what I'm made of.

"Action!"

In her new dress, Melissa lurched out from behind the mirror. Matthew looked up. For a moment he looked alarmed, but then his suave, sneaky smiled returned.

"Hello, honey," he said. "I was just coming to look for you."

"I'll bet you were," Melissa told him.

"That's right," Matthew said, tipping the powder he'd been grinding into a glass of water. "I've made you a drink."

"Is that how you got rid of the others?" Melissa asked, with a sneer. "You poisoned them?"

"I've used it once before," Matthew admitted casually. "I made it look like heart failure."

"And the other deaths?"

"I arranged ... accidents for them. However, in your case, the poison you'll be taking is very easy to detect. So, you see, I have to make it look like suicide."

"And how," Melissa asked, sardonically, "do you plan to do that?"

"Why," Matthew replied, "you're going to make it easy for me. You're going to sign this note."

He pointed to a sheet of paper sticking out of his typewriter. "Take it out," he said.

Melissa's body and her voice seemed to shake a little.

"What, and put my fingerprints on it? You must be joking."

Matthew shook his head. "No jokes. Take it out or I'll kill you with my bare hands." He grabbed Melissa and pulled her close to him. "Take it out!"

Without speaking, Melissa did as she was told. She read the note aloud.

"Matthew, my love,

I cannot live with my conscience any more. Now you know that

I have been having an affair with Aidan, there is no hope for me. Aidan made me promises, but he has broken them. You were right about him all along. He's a liar and a cheat. I can't live with the ruin I've made of my life. Please forgive me, my darling. I won't be around to trouble you any more,

Your love,"

"Very sweet, the way you read that," Matthew told her. "Very convincing. Now sign it."

"You're joking!"

"No joke. Just write the one word, 'Melissa', underneath the word 'love'."

"And then you'll kill me?"

"Oh, no, my darling. Then you'll kill yourself. It'll be a quick death. And, believe me, the alternative is far more painful." He lifted her off her feet and pointed to the window. "The alternative is that I throw you out through that window. You'll probably be dead before you hit the ground, from fright."

"Like your third wife?"

"Precisely. Now sign it."

He put her down. Melissa picked up the pen, playing for time. She wrote her name very, very slowly as Matthew coaxed her.

"That's better. That's more like it. It'll all be over very quickly, I assure you."

They stood facing each other after she'd put the pen down.

"Satisfied?" she asked.

"Not yet," Matthew said. He picked up the drink.

"I'll be satisfied when you've drunk this," he told her. She took the drink from his hands.

"Why?" she asked him. "Is it because of me and Aidan? Or were you always planning to do this?"

"I meant to do this all along," Matthew admitted, without any sign of guilt. "My son's involvement only made it happen sooner." He smiled, then added, "Don't worry. He's next. Now, drink."

Melissa lifted the glass to her lips while Matthew continued to gloat. Then, with a quick jerking motion, she threw the drink all over his face.

Matthew took a step back, turning red with rage. "Young lady," he said, "you just made a big mistake."

"No," said Aidan, stepping into the room with a gun in his hand. "You're the one who made the mistake, Father!"

"Don't kill him!" Melissa shouted. "He's not worth it."

"Justifiable homicide," Aidan announced, pointing the gun. "The worst I'll get is a suspended sentence."

Matthew's face turned pale. Melissa waited awkwardly. The script called for Matthew to leap at Aidan just as he fired, making the shooting seem more justifiable. But it didn't work out that way. Just as Aidan squeezed the trigger, Matthew grabbed Melissa instead, pulling her in front of him.

Sarah didn't hear the gun go off. The next thing she felt was a searing pain across her chest and she was falling to the floor. There was a red patch spreading across her chest. Only this time it wasn't tomato ketchup. It was blood.

18

"Stupid move, sucker!" Matthew announced. "You won't get a suspended sentence for that."

"Cut!" Fitzgerald called. "Great work. I'm really glad we got that twist in. Sarah, you were superb. I'm sorry that I didn't warn you or Jon about the grab. I wanted a look of real surprise. Hey, Brett, did you have to burst such a big blood bag on to her?"

"It was a normal size one," Brett said.

"What I don't understand," Jon said to the director, "is what happens after this. I mean, it can't just end there, can it?"

The director tapped his nose with his finger.

"There might be a little more, but that's all I'm going to tell you. You'll have to wait until you see the final cut. Sorry, but I don't want any rumours leaking out."

"Killing the girl at the end is a brave move," Brett congratulated Leo. "A real anti-Hollywood ending. Do you think you can make it sell?"

"After what happened to Luke?" Fitzgerald said. "And with the way people feel about Sarah at the moment? They'll be cheering."

Jon felt angry at the way Fitzgerald had duped them. It seemed like the director was able to turn anything to his advantage. He walked over to his sister. There was still a pool of red liquid spreading around her. She hadn't got up.

"Sarah," he said, "are you all right? Sarah?" He leant over her. Blood was still pouring from her left breast. "Sarah?"

Her eyes flickered open for a moment but he could tell that she didn't really know what was going on. Jon began to yell.

"Get a doctor!" he screamed. "Call an ambulance! She's been shot! She's really been shot!"

19

Finally, the police let Jon go. He hurried to the hotel, where he changed and picked up his mail, then he took a taxi to the hospital. The surgeon who had operated on Sarah accompanied him down a corridor to the ward she was in.

"Your parents are already in there," she told him.

"Thanks."

"At least the press haven't got their hands on it," the surgeon went on. "The last thing your sister needs right now is to be hounded by the newspapers."

"Sure," Jon agreed.

It was funny, he thought, how Leo Fitzgerald could keep things out of the newspapers when he wanted to. Not a word had appeared about the accident which killed Karen either.

"Basically," the surgeon said, "it was a flesh wound. She lost a lot of blood and she needs time to rest and recuperate. Then she'll have a small scar, that's all."

"You're sure?"

"I'm sure. Now I'll leave you alone with your family."

She showed Jon into the room. Jon couldn't see his sister for the flowers which surrounded her. His parents stood up and greeted him. They hugged. Sarah smiled weakly. She was very pale. For once, she looked younger than her age.

"Hello," she said. "Sorry I can't get up to kiss you."

He embraced her.

"Did you get them?" she asked.

"What? Who?" He had no idea what she meant.

"Your A-level results. Did you get them?"

"Oh, that." He nodded. "An A and two Bs."

"That's brilliant!" Sarah said. "Congratulations."

Mum and Dad told him the same thing.

"How do you feel?" he asked Sarah.

"I'll survive," she sighed. "I guess this is one way of forcing myself to take a rest, decide what to do next. I've just been talking to Mum and Dad about it. I'm thinking of going back to school."

"Really?"

"Yeah. Why should you be the only one in the family to get a degree?" Sarah smiled weakly.

"Do they know what happened?" she asked.

Jon shook his head. "Not really. Somehow, the prop gun got switched with one belonging to a security guard. He left his holster in an office when they were chasing those girls who invaded the set. But no one can explain how they got switched. The police interviewed me for hours. I think they suspected me of wanting to kill you!"

"Where did you pick up the gun?" Sarah asked. "Didn't you notice that it was different?"

Jon shook his head. "As I told the police, I picked it up from a table by the door, just before I shot you. It was where it was meant to be. I took the safety catch off as I walked into the room."

"Could it have been an accident, a mix-up?" Mum asked.

"That's what Leo says, but I don't see how. The way I see it, someone switched those guns deliberately."

"But who?" Dad asked. "Who has a motive?"

Jon shrugged. "The police are trying to get hold of the fans who charged on to the set. They had it in for Sarah. But to switch guns, they'd have had to have known what was in the final script, which is more than I did."

"Can you think of anyone else who might have a motive?" Mum asked Sarah.

She thought for a minute. "The only person I can think of who'd consider doing a thing like that is Luke Kelly. And he's dead."

February

20

Unshaven, Jon got to the Arts faculty corridor at nine precisely and put his essay into Professor Cobain's pigeonhole. He had been up all night, but he had made the deadline. He had lectures to go to but he could borrow someone else's notes. All he wanted to do was get back to his Hall of Residence and catch some sleep.

Before going up to bed, he checked his own pigeonhole. There was an expensive-looking, cream-coloured envelope waiting for him. He took it up to his room and opened it.

You are invited to a charity première of a Leo Fitzgerald film, This Year's Model, *starring Brett Johnson and Luke Kelly in the presence of HRH...*

Jon threw the embossed invitation to the floor. It annoyed him that the two men were listed as starring in the film, but Sarah wasn't. He got into bed. Should he go to the première? He wanted to see it, of course, but maybe he could wait until it showed up at the local cinema. He had no desire to meet members of the Royal Family. Then again, Sarah might want him there.

Jon's sister had changed since making the film. She had wound down her modelling career and was doing a one-year "A" level course in Drama and English Literature at the same college as many of the friends she went to school with. At first, it had been hard for Sarah. For a while there, Jon thought that she was on the verge of some kind of breakdown. She got a lot of press harassment. She took to wearing ugly glasses and baggy clothes so that editors were reluctant to publish photos of her. Then things loosened up. By the time she appeared in a college production of *Volpone,* a month ago, the press had totally lost interest in her.

Jon thought that Sarah was very good in the play. At Christmas, and at the party after the play, he'd been amazed by how relaxed she looked, and how ordinary. The aura of glamour which had descended on Sarah when she was barely a teenager had somehow been lifted. She looked much happier for it.

Jon was happy too. Working on *This Year's Model* had convinced him that he wanted a career in the film industry. He wanted to write screenplays and, if possible, to direct them too. But it was a hard world to break into. There was no British film industry worth speaking of and he had only limited contacts. If he was going to get anywhere he'd have to work hard at it.

Already, he'd invested much of the money Leo gave him for doubling Luke Kelly in buying Super-8 film equipment. He'd started making a film featuring some student friends at weekends and during vacations. Hopefully, by the end of his course, he'd have a portfolio of work impressive enough to get him into the National Film School.

As Jon lay in his bed, trying to get to sleep, his mind whirred over the events of the previous summer. It had all been so dramatic, yet, looking back, he felt like he'd been an observer most of the time, like he was standing outside the action. But Jon often felt that way in life. Maybe that made him a natural writer/director. He noticed things that other people were too involved to pick up.

Sarah, when Jon last spoke to her about it, still thought that all the things which went wrong during the film shoot were accidents. Maybe, in her position, that was the only sensible thing to believe. Otherwise, she would still be worrying that someone was going to kill her at any moment.

But Jon wasn't so sure. After all, there had been five "accidents" during the making of the film. All but one – Luke Kelly's death – took place in suspicious circumstances. Jon figured that Luke had committed suicide as a way of getting back at Sarah. It showed how unbalanced the star was.

But that left four other "accidents", all of which could have killed his sister. OK, maybe some of them were coincidences, but *all four*? Jon resolved to go to the première if Sarah was going. The danger wouldn't be over until the killer was captured. At last he slept, dreaming of anonymous serial killers stepping out of enormous cinema screens.

* * *

Sarah didn't really want to go to the première, but it was for charity and she felt obliged. Once her health returned, she'd enjoyed being out of the public eye. And she'd applied to join RADA next year. She knew that if she wanted to be a good actress, she'd have to work hard at it.

Giving up modelling had been easy. All the bad publicity had cost her a lot of jobs. Anyway, since then the look had changed. No one wanted thin nymphets with flat chests any more. They wanted older, more full-bodied girls. Sarah didn't care. She'd made a load of money. She knew how little glamour there was in the fashion world. Now she wanted to get on with her real life.

Yet here she was, about to attend a press conference for *This Year's Model*, to be followed by a charity première that evening. Luke's death had created massive publicity for the film. A record number of prints had been made. In America, where it had been released two months ago, it was already a huge hit. But all the publicity had focused on Luke and his legend, not Sarah's performance.

Sarah ignored Leo Fitzgerald as she walked up the stairs to the table. Brett Johnson leant across and squeezed her hand. "You look great."

"I wish I didn't have to be here."

"Baptism of fire. You'll get used to it."

The conference began. Leo Fitzgerald gave a spiel about what a privilege it was that his film had been chosen for the charity event and pleaded with the press not to give away the movie's shock ending. Then Brett spoke about what a great privilege it was to work for Leo. He said he'd had a rough few years but now he was on the track to recovery. In response to a question he grinned and admitted that, yes, he was about to star in a major new TV series, but he wasn't at liberty to reveal the details just yet.

Then it was Sarah's turn.

She tried to keep her voice calm as she spoke into the microphone. But it was hard not to be aware of all the television cameras, to be conscious that millions of people across the world would be watching if she made a fool of herself. Sarah spoke briefly about what a big break the film had been for her and how she hoped eventually to have a career in acting.

"Wait until you see her performance," Brett broke in. "And

you'll see that she doesn't have to hope. After this film, she'll be a major star."

Sarah smiled bashfully. "Thanks, Brett."

"We have time for a couple of questions," Leo said.

"Sarah," a woman from a TV news crew said, "now that you've had time to reflect on it, do you feel responsible in any way for Luke Kelly's death?"

"There's no need for her to answer that," Brett interrupted. "That's insulting."

"It's all right," Sarah said. "I'd like to answer it. My reply is: no, I am not responsible for what happened to Luke. It's true we argued that day, but I did not treat him badly – the reverse. I'm sorry about what happened, but we are all responsible for our own actions, and must take the consequences of them."

"Sarah, how have you dealt with the feelings of hate from Luke's fans? There's even a rumour that one of them *shot* you."

Sarah smiled sadly. "I'm not going to comment on rumours. And, as I said, I feel sorry about Luke and sorry for his fans. They want someone to lash out at. I can understand that. But I don't read the hate mail. It would be too upsetting."

"That's all we have time for from Sarah," Leo announced. There was a shuffling noise as the media prepared to leave.

"But please don't turn your cameras or microphones off yet," the director pleaded. "Because we have a special surprise guest."

Sarah had no idea what the producer was talking about. They were bringing someone out from behind the curtain which served as a backdrop to the stage. There was an audible gasp.

"The fool!" Brett Johnson said, in a whisper loud enough for Sarah to hear. "A stroke like this might get him some cheap publicity, but it'll ruin his career at the same time."

Every reporter in the hall was yelling. Sarah looked around, curious to see who they had brought out. She was faced with a familiar, sickeningly smug grin. The object of everybody's attention walked towards her.

"You!" Sarah said, in a kind of hiss. Then she fainted.

21

Jon didn't usually watch television in the afternoon, but he was getting changed to go down to London for the première of his sister's film. He had rented a tuxedo from a costume hirer's and felt like a complete idiot.

He'd turn the set off in a minute, when children's programmes began, but in the meantime he might as well just take a look at the news headlines. For a while, in the summer, he'd not been aware of anything going on outside the tiny area of a film set. It was easy, he thought, for film people to think that they were the centre of the world, when all around them were wars, famine, corruption and other things which needed changing.

But today the main story wasn't about any of those things.

"Amazing scenes today at London's Metropolitan Hotel," the newsreader said, "as a film star literally returned from the dead. Luke Kelly, who co-starred alongside Brett Johnson in the new Warner's release *This Year's Model*, was thought to have died six months ago, when his car fell into a disused quarry. However, the body was never recovered, and today Kelly used the occasion of the British première of the film to announce his return. Mark Briggs reports."

The picture showed not Luke, but Sarah. She was talking at a press conference. However, the voice-over told another story.

"Luke Kelly's death was a secret which he kept from everybody. Even his ex-girlfriend, former supermodel Sarah Wood, was obviously in great shock."

The screen showed Sarah turning round, seeing Luke, and fainting.

"But Kelly, characteristically, made no apologies..."

The picture cut to Luke, dressed in black, smiling soberly as he faced the cameras. He spoke from a script.

"Films have been my whole life for five years now. It's difficult for me to exaggerate the pressures of stardom. This film, for various reasons, was very difficult for me. After it, I was due to return to the States to make another in a series of movies I hated. I couldn't take the pressure any more. I wanted out and I took the only escape I could think of. I pretended to die."

"What about all the people you upset, Luke?"

Kelly glared at the camera.

"I made sure that the people who were closest to me knew what was going on. As for my fans – well, I'm grateful for their support, but I never asked them to make me some kind of a god. I'll understand if some of them feel let down by what I've done. But, you know, they don't know me, and they certainly don't own me. I did what I had to do."

"What exactly did you do, Luke? Where did you go?"

Luke smiled lugubriously.

"I went on a long journey – finding myself, if you like. I decided that I'd come back when I was ready. And now I am."

"Would it be fair to say that what you did was a stunt to get you out of a contract you hated and revive a fading career?"

"That's pathetic. I won't answer that."

A more enthusiastic voice shouted out, "Have you sold the film rights yet, Luke?"

He laughed and shook his head. "No, but as soon as we're through here, my agent will be very happy to deal with enquiries for the rights to *Vanishing Trick – The Luke Kelly Story*."

"Will you be at the première tonight?"

"I wouldn't miss it for anything. I'm a big fan of your Royal Family."

Jon noticed that Sarah and Brett had left the stage. Presumably they were as sickened by the whole thing as he was. On TV, even the newsreader looked a little disapproving.

"Tell me, Mark," she asked the reporter, "how has the film world reacted to the news of Luke Kelly's resurrection?"

"Well, Anna, a lot of people are saying that Kelly has gone just a bit too far this time. They're saying that the only role he's likely to pick up in the near future is that of Lord Lucan."

"Mark, thank you very much. And now the rest of the news..."

Two hours later, Jon spent nearly as long finding a parking place in the West End as it had taken him to drive there. He was meeting his sister inside. He wore his wire-rimmed spectacles, not wanting anyone to confuse him with Luke Kelly.

There was a throng of people outside the Warner West End, noisily waiting for the celebrities to arrive. Most of the people watching the film, however, would be ordinary punters who had paid a fortune for their charity ticket. Jon walked into Ruth who looked very different with her hair down. He'd read that she was about to make her first full feature. Ruth's boyfriend was a dark-haired man with a black beard. He was the man Jon had heard discussing Sarah's death with Leo in the trailer. The press collared him.

"Mr Costello, you wrote the original script for this film. Are you happy with the final cut?"

"I haven't seen it yet," the scriptwriter said, in a disenchanted tone. "I have no further comment."

No one said a word as Jon walked in himself, wishing that he hadn't had to wear a dinner jacket. To his surprise, Sarah was already in the cinema, waiting for him in their seats. She wore a striking, backless red dress.

"Why're you here so early?" he asked her.

"I wanted to avoid the crowds, and certain other people..."

"I understand. Mind you, now that Luke's alive, presumably your hate mail will stop."

Sarah grimaced.

"Presumably. But I wish that I could pay him back for all the grief he's caused me."

"You don't think..."

"What?"

Jon shook his head. "Nah, it's crazy. Only with him still being alive, I thought that maybe the shooting..."

Sarah finished the sentence for him.

"...was Luke taking revenge on me? That's ridiculous. He's a spoilt, silly brat, but he's not that vindictive. No. I've convinced myself that all the odd things that happened on the shoot were just that – odd accidents. So please don't start up about it again. After tonight, I want to put everything to do with *This Year's Model* behind me."

"After tonight, you might be a star."

"*Please!* I haven't had any offers since it opened in the States. The reviews only mention me as a sinister sex object. My movie career was dead before it started."

Seats filled up. Jon spotted a familiar face.

"Yo, Slacker! You couldn't stay away, huh?"

The long-haired youth came over, smiling bashfully. It was odd to see him dressed in a jacket and tie.

"You're right," he said. "I couldn't resist seeing how it all turned out, though the ticket cost me an arm and a leg. What about Luke Kelly, eh? He sure had me fooled."

"Me too," said Sarah. "Look, I never got the chance to thank you ... for what you did. I didn't find out about it until..."

"No sweat," Slacker told her. "You know, I was just hanging around, looking for some action. Anyone would have done what I did. I'm only glad that I managed to do something useful for once."

"Anyway," Sarah said, kissing him on the cheek, "thanks."

"You're welcome. Hey, aren't you meant to be meeting the Queen or something?"

"Oh, God!" said Sarah, checking her watch. "You're right."

Sarah got to the lobby in time to see Luke arriving, a beautiful, buxom starlet on his arm. Brett distracted Sarah.

"Don't look," he said. "He's not worth it."

Sarah smiled gracefully.

"You're right. I just want to make sure that I'm standing at the opposite end of the line from him."

"Come with me. I'll protect you. You know, you're looking particularly ravishing tonight. If I was twenty years younger..."

"You'd still be too old," Sarah told him.

Brett laughed.

"I like a woman who speaks her mind. Got any work lined up?"

Sarah shook her head.

"I've not looked. I'm thinking of going to drama school."

"Don't. Keep your talent fresh, untrained. The shadow's gone from your reputation now. You'll get lots of offers. Believe me."

They were interrupted.

"Mind if I stand between my two favourite stars?"

Sarah frowned at Leo Fitzgerald, but said nothing. The Royals would be arriving at any minute. The hall was already quietening in anticipation.

"That was a stupid stunt, Leo," Brett muttered.

"Don't complain," Leo replied, under his breath. "It gave you the biggest hit of your career."

"At what cost?"

"Look," Leo hissed. "It wasn't my idea, but I went along with it. I'm annoyed with Luke, too. He was meant to hold back his reappearance until the film had had a full theatrical release. I think that he wanted to get back at Miss Goody Two Shoes here."

Sarah smiled. She was glad that she still had some power over Luke Kelly.

"But look at it this way," Fitzgerald went on. "You've got your TV series. Sarah's career will recover. The only person who'll suffer is Kelly. It's his funeral. Who's going to hire him after a débâcle like this? He's committed commercial suicide."

"The witness," Sarah whispered, suddenly curious. "The motorcyclist. Did you pay him off?"

Fitzgerald nodded. "Luke did. The motorcyclist was an actor. The police won't be able to trace him. Mind you, they've already said that they want to interview Luke tomorrow. I hope he doesn't try to drag me into this. After all, I've already lost my favourite car."

There was a sudden hush as the Royal couple arrived. Sarah stood in line. Why was it, she wondered, that the Americans seemed more in awe of royalty than the Brits? When her turn came, she politely answered a question about modelling. Leo offered the Princess a role in his next film. Brett, however, got all tongue-tied. Then, mercifully, it was over. At last it was time to see the film.

22

Sarah slid into her seat next to Jon, then everyone had to stand up again as the Royal couple entered their box. Finally, the film began. The credits rolled, superimposed over the catwalk sequence, as Elvis Costello sang the title song. It was very sexy, very impressive. Sarah had avoided the cinema since making the film. She'd almost forgotten how mesmerizing an experience it could be.

The camera panned over the models on stage at the fashion show. As Prince sang "I wanna melt with you", the camera slowed down and zoomed in on Melissa. Sarah had seen herself in magazines and on television, but never like this: dressed to kill and two hundred feet tall. She didn't know how to react. The picture cut to Matthew.

"That one," he was saying. "The girl in yellow. I want her. What's her name?"

"Melissa. She's beautiful," the hard-looking woman next to him replied. "A little young maybe."

"I like them young. Get her on the country house shoot."

There was a short scene establishing Melissa, where she was offered the job at Matthew's friend's mansion. Then the film moved on to location. Bradlington Hall and the country surrounding it looked very different from the way Sarah had experienced it. She'd found the landscape boring, but on screen it looked quintessentially English. No wonder the Americans had lapped it up.

It was interesting for Jon to see it all on the big screen, slickly edited: Matthew's "accidental" meeting with Melissa (none of the fatal overhead shots were used) in the rain, then his careful seduction of her. Hitchcock would have done it better, Jon thought.

He would have made Brett more sympathetic, more ambiguous. The way Leo had filmed it, you guessed that Matthew was a sleaze-ball from the start and the only issue was how corrupt he was. Had he actually killed his wives? And, if he had, would he do the same to Melissa?

The story unfolded. Sarah looked quite impressive, Jon thought, but it was hard for him to be objective about her performance or the film itself. Jon was too close to both. He knew exactly what was going to happen. The ballroom scene dragged, and the way in which Fitzgerald developed the relationship between Aidan and Melissa seemed laboured. But maybe that was because Jon disliked Luke so much.

Finally, it got to the parts Jon was most interested in seeing. The fire scene looked dazzling. On the score, the composer had used powerful gothic chords, like the ones Bernard Hermann used in *Psycho,* to build up the tension. The director kept cutting between Melissa trapped in her room and Aidan trying to get to her. Aidan knocked out his father in a fight, then you saw him battling his way through the flames. It annoyed Jon, though, to see Sarah in the role of weak victim, waiting to be saved. In real life, she hadn't panicked, as Luke had. She'd waited bravely until she didn't have the strength to escape.

In real life, Luke never actually got to Sarah, but the director got around this in a clever way. All you saw on the screen was a blazing inferno, but the music, along with Aidan's empassioned cries and coughs, convinced the viewer that he was still courageously fighting his way through the fire; that he got to Melissa; and, finally, that he was carrying her out of the building. At the end of the sequence, you saw Aidan and Melissa emerging into the daylight in their fire-damaged clothes. Aidan carried Melissa over his shoulder, then collapsed as soon as he was away from the burning house. It was very effective.

Jon was less convinced by the love scene. In the seat next to him, Sarah began to giggle. The pair of them had found it hard to keep a straight face while performing this very tame bed scene. The close-ups of Melissa showed the stress Sarah was under after Luke's death. For obvious reasons, there were no close-ups of Jon, until the very end of the scene, when, suddenly, Aidan stood up and walked over to a window to say his lines. Jon blinked. There were hairs on his chest where he didn't have any. Sarah poked him in the ribs.

"That's not you," she whispered. "That's Luke. Leo must have got him to film some pick-up shots in LA when he was in hiding."

That was Luke Kelly summed up, Jon thought: the actor couldn't resist taking his shirt off, even when he was supposed to be dead.

Sarah wasn't enjoying the film. She found watching her own performance excruciating. Everything on the screen reminded her of things she'd rather forget. However, she was curious to find out how it would end. She knew that she wasn't in it after the shooting, but didn't know what Fitzgerald had put in after that. The very end of the movie had been filmed in the studio, and Sarah wasn't needed. Her only involvement in the post-production process had been to dub a few lines of dialogue at a London studio.

The end was near. The film got to the part where Matthew was preparing the poison with which he meant to kill Melissa. The picture cut to Melissa, watching her husband from behind a full-length mirror. Sitting in the audience, Sarah didn't look at herself on the screen. She hated looking at herself. Instead, she focused on the mirror. To her surprise, she saw a fleeting image of somebody reflected there, somebody who wasn't supposed to be there. He had something in his hand. It looked like a gun.

Sarah froze in her seat. If this were a video, she could rewind it, make sure. But this was a Royal Command Performance. She remembered what had happened, how the filming of that sequence had been interrupted. There had been an invasion of irate fans. The person she thought she'd seen could have instigated it, could have sneaked in with them then, and switched the guns. Sarah began to feel scared. If what she saw was real, then that person really had tried to kill her. Her life was in danger. But that didn't make sense. Not unless…

Jon didn't notice his sister's distraction. He was anxious now to know how the film ended – whether Fitzgerald had gone for the traditional happy ending or something more cynical. On screen, Jon saw himself shoot his sister, exactly as it had happened. Then there was Matthew's triumphant smile. It seemed that he had managed to kill two birds with one stone: Melissa was dead and Aidan would go to gaol for the killing. But surely the film couldn't end that way? Jon half expected Aidan to appear again, with the same gun. He expected to see Aidan blow Matthew's brains out.

Aidan did appear again, played by Luke Kelly. But he was standing behind the dock in a studio court room. The judge was saying:

"You have been found guilty of murder in the first degree. Your crime was a dreadful one, that of killing your own stepmother, and you have compounded that crime by your defence, in which you have slurred the reputation both of your stepmother and your own father. I have nothing but contempt for you, young man, and there is only one sentence suitable for you. That sentence is death."

Aidan looked in shock. The picture cut to Matthew, trying to suppress a smile.

Next to Jon, Sarah was trying to get his attention.

"It's important. We've got to get up, *now*!"

"Hold on," he whispered.

"Jon. Move!"

Sarah was standing, pushing her way along the row. Reluctantly, Jon stood too, his eyes still glued to the picture. On the screen, Matthew was at another fashion show, with the hard-faced woman who'd appeared in the opening scene. The camera scanned the catwalk and focused on a young woman, very tall, with wide shoulders and an aristocratic expression.

"That one," Matthew said to the woman next to him. "I'd like that one."

The words "The End" appeared on the screen. People began to clap. To his surprise, Jon found himself clapping too. He was pleased that Fitzgerald had chosen a dark ending. It was more realistic.

"Jon!"

Sarah tugged him after her, into the aisle. Other people were beginning to stand up now, applauding enthusiastically.

"What is it?" Jon asked.

"We've got to get to Brett," Sarah shouted. "I think he's in danger."

"Brett? Why's Brett in danger?"

"I don't know why, but I think that it's Brett he's been after all along. Come on! We've got to warn him!"

Jon was confused. "Who's been after who?" he asked.

But Sarah was already pushing her way down the aisle as the audience began their standing ovation. The picture was a big hit, with this crowd at least. People tried to congratulate her.

"You were wonderful!"

"You're going to be huge!"

"When you got shot, it was so convincing!"

Sarah ignored them and continued pushing her way through the crowd.

"Where's he sitting?" Jon asked her.

"Over there. At the end of the row."

Jon wished that Sarah had time to explain why Brett was in danger. He could see the actor now. Brett wasn't standing or applauding. But then, you wouldn't, not when you were the star.

"Brett!" Sarah called, but he didn't seem to hear.

A woman was leaning over Brett, telling him how wonderful his performance had been, how he was bound to get an Oscar nomination for it.

"Brett, you've got to get out of here," Sarah said, elbowing aside members of the gathering crowd in order to get to him. Suddenly, the woman talking to Brett became distraught.

"He's been cut. He's been stabbed. Oh, God! There's blood all over him! He's dead!"

Sarah stopped. She turned to Jon. The colour had drained from her face.

"We've got to find Security. They can stop him, if he hasn't escaped already."

Her presence of mind amazed Jon.

"Who?" he asked. "Who did this?"

But Sarah was running over towards one of the exits. Jon followed her, looking around him. Upstairs, the Royal couple were being ushered out. If there was any risk, they would be the first to be evacuated. Jon guessed that most of the police officers present were with them. He could hear the woman who had found Brett explaining what had happened to anyone who would listen.

"He spoke to me just before the film ended. But, as it finished, this man came over and said something to him. He got really close. I thought that Brett knew him. I thought…"

"What did the person look like?"

"It was dark. I couldn't really…"

Sarah had found an usher. "Where's Security?" she yelled.

"With the Royals. What's going..."

"He's only just got away," Sarah yelled. "The police need to seal the building."

Behind her, there was pandemonium.

"They'll never find him," Sarah said to Jon. "He'll slip away in the confusion."

She turned to the usher. "Did anyone leave as the film was finishing?"

"There was a bloke, yeah, went down the front left exit." The usher pointed at some fire doors a few metres from where they were standing.

"He'll be well gone by now," Jon said.

"Hardly," the usher replied. "All the exits are locked until the Royals are away. We don't want people sneaking in and trying to bump them off."

"In that case..." Jon said.

"Come on," Sarah told him. "We're going after him."

"Why?" Jon asked. "Surely it's dangerous? Why can't the police...?"

But Sarah was already on her way, hurrying towards the exit on the left of the screen. In the audience, no one was leaving. The manager was standing in front of the screen, appealing for calm.

"Get the police," Jon told the usher. "Tell them we've gone after him."

Jon hurried after Sarah, shouting for her to be careful. By the time she'd pushed her way through the crowd to the exit, he had caught her up.

"He's got a knife," Jon said. "He's dangerous."

"I don't think he'll hurt me," Sarah said. "Not deliberately."

"You still haven't told me who did this," Jon complained. "It's Luke, isn't it?"

Sarah didn't reply. They walked down the corridor marked EXIT. It was a dark, narrow warren, deep beneath the cinema. All of the exit doors led either to this back entrance or to the front of house. Jon and Sarah were nearly at the back door now.

"You still haven't told me who it is," Jon complained again.

"Haven't you worked it out?" Sarah asked him. "I thought you were the boy detective and I was the unsuspecting girl victim."

"If it isn't Luke," Jon reasoned, "it has to be Leo."

Sarah didn't speak. They turned a corner. The back door was right in front of them. Four different corridors converged here. The killer, Jon knew, was in one of them. In the distance, he could hear doors being opened, people coming. In a moment, the back door would be electronically opened. People would begin spilling out into the West End. If the usher didn't get to the police in time, the killer would be able to merge with the leaving crowd.

Jon looked down each corridor. They were dark, but he couldn't see anyone. Maybe the usher had been wrong. Maybe…

"Jon!" Before Jon had time to react to Sarah's warning, someone grabbed him.

"Stay still," a familiar voice said. An arm was locked around Jon's shoulders. He felt a knife being pressed to his throat.

"Let him go," Sarah said, calmly. "You know it won't do any good."

There was blood on the knife: Brett Johnson's blood.

"Give me the knife," Sarah said. "I know you had a reason for what you did. Jon and I will help you explain it."

"Please," Jon said.

Shivering in the dark passageway, Sarah took a step closer to them.

"Give me the knife," she said. "It's over. You got the one you wanted to get. It was only Brett you were after all along, wasn't it?"

"Yes," the boy replied, gruffly. "I never meant to hurt you or the lighting woman." His grip on Jon loosened slightly.

"I thought not," Sarah said calmly. "Tell me what happened."

Slacker took a deep breath. Jon could feel it against his neck.

"The day after the camera plot went wrong, I broke into your room while you were asleep and stole a script. I needed to know where best to get at Brett. First I rigged the engine in the boat, trying to make his death look like an accident. Then I poured extra petrol on the fire at the studio. I knocked Brett out when all the attention was on you. Only he got rescued from the fire and you didn't. Then I persuaded those girls to invade the set on the last day of filming. I switched the guns. But I never meant to hurt you then, either. In the script I had, it was Matthew who got shot."

"I know," Sarah said, holding out her hand for the knife, so that her fingers were only centimetres from Jon's neck. "I worked that out. You saved my life once, didn't you? I'll make sure I tell everybody about that. Please give me the knife now. You're scaring my brother."

For a moment, Jon felt the cold steel brush against his neck. Then it was gone, and Sarah was holding the knife and Slacker was releasing Jon.

"Why?" Sarah asked him. "Why did you do it?"

Slacker spoke shakily, slowly.

"I ... I had a sister, Emily. She was an actress, got a small part in a film in Hollywood four years ago. Brett Johnson dated her. She wasn't really his girlfriend. She was just a bit of fun for him. He took her for a drive. He'd been drinking, taking drugs. He turned the car over somehow. Emily broke her neck, died instantly. Johnson wasn't hurt at all. He got a suspended sentence." Slacker began to cry.

"She ... she was twenty-one years old. I was fourteen when it happened. I worshipped her. She had her whole life ahead of her. Emily said that when she made it in the movie business, she'd help me find a job there too. We'd make it together. I miss her so much. She ... she..."

He stopped trying to talk. Sarah dropped the knife on the floor and held him.

"It's all right," she told the boy. "What's your real name?"

"Paul."

"It's all right, Paul. It's all over now."

Jon had stopped shaking now. He watched the boy sobbing in his sister's arms, fixing the image in his mind. He could hear the police coming down one of the corridors and he meant to capture every detail, to hold each one in his memory.

One day, Jon knew, he'd want to make a film about this story, or something like it. He'd want his sister in it too, because she was a good actress and a brave one, as she had just proved. And when he made the film, this would be the final image: the beautiful model in the red dress hugging the long-haired killer in the shabby sports jacket, both of them crying their eyes out.

The audience could work out the rest of the story for themselves from there on.

Cut.